Spiral Into Darkness

Joseph Lewis

Black Rose Writing | Texas

The author grants the final approval for this literary material.

First printing

This is a work of fiction. Names, characters, businesses, places, events, and incidents
are either the products of the author's imagination or used in a fictitious manner.
Any resemblance to actual persons, living or dead, or actual events is purely
coincidental.

ISBN: 978-1-68433-209-0
PUBLISHED BY BLACK ROSE WRITING
www.blackrosewriting.com

Printed in the United States of America
Suggested Retail Price (SRP) $21.95

Spiral Into Darkness is printed in Plantagenet Cherokee

Acknowledgements

Whenever I sit down to write this page, there is a fear that I might forget someone. For this possibility, I want to apologize in advance.

I want to thank a trio of editors: Theresa Storke and Sharon King who have been there from the very beginning and have had their hand in every book I have written. I also want to thank Melissa McArthur, Editor/Owner of Clicking Keys Writing Services for the exacting editing she performed on *Spiral into Darkness,* and to fellow author, Darin Kennedy, for recommending her to me. I want to thank Bob Favarato, an editor with Black Rose Writing for not only the final edits but for teaching me along the way.

I want to thank Sheri Pierce, psychology instructor extraordinaire, for fact-checking a couple of crucial parts of the manuscript, to Pete Augrom for guiding me on running, to James Dahlke for sharing his Forensic Science Background with me, and Jamie Graff who is the Assistant Chief of Police for the force in Kaukauna, Wisconsin. I have given him, perhaps, a more glamorous position as a detective, but in any case, his insight and help have been instrumental in crafting police procedure in my crime thrillers.

I want to thank Reagan Rothe and the publishing team for giving me a home and for their continued support and direction. I have enjoyed my partnership with them.

I want to thank my wife, Kim, and my two daughters, Hannah and Emily, for cheering me on, for helping to keep me going, and for propping me up when it seemed this dream of mine was elusive at best.

Lastly, I want to thank all of you, the readers and fans, who have followed along on the journey and adventures of my characters. You have been more than loyal, and your number has grown, it seems, with each book. Thank you!

If you wish to connect with me, feel free. I am on Facebook at: https://www.facebook.com/Joseph.Lewis.Author/?ref=aymt_homepage_panel and on Twitter at @jrlewisauthor

Until we meet again in and amongst the pages, be kind, make a positive difference in the lives of others, and live your life and your dream.

~Joe

This book is dedicated to two teachers who changed my life: Mrs. Gerald Mehring, my fourth-grade teacher, and Sr. Josephe' Marie Flynn, S.S.N.D., my sixth grade teacher. They saw something in me that no one else did, not even myself. Without them, I would not be where I am today.

Spiral Into Darkness

"We carry these things inside us
That no one else can see
They hold us down like anchors
They drown us out at sea."
~Unknown

"No man chooses evil because it is evil; they only mistake it for
happiness, the good he seeks."
~Mary Shelley

"The pendulum of the mind oscillates between sense and nonsense,
not between right and wrong."
~C.G. Jung

Chapter One

Milwaukee, WI

Vincent O'Laughlin was the youngest partner of the firm. Just four years out of grad school, he had skyrocketed up the food chain, leaving several dead bodies in his wake. Well, not actually dead. Just dead in the firm. Three of the four went on to different advertising outfits, one in Minneapolis, one in Chicago, and one in Kansas City. The fourth was still unemployed, as much to do with his age as it was his lack of creativity.

O'Laughlin rose up the ladder by capturing the Midwest Seed account, the Party Time USA account, and the Grand National Foods account, along with a nationally operated grocery store chain. And because of these acquisitions, his client list went from lackluster to golden, raking in money, accolades, and envy from the big boys in the advertising industry.

With his blond hair, blue eyes, and a dimple when he smiled, Vincent was a natural at sales. But his greatest strength was as an art director, the title he held before he moved to partner. He was a visionary, and because of this talent, he still oversaw the four biggest accounts in the firm. He wined and dined the CEOs of those companies and corporations, and he was given the luxury of hand-picking the art directors and had final approval on all TV, radio, and print advertising on those four accounts. And now with a corner office and a full-time personal assistant, he sipped Evian and gazed out of his fourteenth-floor window overlooking Old World Third Street and the Milwaukee skyline, small as it was, and pondered where he would go from here.

Billy Joel sang it, and Vincent believed it: *New York State of Mind.*

With every breath, every pulse beat, his *only* goal was to make it as big in New York as he did in sleepy, little Milwaukee. The *only* goal he had. There was not enough money or women to hold him in Milwaukee. Not even the 3700 square foot, lakeside condo in Whitefish Bay, a rich, upscale northern suburb of Milwaukee could contain him. His only focus was to get to New York and make his mark there, just as he had in Milwaukee.

Vincent opened his briefcase and placed his checkbook, his wallet, three empty manila folders, a yellow pad of paper in a leather pad protector with his initials embossed in faux gold lettering, and a small calculator neatly inside. He did not have anything to take home, and he did not need a briefcase, at least not one this expensive. But because he was now a partner, he thought the soft, brown leather briefcase gave him legitimacy. He felt it made him look important, just as the tailored Brooks Brothers cashmere suits, silk shirts, and the tan cashmere top coat and matching leather gloves did. The gloves did not keep his hands warm, but they looked good, and looks were everything.

The last thing Vincent did before leaving his office and turning off his light was to pick up the Kodak box holding his portfolio. He preferred a hard copy in addition to the disk and thumb drive. With the hard copy, he could sit across from someone and talk him or her through it. Vincent placed much confidence in his ability to talk someone into just about anything. So as a consequence and precaution, he carried it with him everywhere. It was his present life and the key to his next life. He used the Kodak Film box as a disguise because he could not afford for anyone to know he kept his portfolio updated and ready. And he was *so* ready.

Like he did each day after work, he took the stairs down fourteen flights instead of taking the elevator. He reasoned it was an inexpensive way to get a cardio workout in before he got to the gym.

After signing out at the front desk and wishing a good evening to the portly and elderly night security man, he paused at the door, buttoned up his top coat, clamped his portfolio under his arm, and then stepped into the sub-zero late afternoon.

So cold, his nose hair froze. The dirty snow and ice that had melted in the early afternoon sun now crunched under the soles of his leather slip-ons. The shoes, like his gloves, looked good, but for all the warmth they provided, he may as well have been barefoot.

Vincent emerged between two cars, dodged a bus, and jay-walked across the street and then jogged into the parking garage. He had parked his silver Lexus on the fourth floor. Because it was so cold, he took the elevator which had a faint cigarette and urine smell to it. He tried breathing through his mouth. It did not work because then he could taste it. The slow-moving elevator opened and he quick-walked toward his car. It was within sight at the far end of the garage. The sound was his loafers echoed off the cement and cinder block walls.

The garage was dark. Two of the overhead lights were out, which made him curious. He remembered them working when he had arrived.

He slowed down as he neared his car, tucked his portfolio under his arm, slipped off his glove and held it in his mouth and dug into his pocket for his key fob.

"Excuse me, sir."

The voice came from behind and to his left.

Startled, Vincent jumped and spun around, his heart rate ratcheting up twenty beats. The glove fell out of his mouth and he dropped the key fob.

"Excuse me, sir. Are you Vincent O'Laughlin?"

Vincent squinted into the shadow and took a step back, the safety of his car forgotten. The voice sounded middle-aged, curious and almost friendly, not at all threatening.

"Who's there?" Vincent said, angry this person caused him to drop his glove in a filthy puddle of melted snow and street grime.

"Are you Vincent O'Laughlin?" the voice asked again.

"Yes, I am. Who are you and what do you want?" Vincent asked. He did not like talking to someone he could not see in the freezing, dark, and dirty garage.

"That's what I thought. It should never have happened. You shouldn't have done it."

"Done what?"

The muzzle flashed bright, the report loud, echoing off the concrete walls.

The first shot had done the work, but the second shot was for fun.

Chapter Two

Greenfield, WI

Shirley Bodencamp loved middle school kids. She loved their unpredictability and goofiness. She loved being a middle school principal except for the meetings, the bureaucracy, the politics, the infighting, and the paperwork. All the bullshit that went with being a principal. But even after almost thirty years, it was all she could see herself being.

Although she had a pleasant and comfortable enough office, she was seldom in it. Instead, she would wander hallways during and between classes, peeking into a classroom, maybe playing a game of ping pong in physical education class or cutting boards in carpentry. Each day, she supervised the cafeteria during each of the three lunch shifts, because she loved being around the kids.

The kids loved her. Her staff adored her. And the parents admired her.

She had a way of turning an angry parent into one who laughed as together they left her office. She had a special way of listening to a middle-aged staff member going through a tough divorce or a young worried teacher facing financial troubles or an older distraught custodian who had not gotten over burying his wife.

When she had won Principal of the Year the previous year, one of the recommendation letters read in front of the board of education called her - "gifted." - Heads nodded. Another letter called her - "a kind, caring and a consummate professional who put the needs and interests of children above all else." - Her staff and parents present in the audience stood up and cheered, breaking all decorum.

Fifty-four years old, she wanted two things: to be the best wife possible and the best-damned principal she knew how to be. She and her husband of thirty-one years had never had children of their own. They tried. They discussed adopting, but decided they had a good life, a *great* life, and though they both had wanted children, together they had decided their tabby, Sasquatch, and their toy poodle, Buster, were enough for them. They had each other and life was more than good.

As was the case many times at the end of a busy week, she sat in her office finishing the report the District Office had needed by noon on Monday. It was late on this Friday afternoon and everyone had long ago left. The last to leave was Curley, the older custodian, who she had sent home over an hour before. The plan was for Shirley to meet her husband at *Sallies* for a nice Italian dinner to cap off a great week and start a relaxing weekend.

She saved the report to her desktop, knowing she should have saved it to her hard drive that was district policy. She smiled and shrugged, satisfied she had, at least in a small way, defied authority once again.

Shirley closed down her computer, grabbed a clean mug, and watered her plants sitting on the windowsill. As she did, she glanced out the window and thought she saw someone in the courtyard standing in the shadows. Puzzled, she wondered who would be out there on this cold early evening. The water ran out from under the small clay pot, so Shirley grabbed a paper towel and wiped up the spill and looked out the window again. No one and nothing other than the picnic tables, the decorative stone garbage receptacles, and the shrubbery.

Shirley grabbed her purse, her scarf, coat and gloves, turned off the light and locked up her office. She moved through the outer office and locked the door behind her and picked up her pace down the short hallway, heels click-clacking as she walked on the clean and shiny linoleum.

She stepped outside, and the cold took away her breath. She turned toward the door and pushed against it, making sure it was locked.

"Excuse me, ma'am. Are you Shirley Bodencamp?"

Startled, Shirley spun around and gasped.

"Are you Shirley Bodencamp?"

Shirley did not recognize her visitor, but she recovered enough to say with a smile, "Why, yes, I am. And who might you be?"

"That's what I thought. It should never have happened. You shouldn't have done it."

"I beg your pardon?"

The gun went off once, then twice.

A dog barked and then another.

The shooter walked away with a smile and without a worry, satisfied because Shirley's face had dissolved into an indistinguishable mass of blood, bone, and brain.

Chapter Three

Waukesha, WI

Jamie Graff slept in until his back ached. A stiff neck did not help because it gave him a headache that four Motrin could not chase away. Sleeping in meant getting up at eight instead of six-thirty, but an hour and a half extra did not hurt. Except for his back, his neck, and his head.

Kelli had already left for work at the insurance agency. As she and Jamie had planned the night before, she would drop Garrett off at the daycare on her way. As a result, the house was dark and quiet and smelled of freshly brewed coffee. Jamie enjoyed the smell as much as he did the taste, and part of his routine was to drink two cups before he left for work and another on the way. Not that he ever kept track.

He got up, stretched, and walked stiffly to the bathroom for a quick shave and shower.

Thirty minutes later, he sat at the counter in the kitchen eating an egg sandwich while he drank his second cup of coffee. He hunched over the paper, but there was not much he did not know already.

He spent most of the time on the sports page reading about the Bucks, and then the high school sports round up. Waukesha North sat in second place and a half-game out of first. Everyone was astounded that five freshmen could play that well and that consistently. Ever since Brian Kazmarick, who was soon to be Brian Evans, and Randy Evans were inserted into the starting lineup, North was on a roll. The two boys joined Brett McGovern, Billy Schroeder, Randy's twin brother, and Troy Rivera. Five freshmen. Four from the same family.

The old timers thought they had done so well because the five freshmen did not know any better. Others thought they had done so well because four of them were brothers, and because of that, they had their own language and a way of communicating. Still, others felt it was because the four brothers were adopted or soon to be adopted by Jeremy Evans, the school counselor and former basketball coach who had worked with them on the side. Whatever the reason, Waukesha North was in the midst of a seven-game winning streak and was perhaps the hottest team in the conference.

Graff smiled. Jeremy Evans was his best friend, and he loved Jeremy's and Vicky's boys almost as much as they did. He ought to since he was godfather to two of them, Randy and Billy.

His cell buzzed, and Jamie glanced at the caller ID and saw it was the captain. O'Brien seldom called his cell, and when he did, it was because of an emergency.

"Captain."

"How soon will you be in?"

No pleasantries. Formal like his uniform and clipped like his bald head. O'Brien was never that abrupt, so Graff knew it was serious.

"Give me twenty minutes."

"Make it fifteen or sooner," and the call went dead.

Graff threw out the rest of the coffee, rinsed off his plate and put it in the sink, thought better of it, and placed it in the dishwasher. He grabbed his keys and his coat and walked out the door heading to the garage, locking the door behind him. He hit the garage door opener, hopped into his Pathfinder, backed out and drove off. Fifteen minutes later, he walked through O'Brien's door.

O'Brien was bald and on the short side but thick. His arms bulged out of his sleeves, and his chest strained the buttons on his crisp uniform. He seldom smiled, but when he did, people shied away because his smile was downright scary.

Among the officers, he was known as "Mr. Clean" because he resembled the animated pitchman for disinfectant. No one, however, dared call him that to his face.

"I'm thinking of making you COD," the captain said as soon as Graff sat down.

A thousand thoughts tumbled around in Jamie's head, all fighting for attention. Chief of Detectives meant politics and paperwork, and

Graff was not a fan of either. He wanted police work, loved being a detective, and was most at home at a crime scene.

Jamie said nothing.

"You would still be out in the field."

"But I would have to do the paperwork. It would limit me."

"Only as much as you allow yourself to be."

Looking out the window and off in the distance, Jamie shook his head.

"It comes with a raise."

Jamie turned back to O'Brien but said nothing. Yes, he and Kelli could use the extra money, but he did not want the extra headache associated with the position.

O'Brien sighed and pushed a typed piece of paper at Graff and then leaned back with both hands behind his shiny head.

"Okay, your choice. You select the detective you want to take orders from." He gestured at the typed sheet and said, "Pick someone."

Graff read over the list and pursed his lips. He had to admit that the seven names on the list were weak investigators. He did not like to set himself above the others, but there was not anyone he thought he respected enough to take orders from. The group was not close to good, which was why O'Brien tapped him for anything presenting even the slightest difficulty.

The best detectives were in the Waukesha County Sheriff Department, not in the Waukesha City Police Department. Pat O'Connor and Paul Eiselmann were the first two who came to mind, followed by Tom Albrecht, Brooke Beranger, and Ronnie Desotel. Graff had worked with all five during the summer of death.

Eiselmann and O'Connor had led a team who freed kids from a brothel in Long Beach, California. On the same day, Albrecht and Desotel led a team freeing a different set of captive kids traveling on a circuit catering to perverts. Desotel was shot and ended up with a permanent limp. Later that same summer, Beranger and Albrecht protected Jeremy Evans and his kids as they traveled across the country toward a deadly showdown in the Arizona desert. And more recently, Jamie had worked with O'Connor and Eiselmann as they shut down a drug ring involving high school kids and staff. They cut off an arm of MS-13, a violent gang out of El Salvador who ran the drug, gun, and skin trade along the I-43 and I-94 corridor from Chicago to Door County.

He glanced back at the list and knew there was not anyone he saw as anywhere close to being in a class with the five sheriff detectives. He frowned and pushed the sheet of paper back at O'Brien.

"You see the problem I have? Or should I say, *we* have?"

Graff bobbed his head from side to side. He did not want to agree with him, but deep down, he knew the captain was right.

O'Brien pushed two stapled sheets across the desk and said, "Here's a list of our patrol officers. Look at this list and identify two or three of the best we can promote to detective."

Knowing O'Brien had won, Graff made the most of it. He read over the list of names. There were some he knew and had worked with at various crime scenes, but many were unknown to him.

"Do I have to decide right now?"

"How much time do you need?"

It was easier to promote than demote, so he would like to talk with them and spend time getting to know them.

"Is anything pressing right now? Can I have until the end of the week? Maybe until Monday?"

O'Brien frowned and said, "Perhaps. Maybe."

"What's up?"

"I'm assuming you've heard about the series of murders. Same MO, no leads. Most have been in or around Milwaukee, but there was a middle school principal shot and killed this past Friday in Greenfield."

Graff nodded and said, "I've read about 'em. I think there were six so far."

"Seven. A task force is being put together, and you were asked for by name."

Graff blinked. "By who?"

"Summer Storm."

"Wow! I haven't heard her name since ..." He did not finish, because he, Jeremy, and Jeremy's kids all referred to it as the summer of death, and Jamie did not think O'Brien would appreciate that." So he asked, "Why is the FBI involved?"

"We might have a serial on our hands."

"But not actually on our hands."

O'Brien nodded and said, "Correct, not us. But the FBI wants a task force made up of the best from local police and sheriff departments around the Milwaukee Metro, and I want us involved before it gets to us."

"Is Pete Kelliher or Skip Dahlke coming with Summer?"

O'Brien shrugged and said, "Not sure who the FBI is bringing. I doubt Pete would come because he works crimes against children, but who knows."

"Anyone from the county involved?"

"Not yet, at least not that I know of. Give me who you'd like to work with, and I'll give Myron a call and see if he can spring them loose."

Myron Wagner was the county sheriff in the last couple of years before he hung up his pistols. He was short and round, and Graff did not think much of him. Graff figured O'Brien did not either.

"Eiselmann and O'Connor."

"They're drugs and gangs, though."

"They're great detectives. And Eiselmann is a techie, and that's always a plus."

"Okay, I'll give Wagner a call." He reached into his top drawer and pulled out a press release and said, "Read this over. I'd like to get it to the paper this morning."

Graff read it without enthusiasm.

"Any politics with me taking COD?"

O'Brien said, "Of course. That's half the fun. But do you care? I don't."

Chapter Four

Milwaukee, WI

The Milwaukee County Safety Building hunkered down in the heart of the city, surrounded by the Milwaukee Area Technical College, Marquette University, the County Court House, and the Bradley Center. It sat just off three of the main arteries in and out of the city: I-43 ran north and south, and I-94 and Bluemound Road ran east and west.

It sagged, maybe under the weight of a lack of care and concern. Perhaps it sagged because it housed the force losing the never-ending battle to rid the city of crime that had been increasing with each passing day. It was made of stone, and the color was gray. Hard to tell if the color came from the dirt and grime kicked up from the comings and goings of the thousands of cars on their steady journey into and out of Wisconsin's largest city or from the throaty belches of soot from downtown factories.

Three attending deputies stood at the doorway and metal detector. He handed over his ID and was processed through the security entrance.

"There's a multiple-jurisdictions meeting in here somewhere."

The largest of the three, a heavy-set and deep-voiced deputy, glanced at him and said, "Second floor, end of the hall on the left. Room 214."

Graff took the steps rather than the enclosed and slow-moving elevator, the soles of his shoes soundless on the cracked and yellowed linoleum. He walked down the hall to his destination and pushed through the heavy wooden door and stepped inside but stayed in the back next to a table filled with pastries, coffee, Styrofoam cups, paper plates, and napkins. A couple of cops gathered around. Jamie felt he was in the way, so he moved.

There were suits at the front of the room. He recognized Summer Storm standing among them, though her blond hair was shorter and she seemed thinner and tired. She was still as tall and as beautiful as he had remembered. He did not see Pete Kelliher, but he saw Skip Dahlke, and he smiled.

Dahlke had not changed. He did a little math and guessed Skip was pushing thirty, but looked no older than seventeen. His blond, almost white hair matched his complexion. He spoke with a youngish black man with short-cropped hair and a thin mustache. He stood a solid six or six-one, and not an ounce of fat on him, and moved like an athlete. With Dahlke and the black guy was a short, slender female with short dark hair and dark eyes who did more listening than talking. Not much weight to her and Graff wondered if a good stiff breeze would knock her over.

Cops and deputies had gathered in small groups and spoke just above a whisper or munched on pastries and sipped coffee. Graff recognized a face or two, but not their names. He was never great with names. He recognized two suits from the Milwaukee FBI office whom he had had dealings with over the years.

"I hear we have you to thank for us getting mixed up in this cluster fuck."

Jamie turned around and said, "Hi, Paul. Been a while."

"Yeah, sure. Since ... the last North game?"

Paul Eiselmann stood a compact five-nine or -ten with dark red hair, green eyes and a billion freckles. He smiled and shook his head as he gazed at the room full of officers.

Pat O'Connor, who had been standing behind Eiselmann, said, "I recognize a couple guys."

O'Connor was tall and thin and wore his brown hair shoulder length. He looked more like a drug dealer who used more than he sold. As a consequence, he caught curious looks from several of the cops who wondered who in the hell he was, but O'Connor was used to it, and he did not give a damn, anyway.

Summer Storm stepped to the microphone at the front of the room and said, "If you can take your seats, we'd like to get started."

The cops, about thirty, shuffled to the uncomfortable metal folding chairs and sat down. He, Eiselmann, and O'Connor sat together in the back with Graff taking the chair on the aisle. Suits walked down the outside rows and handed out manila folders, which were passed from cop to cop so each could have one.

Graff opened his and found crime scene reports from unsolved murders and photographs of each of the corresponding victims.

"Show and tell," Eiselmann whispered.

Storm spoke. "I'm S.A.C. Summer Storm. I am the Associate Director of the Criminal Investigation Division. With me are Special Investigator Cleveland Batiste from ViCAP, Special Agent James Dahlke, who works out of Quantico in Forensic Science, and Special Agent Jo Weist out of the Behavioral Science office also out of Quantico." Each agent raised a hand and nodded when their name was called.

"ViCAP?" whispered Eiselmann.

"The Violent Criminal Apprehension Program deals with serial murders, among other things," Graff whispered back.

"Also with us is Dr. Nelson Alamorode, a local psychiatrist some of you may know who has agreed to provide consultation for us."

Graff had heard of the man. He was not at all remarkable looking. Average height, maybe a little taller, and doughy, with thinning dark hair graying at the temples. Summer had assembled an impressive team, Jamie thought.

"We asked law enforcement agencies in the Milwaukee Metro Area to send us their best detectives and investigators. Thirty-five of you, give or take. So each of you is now part of a task force to find who is behind the series of unsolved murders in and around Milwaukee. If you can open your folders and follow along, please."

One of the Milwaukee agents ran the projector and laptop showing the victims' before and after photos, followed by the crime scenes of each victim. A little redundant since each folder contained the same photos.

"We have eight victims so far. The most recent was last night." She paused, looked down at her notes, and said, "It took place off Forest Home on South Twenty-Eighth Street. The victim was a thirty-six-year-old mother of two. According to her husband, David Fortune, their two children were in bed and he and his wife, Gwen, were watching TV. The doorbell rang, and she went to answer it. He heard a conversation and presumed someone was selling something, but he could not make out what was said. He heard a gunshot and ran to the door and found his wife dead from a single shot from a .38 caliber handgun. Like the others, in the face. The shooter had disappeared."

Summer paused and said, "The unsub followed the same MO as each of the other victims."

"Is the husband credible? How do we know he didn't shoot his wife?" a cop asked from the middle of the room.

Summer said, "He was tested for GSR, and there was no trace, and he has an alibi for six of the eight murders, so we know it wasn't him."

"Are there any leads? Do we have anything to go on?" a female cop asked from Jamie's right.

Graff recognized her as being a detective from the East Side. He assumed the lady cop on her left and the older male cop on her right were from the same precinct.

"Not much," Summer said. "That's why we need each of you. You know your cities and your counties."

"But how do we even begin if we have nothing to go on?" an older cop who Graff did not know asked.

"Dr. Alamorode, you and Agent Weist put together a tentative profile. Would you care to share it?"

The shrink stood up, moved to the microphone, and cleared his throat.

"I believe we're looking for a male between the ages of thirty and fifty, more toward the younger end. He's either single or divorced. He's more than likely educated and a professional who blends in and functions well in society. Somehow, at least in the unsub's mind, each one of the victims are connected, and the unsub has created a pattern."

"What pattern?" an older cop asked.

"Well, he shoots his victims once or twice, never more than that. He shoots them in the face. And we know at least in the last instance, the unsub had a brief conversation with the victim, Gwen Fortune. We can assume he had a similar brief conversation with each of his victims."

"But we don't know for sure," the female profiler, Agent Jo Weist, said.

Alamorode smiled, nodded and said, "It is an assumption, not a fact."

"Why the face?" a young cop asked from the front.

Alamorode thought it over and said, "It could be as simple as a convenience, but I ... we believe there's more to it than that. We think he's trying to erase them."

"Erase them?" another cop asked.

The shrink nodded and said, "By shooting them in the face, he alters their identity. Think of it as erasing their existence."

"But even with what you told us, there isn't anything to go on," the older cop said. "We can't investigate a conversation with dead people unless it was recorded. So where do we begin?"

Summer sighed and moved back to the microphone. Alamorode sat back down.

"I'm asking each of you to search your files and look for any similar cold cases. That's where we begin. It's possible the unsub could have started earlier, and the pattern, as Dr. Alamorode calls it, wasn't recognized. I'm asking you to interview any witnesses, neighbors ... anyone who might have heard a gunshot or unusual noise and who might remember the smallest detail. Agent Dahlke will review all the crime scenes. It will take an effort from all of us to solve this. But until we solve it, more people will get killed."

"Mission Fucking Impossible, if you ask me," a young cop sitting in front of Graff grumbled.

Graff could not help but agree.

The meeting broke up, and the cops drifted off in groups of two or three. Graff, Eiselmann, and O'Connor stayed behind. When most everyone had left the room, Summer spotted them, waived, hooked Dahlke by the arm, and the two of them met Graff, Eiselmann, and O'Connor halfway. Weist and Alamorode had their heads together with Batiste in the front of the room.

She embraced Graff and said, "Jamie, thanks for coming! It's been what ... a year and a half?"

"Something like that," Jamie said with a smile.

She turned to Eiselmann and said, "Paul, thanks for coming," and embraced him and did the same to O'Connor.

Dahlke got a man-hug from Graff and shook hands with Eiselmann and O'Connor.

"You haven't changed any, Skip," Graff said. "You still look like you're in high school." He laughed, as did Dahlke. "Is Pete here somewhere?"

"He might come later," Dahlke said. "He's teaching a class at the academy."

"What?" Graff asked. "Teaching?"

"Yup," laughed Dahlke.

"We have so much to catch up on. How are Jeremy and the boys? Pete told me he's getting married to Victoria McGovern. Did I hear that correctly?" she said.

Graff smiled and said, "She's changed a lot."

"God, she must have," Summer said with a shake of her head. "I didn't see that coming."

Graff laughed and said, "It started slow, but then it took off. They're good for each other and good for the boys."

Summer bit her lip and then said, "How are the boys? Are they doing okay?"

It was Eiselmann who answered. "Better than okay. They've grown so much, I don't think you'll recognize them."

"Brett is like the older brother to all of them," O'Connor said rolling his eyes. "Almost a nag."

"I can see that," Summer laughed. "He was a bit stubborn."

"A bit?" Graff said. "Hell, a mule has nothing on him."

They all laughed.

"I'd like to see them again," Skip said.

"I let Jeremy know we were coming to your little party this morning, and he said to tell you to pick a night when you can come to dinner," Jamie said.

"Did I hear you mention the name McGovern?" the black agent asked.

Summer introduced him. "Guys, this is Cleveland Batiste."

"Just call me Cleve," he said as he shook hands all around.

"Cleve, this is Jamie Graff, Paul Eiselmann, and Pat O'Connor. Jamie and Pete led the team in Chicago setting Brett, Mike Erickson, and Stephen Bailey free. Paul and Pat led the team in Long Beach. Guys, Cleve ran protection for the McGoverns when Anthony Dominico was on the loose."

Batiste hung his head and said, "I wish I could have been around to help MB."

"It wasn't your fault, Cleve. You weren't on duty," Summer sighed.

"And as I understand it," O'Connor said, "Thomas McGovern had as much to do with her death as Dominico did. Indirectly, at least."

Agent Mary Beth Wilkey or as everyone had called her, MB, shared protection duty with Batiste. He took it during the day while she had it at night. When Thomas McGovern insisted on going to the university, he left a door unlocked. Tony Dominico entered and ended up shooting Wilkey. She did not survive the emergency surgery. It was Brett who shot and disabled Dominico using Wilkey's gun, which was the finest of ironies. It was Dominico who had taught Brett how to shoot.

"How is Brett's shoulder?" Batiste asked.

"There's a scar, but he has full function and range of motion," O'Connor said.

"He's a tough kid," Batiste said.

"One of the toughest," O'Connor agreed. "He made second team all-conference in football as a freshman, and he starts at point guard on the varsity basketball team."

"I knew he was an athlete. I think his little brother will be a good one, too."

"Listen, I know we need to catch up," Summer said. "And we will take Jeremy up on dinner. But I'd like to get you guys back in the field."

"I'd like to start with the Forest Home crime scene, if that's okay with you," Graff said, looking from Eiselmann to O'Connor. Both men nodded.

"Start there then," Storm said. "We need to end this."

Chapter Five

Milwaukee, WI

The Fortune home sat on a quiet residential street of middle- to lower middle-class homes. Blue-collar type homes of the silent, sometimes struggling working class. Or maybe homes of young couples starting out who lacked the money for a newer home in the burbs.

David Fortune's eyes were red and his face puffy. His dark hair mussed and his five o'clock shadow prominent. He sat with his forearms on his knees, but his head hung low, and now and then he snagged a tissue and wiped his eyes.

They were in the small living room. Graff and Eiselmann sat in stuffed dark gray or ruddy brown chairs. Fortune sat on the couch facing them. The volume on the TV was turned down, and Graff did not recognize the show. An older woman, who Graff assumed was a mother or mother-in-law, stuck her head into the room from time to time, and was rebuked by an older man, who Graff assumed was a father or father-in-law, and when he did, the older woman would disappear back into the kitchen.

"I don't know anything more," Fortune said, throwing his hands up in the air.

They had been there for twenty minutes, and what the two detectives found out was that David Fortune was thirty-three years-old and worked in IT at Associated Bank on East Kilbourn Avenue. It was the fourth largest bank in Milwaukee, and Fortune was one of six computer guys making sure the network ran without a hitch. It was not the type of job that would piss someone off enough to pull a trigger on his wife.

He was lean and lanky, and Eiselmann pegged him as a runner. He looked like he had not slept all night. In fact, his t-shirt could have been the shirt he had worn the night before. He wore jeans and had white athletic socks on his feet stuffed into some well-worn brown suede slippers.

Gwen Fortune was a dental hygienist at a family clinic. On the side, she did medical transcription from home. Between David's income and both of Gwen's incomes, they did okay.

She was one month shy of her thirty-third birthday. A two-sport athlete at a rival high school, she and David had met their junior year on a blind date set up by one of David's friends. They had dated on and off, but got serious their sophomore year in college, she at UW-Milwaukee and he at Marquette. They got married a year after they had graduated.

Their two girls, four and two, were with Gwen's sister and brother-in-law. Given their ages, there was no way they could comprehend what had taken place, Graff thought. At any rate, Graff felt for the guy. He wondered how he would raise Garrett by himself if something tragic had happened to Kelli. He shuddered involuntarily.

Later in the day, Fortune would be surrounded by family and friends, and they would try to lift the burden of grief and despair off him. Grief shared sort of thing. Still. Graff shook his head.

"I know this is hard for you," Paul said. "It's gotta be. We're sorry to be asking these questions, but it's the only way we'll catch whoever did this."

"Did your wife, Gwen, have any enemies? Anyone with whom she might have had a disagreement?" Graff asked. He knew the answer to the question before he asked it.

Fortune shook his head. His hands moved dismissively. "No one I can think of." He looked up at the two detectives and said, "Why? Why would someone do this?"

His voice caught, and his hands covered his face as he sobbed. In response, the older woman's head appeared in the doorway, but this time, the older man said nothing to call her back.

"David, can I get you anything?"

"No, Mom. I'm okay," he whispered, breathing in short gasps.

She hung in the doorway. Dabbed at her eyes with a tissue and then disappeared back into the kitchen.

Eiselmann and Graff exchanged a look of resignation knowing there were not going to be any great revelations. How could there be? He was in one room while his wife was shot at the front door.

"Mr. Fortune, here is my card. It has my cell number on it. If you remember anything, even the slightest detail, anything at all, no matter how small or insignificant it might be, please call me," Jamie said, standing up and handing Fortune his business card.

Eiselmann had already powered down his laptop. He stood up and fished out one of his business cards from his breast pocket and gave it to Fortune.

"If you can't reach Detective Graff, call me."

Fortune stood up and took both cards, glanced at them, and then stuffed them into his jeans pocket. Graff had a hunch Fortune would not call except to find out what, if anything, was happening with his wife's case.

"How are you going to find this guy? I didn't help you any."

"Mr. Fortune, because of you, we know it was a man. We didn't know that," Eiselmann said. "It's a start."

"We take your information and combine it with other bits and pieces of information we gather from others. There's a large team of us working on this. The FBI is involved. We'll find him," Graff said.

"It might take time, but we'll get him," Eiselmann added shaking the man's hand.

Fortune looked doubtful, but he nodded, and his eyes remained downcast.

"We'll finish up out here, and then we'll take off," Graff said as he shook the man's hand.

The older man and the older woman appeared from the kitchen, and the older man said, "Thank you for coming. Please catch this son of a bitch. Please!"

Graff and Eiselmann nodded and left the living room.

Dahlke and a heavy-set black woman, one of the Milwaukee County forensic techs, were in the foyer squatting down examining the little woven rug.

She pointed to a large, round, dark stain and said, "We gathered her DNA from this."

Dahlke was not as interested in the forensics from inside the house as much as he was in the forensics outside the house. Yet, he always started in and worked his way out. It was similar to what he might do on an outdoor scene. He would begin at the center point and spiral out, gathering whatever was pertinent to the case.

James Dahlke, christened "Skip" by Pete Kelliher, worked in the Wisconsin Crime Lab operating out of Wausau in the North Central part of the state. Storm and Kelliher had met him when he worked a crime scene near Goodman in the North woods. A naked boy and two men were found dead. The FBI was brought in because the boy was a victim of a ring of kidnapped boys used as sex slaves. The same ring was responsible for abducting Brett McGovern and forcing him to acquiesce to perverts for twenty-two months.

The two men had been identified as being behind some of the kidnappings. Dahlke ended up being part of a raid led by Graff and Kelliher freeing Brett McGovern, Stephen Bailey, Mike Erickson, and other kids held captive in a warehouse in Chicago.

When the Northern Crime Lab closed due to budget cuts, Dahlke was snagged by the FBI based upon Pete's recommendation. He ended up at the academy and became an agent specializing in Forensics.

Eiselmann and Graff watched the two techs, got bored, and went outside where they found O'Connor.

"What are you doing?" Eiselmann asked his partner.

O'Connor ignored him. He stood on the small cement stoop. He faced the door, extended his arm and pointed, and then turned his back to the door and faced the street.

"The door was open."

"Yeah, so?"

"How tall is ... was she?" O'Connor asked.

Graff opened his folder, scanned the lab report, and said, "Five-foot-six."

O'Connor nodded and said, "So she's in the doorway. If you're the shooter, where do you stand?"

Eiselmann shrugged and said, "On the porch."

O'Connor faced the door and extended his arm, pointing at the front door, and asked, "What was the angle of entry? Up? Down? Straight?"

Graff read and reread the report and then shook his head. He opened the door and asked the Milwaukee County crime tech to step outside. Dahlke followed her.

She said, "What?"

"The autopsy report. What was the angle of the entry wound? Up, down, or straight?"

"Don't know. That's not my thing," she said.

"Can you call someone whose thing it is?" Eiselmann asked.

She frowned and said, "I don't like your 'tude," but she pulled out her cell, checked her contacts, and dialed a number.

"Oscar, this is Na'Lah. Can you find the autopsy report on Gwen Fortune?" There was a pause, and then she said, "I'll wait."

"What are you thinking?" Graff asked O'Connor.

"If I shoot someone, my arm is straight, right?" He demonstrated.

"Generally, yeah."

"The shooter stands on the stoop, and Fortune stands in the doorway. The step up is what, six inches? She's five-foot-six. I'm six-foot-two. If I shoot her in the face, the bullet would have a downward angle. Paul, you're five-foot-eight, two inches taller than she is. But she's standing up an additional six inches. Your bullet would have an upward angle."

"Using the angle of entry, we can figure out approximately how tall the shooter is," Graff said.

"Okay, thanks." Na'Lah Fleming turned off her cell.

"The angle of entry was straight with a slight upward angle. Figure straight on, just below her right eye, closer to her nose."

"Okay, so Fortune was five-foot-six. Give her another six inches, but subtract three, maybe four inches from the top of her head to just below her eye," Dahlke said, "we're looking at a guy about six-foot to six-foot-two."

"Sounds about right," Na'Lah said, nodding her head.

"We need to call this in to Summer," Dahlke said.

"Not yet," O'Connor said. "I want to double check this with the shooting in Greenfield."

"Let's go," Graff said. It was not much, but it was a little more than what they had.

Chapter Six

Greenfield, WI

The mood at the middle school was somewhere between sad and sadder. Teachers and staff kept it together in front of the kids. The kids registered all of it though in a way that all kids do. Some kids looked up. Other kids could not make eye contact because it was too painful for them. In all cases, they registered the pain coming off them in waves.

A small memorial of pictures, cards, and unlit candles garnished the walk approaching the front door where Bodencamp was shot and killed the previous Friday. The chalk outline and blood had been cleaned off the sidewalk, though there was a faint stain. The custodial crew had done a nice job getting the school ready.

O'Connor was in awe of the display. Of course, he had seen it before, but nothing like this. Hell, he could not even remember who his middle school principal was. And it was not a middle school. He and Eiselmann attended Holy Angels Grade School, and it ran from first through eighth grade. The teachers were nuns for the most part.

He shut his eyes, squinted, and tried to picture who the principal was when he was in eighth grade. Nothing came to him except the mandatory penguin outfit of black and white that nuns wore.

And then his mind did what his mind often did. It flipped back through his childhood and dwelt on the ugly parts.

O'Connor was the youngest of three brothers. His father split after he beat up his oldest brother. When his mom tried to stop him, he beat her too. His father left, and they never saw or heard from him again, which was pretty much okay with O'Connor. His mom was not happy though. After that, they never had much. Hell, even before that, they never had much.

His two older brothers dropped out of high school when he was in seventh grade, and they started running drugs ... weed and coke, a little meth, some heroin. They would come home and get high and try to get him to use. O'Connor refused, so his brothers took turns beating him. His mom found out and threw them out of the house.

His mom worked three jobs the whole time he was in high school, and he hardly ever saw her. He ended up putting himself through college, and after that, joined the sheriff's department. The last time he saw his brothers was when he worked a drugs and weapons case and arrested both of them. His mom died shortly after their trial.

He could have followed his father down the road to who-in-the-hell-knows, or he could have followed his brothers down the rabbit hole. He did not. He didn't because he knew both choices were wrong, and it was not what he wanted to do. Mostly because of his partner's family. Mostly, because of his partner's dad. Eiselmann and he were already friends, but Eiselmann's family looked out for him. His dad cared about him. Gave him an example and became a role model.

Then his mind did what it often did, and another picture and thought came into focus. He thought of Jeremy Evans taking in George after adopting Randy and Billy. He pictured Brett, Bobby, and Vicky. He pictured Brian Kazmarick, who would soon be Brian Evans, because Jeremy was adopting him too.

Life was funny that way. As sad and as ugly as it sometimes was, there was often good that came out of it. As ugly as O'Connor's life was once upon a time and as ugly as the world was when he put on the badge, he embraced and sought out all the good he could. He needed to in order to keep his sanity.

O'Connor took a swallow of water. His eyes had a faraway look.

Clint Sidowski, a member of the Waukesha County Crime Tech crew stood out of the way while Eiselmann worked the scene with Skip Dahlke. Graff read the crime scene reports in silence.

"Hoss, you okay?" Eiselmann asked his partner.

"Yeah. Peachy," O'Connor answered. He took another long pull from his water bottle.

Eiselmann frowned, wondering what was running around in his friend's head, but asked Sidowski, "Do you have a height for Bodencamp?"

Sidowski glanced at his notes and said, "Five-five and a half."

"Angle of entry?" Dahlke asked.

"Downward under her left eye near her nose."

To be sure, Eiselmann glanced at the front door. Upon confirming there were no steps and no porch or stoop, he said, "Well, that confirms it. Our guy is between six and six-two."

Graff raised his head, pointed to the camera, and said, "I want to see some film."

Graff led the little group to the front office where they identified themselves once again. As she did when they had arrived, the woman behind the counter glanced nervously at Graff's sidearm and did not offer any smile.

"Your camera system, is it working?"

She nodded and said, "The police already watched it."

"I was wondering if we might be able to view it," Graff said with a smile. "Just to be sure."

She shrugged and led them through the office, past the staff workroom to a small room adjacent to a staff restroom and water fountain.

Teachers watched the little procession and stopped what they were doing, frozen like in the little kids' game of statues. The group of cops ignored them as best they could.

"I'll get someone from security to run this for you."

"Thank you, ma'am," Graff said.

The cops cleared a path so she could leave. A few minutes later, a young guy wearing a security uniform entered and sat down at the system without any introduction. He fiddled with this switch and that switch, and Bodencamp appeared on the computer screen.

They watched her lock her office door and walk down the hallway to the front door. She pushed it open, shut it, and leaned against it.

"Okay, there he is," Graff said. "Run it in slow-mo."

"She jumped," O'Connor said. "She never heard him."

"It looks like they're talking," Eiselmann said.

"He's talking. She's listening," O'Connor said.

They watched him raise his .38 and fire two shots, the muzzle flash bright against the darkness of the night. The shooter did not linger, but turned around and walked away. He did not run, and he did not even walk very quickly.

"Is there another camera where we might see the guy's face?" Eiselmann asked.

The young security guy shook his head and said, "No. Only one camera on this door."

O'Connor said, "Hmmm."

"What?" Graff asked.

O'Connor shook his head and said, "Not sure."

Graff considered his response and knew from experience something was tickling his brain. Not wanting to disturb him, he changed the subject and said, "How long does this system store video?"

"The district has it set for thirty days. I can extend it if you want me to," the nervous young security guy said.

"All cameras, all video?" O'Connor asked.

"Yes, they're all tied to the same system."

Eiselmann dug into his laptop bag and pulled out a thumb drive.

"For now, can you download the footage to this?"

"Any particular file?"

Eiselmann shook his head and said, "I'll organize it when we get back."

It took the tech less than ten minutes to download it beginning with locking the front office door to the shooting to the shooter's departure.

Graff was pretty sure he noticed the security guy had shut his eyes through the shooting.

Chapter Seven

Milwaukee, WI

They had gathered in an office back at the Milwaukee County Safety Building that smelled unpleasantly of disinfectant. The floors had a waxy shine, and the temp in the room was almost too warm. Still, Eiselmann wore his sports coat with his t-shirt and jeans, just as Batiste and Dahlke did. Alamorode wore an expensive tailor-made three-piece suit. Weist and Storm wore nearly matching pantsuits with a white blouse on Storm and a cream-colored blouse on Weist. Graff had dressed down to khakis and a police polo. O'Connor did not bother with any formality. He wore what he always wore: a t-shirt and jeans.

Papers and photos covered the surface of the beaten and battered wooden table. Matching photos, along with the names, the cities, and where the victims had died lined a tack board on one wall. A whiteboard faced them, and someone had taken the time to organize a timeline.

Eiselmann sat next to Dahlke, and both worked at their laptops, talking. Joe Weist and Dr. Nelson Alamorode sat across the table reading the various reports that came at them via email from law enforcement in the field. Graff sat next to Summer and exchanged ideas and posed questions to which neither had satisfactory answers. Yet.

O'Connor stood against one wall with his arms crossed, alternately staring at the timeline and the picture and crime scene board. He would stare, shake his head, and stare some more.

Batiste watched him, gave in to curiosity, and asked, "What are you looking at?"

Eiselmann and Dahlke glanced up from their laptops in time to see O'Connor shake his head once.

"What?" Graff asked. No offense to Summer, Eiselmann, or Batiste, he knew O'Connor was the best investigator in the room, himself included.

The question and the resulting silence of the room were enough to cause Alamorode and Weist to watch and listen.

O'Connor made a face, said, "I," and stopped. Graff and Eiselmann were used to this little quirk.

"What?" Summer asked.

"I," he began again, then continued. "The shooter is organized. The crime scene is organized. He plans each murder. This guy is intelligent. Something is driving him. We just don't know what it is, but it's right there," he said gesturing at the crime scene board.

"Why do you think this?" Alamorode asked. "I'm not doubting you. I just want to understand your reasoning."

"We watched the tape of the Bodencamp shooting. The shooter was waiting for her. He knew she would be working late. He had to have surveilled her and knew her movements. Same with the O'Laughlin shooting in the parking garage. The shooter knew where he had parked and at what time O'Laughlin would be in the parking garage after work. There was evidence that the overhead lighting in the garage had been tampered with, so the shooter had that planned too."

"How do you explain the Fortune shooting?" Weist asked. "It was chancy walking up to the door like he did. What would have happened if her husband had opened the door?"

O'Connor shrugged and said, "Don't have an answer for that."

"I was hoping for a crazy," Eiselmann said. "In some respects, crazy is easier to deal with."

"We definitely have crazy," Weist said. "But I think this crazy is smart. The organization and detail he put into this, points to smart. It points to control. There is some sort of plan this guy is following."

Summer nodded and said, "I think so too." She pushed through some of the paper on the table and picked up the O'Laughlin crime report.

"Did anyone interview Gustnecky? The guy who found himself out of a job in the advertising agency where O'Laughlin worked? There were reports he blamed O'Laughlin."

"Yeah, he was interviewed at his home in Richfield." Eiselmann found the report on his laptop. "He was out of town visiting his daughter and son-in-law in Fond du Lac."

"Could they be covering for him?" Batiste asked.

Eiselmann shook his head and said, "The cops put in an aside that the guy had no registered weapons and didn't seem the type.'" He looked up and said, "They wrote that."

"What does that mean, 'doesn't seem the type'?" Alamorode asked.

The cops looked from one to another to see who would explain, each not caring to. It was Batiste who said, "When you work a possible perp, you get a feeling. I'm assuming that's what they meant."

"A *feeling*? They based their decision to rule him out on a *feeling*?" Alamorode said with a dry chuckle.

"Sometimes a feeling is enough," Graff said.

"Maybe Pat and I should interview him again," Batiste offered.

"Wouldn't hurt," Summer answered. "Just to rule out possibilities."

"Where is Richfield from here?" Batiste asked.

"Not far. Maybe thirty, forty minutes?"

"Up for a road trip?"

O'Connor shrugged and said, "If you buy dinner."

"Deal!" Batiste said with a smile.

"Summer ... Chief?" Weist said.

"Yes, Jo?"

"I think it's important that everyone understand that this guy isn't going to stop any time soon. He's on some sort of mission. Real or imagined, he's on a mission."

"Shit," Eiselmann muttered. He had been thinking the same thing, but hearing it out loud was depressing.

Graff stood up, stretched, and said, "We've done about as much as we can do today. I'm heading home."

"Yup, same here, except my home for the foreseeable future will be a Holiday Inn Express," Summer said. She glanced at her watch and sighed. "And I have to do a press briefing in about thirty minutes."

"Better you than me," Graff said with a laugh. "Do you want anyone with you for that?"

"No, I'm good. No sense anyone else has to suffer through it." She turned to Batiste and said, "Cleve, can you give me a call with what you and Pat find out?"

"Will do."

Graff looked over at Summer and said, "North plays South tomorrow night. Big game. Brett, Billy, and Randy will be playing. Jeremy, Vicky, and Jeff Limbach will be there."

"I'd like to go ... if that's okay with you," Batiste said to Summer.

"I would like that too." To Graff, she asked, "What time?"

"Seven-ish. I would get there about an hour early. The place will be packed," Graff said.

"I might have to do another briefing, but text me the address, and we'll be there." She turned to her team and said, "If you guys want to, that is." To Graff, she added with a wry smile, "And, I think I might have a surprise for you."

Chapter Eight

Milwaukee, WI

They had gathered in the same room where that morning, Summer had met with the representatives from Metro Milwaukee law enforcement. *ABC, NBC, CBS, FOX,* and several independent networks had their cameras rolling. Several radio stations had their microphones mounted at the podium. Print media were also present, headed by the flagship, the *Milwaukee Journal Sentinel,* with smaller community papers following along like ducklings chasing their mother.

The briefing had been going on for twenty minutes, but of course, Summer knew whatever she said would be edited to a minute-and-thirty-second sound bite, if that. Media wanted live footage for their five o'clock broadcast. It would be repeated on the ten o'clock and eleven o'clock newscasts. Newspapers would post it online yet that afternoon and plaster it all over the front page in the morning.

The popular two-term Milwaukee mayor, Democrat, kicked it off by thanking the Milwaukee Chief of Police and the Milwaukee County Sheriff, a far right, controversial Republican, for putting the task force together. He praised cops and law enforcement up and down the shores of Lake Michigan for working together, and then he thanked the FBI for their willingness to help with the investigation.

He introduced her as Agent Summer Storm, Associate Director of the Criminal Investigation Division of the FBI. When she took the microphone, she stated humbly that she was one member of the team and thanked the mayor, the chief, and the sheriff for inviting the FBI onto the case.

She provided an update on the investigation, including the preliminary profile, but deftly downplayed the role of the FBI and talked up local law enforcement instead. The media did not buy it because neither the chief nor the sheriff said anything, and they had no intention of doing so. In fact, both stood behind the mayor. If they could have left the room or hid behind curtains, they would have. It was as if they expected the investigation to fail and did not want to get any dirt on them. Of course, if it did succeed, it would get several degrees of ugly before the case was closed, and in the end, they would fight each other for the credit.

"Do you have any leads at all?" a talking head from *Channel Six* asked. Though it was asked in different ways, it was still the third time Summer was asked, and she gave the same answer as she had the first two times.

"I can't answer that just yet because I don't want to jeopardize the investigation."

"Is there any connection between the murders, or are the murders random?" asked an expertly coiffed reporter with too much lipstick.

"We're sure there's a connection," Summer said, unwilling to elaborate because there was not much more to say.

"Can you share what that connection is? For the safety of the public?" someone had shouted.

"I'm sorry, that might jeopardize the investigation," Summer said with a smile. It was her favorite answer, and she stuck to it like shit on toilet paper.

"Unwilling or unable?" the same reporter asked.

"Next question," Summer said.

"The killer ... would you classify him as a psychopath?" an older gentleman asked, waving a pen in one hand and a notebook in the other.

"I'm not qualified to give a psychological evaluation, but I would say that anyone who has murdered seven or eight individuals coldly and callously is not in his right mind."

"So, we're talking about a crazy person who is running around killing people," the reporter said with a smile.

Summer nodded at the mayor and said, "That's all for now. We will update you when there are any developments."

The mayor stepped to the podium; thanked Summer, the Chief of Police, and the County Sheriff and law enforcement again; and led the little group to a back room.

He sighed and asked, "Do you have any idea how long this investigation might take? Off the record, that is?"

With a practiced smile, Summer said, "As long as it takes."

Chapter Nine

Shorewood, WI

He rarely displayed emotion except when the appropriate social situation called for it. On demand, he could feign anger, surprise, shock, or doubt. Even happiness and joy though they took more work. Like an actor. However, he viewed himself to be more of a chameleon than an actor.

He watched the news conference and concluded they did not have a clue. None. The blond FBI agent was no match for him. Beauty over brains, except he did not think she was all that good looking either.

Free and clear, just as he had been and always will be, forever and ever, amen. He chuckled at his little joke, the smile disappearing as quickly as it appeared.

The Man sat down at his dark cherry wood and oversized desk. He opened the bottom drawer and from the back, buried under two one-inch, black, three-ring binders, pulled out a small black leather-bound notebook.

He set it on top of the plastic blotter. A framed picture of a toy poodle and a silver pen and pencil set were the only ornaments on an otherwise barren desktop. He liked his desktop like his life: neat and orderly, free from anything extraneous.

He gazed around the room. A cozy fire, though it was of gas and fake logs. A small decorative candelabra with three small candles sat on mantelpiece. Of course, the candles were never used. The wick would deform the candle making each untidy and therefore unsightly.

He flipped open the book and studied his next query, though he did not have to. He knew all there was to know. Pictures. Daily routines. Habits. The tiny meaningless minutia of her life. Her friends. Her husband. Her job.

All of it would end. All of it. As soon as he pulled the trigger. Easy. Just like the others.

Chapter Ten

Cudahy, WI

Jenna Meyers looked like a twenty-two,-year,-old, not like the forty-two,-year,-old she was. And she looked as good as she felt. She had cut out carbs, soda, and alcohol a year earlier. She ate red meat sparingly and desserts even less.

Jenna began running and Pilates when her mother was diagnosed with Alzheimer's. A sad day for Jenna because Marion was her mentor and her role model and her closest female friend. She had confided in her mother more so than her husband, Russ. But it was not because she did not love him. From little on, Jenna had developed a deep love and friendship with her mother.

Each night after work, Jenna would slip into her black Under Armour Cold Gear Tights and matching jacket with reflective tape. Then she would drive to Warnimount Park just north of Cudahy, do some light stretches, and run. Some afternoons, she would run three miles. Other nights, she would run six. On weekends, eight to ten. When finished with the run, she would stretch and then drive home, which was a short five-mile drive, as long as traffic cooperated. It did most nights.

There were two other cars parked in the smallish lot adjacent to the blacktop path. The lack of cars did not cause her to worry since there would be other runners who had parked farther south. Jenna sat in her car long enough so Kenny Chesney and Pink could finish "Set The World On Fire." She turned off her car and stepped into the cold night air. She did some easy stretches and started on her run, eager to get going.

Three miles and just over twenty-six minutes later and hardly winded, she stood in front of her car and stretched again. Two more cars had appeared in the same lot since she started on her run.

"Excuse me, are you Jenna Meyers?"

"What?"

"Are you Jenna Meyers?"

"Do I know you?"

The Man moved closer. He already had his hand in his pocket gripping his .38.

"Jenna! I thought that was you! I tried to catch up to you but couldn't quite reach you!"

Another runner had come around the bend and over the hill. Huffing, he stepped between Jenna and The Man.

Recognizing him, Jenna smiled and said, "Stan! I haven't seen you in ages! I thought you had quit running." She laughed and embraced him.

"I did for a while. I tweaked my meniscus and had to lay off it. I hate stationary bikes." Stan laughed.

He turned to The Man and said, "I'm sorry, I'm interrupting."

The Man took a step back and said, "No, I'm sorry. I was mistaken," and he hurried off to his dark BMW.

Puzzled, Jenna and Stan watched him get in and drive away.

Stan shrugged and said, "Who was that?"

Jenna hugged herself. A chill ran up and down her back that had nothing to do with the cold night air. She shook her head and said, "I have no idea."

Still staring after the car that had disappeared, she whispered, "But he knew my name."

Chapter Eleven

Richfield, WI

"I don't think he's our guy, but there's something there," Batiste said.

Pat O'Connor and Cleve Batiste were heading south on Highway 41 towards Milwaukee. O'Connor had Bluetooth in his car, and they used his phone to contact Summer.

"Both of you feel that way?"

Batiste stared at O'Connor, waiting for him to respond.

"Um ... there's." He stopped, glanced out the side window and then his eyes were back on the road. He shook his head and said, "Not our guy, but ... something."

Summer sighed and ran a hand through her short hair. "Well, we kind of figured it was a long shot."

"We pressed him pretty hard, and he held up," Batiste said.

O'Connor nodded.

"So, what are you guys going to do now?"

"Eat. I'm starved." Batiste laughed.

"Do you want to meet me somewhere? I think there's a Fuddruckers down ... what's this road? Where the Holiday Inn is?"

"Bluemound," O'Connor answered.

"Yes, on Bluemound. Just down the road."

"Give us about twenty minutes," O'Connor said. "Are Skip and Jo coming?"

Summer smiled. She did not see O'Connor as being interested in the young profiler or anyone else for that matter. He was a lone wolf. But stranger things have happened. Take Jeremy Evans and Victoria McGovern for instance. That still baffled her.

"Summer, are you there?" Batiste asked.

"Yes ... sorry. Just thinking. I'll give James and Jo a call and see if they want to come along."

She ended the call, glanced at her watch, and decided she had time for a quick shower. She kicked off her shoes and dug around in her suitcase for some casual clothes. Barefoot, she walked into the bathroom and shut the door.

Summer speed-dialed Skip Dahlke and said, "Hungry? Cleve, Pat, and I are heading to Fuddruckers. Do you want to join us?"

"Sure. What time?"

"About twenty minutes or so. I'll call Jo and ask her."

"She's with me. We were going over crime scene reports, and we were talking about getting something to eat."

Summer smiled. *Jo Weist and Skip Dahlke?* She shook her head and smiled at the wonder of it.

"Okay, I'll meet you in the lobby in twenty minutes."

Chapter Twelve

Waukesha, WI

In the study on the left side of the couch was Jeremy's favorite spot in his favorite room of the house. Add an opened Diet Coke on the coffee table and Jeremy was in heaven. Vicky McGovern, the future Vicky Evans, sat on the other end of the couch, her bare feet tucked under her, a thin Navajo blanket covering her lap as she alternately read the latest Patricia Cornwell novel and watched a rerun of *NCIS*. Every now and then, she would sip from a mug of hot herbal tea. Momma, part Husky and part wolf, lay on the rug in front of the cozy fire. Jasper, one of her two puppies, lay with his head resting on Brian's thigh.

As he did most often, Brian sat cross-legged on the floor, leaning against both the couch and Jeremy's leg. As much as Jeremy and Vicky could tell, Brian never strayed too far from either of them in the two months he had lived with them. Yes, he got along just fine with the five other boys. They were best friends. He had known them long before he had moved in after his parents' death. He would go hunting and fishing with Brett and George, and work the horses and shovel the driveway with George. He started and played on the same basketball team as Brett, Billy, and Randy, and he shared a room with Bobby by mutual choice. Still, where Jeremy or Vicky was, he was not too far away. And where Brian was, Bobby could be found.

Brian read *Lord of the Flies* and would jot notes after every passage or two. Bobby leaned up against him, sometimes resting his head on Brian's shoulder while he watched TV with Jeremy.

"Where is everyone else?" Jeremy asked.

"Randy's in the living room working on a song." Bobby turned around, grinned at him and said, "It's sounds good, but he won't let me sit and listen to it until he's finished. He's a perfectionist."

"Where are the others?" Vicky asked.

"In the kitchen. Billy's working on science, and Brett's helping George with algebra," Brian answered, not looking up from his paperback.

"You want anything?" Bobby asked Brian.

"Water."

"That's it?"

Brian wrote a couple of sentences and answered, "A cookie."

"That's refined sugar."

"That's why I like cookies."

Jeremy laughed, and Vicky smirked. Bobby glared at them both.

He sighed, turned back to Brian, and said, "But we're going to bed in about an hour, and a cookie is going to sit in your stomach and do nothing for you."

"It will taste good."

Bobby was a year and one grade younger than Brian and the other guys. He was also Brett's brother and Vicky's son by birth. Brett and Bobby looked remarkably alike, and most everyone would say they looked like Tom Brady without the cleft chin. The two boys had chestnut brown hair with matching eyes. The biggest difference between the two was that Bobby smiled and talked more. He was also one inch taller, and Brett was not happy about that.

Randy and Billy were identical twins, who had been separated at birth but had joined back together two or three years previous and were adopted by Jeremy. Like the McGovern boys, they had brown hair and brown eyes, but were taller than the McGovern boys. George had been adopted by Jeremy just after the summer of death, the same summer the McGoverns moved to Waukesha from a suburb of Indianapolis. George had no one and nowhere to go because his family had been murdered. A full-blooded Navajo and originally from Arizona, he wore his black hair long to his mid-back. Sometimes he would braid it. Other times, he would pull it back into a bun. His preference was to wear it long. His eyes were dark and missed nothing. He had learned to be observant from his grandfather, and it had saved his life and the lives of his adopted family several times during the summer of death.

It had been quite an adjustment for each of the boys. To one degree or the other, each struggled in his own way. But each of the boys thrived because they had Jeremy and Vicky. They had each other.

"But it isn't good for you," Bobby continued.

Brian looked up at Bobby and said, "You asked what I wanted, and I would like water and a cookie."

Jeremy and Vicky listened to the exchange thinking once again that of the six boys, Brian and Bobby sounded like an old married couple.

Bobby pushed himself up to his knees and said, "I'll bring you a cookie, but I'll bring you something good for you too."

"I'm not that hungry."

Ignoring him, Bobby smiled and said, "Butterflies."

Brian and Bobby leaned together and put first one eye together and fluttered it, then the other eye and fluttered it.

"Eskimo," Bobby said.

They rubbed noses.

"Regular," Bobby said.

They kissed each other's cheek. Bobby stood up and left the study.

After he had gone, Vicky said, "If you get tired of that and want Bobby to stop, just tell him."

Brian shook his head and said, "No, it's okay. I don't mind." He smiled at her and said, "He's like the perfect little brother. I like him a lot."

Brian had longish dark wavy hair that Jeremy teased him about, saying he looked like one of the Beatles. His eyes were greenish-hazel, and he had a smattering of small freckles under his eyes and on his nose. He, George and Brett were the quietest of the boys, but every now and then, Brian would lighten up and flash a quick wit.

"He remind you of Brad?" Jeremy asked.

Brad was Brian's twin, who had died during the summer of death. His parents had never recovered from his death, and it led to his mother killing Brian's father and her committing suicide. Police found them in Brad's bedroom, lying on Brad's bed with Brad's rifle clutched in his mother's hands. Concerned and watchful, Jeremy was sure Brian was not over Brad's death much less his parents' death.

Brian smiled, shook his head and said, "In some ways. He's just Bobby, and I like him a lot."

Jeremy was not sure if the time was right or not, but on impulse and a hunch, he asked, "Bri, are you doing okay?"

Brian stared at the fire and said, "Most days are good, and some days aren't. Kinda like you said they would be. Sometimes I wonder why my mom and dad did that and I get pissed off. Sometimes I'm just sad. Most times, I try not to think about them."

Jeremy smiled. For a fifteen-year-old kid, Brian was self-aware. Mature. The same could be said about any of his boys. Forced to grow up because their childhood had been stolen from them along with their innocence.

"Are you happy here?" Vicky asked. "I mean, living with Jeremy and me? With the guys?"

Brian nodded, turned around, smiled sadly, and said, "Sometimes I feel like I'm visiting, you know? But there's no place else I'd rather live. I like Sean and Gavin. They're my friends, but I don't want to live with either of them. The guys live here. You're here," he said looking at both Vicky and Jeremy.

"You're not just visiting, Brian," Vicky said. "You belong here as much as anyone else."

He shrugged and chose not to reply.

"Are you still okay with me adopting you next week?" Jeremy asked, tugging on Brian's hair.

Brian stuck his finger in his book, turned around, and said, "Yes, but my uncle doesn't want me to change my name. He wants me to keep Kazmarick."

"How do you feel about that?" Vicky asked.

"I don't want to be remembered as that Kazmarick kid whose parents ..." His voice trailed off, but he regained his composure and said, "Pretty much everybody knows me as Brian Evans except for Mr. Coggins, who can't get anything straight anyway."

Jeremy did not think much of the business teacher. More kids trying to get out of his class than in it, and it had nothing to do with the subject matter.

"So, you want to change your name?" Jeremy asked.

Brian nodded and said, "If that's okay with you. I want to be Brian Evans. Brett and Bobby want to change their last name, too."

"I'm working on that," Vicky said, shaking her head. "Their father can be hard-headed."

"They know," Brian said with a smile.

Even though Randy and Billy were twins, Randy chose Jeremy's last name, while Billy chose to remain Schroeder out of deference to his first adoptive father who had passed away from a heart attack. George remained Tokay, choosing to keep his Navajo name.

Bobby came back into the study with a glass of ice water and a plate of orange slices and a single cookie and sat down next Brian.

"Here's your cookie. We'll share the orange."

"You and Brett and oranges," Brian laughed.

"Vitamin C. Oranges are good for you."

"Won't taste as good as a cookie."

Chapter Thirteen

Shorewood, WI

The Man sat at his desk with his manicured hands folded in front of him. His eyes were shut. He breathed in, would hold it, and would ease it out. He was in control and had been sitting this way for thirty minutes.

He thought over his evening.

True, for the first time, one of his victims had lived. True, he was seen by both the woman and the man, the intruder. True, they had seen his car. True, they might be able to identify him.

However, it was dark, and darkness hid things. Even though the intruder and the woman had seen him, he had done nothing nor said anything that would incriminate him. The only suspicious thing he had done was talk to the woman.

Yes, he had used her name. But that could be explained as a misunderstanding. The Man would invent some excuse, some reason for being at the park and for speaking to her.

He opened his eyes. He reached into his drawer and extracted the leather-bound notebook. The Man opened it to stare at the woman and then, reluctantly, flipped to his next victim. It troubled him that his victims were no longer in order. Troubled him greatly.

Of course, he knew his next victim just like The Man knew all of the other victims, dead or alive. But he read and reread and studied him just the same.

On impulse, The Man checked his pulse. Ninety-three.

The Man grit his teeth, angry that, he was unsettled. At least on the outside, he did not appear to be.

This next victim might give him some trouble. Fifteen-year-old boys ran in packs. There might be witnesses. But though he did not like taking any life needlessly, he would not leave any witnesses again. He should have shot both the woman and the intruder. Then, every victim would be on schedule. It would be orderly. Tidy.

For his next victim, The Man would take his time and make sure it was done right. He would complete his task and not let anyone interfere with his goal.

Unlike the lady, the fifteen-year-old boy would die.

Chapter Fourteen

Waukesha, WI

Instead of heading off to bed, they had gathered in Brett's room. Teeth had been flossed and brushed. Faces, necks, and ears washed and lotion applied liberally.

His bookshelf had autobiographies of athletes. On his nightstand was an autographed copy of the latest Jeff Limbach novel. On one wall was a framed and autographed Peyton Manning jersey. Next to it was an action poster of Usain Bolt. Just inside the door was a corkboard that had medals from his track meets along with pictures of Tim and Patrick, guys he was captive with in Chicago. He also had pictures of Mikey, Stephen, and Big Gav, and of course, the twins, Brian, George, and Bobby. Billy had remarked more than once that Brett had displayed track medals and none of this basketball or football trophies.

Brett sat against the headboard with one of his pillows on his lap. Brian sat on his left. Bobby used Brett's other pillow with his head toward Brian while he stretched out with his feet in George's lap. George ran his fingers up and down Bobby's back and shoulders, and goosebumps covered Bobby's torso. Randy sat opposite Brett and Brian, while Billy mirrored Bobby and George on the other side of the bed.

"Who was your favorite character?" Brian asked.

"I liked Sam and Eric," Billy answered with a laugh. "I liked how they talked at the same time and finished each other's sentences."

"Like you and Randy," Brett laughed. "And Brian and Bobby."

The boys laughed.

Billy was more talkative than Randy. Both boys were beyond little boy cute and were well on the road to young man handsome. Billy was the joker, while Randy was more serious. But it was Billy who was the peacemaker who worked hard at lifting spirits and mending fences, his or others.

"I liked Simon," Randy said.

"He didn't do much, though. He was always alone," Bobby said.

"Why did you read the book?" Billy asked. "You didn't have to."

Bobby shrugged and said, "Everyone else was reading it, so I thought, what the hell?"

"Why did you like Simon?" George asked Randy.

"He was gentle. He was a thinker, and he didn't follow along with either group. He was more of a loner."

"I didn't like any of them," Brett said. "But if I had to pick a character to like, I'd say, Ralph."

"Why didn't you like Ralph?" George asked.

Brett shrugged and said, "Ralph was a coward. He didn't stand up for Piggy. There was nothing to like about any of the other characters though."

"Piggy was annoying," Brian said.

"But if you're a friend, you have his back," Brett said.

"So, what are you going to write your comparison paper on?" Brian asked as he looked around at his friends, his soon-to-be-brothers.

"I've been talking to Uncle Jeff about that," Billy said. "I'm going to compare it to a basketball team."

None of the boys responded right away. Randy, Brett, and Brian cocked their head at him. Bobby asked, "How?"

"Look at our team. On the floor, Brett's the quarterback ... the point guard. What he does, we react to. We follow his lead. Part of it is the style of offense and defense we run, but it's because Brett's the leader. I'm going to compare our team to the guys in the two groups on the island."

"Huh," Randy said.

"I think I'm going to focus on the lack of laws and the lack of order. I'm going to compare it to the start of our nation and how we had to develop our system of laws out of nothing," Brian said. Of the boys, he was the best in social studies.

George nodded. Even though the assignment was in English, it was smart of Brian to go with his strength. Same with Billy, who was into sports.

"What are you going to write about?" Brian asked him.

"The difference between living in *Diné Bikéyah,* Navajoland, and living in Wisconsin and then compare that to living on the island. Adaptation."

"I like the way you say that," Bobby said with a smile, craning his neck back to look at him. "Say it again."

George smiled at him, poked his ribs, and said, *"Diné Bikéyah."*

"That's cool!" Bobby said batting George's hand.

"I'm going to compare *Lord of the Flies* to being abducted and held captive in Chicago," Brett said. "I'm going to compare the guards' rules with our rules and the rules of the island."

"Seriously?" Billy asked.

Brett nodded.

"Does Dad know?" Bobby asked.

"We talked about it."

"Are you going to ... write about everything?" Bobby asked.

Brett shrugged, but nodded at the same time. "Dad and I thought if I write everything, I can always edit things out or leave in what I want."

"Everything?" Bobby asked just above a whisper.

Brett sighed. With his eyes focused on his hands, he said, "I've been thinking about it a lot."

"Thinking about what?" Randy asked. Brett had been talking about it with him on and off, but more so lately.

Brett was silent, and the others imagined his mind whirling and spinning. Brian could almost hear Brett's heart pounding. He placed his hand on Brett's thigh.

"Did you guys know that Ian and Corey tried to commit suicide?"

The boys shook their head while Randy did not react because he had known. In fact, he and Jeremy had spoken with them and their families.

"In that hell-hole, Ian was the funny one. He could turn anything into something funny."

George sat expressionless face. Billy glanced at Randy, who remained focused on Brett.

"Tim thinks he's gay. Hell, there are times ..." Brett did not finish. He set his jaw, though his chin quivered.

"Patrick's still taking anxiety medicine. He says he's still nervous and jumpy," Billy said.

As if he did not hear Billy's comment, Brett said, "I hated all the shit I had to do. We all did. I hated the perverts and the guards. That night we were rescued was when I was the most scared." He wiped his eyes. "I was afraid we wouldn't make it out of there."

Brian tightened his grip on Brett's thigh. Bobby dipped his face into the pillow, and the guys knew he was weeping. George rubbed Bobby's back.

"But we had our own rules. The guards and perverts didn't know it." He paused, looked from one to the other, and said, "This is going to sound ... *wrong*; but I don't know how else to say it."

None of the guys responded. Bobby still had his face in the pillow, but Brian could see one of his brown eyes. He reached out, and finger-combed Bobby's hair, much like Jeremy did to the boys when he talked with them.

Brett stared first at Billy and then at George and said, "You know how you miss Rebecca?"

Billy nodded, but George remained expressionless.

"Not just miss her, but miss being *with* her ... doing things ... you know?"

Each of the boys knew what he meant.

"When we ... Tim or Johnny or Patrick or Ian and I had to do stuff with each other, it was different than doing shit with the perverts. We cared about each other. We ... *loved* each other. We were all we had." This last he said just above a whisper. "I know that's hard for you to understand. It's hard for me to explain, but I hated the shit I had to do with the perverts. I never would have thought of doing that shit with any guy. But ... Tim and Johnny and Patrick ... they were all I had. We were all we had. Sometimes I miss being ... *with* them. I think about the night Stephen and Mikey were taken. Stephen was so scared. We never saw Mikey, but we heard him screaming and crying. If we hadn't been rescued, Mikey would have ..." He stopped and shook his head and wiped more tears from his eyes.

He took a deep breath and plunged on.

"I know Stephen didn't want Tim and me to ... you know. But the guards needed him in a movie, so Tim and I volunteered. We knew the rules, and Stephen didn't. So, I did Stephen while Stephen did Tim while Tim told him the rules. It was the only way we knew how to keep Stephen safe," Brett added, almost begging to be understood.

Brian let go of Brett's thigh and slipped his arm around Brett's shoulders. He pulled him in tight, and Brett let him. Brian brushed Brett's chestnut hair with his lips.

"There are times I want to be held. There are other times I don't want anyone to touch me. No one. Not Mom. Not Dad. Not any of you. It's like I feel dirty."

He looked at Billy and George again and said, "Just like you miss being *with* Rebecca, sometimes, I miss ..." He sighed and said, "I know that sounds sick, and I know that's wrong, but. . ." He let a shrug finish the sentence for him. "I know I'm not gay, but sometimes ..."

The boys were silent.

Bobby wept, and George patted his bare back. Brian held Brett with one arm and ran his other hand through Bobby's hair. Billy struggled to hold back tears.

Randy smiled at Brett and said, "That took a lot of guts."

Brett started to object, but Randy cut him off. "No, that took a lot of guts."

Brett said nothing.

"You've always been tough, Brett. That's how you survived."

Brett met Randy's eyes, but just briefly.

"Enough for tonight. We have a game tomorrow," Randy said.

Billy climbed off the bed, wiped his eyes, and stretched.

Brian and Brett embraced, unwilling to let go of one another. When Brian was sure Brett was okay, did he grip Brett's shoulders, put his forehead to Brett's, and said, "Are you going to be alright?"

Brett nodded.

George tapped Bobby on the shoulder and said, "Come here."

Bobby turned around and sat up, and the two boys embraced.

"Are you okay?" George asked still holding him. He felt Bobby nod his head.

Each of the boys embraced each other and said goodnight.

"What side of the bed do you want?" Randy asked Brett.

Brett did not answer.

"I sleep on the right, and you sleep on the left, so that should work."

"You don't have to."

"I'm going to anyway," he answered crawling under the covers.

"Are you okay?" Brett asked Bobby.

Brian, who stood behind Bobby, slipped both arms around him, hugged him, and said, "I'll take care of him."

Brett smiled at the two of them.

"What time do you set the alarm?" Randy asked Brett.

"Early."

"Works for me."

Chapter Fifteen

Waukesha, WI

It was late, and he knew he should be asleep with the huge game against Waukesha South later that evening. They had lost the first game at South, but that was before he and Randy were put on varsity and inserted into the starting lineup. Since then, they had not lost a game, though some were close. This time, the game would be played in the North Fieldhouse in front of Northstar Nation, so the guys hoped that would make a difference.

Bobby twitched and moaned. His expression was a grimace as if he were in pain. He had his leg thrown over Brian's and his head was half on Brian's pillow and half on Brian's shoulder. A typical night for him. Brian held him in both arms to provide as much comfort as he could.

Startled, Bobby raised his head and looked around the room, then blinked at Brian and put his head back down on Brian's shoulder.

"Are you okay?" Brian whispered.

"Did I wake you up?"

"No, I couldn't sleep."

Brian ran his fingers up and down Bobby's back, while Bobby did the same to Brian's chest and stomach to just inside the waistband of Brian's boxers. Brian felt his heart quicken each time Bobby tickled him on his lower belly, and inside his boxers. He ran his fingers just inside Bobby's boxers on his backside, and Bobby responded by rubbing himself twice on Brian's leg.

"If I ask you something, you can't tell anyone, okay?"

"I won't," Brian whispered.

"Do you think Randy and Brett ... *did* anything?"

Brian shook his head and said, "I don't think so. I don't think Randy would do anything with anyone, and I don't think Brett would either. I could be wrong though."

Bobby dipped his fingers way inside Brian's boxers touching and tickling him and then gripped him.

"Brett said he missed ... *this.*"

"Yeah, but missing it and doing something about it are two different things."

They were silent as Bobby played with him. Brian shifted his hand from Bobby's backside to the front and reciprocated.

"I don't want to get anything on my shirt or boxers," Brian said.

Bobby stopped and helped Brian out of his shirt and then helped him slide his boxers off. Both ended up on the floor at the side of the bed along with Bobby's boxers.

Bobby pushed the covers down exposing their naked bodies in the moonlight.

"Does this ever bother you? I mean, that we do this?" Bobby whispered.

"No. It's not like we do this all the time. We've done this maybe three times in two months."

"I'm not gay," Bobby whispered.

"I know you aren't. I'm not either. Both of us have girlfriends."

"It's just that I don't like doing it by myself."

"Me neither."

"Eskimo," Bobby whispered, and the two boys rubbed noses.

"I'm going to kiss you," Bobby said.

Brian whispered, "You've done that before."

Bobby shook his head just once, rubbed noses, and then tenderly kissed Brian on the lips. Then again, but this time, his lips were parted.

Nervous, Brian answered and then, forgetting it was Bobby, kissed Bobby back with urgency.

Bobby shifted his body to between Brian's legs, and the two boys clung to each other. They picked up a gentle rhythm.

"Stop for a minute," Brian said between kisses.

They resumed kissing, and then their rhythm began again.

"Better stop again," Brian whispered breathlessly.

Bobby kissed Brian's neck, his chest, and continued down Brian's belly.

"Bobby," Brian whispered.

He shut his eyes in anticipation. Bobby had never done this to him before.

"I want to," Bobby whispered as he kissed and fondled him.

Brian could not object even if he wanted to.

"Uh ... God!" Brian whispered. "Oh God!"

He placed his hands on the back of Bobby's head, arched his back, and let loose.

"Jesus!" Brian whispered.

Bobby kissed his way up to eye level and smiled down at Brian.

"Was that okay?"

"Jesus, Bobby."

Brian smiled at him and rolled Bobby onto his back and then kissed his chest and belly.

"You don't have to if you don't want to."

Brian had never done anything with any boy other than Bobby, and it was never with his mouth.

"I've never done this before," Brian whispered.

"Do it like I did," Bobby whispered. His eyes were shut and his mouth open.

Tentatively, testing it, he took Bobby into his mouth.

It did not take long, and like Bobby did to him, Brian slowed down, but did not stop. He laid down between Bobby's legs, and the two boys clung to each other as they kissed passionately. As they did, they picked up a slow rhythm once again. Neither of them felt the need to move, though they rolled onto their side. They clung to each other, neither of them wanting to let go.

"I'm not gay," Bobby whispered again.

"I'm not, either," Brian whispered in return.

"But I love you, Bri. I mean, I think I *love* you. I don't know if that's a good thing or a bad thing."

Brian gave Bobby an Eskimo and another passionate kiss and said, "I love you more than anyone, Bobby. More than Brett and George." He kissed him again. "More than Randy or Billy." And he kissed him again. "And I think more than Mom and Dad."

Tears sprung to Bobby's eyes.

"You don't think I'm weird or anything? I mean, we're brothers."

Brian smiled and said, "We're brothers, but we're not related. It would be different if you did this with Brett. I'm your brother by adoption, not blood." With a smile, he added, "And of course you're weird. But we're all a little weird."

They kissed again as they held each other. Their hands slid between each other's legs.

After, Brian announced, "My balls hurt. I don't think I'm going to be able to walk tomorrow."

"But it was worth it." Bobby smiled.

Brian smiled back at him, kissed him, and said, "Yeah, it was."

Chapter Sixteen

Waukesha, WI

It was controlled chaos each morning before school. Those who had not showered the night before, showered in the morning. Those who were at the tail end had an uncomfortably cold one. Jeremy knew that the next major purchase would be a larger water heater.

Vicky had gotten up before him and had showered and dressed in her nurse's whites ready for a day in surgery. Jeremy was sure that by now, she would be in the kitchen supervising breakfast.

He had just finished with his tie when Brian knocked on the door in his stocking feet wearing khaki slacks with no belt and his white shirt unbuttoned at the top. He held a purple and gray tie in his hand. Even though Brian knew how to tie a tie, it was more about the time spent between the two of them than anything else. It was a game day ritual, and it did not matter if the sport was soccer or basketball.

Brian walked over and stood in front of the mirror and held his hand with the tie backward toward Jeremy. Jeremy stood behind him, lifted up Brian's collar, buttoned the top button, and took the tie from him.

"Were you limping just now? You were walking funny."

Brian felt himself blushing. "Maybe a little stiff."

Jeremy nodded but did not comment.

He snugged the tie up to Brian's neck. Brian turned around; the two stood facing each other. Jeremy playfully grabbed Brian's nose, and then the two embraced.

"Bri, can we talk for a second?"

"Sure." He figured it would be about the game.

Jeremy did not know any other way than to hit it straight on. That was the way he had dealt with kids as a counselor, especially if he had built up a rapport with the individual. He and Brian were already pretty close.

He said, "If you and Bobby are ... experimenting, please be careful."

Brian blushed deep crimson starting at his neck and creeping up to his face. His mouth opened and closed, and he started to speak, to object, but in the end, he shut his mouth without saying word one.

"Just be careful if you do anything risky."

Brian took a step back and said, "Dad, this is private."

"I know it's private."

"We hardly do anything and maybe just three times. Ever."

As uncomfortable as Brian was, Jeremy said, "I just want you to be careful, that's all."

"We don't do anything to be careful about or with or ... anything," Brian said.

"Well, if you do ... *whatever*, please protect yourselves."

"What? How? We don't do anything. Honest."

"Just please promise me that if you do decide to ... do anything ... *more*, let me know, and I'll get you protection."

Brian lifted both hands to his head and walked in a tight semi-circle as he said, "Oh my God, Dad! Both of us have girlfriends. Geez, Dad!"

Jeremy smiled, placed both hands on Brian's shoulders, and said, "Brian, please calm down."

Brian struggled a little.

"I didn't mean to embarrass you. I didn't mean to make you feel uncomfortable. I'm sorry."

The look of horror on Brian's face said it all.

"Brian, I'm sorry."

Brian nodded and said, "It's only been a couple of times, and we don't do much. And, I love him. Wait, that sounds wrong," he corrected himself, shaking his head. He rambled and speed-talked when he was nervous. "Bobby's my friend. He's my brother ... well, not until next week, anyway, but he's my brother. He means as much to me as Brad did ... does."

"I know that, Bri. So does Vicky."

In a second, Brian went from beet red to white.

"Mom? She? Oh my God!" He pulled away from Jeremy, both hands on his head.

"Brian ..." Jeremy said.

"We're not gay! I'm not gay! Bobby's not gay! We hardly did anything!"

Jeremy took him by the shoulders and said, "Brian, we know you aren't gay. And that wouldn't matter anyway. We don't care one way or the other. We just want you both to be careful."

"Geez, Dad, we are careful! We hardly do anything, and we aren't gay! Oh my God!"

"Brian, please stop. I'm good. Vicky's good. And you and Bobby are good. Okay?"

There were so many things flying around in Brian's head, and they either made him scared or sad or sick to his stomach.

"Do you want me to move out? I will if you want me to. I can even sleep in the other room across from Brett ... by myself, I mean. Or I can ask Sean or Gav if I can live with them. I'm sorry. Bobby and I will never do anything again. Promise! But if you want me to move out, I will. I'm really sorry."

And he began to cry. At first a tear or two, but then a full-on storm.

"I'm sorry. I am. I would never hurt Bobby. I promise."

Jeremy held him and let Brian cry into his shirt.

"I'm sorry, honest."

"Shhh, Brian ... there's nothing to be sorry about."

"Please don't say anything to the other guys," he said between sniffles. "I'm sorry, but please don't say anything to them."

"Brian, stop! Just stop and listen to me! Please!"

Jeremy held on to him, and he wondered how this conversation went sideways so fast. He wished he could start over. He felt Brian settle down and nod.

"You're not moving anywhere. You're not changing bedrooms. You and Bobby haven't done anything wrong, and Vicky and I won't say anything to any of the guys. That's a promise."

Brian lifted his head and peeked up at him and said, "If you don't want to adopt me, I understand. And if you want me to move out, I will. Just please don't tell the guys. Please."

"Brian, please stop. I will never lie to you, okay? So listen to me. I want to adopt you. I want to be your dad. I want you to live here. You and Bobby are fine. And this stays between you and me."

"What about Mom?"

"She's okay, Bri. She understands as well as any mom might understand. You and Bobby have done nothing wrong."

"We're not gay."

Jeremy laughed and said, "Brian, we know you aren't gay, and neither is Bobby."

"You won't tell the guys? Please?"

"Brian, we won't tell the guys."

"Promise?"

"Yes, Bri, I promise."

Jeremy thumbed tears out of Brian's eyes and said, "Just remember two things."

"What?"

"No matter what, I love you, and I always will. I love you and Bobby and all of the guys. Okay?"

Brian nodded.

"And I want you to live with us. I want to be your dad, and I want you to be my son. And I'm honored that you want to be Brian Evans. Okay?"

At first, Brian stared at him, trying to read his eyes and his expression. He ran back the words Jeremy had spoken, looking for any fault in his tone or anything lurking behind his words. There was not anything. Nothing. Still, he could not be sure.

"Okay."

They embraced and clung to each other.

"I love you, Bri."

Brian nodded, but that was all.

"And Bobby loves you. He trusts you, so please continue to be his friend and his brother."

Brian said nothing.

Brett stormed into the bedroom and said, "I can't tie my stupid tie. Geez! What the hell?"

Both Jeremy and Brian were startled, but Brian broke free and said, "Come here."

"It's not working!"

Just like Jeremy had done to him moments before, Brian stood behind Brett in front of the mirror and redid his tie.

"What's wrong with me?" Brett said. "I can tie a tie. I know how to tie a tie." He stopped, stared at Brian, and said, "Were you crying? Your eyes are all red."

"I'm fine."

Brett looked over at Jeremy, but Jeremy betrayed nothing.

Brian finished with his tie, turned him around, and took him by the shoulders, just as Jeremy had done to him, and Brian said, "I'm fine, but I need you to listen to me!"

Brett took a deep breath and said, "What?"

"It's a game. That's all it is. We've done this before."

"It's South. If we win, we get top seed and a bye."

"Stop and listen to me, right now!" Brian said raising his voice a little.

Brett blinked. He could not remember Brian ever raising his voice to him like that.

"You can't lose it, Brett. Not in front of Randy and Billy. They go as you go. You're the leader. They follow you. If you're nervous, they'll be nervous. Especially Randy. We need you to lead us, Brett. No matter what you feel on the inside, on the outside you have to be calm and confident. You have to, or we've lost the game before we suit up. Got that?"

Brett nodded, sighed, and said, "I was acting pretty stupid, huh?"

"Pretty much, so knock it off. This stays between the three of us. Randy and Billy don't know. Not now, not ever. Got that?"

"Got it."

Brian nodded and said, "We can't afford for you to have a meltdown. We have a game to play. We have a chance to win. We're a different team, and we're playing on our court."

Brett nodded and said, "You should be the captain, Bri."

"No," Brian said, shaking his head. "We follow you. Maybe Billy a little, but mostly you."

"Sorry I was acting stupid."

Brian smiled and shrugged. "Already forgotten."

They hugged and started to leave the room. Brett continued down the hall, but Brian turned around in the doorway. Jeremy knew he had wanted to say something, but in the end, Brian lowered his head, turned, and left.

Jeremy watched Brian leave, and it dawned on him that Brian was a lot like him in many ways, even adopting some of the same mannerisms, words, and phrases. For all of his confidence, Brian wore his heart on his sleeve, and Jeremy had crushed it. Somehow, someway, he knew he would have to make it up to him.

Minutes later in the kitchen, they filled up their plates with eggs and bacon and whole wheat bagels. Brett added an orange to his plate and tucked one into his backpack.

"What's everyone doing after the game?" Vicky asked as she sat down to her own plate.

"I'm going to Stephen's house with Gav, Garrett, Mikey, and Danny. I'll be home by nine tomorrow morning," Bobby said.

"Chris and Troy and some girls are coming over, if that's okay," Randy said. "I think Chris and Troy are going to spend the night."

Brian did not look up from his plate. He could not. "Sean, Melissa, and I are going to Cat's house. I was going to sleep over at Sean's, if that's okay."

"Bobby, you and Brian should make sure you have clothes for after the game and for tomorrow morning," Vicky said. "And don't forget your toothbrush, toothpaste, and deodorant."

"We did, I mean, we have them. We packed clothes, and Dad's going to put them in his office," Bobby said.

Jeremy walked into the room, grabbed a plate, filled it, and said, "Is everyone about ready?"

Randy stood up and took his and Billy's plates to the sink, rinsed them off, and placed them in the dishwasher. He went to the refrigerator and said, "Who wants water?"

A chorus of "Me!" rang out, some muffled because mouths were full.

Randy passed out water bottles as George, Bobby, Brett, and Brian took their plates to the sink. Brian went back to the table and began to clear it off.

"I have it, Bri," Vicky said. "I have time. You guys don't."

Brian hesitated. His eyes flicked up at Vicky just long enough to see her smiling at him. Cleaning off the table was something he had done ever since he was little. It was part of his routine. Breakfast, lunch, dinner, each and every one, each and every time. That's what he did. He cleaned off the table, did the dishes, or packed the dishwasher.

"I have it," Vicky said with a laugh.

"Let's hit it," Jeremy said. He walked around the table, bent down, and planted a kiss on Vicky and then planted another.

"I love you."

"I love you too."

"Get a room," Billy said with a laugh.

"We have one, and we use it," Vicky said with a laugh. "I can't believe I just said that."

"Oh my God! That's so gross!" Billy said as Jeremy and Vicky laughed at him.

Each of the boys came around the table to kiss her goodbye, except for Brian who wanted to avoid her. He ducked out of the house hoping she had not noticed.

On the way out the door, George said, "Father, I need new running shoes."

Of the boys, he called Jeremy, "Father," something he did because "Dad" was not respectful enough. Vicky insisted on being called, "Mom," and while George did not like it as much as "Mother," he did as she wished.

"And I need new shoes," Bobby said with a big smile. "I'm growing again. My toes are touching the tip."

"It doesn't matter how tall you get. I can still take you," Brett said.

"Ha! You wait," Bobby laughed. He nudged Brett, and Brett nudged him back.

"Hey, are you two limping or something?" Billy asked of Brian and Bobby. "You're walking funny."

Chapter Seventeen

Milwaukee, WI

As much as Jamie was happy to see Pete Kelliher, Pete had an aura of dread and doom associated with him. It brought back too many memories, and most of them were not good. In fact, most were ugly, and most emanated from the summer of death. Though Jamie counted Pete as a friend, there was an air of dread and darkness that was associated with the agent.

In his late fifties, Pete Kelliher wore a clipped gray flattop and a little too much weight. He had a rumpled look to him no matter what clothes he wore. He would not make the cover of *GQ* or any other fashion rag. Yet his mind was anything but rumpled. Together, he and Summer were a formidable team. He had never married and had no close family, though he had looked upon Summer as his daughter and Skip Dahlke as a kind of son. She had fought it, but eventually accepted it, and Skip just went along with it, looking at Pete as a mentor as much as a friend.

Though he spent most of the time teaching at the FBI Academy, he and Summer had convinced Deputy Director Thomas Dandridge it would be good for Pete to get back in the field from time to time to keep his skills fresh. In whispers and in hallways, Pete was considered larger than legend. To Summer and Dandridge, and to Jamie, Skip, and Pat O'Connor, Pete was a friend. Perhaps they were Pete's only real friends.

"What do you need from us to bring you up to speed?" Paul Eiselmann asked.

"A cold beer and a pepperoni pizza," Pete said with a laugh.

"I had emailed and faxed him all the reports as we received them," Summer said with a laugh.

"My nighttime reading. Not as good as Jeff Limbach or Stephen King, though," Pete said.

"Okay, just to make sure you all know, we received reports on three cold cases that match our current case. Right down to shooting the victim in the face with a .38," Eiselmann said.

"What were the locations in relation to the current cases?" O'Connor asked. He pushed himself away from the table, stood up, and positioned himself at the board with pushpins at the ready.

"East Side on the waterfront near the Milwaukee Art Museum," Eiselmann said. "A nineteen-year-old second-year college student at UWM majoring in psychology. Tory Wriblowski, a female. No witnesses. Case open, but no movement on it."

"Where? And how long ago?" O'Connor asked.

"A block west of the museum six years ago."

"We have to adjust our timeline," Cleve said. "She's way before the others." He got up and wrote information on the timeline. "Do you have her picture?"

Eiselmann said, "On the printer now."

Batiste pulled the picture off the printer and stuck it up on the wall.

"Next one?" O'Connor asked.

"Nathan Flock, age twenty-four, a graduate student at UWM in psychology." He paused and said, "Hmmm."

The detectives looked from one to another considering it. It was Pete who asked, "How long ago?"

"Five years and six months."

"Where?" O'Connor asked.

"Lake Park, about four blocks east of UWM. He was dressed as a jogger. Police theorized he went for a run and was shot in the parking lot."

"Picture?" Batiste said.

"Coming now."

As he did before, he went to the printer, grabbed the picture and tacked it up on the board, and wrote on the timeline.

"Number three is Callie Putzer, a female, age twenty-two, an English major at UWM, five years and two months ago in Lincoln Park in Whitefish Bay. She was reading in the park."

Batiste went to the printer, took the picture, and tacked it up with the others.

"There could be others, but these appear to be the first three victims. Like I said, at least the ones we know about," Summer said. "And all three from UWM."

"What is UWM?" Jo Weist asked.

"The University of Wisconsin-Milwaukee. A big school with a large commuter population. Not as big a school as Marquette or UW-Madison, though," Eiselmann answered.

"Paul, we need to look at these three victims. See if there are any connections between the three and then see if there are any connections to the other victims," Pete said.

"Summer, I think we need to get this to the press," Jamie said. "Link these to the others. Ask for any information. Maybe someone saw something, even after all these years."

"Interesting that the three victims were students," Weist said. "Two of the three studied psychology, and English is sometimes studied from a psychological perspective."

"When you're looking for connections, check to see if they had any professors in common," Summer said.

"Maybe check the victims we know about to see if there were similarities in undergrad or graduate studies," Pete said squinting at the board and running a hand over his flat-top. "Maybe look at common courses outside of majors."

"And check to see if they had minors," Weist said.

Nelson Alamorode bustled into the room and shut the door behind him. He shimmied out of his overcoat and scarf, and hung them up on the rack near the door. He set his briefcase on the table and sat down next to Weist.

"Sorry I'm late. Had an appointment early this morning. What did I miss?" He took a closer look at the timeline and pictures and said, "More victims?"

"Three cold cases," Summer answered. "Nelson, this is Agent Pete Kelliher."

The two men exchanged handshakes.

"What did you find out when you interviewed that suspect from Richfield?"

Batiste shook his head and said, "Not much. Neither Pat nor I think he's our guy, but we both agree there's something to this guy. He's on soft surveillance."

Alamorode frowned.

"What?" Weist asked.

"I just thought he looked like a solid person of interest, that's all."

"We're still watching him, but there are too many holes," Summer said.

"Say, where is the forensic guy?" Alamorode asked.

"Out in the field with Milwaukee County Sheriffs. They had the most victims, and he's reviewing crime scenes," Jamie answered.

The room was quiet as the men and women read through and shuffled papers. It occurred to Jamie that Summer had brought Pat, Paul, and him into the tight circle over any of the other cops. Maybe it was her intuition that proved to be uncanny at times. Maybe it was because she was familiar with them more so than any of the other cops on the task force. Whatever the reason, they were the outsiders in the room and the only outsiders who met with her team on a regular and ongoing basis. Not even any agents from the Milwaukee FBI office did that.

He supposed it was a compliment as much as it was extra work. He never minded the work. He liked puzzles, and he liked closing cases. By closing this case, he would help save lives and get answers for those who had lost loved ones. Answers were important to him. So far, the questions outnumbered the answers.

He sighed.

"What?" Pete asked.

Jamie shook his head and said, "Nothing yet. Just thinking."

Chapter Eighteen

Waukesha, WI

It happened almost in the same moment.

Brian was fouled hard and landed on his right knee and elbow, jamming both into the tartan surface. A strawberry blossomed on each, and both threatened to bleed. He got up slowly, tested them, and found they still worked fine, though the elbow was a little sore. The trainer, Caitlin Cortese, would bandage them up during halftime. Maybe give him an ice pack or two.

The team huddled at the free throw line.

"They will finish out the half fast," Brett said to them. "They'll run their set half-court offense, but if they have the chance to rebound and run, they will. Billy, you and Randy and Troy will have to clean up underneath. Bri and I will take care of anything long."

Of course, Coach Harrison had already said all of that in the last timeout. Brett repeated it, but that was Brett's way.

"If we can steal anything cheap like an inbounds, do it," Brian said.

"And steal off the traps," Randy added.

"Take the game to them. Our court. Our game," Billy added. "Make them react to us."

They broke out of the huddle, and Brian went to the free throw line. As he waited for the ball, he glanced into the overflow student section behind the basket. He saw Mikey and Stephen, Garrett and Big Gav. But he did not see Bobby.

The official tossed him the ball. Brian caught it, bounced it twice with his right hand, twice with his left hand, aimed, shot, and swished it.

He took another look to the left where the band was and saw Danny, Sean, and Chris. He looked to the right and there in the back corner on the backside of the bleachers, he spied Bobby kissing Megan O'Donnell. It was not just a peck. It was passionate and deep, and Brian was pissed.

It was not just because Bobby was not watching the game.

Bobby was kissing Megan.

Brian knew he should not have been angry. After all, he and Cat had kissed. They had done more than kiss. Not much, but a little. He did not understand what he was feeling or how he should feel, except that for some reason, he was pissed at Bobby. More than anything, his feelings for Bobby scared him, especially after his conversation with Jeremy that morning.

The second thing that took place was that right after they broke the huddle and just before Brian's first free throw, Brett turned to see if Coach Harrison had any words or if he wanted to change defenses. He did not. In fact, all Coach did was smile at him and give him a nod.

Brett smiled back and then glanced up into the stands at Jeremy and Vicky. Sitting right in front of them were Pete Kelliher, Summer Storm, Skip Dahlke, and Cleve Batiste!

Brett blinked, thinking he was seeing things.

The four of them saw Brett staring up at them, and they waved. Without thinking, Brett waved back. Coach Harrison half-stood and turned around to see who Brett was waving at and so did several of the players sitting on the bench.

Brett recovered and remembered where he was and what he was doing.

He looked up at the scoreboard and saw that there were just over two minutes left in the first half. North had a fourteen-point lead, thanks to Brian's sixteen points ... now seventeen as he sunk the second of two free throws. Billy added nine points and Randy six. They were the primary beneficiaries of Brett's ten assists.

He whistled as he had always done to get the guys' attention, gave them a hand signal, and then he and they went back to work to finish out the half.

And 2:17 later and heading into the locker room at the half, North had increased their lead by six, thanks to three straight steals, two by

Brett and one by Billy, which were converted into points. Four from Brian and two from Randy.

The half gave the guys a chance to rest. It gave Brett a chance to consider why Cleve was in the stands, along with Summer and Pete and Skip. And it gave Brian a chance to think about Bobby, though he should have been thinking about the second half.

Chapter Nineteen

Waukesha, WI

Alamorode stood in the doorway of the gym, jostled and bumped by adults and kids escaping the gym for the concession stand and restrooms. Some of the adults stepped outside to grab a smoke even though the school was a tobacco-free zone.

At first, he could not see them, but as the bleachers behind the home team thinned, they came into view. He walked up the stairs and moved along the row and sat down next to O'Connor.

"Hi, Nelson," Summer said. "I want you to meet Jeremy Evans and his fiancée, Victoria McGovern."

Handshakes were exchanged, and Vicky said, "Please call me 'Vicky.'" She blushed and smiled at him and then at Summer.

Summer smiled back and thought one more time how much Victoria, or Vicky, had changed. She and Jeremy seemed happy, and Summer could not help but feel a bit sad about that.

"I didn't take you for much of a basketball fan," O'Connor said to Alamorode good-naturedly.

He laughed and said, "I have to admit I'm not much of a sports fan. But I didn't have anything else to do, and I knew you guys were coming here, so I thought I'd check it out."

"Good to have you," Jamie said. "Jeremy and Vicky are responsible for four of the North starters."

"Wow!"

"Here they come now," Pete said.

"Number ten is Vicky's oldest. The twins Billy and Randy are numbers twenty-four and thirty-four, and Brian is number eleven," Jamie said.

Alamorode checked them out and said, "They're yours?"

Vicky smiled and said, "Brett, number ten, is my oldest. My youngest, Bobby, is around here somewhere. Jeremy adopted Randy and Billy, the twins. And Brian is being adopted this next week."

"And then there's George. He doesn't play basketball, but he's a runner," Jamie said. "He placed third at state in cross country. Jeremy adopted him a summer or so ago."

"Wow! I admire you for doing that," Alamorode said. "Very selfless of you. Both of you."

Jeremy smiled and blushed and said, "They've given me more than I've ever given them. I love each of them, including Brett and Bobby."

Vicky hugged him and kissed him on the cheek. "They love you too."

North and South traded baskets at the start of the third quarter, and by the start of the fourth, the Northstar Nation still had a twenty-point lead. As Coach Harrison liked to say, "Feed the monster!" or "Ride the horse that got you to the race!" and Brett did just that, feeding both Brian, who led both teams with twenty-seven points, and Billy, who added nineteen.

South started the fourth quarter with another hard foul on Brian, knocking him off his feet and into the first row of bleachers of the Northstar student section. South got a technical, and the player was ejected.

The North fans booed and hollered and stamped their feet on the bleachers. The noise in the fieldhouse rivaled an AC/DC rock concert.

While the officials sorted it out, Brian stood hunched over with his hands on his knees, wincing at the fresh pain in his hip.

"Bri, you okay?" Brett asked holding Brian by the shoulders.

As they often did, the two boys put their foreheads together, though Bri had his eyes shut and had a pained expression on his face.

He winced, but nodded, turned around, and glared at the South bench and said, "Yeah." He limped to the free throw line.

Harrison called the other four players to the sideline for a quick conference.

"Son, are you alright?" the older official asked Brian as he stood alone at the line.

"Yes, sir. I'm fine."

The official shook his head and said, "You don't look fine."

The South coach continued to argue the ejection and was warned that anything further, he would be ejected along with the offending South player. The official suggested that the coach might want to take a timeout to make sure his players understood that.

Reluctantly, the South coach called a short timeout, and Harrison called Brian over to join the rest of the team as the North student section chanted, *"Bri-an! Bri-an! Bri-an!"*

He did not bother addressing Brian's injury. He knew Brian well enough to know that if he was hurt and could not go, he would say something. As he expected, Brian did not say anything.

"It might get ugly out there. Keep your heads and don't stoop to their level. No retaliation. We can't afford for anyone to get thrown out of the game because then you'd miss the next game, and the next game is the first game of the playoffs." He let that sink in and then said, "Got that?"

The boys nodded. With his jaw set and his hands on his hips, Brett glared at the South bench. He caught the coach looking his way, so Brett turned to face him.

The South coach and Brett faced each other until Billy stood between the two of them with his back to the South bench.

"Can't afford that, Brett. Bri is banged up, and if you're out, we don't have a point guard," Billy whispered.

Reluctantly, Brett nodded, though he took one more look at the South coach before turning around.

"I've seen that look a time or two," Cleve Batiste muttered to Pete and to Vicky.

Pete nodded and said, "Oh, yeah! I have too." In fact, Pete had been on the receiving end of it.

The officials brought the teams out of the timeout. The older official called for the captains, so Brett and Billy joined two South players at center court.

"I'm only going to say this once. Anything dirty will get a technical foul and an ejection. Play basketball and play it clean. Understand?"

The four players stared at each other and nodded. Brett was the last to leave, taking one more look at the South coach.

Brian stepped to the line and sunk both shots. The student section took up their chant again, and North took the inbounds. Brett called for a Cowboy, a play Jeremy had used successfully when he had coached. It provided three options, and the offense took whatever the defense gave them.

Randy took the first option and hit Billy for a beautiful lob that Billy grabbed as he leaped high in the air for an easy layup.

The fieldhouse went wild, and the chant changed to *"Bil-ly! Bil-ly! Bil-ly!"*

Brett called for an all-out press. Randy intercepted the inbounds at half court, took two dribbles toward the basket, and hit Brian on the right wing. Brian swished it for a three-point play.

They pressed again. This time, Troy Rivera intercepted it, kicked it to Billy on the baseline, who hit Brett charging hard down the lane, who scored on a nifty reverse layup.

Another press and another turnover with Brian hitting from beyond the arc for another three.

The South coach jumped up from the bench and screamed for a timeout.

North walked to their bench all smiles. Brett never took his eyes off the South coach.

Harrison walked out onto the court to escort Brett to the sideline.

"Hey, Little Man, let's keep it together. I'm going to sub each of you anyway in the next minute."

Brett nodded and joined his teammates.

"We have to keep the pressure on, but we have to keep it together," Brett said. "Coach, do you want the full court press or go to the one-three-one half-court trap?"

Harrison smiled and looked at his five freshmen starters, who had played most of the entire game. Brett, Brian, and Billy had never come out. Randy sat down for a minute or two as did Troy. They were beat up and asleep on their feet, but God, he loved these kids. Tough. Resilient.

Too young to know any better. Freshmen who played like seniors. Hell, outplayed seniors.

"What do you guys want to do?"

The five guys, four of them brothers, looked at one another and it was Brian, the quietest, who said, "Press the hell out of them."

"Balls to the wall," Billy said with a laugh.

"Okay, go get 'em," Harrison said. "But keep your heads." This last he said to Brett, who smiled for the first time since the fourth quarter had begun.

They broke the sideline huddle, and as he did every time, Brett called the boys together. With arms around shoulders, the boys listened.

"No one lets up. No one. I want to run them in the ground. Coach is going to start subbing us out, so play hard until he does."

Billy smiled and said, "I think we're kinda already doin' that."

Chapter Twenty

Waukesha, WI

He hated crowds, and he did not like people. People were boorish and rude. Crude. All of them Huns.

He hated the smell. It reminded him of his middle school gym class and his PE teacher, Hemmalman, the ex-marine. Fake bullshit tough-guy attitude.

Dead.

He hated the locker room. Boys surreptitiously checking each other out as they undressed and showered. *Whose was bigger? Whose was smaller? Who had the most hair, if any of them had any hair other than a few strands or a wisp or tuft?*

The older, bigger kids pushing around the smaller kids. Him. All of them smelling of armpits and ass and feet. Wedgies so hard and so high an ass ... his ass ... might bleed. Bright red welts from practiced towel flicks.

It did not take long to spot the fifteen-year-old. Sweaty like the rest of them. A mask of false bravado, a common facade of youth. Among them, but separate. Quiet. A loaner. An easy target, easy prey. The Man wondered if that was a John Sanford title. *Easy Prey.* Should be. The Man would be the star.

The Man's anger at the missed opportunity in the park surged and threatened to boil to the surface again. He perseverated on the thought that he should have just shot both of them. Could have confused the ignorant cops and agents even more than they already were. Could have. Should have. Would have.

He shut his eyes and controlled his breathing.

Jostled out of his mini-meditation once again from behind. A knee to his back and a sweaty, filthy hand on his shoulder.

He turned around, masked an understanding smile, but the Hun did not bother to acknowledge it or murmur an apology. Why would he? He was an unintelligent heathen. He would probably go out after the game, drink dozens of cans of cheap beer, and drive home drunk. Mount his homely, chubby wife, grunting and sweating until he finished and pulled out and off of her still dripping his fluid and his seed on her belly and legs. An ignorant, filthy heathen who gave thousands of wedgies in his time. Hundreds of towel flicks.

Maybe he would shoot him. The world would be better off. Much better off. One fewer heathen. One fewer Hun.

No.

The Man could not afford to. He had his list. He had his agenda. The Man would remain focused on the task at hand.

The fifteen-year-old would die tonight. One fewer of them in the world.

Chapter Twenty-One

Waukesha, WI

As hard as Jeremy and Vicky were searching the crowd for Brian, he was doing his best to avoid them. It was not hard. When the final buzzer sounded, the student section poured onto the court. The boys knew, however, that they were to report to Coach Harrison for a final word and then line up for the handshake with the opposing team.

Harrison, along with the athletic director, Hal Stuebner, and one of the assistant principals, Bob Farner, took positions to monitor the process in case anyone had ideas that were less than sportsmanlike. The handshakes went well until Brett and the South Coach stood face to face.

"You're a good player, McGovern, but a little cocky."

"You're a good coach, but your team plays dirty."

Harrison overheard it and stepped to intervene.

"He has a mouth on him, Harrison."

"Along with two arms, two legs, and a good head on his shoulders," Tommy said with a smile.

"You know what I mean," the South coach said, jabbing a finger at him.

"Not sure I do, but whatever Brett said was probably accurate. He's known for telling the truth."

The players on both teams gathered around, but Brett and Randy shooed them away along with help from Stuebner and Farner.

"We'll see you in the playoffs, Hot Shot."

Tommy smiled and said, "Looking forward to it."

South headed to their own locker room while the Northstars were engulfed by their fans. Pats on the back. Hugs. Applause and Cheers.

Brett turned back to Harrison and said, "I'm sorry. I shouldn't have said anything."

Harrison considered the statement and then said, "Did you say anything that wasn't the truth? Did you curse or call him a name?"

"No. Nothing like that."

"Then we're good, Brett. You spoke as a leader and as the team captain."

"Thanks, Coach."

He turned around and went to look for Cleve, Pete, and Skip.

Caitlyn Watkins found Brian, threw her arms around his neck, and kissed him.

Cat and Brian had known each other a long time. She was Sean Drummond's cousin, and Sean was one of Brian's best friends. Brian had always thought Cat liked his twin, Brad, but Cat saw Brad as a friend. She and George were friends, and George had hoped for more than friendship, but Cat liked Brian. Always had, but it took a while for Brian to catch on. She reminded him often that he was, after all, a boy and all boys were slow to get most anything.

"You had a great game, Bri." She took her arms off his neck and said, "But you're sweaty. Yuck."

"That's what happens when you work hard," Brian said with a smile. "And I think I did okay."

"Oh, I see. *Okay*, huh? How do you explain your thirty-five points? That is, if you were just *okay*?" she said with a twinkle in her blue eyes.

Brian did not answer but instead studied the freckles sprinkled under her eyes and across her nose. He loved her short blond hair and her smile. They were about the same height, and as she pressed up against him, he liked the feel of her breasts against his chest.

"So you admit you might have been a little better than *okay*?"

Brian smiled, kissed her, and changed the subject by asking, "Are we still going to your house?"

"Why? Do you have something in mind?" Again, her eyes twinkled.

He blushed and did not respond. He was shy around girls, and she knew it. She liked teasing him because he was pretty helpless. They had never gone much beyond a kiss. A little touching here and there, but it was fun to tease him.

"I better go shower."

"Yes, please. You're gross."

He gave her one more kiss, took about six steps and ran into Big Gav, Mikey, Stephen, and Garrett.

"Helluva game, Bri," Gav said with a smile and a hug. "I can't stand South."

"Neither can I," Mikey said giving Brian a hug.

Which was funny because both he and Stephen lived in the South attendance area. Because of the summer of death and because of their abduction, Mike's and Stephen's parents asked for a transfer from Horning Middle School to Butler Middle School with the idea that their boys would attend North and be under the watchful eye of Jeremy. A fresh start for both boys.

Brian promised to talk to them after he showered. He saw Jeremy and Vicky and four other people he did not know talking to Brett, George, Billy, and Randy. One was an older guy, and one was a younger black guy. The black guy had his arm around Brett's shoulders.

Brett saw him and waved him over, but Brian pointed to the locker room and walked there instead. He was not ready to face Jeremy and Vicky and hoped to avoid them as long as he could.

"There you are," Bobby said. "I was looking for you."

Brian's eyes flashed. "Oh? Is this before or after you made out with Megan?" He had not intended to say that, but out it came.

Bobby blinked at him, decided not to respond and instead asked, "What happened to your elbow and knee?"

He reached out to touch Brian's arm, but Brian jerked it away.

"I guess if you were watching the game instead of making out with Megan, you'd know."

Bobby's face fell, and it hurt Brian to see him like that.

"Are you angry with me?"

"Good guess, Sherlock."

"I'm sorry, Bri."

"Yeah, well, whatever. I have to shower," Brian said as he pushed past him, bumping into him on his way to the locker room.

As much as Brian wanted Bobby to know he was pissed at him, Brian was equally pissed at himself for treating Bobby the way he did. Bobby did not deserve it. He had done nothing that Brian had not done.

There were two things had bothered him more than anything else. The first was that he was jealous. As hard as it was for him to admit this to anyone, and to himself, he was angry that Bobby was kissing someone ... else.

And the second thing that bothered him- his feelings for Bobby. He did not understand them. He never felt like this about anyone, especially another guy. Brian knew his feelings were more than just a friend thing or a brother thing. He had never felt like this about Brad, and he and Brad were as close as you could possibly get. It was confusing because he liked Cat and he was looking forward to whatever would happen with her. The only person he could talk to about it was Jeremy, but he could not. He was afraid to. *What if Jeremy would make him move out? What if Jeremy wouldn't adopt him?*

Brian pushed through the locker room door. It was empty, and he was alone. Ignoring the bench, he sat down on the floor with his back to his locker. He drew his knees up to his chest, held his head in his hands, and fought back tears. Mostly, he struggled to push down the rising fear he had about himself.

Chapter Twenty-Two

Waukesha, WI

Michael Staley was fifteen and handsome with dark hair and blue eyes, a few pimples here and there, but nothing outrageous. He lived in a nice two-story home with his parents, John and Lori, and two other siblings. One sib was a seventeen-year-old girl named Stacey and the other sib was a thirteen-year-old boy named Carson.

Whenever Michael walked home from school, he took the same route, a shortcut lined with garbage cans and recycling bins. The Man counted on Michael not deviating from his routine.

There was a parked car or two. Not expensive cars because they would be easy pickings for anyone interested in CDs, spare change, or anything else of value. Waukesha did not have many stolen vehicles, at least in this neighborhood, but if there was a car worth taking, it could end up missing.

The Man parked almost at the end of the alley facing the direction the boy would walk. He stood in the shadows against a wall and behind two stink-filled garbage cans.

And waited.

Michael stepped off the fan bus, hoping he would be invited to a party, but that never happened. Never. His sister got a ride to the game from her boyfriend, and she would end up with friends somewhere and then come home at midnight, her curfew. Carson got a ride to and from the game with his parents. They had offered to take Michael, but Michael declined because it was lame to ride with his parents anywhere other kids were.

Still, the sad part was that Carson and his parents were already home eating pizza. Carson would have a Pepsi, and his parents would drink a

Bud Lite or two. Kind of a Friday routine. They would save him a piece or not depending upon how hungry they were.

Whatever. He did not care much anyway.

Michael rarely smiled because he did not have much to smile about. No friends. Only average grades and it was not because he did not try, and it was not because he was not interested. He never caught on to school, and school never caught on to him. He would raise his hand, and a teacher would call on someone else. He would have a question, and a teacher would tell him to figure it out and then walk away from him. He tried, all right. It seemed he tried harder than his teachers.

However, there was one, Penny Faulkner, his English teacher. She read two of his poems and encouraged him to write more. She told him he was a natural. So, without his parents knowing it, he kept a notebook filled with poems. He even wrote a short story or two. Faulkner was the only person who had read them, and she seemed to be the only one who cared about him.

He never complained because his parents would not listen anyway. Rather, they took the side of the teachers. Always and under any circumstance. They would urge him to try harder. To make an effort. Never once did they see that he had been doing just that.

Friends? No one. Did not have anyone to call, and no one ever called him. Stacey did not even talk to him except to ask him to pass the potatoes. Carson would try, but there was not much in common between the two of them.

The night was cold. He had his cell in one hand with the other in his jacket pocket and then would alternate when the hand with the cell turned red and purple. His shoulders were hunched, and his collar was up. A stocking hat sat on top of his head and covered his ears, but he still shivered.

He almost walked right into him.

"Sorry. Excuse me," Michael said.

"Are you Michael Staley?"

Michael took a step back ready to bolt. He did not know if he was going to get hit on. It used to happen when he was younger. Not so much now.

"Are you Michael Staley?" The Man asked again.

"Yes, who are you?" Michael said as he took another step back.

Michael's legs refused to work when The Man brought the gun up to his face.

"You shouldn't have done it."

Two quick shots, though Michael's body fell backward after the first. Dead before he hit the pavement. In a heap, spread-eagle.

The Man walked away, but not at a run. Just before he got into his car, he heard a neighbor yell out the backdoor to stop lighting firecrackers.

The Man chuckled, shut the door, started up his BMW, and drove away. Another one to cross off his list.

And speaking of the list, he might have to rearrange it some. He had some new names to consider.

Chapter Twenty-Three

Waukesha, WI

The TV was on low, but neither of them had paid any attention to it.

Brian and Cat were snuggled under a blanket on the floor in the basement family room. Cat had her shirt up and her bra off and her jeans open. Brian had his left hand on her breast. She had guided his other hand between her legs to the magic spot as she called it, and Brian rubbed it. She arched her back, squirmed, and wiggled rhythmically, almost spastically.

Brian had his shirt pushed up and his jeans down to his knees. She had played with him once, and the sticky results were on his lower belly and on her hand that was pressed against his butt cheek. He was hard again, and he waited impatiently for her to do something to him. Anything, at this point, would be great.

Panting, she kissed his neck and then his lips, and said, "Let's."

Brian knew what she meant, but hesitated.

She caught his look and said, "I'm on the pill, if that's what you're worried about."

It was not that Brian was unwilling. In fact, if it was physically possible, his erection grew as she played with him. Still, he hesitated, but kissed her. In his head, he heard Jeremy's admonishment to wait and make sure it was love. It was one of Jeremy's laws of life and love.

"Sean and Lissa are doing it in the other room."

They had disappeared in a room a few feet away almost as soon as they had gotten there and had not come out since. Brian had heard some murmuring and some laughter, along with a moan or two on the other side of the door, but he figured that they were doing what he and Cat were doing.

"Help me with my jeans," Cat whispered.

"Are you sure?" Brian said in equal parts of anticipation and anxiety. She kissed him and then repeated, "Help me with my jeans."

He kicked his off altogether. Cat raised her hips, and he slid them off, and the two of them were naked except for socks.

"What if someone comes down here?"

Cat smiled and said, "They won't."

She spread her legs, and Brian slid between them and together took up a quick rhythm.

"Slow down," Cat whispered.

"I'll try," Brian whispered breathlessly. He could not. "God, Cat."

She had one hand on the small of his back and the other on his butt pushing him in farther.

"Jesus," Brian whispered as he emptied himself. He had his hands on her shoulders but shifted them to her breasts and played with her nipples.

"Stay in, keep going," Cat said breathlessly. She began her spastic dance beneath him again, and she arched her back and murmured, "Ahhhh ... oooooh."

Brian hung on but slowed down, and before he knew it, he had gotten hard again.

"Again," Cat said.

Brian picked up his rhythm, more urgent this time, and then finished. They clung together sticky and sweaty and panting. His face was buried in her neck.

"I have to go to the bathroom," Brian whispered.

He pulled out of her but knelt between her legs.

She smiled at him and said, "I wanted this for a long time."

He smiled at her, bent down, and kissed her and then kissed each breast, taking her nipples into his mouth.

"You're hard again," Cat whispered.

"I can't help it, but I have to go to the bathroom."

"Can we do it again?"

"I can try." He wanted to, but his balls ached.

Naked except for the gauze bandages on his elbow and his knee and the leather and turquoise bracelet he wore on his right wrist, Brian stood up and tiptoed to the bathroom that joined both the family room and the bedroom Sean and Lissa had been in. He walked in on Sean who was removing a used condom.

They stood staring at each other and then both smiled.

"Did you?" Sean asked.

Brian nodded, unable to take his eyes off Sean. He had seen him naked before, many times, but had never seen him with an erection or a sort of erection.

"You used a condom?"

Sean nodded and said, "Lissa isn't on the pill like Cat."

The two boys stood facing each other in front of the sink.

"Did you know?"

Sean laughed and said, "What? That she was on the pill or that you were going to do it tonight?"

"Both." For cousins, he knew Sean and Cat were close and shared most everything.

He nodded and said, "She gets bad cramps, and the pill helps. She told me she wanted to do it with you."

Sean managed to pull off the condom without much fluid escaping and flushed the contents down the toilet and hid the used condom in the garbage can under some tissue. He used some clean tissue to wipe himself off. He handed over a couple for Brian to do the same.

The boys were almost the same height. Sean was a little taller and a lot narrower. There were a few freckles on his chest and shoulders just as there were under his bright blue eyes and on his nose. His sandy blond hair matched the hair under his arms and between his legs. Still hard, Brian judged Sean's to be about the same length, though he thought his was thicker. Of course, his dark wavy hair matched what was between his legs and under his arms.

"You ever use a condom?" Sean asked.

Brian shook his head.

"Do you know how?"

Brian shook his head again.

"It's tricky." He had intended to use the fresh one on the counter, but instead opened it up and gave it to Brian. "Here."

Brian took it but did not know what to do with it.

Sean took it from him. He placed it on Brian and rolled it down. "You have to make sure it's snug."

"It is," Brian answered. He did not like the feel of it.

Sean touched him and said, "You can still feel ... *it*, but not as much as if you don't use one. See?" he said playing with him.

Brian nodded.

"Are you going to do it again?" Sean asked.

Brian nodded and said, "Cat wants to."

Sean grinned and said, "Me, too. But we need to hurry so my mom doesn't get suspicious. I have to call her to come get us."

He helped Brian remove the condom, showing him how to do it without spilling the contents.

"Of course, when it's full of stuff, it's different. But you won't have to worry about that with Cat."

Brian nodded and then both left the bathroom, Sean to Lissa and Brian to Cat.

Cat smiled at him and said, "You ready?"

Brian smiled and said, "Can't you tell?"

Chapter Twenty-Four

Waukesha, WI

At first glance, it looked like the boy tried to make a snow angel but gave up after he laid down. When the patrol cop looked closer, he saw the holes in his face and the blood in a dark chocolate syrupy halo on the ice around his head.

They had responded to a late call from an elderly woman who thought kids were lighting firecrackers.

What kind? Dispatch had asked.

Loud ones! She had answered.

Lorenzo and Gonnering were in the vicinity, so they responded to the call.

"Better call Graff. He's working the serial case, and this fits the MO," Greg Gonnering said.

Carlos Lorenzo turned around and, using his lapel mic, called dispatch to have her relay it to Graff. He checked his watch. 11:27 PM. He knew Graff would get there with the cavalry and crime scene tech.

"Any missing kid reports?" he asked dispatch.

There was a moment of silence and then, "Not so far."

He turned to his partner and asked, "Greg, is there any ID on the kid?"

Gonnering considered fishing the kid's wallet out of his back pocket but decided to wait until Graff and company showed up. He did not want to be the one to mess up the crime scene.

"Let's wait. Carlos, walk the perimeter. Look for footprints, cigarette butts, anything. Tire tracks would be good, too."

Lorenzo took out his Maglite and walked up the right side of the alley. He stopped and said, "Greg, come here and tell me what you see."

Gonnering stood up, walked to his partner, and followed the beam of light shining on the ground and against a garage. There were two footprints. Lorenzo trailed the prints to the alley. They were the deepest directly in front of and facing the boy.

He took out his own Maglite and shined it against the garage, hoping for a bit of fabric or a cigarette butt. Not seeing anything but weathered wood, he shined it on the footprints leading to the middle of the alley and then on the footprints in front of the boy.

"This might be Graff's guy. Look how deep they are against the garage. Lighter as he walked out in front of the boy, but deeper again as he stood in front of him."

Lorenzo nodded and said, "He was waiting for him like he knew he'd be coming this way."

Gonnering said, "I'm thinking size nine. Dress shoe."

"That's what I'm thinking."

"Okay, careful now, but follow the prints up the alley. Unless he walked out on foot, my guess is that there will be tire tracks."

Lorenzo followed the footprints to the other side of the alley about twenty yards away. The same prints initially, but then they disappeared.

"Tire tracks. Nice clean tread. Drove out nice and slow."

"Okay, block off that end of the alley, and I'll take care of this end," Gonnering said. "I think this is Graff's guy, Carlos."

Graff appeared fifteen minutes later ahead of the ME. Just after he arrived, a host of others showed up. The FBI crew of Kelliher, Storm, Skip Dahlke, Cleve Batiste, and Jo Weist drove in one car. Pat O'Connor showed up in his beat-up Ford. Nelson Alamorode drove up in his Cadillac CTS, and Paul Eiselmann arrived in his black Chevy Malibu.

Dahlke asked all of them to stay clear of the scene until he was finished. He compartmentalized his task keeping his emotions out of it and bent down over the dead boy.

"Can someone get the camera and video recorder out of my trunk?"

Eiselmann was already trotting to retrieve it. He returned and at Dahlke's direction, snapped pictures. Gonnering had followed him to the car, grabbed the video cam, and recorded the scene.

"Carlos, can you walk me through what you and Greg found?" Graff asked.

Lorenzo walked him, Kelliher and Storm up the alley using his Maglite. O'Connor, Weist, and Alamorode stood back and watched. Batiste assisted Dahlke. At times the two conversed quietly.

Graff, Kelliher, and Storm huddled off to the side and O'Connor, Weist and Alamorode joined them.

"I'm thinking of calling Jeremy and having him bring George and Brett here," Graff said.

Summer did not respond but folded her arms in thought. Kelliher tugged at his lower lip and ran a hand over his flattop.

"Why? What's the point?" Weist asked more out of curiosity than opposition.

"We already know the boy ... Michael Staley is fifteen-years-old. I would like to get George's and Brett's take on it. Give us an insight into what might have been going on in the boy's head."

Summer glanced at Pete, but she already knew his opinion. Her years of working with Pete and his unorthodox methods did that.

"Jamie, make the call," Summer said. "If Jeremy wants to speak with me, I'm here."

Jamie walked away from the group to the other end of the alley and had a rather lengthy conversation with his best friend. O'Connor watched him nod and gesticulate, but could only imagine what was being said.

"I don't understand this at all," Alamorode said shaking his head. "Not at all. Bringing kids to a crime scene?"

"These aren't ordinary kids, Nelson," Summer said. "It was George who helped solve the trafficking ring. He is responsible for saving the lives of his father and his brothers three separate times, not to mention helping bring home thirty boys held in captivity. And Brett? He saved Pete's life in Chicago and took a bullet for it."

"Brett also saved his mother and brother and disarmed his uncle who had shot and killed two FBI agents," Pete said.

"But they're kids," Alamorode said. "There's something unethical about this, if not immoral."

Neither of the agents nor any of the detectives had an answer for that.

Jamie came back to the group and said, "Jeremy will be here in twenty minutes."

"And?" O'Connor asked.

"He's not sure about this, but he left it up to George and Brett, and they agreed to come."

Alamorode shook his head, turned his back on the group, and walked a short distance away.

Chapter Twenty-Five

Waukesha, WI

Jeremy's eyes betrayed his feelings. Jamie met him, George, and Brett at the entrance of the alley and shook hands with him and hugged the boys. Pete, Summer, Cleve, Weist, Alamorode, and O'Connor drifted over that way and greeted Jeremy and the boys, though Alamorode was a bit frosty.

"I'm sorry to bring you out here tonight, since you had a group of friends over," Graff said. To Jeremy, he asked, "How much did you share with them?"

Jeremy shook his head and folded his arms across his chest.

"Okay." He turned to the two boys and said, "We have a fifteen-year-old boy from South, a freshman like you, who was shot in the face twice. We think he died instantly."

"What do you want from us?" Brett asked.

Both boys were about the same height, and neither seemed shaken or displayed any emotion other than curiosity. Brett had his collar up to shield his neck, and his shoulders were hunched. His short chestnut hair was uncovered. He wore fingerless mittens on his hands, but his fingers were red turning to purple. He blew on them to keep them warm, but it did not seem to help.

George's shiny black hair, which normally lay way down on his back, was in a single braid. He did not show any sign he was cold, and that was typical for a traditional Navajo who did not show any emotion. Yet, his eyes indicated he was listening intently, if not out of curiosity.

"I'd like the two of you to walk the alley just as he did. Officers Lorenzo and Gonnering will meet you at the body, but I asked them and Skip Dahlke not to say anything to you. George, you have more experience with crime scenes. I want you to use your skills to see what

102 Spiral Into Darkness

you can see, but I want the two of you to tell us what you think the boy might have been doing and feeling." He shrugged and made a face, not liking his directions to them.

Alamorode shook his head and grunted.

George frowned at him and then nodded at Jamie.

Brett shrugged and said, "Okaaay." It came out as a kind of question.

Pete and Summer backed the little group up about five yards leaving the two boys alone. George knelt and bowed his head.

"Is he sick or is he scared?" Alamorode asked loud enough for George and Brett to hear.

"George is traditional Navajo," O'Connor explained. "He's asking the boy's *chindi* for permission to approach."

"The *what?*" Weist asked.

"The *chindi* is a spirit," O'Connor explained. "The Navajo believe that when a person dies violently or unexpectedly, that spirit or *chindi* remains behind until there is satisfaction."

"Satisfaction?" Alamorode asked.

"The *chindi* will want answers, and George is asking permission to help him, or it will get them."

George stood up, brushed off the knees of his jeans, and turned around, smiled at O'Connor and then stared at Alamorode impassively before he and Brett walked down the alley side by side. Jamie had given them a Maglite to use, but George motioned to Brett to turn it off.

Every so often, George would squat and point at something. He spoke just above a whisper. Brett would nod or blow on his fingers. The cold did not seem to bother George.

It took some time with all of George's stops, but they reached the body. Both boys nodded at Skip and the two officers.

Back at the start of the alley, Alamorode muttered, "This is ridiculous."

The FBI and cops did not pay any attention, but it was clear that George had heard him. He turned around, cocked his head, and then turned back around. He said something to Brett who chuckled. It was Brett who motioned to Pete and Graff.

"What?" Pete asked.

"We think he wasn't paying attention. He was distracted and didn't see the shooter," Brett said.

"Why do you think that?" Summer asked.

The body had been covered partially by a sheet, but the boy's arms and feet were visible.

George pointed to the boy's cell still grasped in his hand and said, "I think he was looking down at his cell." He pointed at the boy's footprints and said, "He shuffled his feet and then stopped and then took a step back. He did not know the shooter. It was dark and cold. The boy was by himself. He was startled, but not necessarily scared. He took a step back, in order to escape, if needed. When the shooter pulled out his weapon, the boy froze. The force of the bullet knocked him backward."

Brett said, "We think the shooter stood right here," pointing at the footprints facing toward the boy. "He shot him and then walked away." He pointed at the set of footprints walking in the other direction.

Speaking formally, George continued, "There was not anyone around. No witnesses. The shooter walked to his car and drove away."

"How do you know he drove away? You didn't walk up the alley far enough to say that," Alamorode said.

Brett smiled, looked at Jamie, and said, "Is George right?"

"Yes, he is."

Neither Brett nor George bothered to look over at Alamorode.

"What else can you tell us?" Pete asked.

"The kid was in high school. South, right? Was he at the game?" Brett asked.

"We believe he was, but we haven't confirmed it," Graff answered.

George nodded and said, "He was lonely. Sad."

"How can you tell that?" Alamorode asked.

George turned around to face him and said, "He was by himself after the game. An important game. There were not any friends with him, and he was not with anyone. He was not with his family. This was a shortcut to his home. A path that was familiar with him. He was not expecting anyone on this route. Maybe he wanted to be alone. Maybe he did not but was alone anyway."

"But ..."

"The shooter waited for him. The shooter knew the boy would take this route home." He turned to Jamie and asked, "The shooter must have known this about him. Did you find where the shooter was waiting?"

Jamie nodded at Lorenzo and Gonnering.

"Over here," Gonnering said.

"Follow his footprints," Lorenzo said.

The four of them walked to the garage, and there behind the garbage cans was a set of footprints. George, wearing his cowboy boots, placed one boot next to one of the prints.

"Size nine?" he asked.

"That's what we think," Gonnering said. "Dress shoe."

"Did you get pictures of the footprints and the tire prints or whatever you call them?" Brett asked.

Lorenzo smiled and said, "Yes, we did. We're running them through the computer as we speak."

"Okay, guys," Jamie said. "I think we took you from your friends long enough. Thank you for coming. I ask that you keep this confidential. This is an ongoing case, and we can't afford any leaks."

"Got it," Brett said.

George nodded, stole a glance at Alamorode, and frowned and then the two boys left with Jeremy.

After they had left, Lorenzo said, "Holy shit!"

"I heard the stories, but I didn't believe it until tonight," Gonnering said.

Summer called everyone into a tight huddle.

"We need to split the duties up. Jo and Cleve, can you go to the boy's home and interview the parents? Find out anything you can. Any information would be helpful. Friends, contacts, anything. Paul, we'll need to dig into his cell. If the kid had access to a computer, we'll need to dig into that too."

"I'd like to go to the boy's house too," O'Connor said.

"That's fine," Summer said. "Skip, work with the ME on the autopsy." She turned to the two patrol cops and said, "Can you do another once over here. Bag and tag anything you find. Make sure you follow the chain of custody protocol."

"I'm heading home. I have an early morning appointment, but I'll call at some point to get caught up," Alamorode said.

"Thank you for coming tonight," Summer said. "I appreciate all the help you're providing."

She turned back to the group and said, "I know tomorrow is Saturday, but can we meet in the morning, say eight or eight-thirty?"

"We can meet here at the station if you want," Jamie suggested. "The freeway construction in Milwaukee is nuts. Carlos and Greg, I'd like you to come too."

"Jo, get what you can from the parents. If there's a brother or sister, you might want to talk with them separately," Pete said. "They will be more apt to talk if no one else is around."

"Pat, if you can get the parents to let you into the boy's room, do so. See what you can find. I don't know what if anything you might find or what you might be looking for, but anything might help."

"George and Brett didn't think the boy knew the shooter," Cleve said.

Summer shrugged and said, "Let's see."

"This is our youngest victim," Eiselmann said.

"Hopefully," Jo said, though she was not sure why she said it.

Chapter Twenty-Six

Waukesha, WI

The two boys lay on the sofa sleeper in the basement with the door shut. Sean's mom had picked them up without any questions, and the only comment she had made was, "Great game tonight, Bri! Nice win!" to which Brian had responded, "Thanks!" No other commentary until they pulled into the driveway and entered the backdoor off the kitchen when Lydia Drummond asked, "You boys hungry?" to which both boys responded, "No thanks." With that, she went off to bed leaving the boys alone.

The Drummond basement was finished as a family room complete with a stocked wet bar. A refrigerator was filled with water, Coke, Diet Coke, and Sprite, along with Gatorade and Propel. For the adults, Bud Lite, and Corona. A full bath was off in a corner, and there were two extra bedrooms. Life was good on an orthodontist salary.

They had played *FIFA,* and Sean had hammered Brian in the first game, squeaked out a win in the second game, and Brian squeaked by in the third game. It was way into the night, but neither could fall asleep. Sean tossed and turned, and Brian lay on his back with his hands under his head. Both boys had their legs spread a little more than normal. It ached to move too much.

"Are you awake?" Brian asked.

Sean rolled over onto his side, faced Brian, and said, "Yeah. Can't sleep."

The two boys had been friends since third or fourth grade. Brian and his brother Brad and Sean had been constant companions spending as much time at each other's house as they did their own. Randy and Billy arrived when the boys were in the fifth or sixth grade, and it was the five of them. Brad's death affected all four boys in various ways, but Brian was hit the hardest.

The same summer Brad died, Brian met Brett and Bobby, Big Gav, Mikey, Stephen, and George. Brett, George, and Big Gav had become Brian's fishing and hunting buddies. Still, Brian's closest friends were Sean and Bobby, but neither of them could take the place of Brad.

Brian turned his head to get a better look at Sean, his green eyes staring into Sean's blue ones.

"How many times have you and Lissa done it?"

Sean grinned and whispered, "Tonight or total?"

Brian smiled back and said, "Both."

Sean bounced a finger on Brian's pec and said, "Twice tonight, but she beat me off once. And I think we've done it ... a lot." He laughed. "We started last year around Easter, so maybe thirty times. Something like that," and he laughed again.

"Seriously?"

Sean grinned, tweaked Brian's nipple, then stuck a finger into his belly-button and said, "I'm not sure of the exact number, but we've done it a lot."

"Do your parents know?"

"Well, not really. At least, I don't think so, but I think they suspect. One day I came home after school and found a box of condoms on my dresser." He laughed. "I keep them in my underwear drawer."

"Oh, wow! Seriously?"

Sean grinned, chuckled, tweaked his nipple again, and said, "Seriously."

Brian did not have to wonder what Jeremy and Vicky might say if they knew he had sex with Cat. He thought they would be angry and disappointed. Maybe more disappointed than angry, but they would still be angry. But disappointing them was worse than making them angry. He would take their anger over their disappointment any day.

"What?" Sean asked.

"How did you know how to put on a rubber?"

"I practiced. But sometimes I worry about it ripping or it coming off."

"That can happen?"

Sean said, "Oh yeah. I don't think one would come off you because you're thicker than me."

He studied Sean.

"What?"

"A rubber can break or come off?" Brian asked.

"Look at your dick." When Brian hesitated, Sean repeated, "Look at your dick."

Brian lowered his boxers and looked at himself as Sean did the same.

"See how much thicker yours is. Mine's skinnier. See?"

The two boys studied each other and then pulled up their boxers.

"Do your balls hurt?" Brian asked. "Mine ache. Is that normal?"

"Shit, yeah! Especially after you do it two or three times like we did."

"Feels like I have a bowling ball between my legs."

Sean laughed, pulled down Brian's boxers, and said, "They're big, but not that big."

Both boys laughed.

Brian asked, "Have you ever done anything with a guy?"

Sean laughed and said, "Yeah."

"Who?"

With a little hesitation, Sean whispered, "Brad."

"My brother?"

Sean grinned and said, "The same one. Lots of times."

"Seriously?"

"Yup."

"What did you do?"

Sean thought it over and said, "Hand jobs. We gave each other a blow job a couple of times. His idea."

"No way!"

Sean laughed and said, "Yes way."

"Where was I?"

"Sleeping. We would wait until we were sure you and everyone else was asleep and then, you know, we'd do it."

"You're making this up!"

"No, I'm not," and Sean laughed again.

Brian was not sure if he could believe him. He frowned and said, "Why didn't you ever do anything with me?"

Sean touched Brian, shrugged, and said, "I don't know. I guess I didn't think you'd want to. I mean, I know guys do it, but nobody talks about it."

"We're talking about it," Brian said.

Sean chuckled and said, "And I have my hand on your dick. But my balls ache. My back and legs too," Sean said with a smile.

Brian said, "Me too. I ache all over, but I liked it."

Sean laughed, "Yeah, I know. I can't do it enough. I think about it, and I get an instant boner."

Brian waited a beat and said, "When you and Brad did it, did you ever wonder, you know, if you were gay?"

Sean rolled over onto his side to face Brian, and laid his hand on Brian's stomach and said, "No, never."

"Did Brad?"

"He never said anything, but he never acted like it."

Brian considered this new information. Brad and Sean doing stuff while he slept. He had done it with Bobby three or four times. While the other night was the exception, each night was just one time. And the last time was the only time they had really kissed. Made out, actually. He looked over at Sean.

"What?"

"I like Cat a lot. *A lot!*" he said for emphasis.

"She likes you *a lot*," Sean said mimicking him.

"I've done it with a guy like four times. I liked it each time. But I liked having sex with Cat, and I'd do it again."

"I know she liked it."

"How do you know?"

Sean grinned and said, "She texted me. Just an emoji, but I knew what she meant."

Brian grinned back at him.

Sean said, "What guy have you done it with?"

Brian shook his head. "That's kind of private. I'd rather not say."

"I have too. Besides Brad, I mean. And yeah, it's private."

Brian turned and faced Sean and said, "But did you ever think you might be gay, you know, because you did it with a guy?"

Sean smiled, shook his head, and said, "You worry too much, Bri. What's the difference if I do it by myself or if I do it with someone else? What's the difference if Lisa or Brad or you do it to me?"

Brian pursed his lips and thought about it. It sounded logical. "Nothing I guess."

"You're not gay, if that's what you're worried about."

"You don't think so?"

"Not even a little. You're ugly, but not gay," Sean said with a laugh.

Brian smiled at him. It was like a load fell off his shoulders, and all at once, he felt a little more at peace.

"Thanks."

Sean smiled at him and rolled onto his back.

"I'm glad we're friends, Sean. I mean, I don't think I can talk to anyone else about this stuff."

"Anytime, and I'm glad we're friends too."

Chapter Twenty-Seven

Waukesha, WI

"Why? I don't understand. Why would someone do this?" Lori Staley asked. Though the shock was palpable, there were not any tears. None. Not from Michael's father, John, either. Not from Michael's sister, Stacey. And not from Michael's brother, Carson, though of the four, Carson was the closest.

"Your name is Carson, right?" Jo Weist asked.

He nodded but kept his eyes on the floor.

She turned to John and Lori and asked, "Do you mind if Carson shows Detective O'Connor and me Michael's room?"

Lori never answered or indicated she had heard the question. John sort of flipped his hand dismissively, so Jo took that as an invitation to go ahead. She extended a hand to Carson, who ignored it but stood up. Carson led Jo and O'Connor out of the living room, leaving Cleve Batiste to finish interviewing Michael's parents and sister.

She glanced back over her shoulder and saw Cleve lean toward them with his elbows on his knees. He tried engaging them with open-ended questions, but it was not happening. Lori looked off in space. John stared at him and shook his head every five or six seconds. Stacey, who seemed to be a little high or drunk, kept checking her cell.

The cumulative effect pissed Cleve off. He supposed he could understand the shock with Michael's parents, but where was the sadness? Maybe that would come when the shock wore off, but somehow Cleve did not think so. The total indifference and lack of compassion Stacey displayed mystified him. In actuality, he had the sustained urge to slap the shit out of her.

Jo, Pat, and Carson trudged up the stairs and walked down the hallway. Carson stopped and stared at the door in front of him, not wanting to enter.

"It's okay, Carson. Is this your brother's room?"

Carson nodded.

O'Connor reached around him and said, "Excuse me," as he opened the door and entered.

Carson's feet were glued to the spot. Jo gave his shoulders a little squeeze for encouragement.

"Can you show us around?"

It took a while, and without a word, Carson entered the room.

First, he stared at the bed. It was made up as any teen might have made it, and Jo suspected that Michael had pulled the comforter up, leaving the rest unmade. Yet for a teenager's room, it was clean and tidy. On impulse, she pulled down the corner of the comforter and saw that, indeed, the bed was made up, sheets tight and pillow fluffed. Not quite military grade, but pretty good for a high school freshman.

"Huh."

"Not what you expected?" O'Connor asked. He had his back to her and was thumbing through a notebook on the desk. Jo did not respond.

"That's Mike's," Carson said.

"It's poetry," O'Connor said. "Nice writing. I have a friend who writes. An eighth grader named Bobby. He's writing music too. I think he would like to read this."

"But it's Mike's."

To distract him, Jo asked, "Carson, can you and I sit on the bed and talk?"

Carson nodded but never took his eyes off O'Connor, who had closed the notebook and had started on the desk drawers. Carson watched as Pat looked over the contents of each without pulling anything out. When O'Connor finished with the desk, he moved on to the closet.

"Can you tell me, what was Michael like?"

Carson brushed a tear from his eye and said, "Mike. Mom and Dad called him Michael."

"I'm sorry. What was Mike like?"

Carson shrugged.

Jo tried again. "Who was his best friend?"

Carson's expression clouded over, and it was clear to Jo he was struggling with something. She let him wrestle.

He said, "I don't know."

"Who did he hang around with most?"

Carson shook his head and said, "No one. He was by himself a lot."

"What kinds of things did Michael ... I mean Mike, like to do?"

Carson shrugged again and said, "Normal stuff. He liked to write, but he never talked about it."

Jo smiled at him and said, "But you might have snuck into his room and read some of it?"

The blond boy's chin lowered to his chest, and he fidgeted.

"It's okay. I think that's why Mike left it on his desk. You know, so someone would read it."

The hope on Carson's face was visible to both Weist and O'Connor, and O'Connor was impressed with the FBI profiler.

"Sometimes, quiet kids, even adults, will leave things out in the open. Something personal like poetry, for others to read."

"Mom and Dad never came in here. Much anyway. Mike and I talked a little. I liked him."

"What about Stacey?" O'Connor asked.

Carson shook his head, and his face clouded over. Jo knew she had hit a note with that question. She might circle back to it in time.

"What did you talk about, if I could ask?" Jo asked.

"Stuff. Music and books. He liked to read. I like sports. He doesn't."

Carson got up off the bed, went to the bookcase, and pointed. Jo followed him the short distance.

"Mike liked the *Divergent* series and the *Maze Runner* series. See?"

"I bet you like to read, am I right?"

Carson nodded.

"Can I ask you a tough question, Carson?"

He nodded.

"Your parents didn't spend much time with him, did they?"

His chin rested on his chest.

"That's what I thought. Same with Mike's sister?"

Carson's eyes flashed. Something was behind them that Jo could not read, and it caused her to mutter, "Huh." She considered that she had just struck the same chord as before.

"Carson, if I promise to bring this notebook back, and I do promise, can I take it so I can read it?" O'Connor asked. He was not sure, but there was something in it. If he could not understand what it was, perhaps Bobby or Randy might be able to decipher it.

Defiantly, Carson met O'Connor's eyes and said, "Don't let Mom and Dad know."

"I promise."

"You'll bring it back?"

"I promise."

O'Connor fished a business card out of his pocket, grabbed a pen off Michael's desk, and wrote his cell number on it. He walked over to the bed and sat down next to the boy.

"I want you to take this. You don't have to show it to your Mom or Dad or your sister. This is between you and me. Anytime you want to talk, call me. Day or night. It doesn't matter when."

Carson took the card and studied it and then looked up at O'Connor.

"I mean that. You call me anytime. Day or night. I'll answer. We can talk about anything you want. If you want to get a burger or a soda, I can come get you, or we can meet somewhere. I like sports too, though I pretty much suck at them."

Carson smiled, and then the first of many tears fell from Carson's eyes. That's when Jo and Pat heard Mike's story through the eyes of a thirteen-year-old.

Chapter Twenty-Eight

Waukesha, WI

"Do you think he'll call?"

Pat knew what Jo meant.

"Don't know. Hope so."

Cleve sat in the backseat still fuming about the sister, so he did not catch the significance of the question.

They drove on in silence until Pat's cell buzzed. His Bluetooth picked up the call and ran it through his audio system.

"O'Connor."

"Pat, this is Paul. Did you guys find anything?"

"Nothing much. Kind of drew a blank. Interesting family dynamics though. We have Mike's cell, laptop, and a notebook full of poetry and short stories."

"Poetry?"

"Yeah. I'm going to read it over and then give it to Bobby and Randy to read. Maybe they can make some sense out of it." He knew he would not, that was for sure.

"Where are you?"

"On Bluemound just out of Waukesha heading to the Holiday Inn Express. We're calling it a night."

"Me too. Heading to Sarah's, but I want to run past Mikey's house. The guys are staying there."

"I know. I drove past. Bri is at Sean's house. I checked on him too."

"See you in the morning."

The call ended, and O'Connor drove on.

Jo asked, "Why are you and Paul checking on kids?"

O'Connor shrugged, glanced out the side window, and said, "With this crazy shit running around killing people ... now a kid ... we're playing it safe."

Jo caught Cleve's expression from her passenger-side mirror. Thoughtful. Almost worried. And she wondered what was going on and why.

Chapter Twenty-Nine

Shorewood, WI

Satisfied, The Man took a long pull from his bottle of Evian. He shut his eyes and slowed his breathing, willing himself to calm down. A smile crept across his lips.

The FBI did not know anything. He was sure of that. The cops knew even less.

He finished off the Evian, stood up, and walked to his desk, and sat down. He pulled a yellow legal pad from the drawer, and then picked up his favorite pen. He held it to the pad but did not write.

The Man had a decision to make.

Who would his next victim be? Typically, he was decisive. Daring and confident. It was not that he was not confident. Not at all.

He had two potential targets, one being as meaningful as the other. Any other time, he would just follow the names in his notebook, but he had the feeling that he needed to speed things up so he could take an extended vacation. Maybe move out of the area and start again. Not yet, but soon.

The Man stared at his yellow legal pad. He could not decide who would be first. But both would die. He was certain of that. And then two more would be removed.

Chapter Thirty

Waukesha, WI

Two things were accomplished on the cold gray Saturday morning. One was an empty pot of terrible-tasting coffee that had to be refilled twice, and the second was that two of a dozen donuts escaped being eaten. Both of them were maple, and no one liked maple donuts, so that hardly counted as an accomplishment.

Sadly, while there was much to report about Michael Staley, not much of it was readily applicable to the investigation. At least that they saw at a surface level. There were not any apparent tie-ins to any of the other victims, and that was pointed out by a frustrated Paul Eiselmann.

"I mean, how much in common does a fifteen-year-old freshman in high school have with a fifty-ish middle school principal and an advertising exec in his thirties or a similarly-aged dental hygienist? It doesn't make sense. Nothing makes sense."

"The first couple of victims were students, but they were college kids," added Batiste.

"There's got to be something. There has to be something that ties each of these victims to the shooter. Something," Pete said. "We're just missing it somehow."

"I agree," Summer said. "I don't know what that something is, but I believe as Pat does that we need to look at the Staley boy for the answer. There is something about Staley that ties to the other victims."

"I've read through the notebook once, but I'm not into poetry," O'Connor said.

"Words have too many syllables?" Eiselmann asked with a laugh.

"I didn't bring my decoder ring with me," Graff added with a straight face.

Ignoring them, Pat said, "I'm going to take it to Randy Evans and Bobby McGovern for them to read over. They're the same age or thereabouts, so maybe they can make heads or tails of it."

"You mentioned that in the notebook, there were several comments from his English teacher, Penny Faulkner," Summer said. "Cleve, can you and Jo interview her? Anything you can find on the boy would help."

"Is there anything you'd like us to do?" Greg Gonnering asked with a slight nod to his partner, Carlos Lorenzo, who sat beside him. Up until that moment neither had contributed to the conversation.

"Yes," Jamie said. "I want both of you to change into street clothes and interview Michael's counselor, principal, and assistant principal. It's possible that one of them might give you a name of a kid, a friend, someone he hung out with. If so, follow up on that."

"Got it," Lorenzo said.

"As of now, both of you are in plain clothes and attached to this unit. Anyone asks, refer them to me."

"Given what his brother ..." Pete stopped, searched his notes, and found what he was looking for, "Carson told us, I think we should take another run at his parents."

"But how can we do that without them finding out it was Carson who shared it with us?" Pat asked. "I don't want to burn him."

Summer said, "Let's wait until Carlos and Greg get back to us with what they find out. We dress up what Carson told us with what Carlos and Greg find out. That way he's shielded."

"Might work," Eiselmann said.

"Go over again what Carson shared with you," Pete said to Jo.

"It's sad," Jo started.

Michael Staley had been adopted when he was twelve. Carson was nine, and Stacey was fourteen. Of course, Carson could not shed any light on why they adopted Michael, but it was pretty clear from the start that Michael didn't fit in. In Carson's view, his mother did not want anything to do with him, and either gave him orders to do this or that or ignored him. His father was worse. He was on Michael from day one. Michael could not do anything right. He would try, but nothing was good enough. Carson called his father an ass. Stacey did not like him and made it known. Snide comments, or in Carson's words, rude comments. Other than that, she ignored him, like Michael's mother.

Michael was silent through all of it and, at least on the surface, did not seem to be bothered by it. Carson never saw him cry. He never saw him angry. He never saw him use drugs or alcohol. In fact, Michael would talk to Carson to be careful about who his friends were.

"Carson made him sound like a great big brother who didn't let much get to him. Of course, the notebook might give us a different picture," Jo said with a sigh.

"My God! How sad is that!" Summer said.

"I look at the six boys in Jeremy's and Vicky's family and think, how did they manage?" Pete said. "I mean, if any of them had a reason to be a mess, they did."

"Knowing Jeremy and Vicky, they made it because they were provided love and support," Jamie said. "They were given what Michael Staley wasn't."

"Paul, I need you to dig into Michael's birth and the pre-adoption history," Summer said.

"He's a juvenile, so records might be sealed."

"I'll get the local FBI office to get a hold of a judge to unseal them," Summer said, already making a note. "We need to know the circumstances behind why he was adopted at age twelve. That's atypical for adoption."

"It happens, but not often," Graff said. "Might be something there."

"Skip confirmed time and method of death. Bullets came from a .38, same as the others. This is our guy," Summer said.

"Asshole," Eiselmann muttered.

She looked around the room and said, "Anyone have anything else to offer?"

Nothing from anyone.

"Okay, I guess we've done all we can this morning. Everyone, please keep all of us in the loop on what you uncover. Carlos and Greg, do you have everyone's contact information?"

"Yes, ma'am. Jamie gave it to us," Gonnering responded.

"Okay, welcome to the team. Let's get on this. Too many people are getting killed, and now he's onto kids. We can't have that," Summer said.

Eiselmann had no intention of leaving anytime soon. He wanted to dig into the Staley boy's background. Gonnering and Lorenzo left, taking their mugs of coffee with them. Graff knew they would pour it down the nearest drain.

"Oh, I forgot. Jeremy and Vicky invited us to a mid-afternoon dinner tomorrow at their house. I'll text you their address and their cell numbers. They were thinking three-ish," Graff said.

"I'll make sure Skip knows," Pete said. "I'm looking forward to seeing them and the boys."

"Do we invite Nelson?" Summer asked.

Graff shrugged. He did not much care either way. In some respects, it was hard to tell if he was a member of the team or not. He was in and out, mostly out.

"I guess it wouldn't hurt," he answered.

O'Connor made a noise and covered it by coughing. The others did not notice except for Eiselmann, who ignored it and Jo, who suppressed a smile.

Chapter Thirty-One

Waukesha, WI

Brian leaned against the wall, shut his eyes, and took a deep breath. He knew both Jeremy and Vicky were on the other side of the wall in the office drinking coffee and reading the newspaper. It was a ritual performed every Saturday morning after breakfast. The two of them alone on the couch in front of a fire reading the newspaper and drinking coffee. No TV. No music. Silence. And each other.

George was in the kitchen eating a late breakfast. The other guys were still upstairs. No one was around, so this was his time.

Having built up as much courage as he could muster, he took another deep breath and knocked on the open door.

"Can I come in?"

Just as Brian knew they would be, Jeremy sat in his favorite spot on the left side of the couch wearing a plaid flannel shirt, blue jeans, and slippers. Vicky was curled up on the other side of the couch with one leg under her, wearing her favorite dark blue sweater, sweatpants, and socks. One hand held the folded front page of the paper, while her other held a cup of coffee.

Jeremy looked up in surprise and smiled.

Vicky smiled at him and said, "Good morning, Brian. When did you get home?"

Brian, who still had not entered the room and was hesitant to do so until invited to, said, "A little bit ago."

"Come in," Jeremy said. "What's on your mind?"

Brian turned around and shut the door. Jeremy and Vicky exchanged a look and shrugged at one another before he turned back around.

He took another deep breath, limped over to the couch, and sat down as close to Jeremy as he could without sitting on his lap. He sat staring at his hands.

Jeremy slipped an arm around Brian's shoulder, kissed the side of his head, and said, "What's up Bri?"

"I don't know how to start," he answered just above a whisper.

Vicky pursed her lips and waited, while Jeremy gave his shoulder a squeeze for encouragement.

"I'm not gay. I don't think I am."

Jeremy sighed, gave his shoulder a squeeze, kissed the side of his head, and with his lips still in Brian's hair, said, "Bri, Vicky and I don't think you're gay. We never thought you were gay. Not you and not Bobby."

A tear fell from Brian's eye, followed by another, and he brushed them away.

He turned to Vicky and said, "I would never hurt Bobby. Never. I love him more than anyone."

Vicky reached over and took hold of Brian's hand and said, "I know that, Brian. We both know that. So does Bobby."

"We did ... a little. Only three or four times. I promise," Brian said wiping away more tears. "I know technically we're brothers, but we're not *brothers*, if you know what I mean."

Jeremy looked over Brian's head at Vicky, who shook her head.

"Brian, you don't need to explain this to us. We trust you, and we trust Bobby."

He shook his head and said, "Last night I ... I ..."

Jeremy waited for what seemed like an hour, but in reality, was six or seven seconds. Brian said, "Last night ..."

He took a deep breath and said, "I had sex with Cat."

Vicky blinked at Jeremy and blinked again. Jeremy brushed his lips in Brian's hair.

"It just happened. We weren't doing ... much. You know. And then ... we did. *It.*" He took another deep breath and said, "Three times."

Jeremy felt himself blush, and he said, "Brian, I appreciate your honesty, but you don't have to go into details."

Brian wiped off the rest of his tears, which had slowed to a trickle. He had gotten most of it out. The worst part, anyway. He was still scared of what they might say or do.

"I know you're angry. And I know you're disappointed. I'm sorry."

"Brian," Jeremy started, but could not finish. He ended up hugging Brian.

"I need to finish," Brian said.

Vicky had never let go of Brian's hand. She moved over closer to Brian, kissed his hand, and then hugged the boy.

"Brian, we're not angry with you. Yes, we're disappointed, but we're not angry."

Brian's shoulders sagged. He tried to pull his hand away from Vicky, but she would not let him. Brian gave up.

"I feel so fu ... screwed up," Brian said, and he began to cry harder.

"Brian, how much of this is my fault?" Jeremy whispered. "I mean, how much of this comes from my conversation with you yesterday morning?"

Brian shook his head and said, "Nothing. It's all on me. It's my fault."

"I don't believe that," Jeremy said. "I think I played a big part in this."

"Bri, what are you scared of? What's going on?" Vicky said.

As if Brian had not heard her, he said, "I never thought I was gay. Ever. Then we talked yesterday morning, and I thought, *am I?* I mean, I love Bobby. More than anybody. I *love* him. We talk about everything. He understands me. I like being with him, and I miss him when he isn't." Tears rolled down his cheeks as he looked first at Jeremy and then at Vicky and said in a small, terrified voice, "I love him. I want him near me."

"I know you do, Brian. Both of us know that," Jeremy said.

"But I like Cat. I liked what we did last night. It was ... *good.* But I liked what Bobby and I did." He looked at Vicky, and his face crumbled. "I'm sorry, but I did. I'm sorry if that sounds weird."

He sighed and said, "Does that mean I'm gay?" Without giving them an opportunity to respond, he asked, "What's wrong with me?"

"Brian, please look at me." When Brian did not, Jeremy again, "Please look at me."

Brian shook his head and mouthed the word, "Can't."

Jeremy looked at Vicky for help, and she responded, "Brian, I'm Bobby's mother. I gave birth to him."

"I know. I'm sorry."

"Brian, let me finish. Please? Okay?"

Brian nodded, though he was not sure he wanted her to.

"I can't think of a better friend for Bobby than you. No one."

Brian started to object, and she said, "Please let me finish. You need to hear me out, okay? You need to listen to me."

Brian nodded.

"I know you and Brett and George are close. I know George and Billy are close. I know Randy and Billy are close. And I know Randy and Bobby are close."

"I love them all," Brian whispered. "We love each other."

"I know, Bri, just let me finish."

Brian nodded and said, "I'm sorry."

Vicky kissed his cheek and said, "Stop with the, *I'm sorry*, okay? It isn't necessary. Just listen to me."

Brian nodded, started to say *I'm sorry* again, but shut his mouth in time.

"I'm Bobby's mother. And I'm your mom, too. I'm mom to all of you guys whether I gave birth to you or not. I wouldn't change that for anything in the world." She gripped his hand a little harder and shook it once for emphasis. "There are two things I want for each of you. Just two. The first is that I want my boys to end up more successful than I am. The second is that I want each of you to be happy. To have a happy life. Whatever that means to you. Not to me. Not to Jeremy. But to you. I want each of you happy."

Jeremy kissed the side of Brian's head and said, "What she said, Big Guy."

"But what if I'm gay?" Brian asked.

Vicky smiled at him and said, "We're going to love you either way. That's a promise. But I want you to think for a minute. Up until yesterday, that thought never entered your mind, did it?"

Brian shook his head.

"So, what if you aren't?" Vicky said with a smile. "Yes, you and Bobby experimented a couple of times. Boys do that. But it doesn't mean you're gay. It means you're exploring your feelings, that's all."

"Your mom and I can't read your mind, Brian. We don't know your heart except for what you share with us. The only one who fully knows is you," Jeremy added.

Brian shook his head and said, "I feel so fu ... screwed up."

"Until yesterday morning, Brian, did you ever, *ever* think you might be gay?" Jeremy asked.

"No! Never! Honest!"

"And last night with Cat. Did it occur to you that you might be gay?"

He blushed and said, "No. I liked it. It was ..." He searched for the right word. "It was normal." He looked from Jeremy to Vicky and said, "But I like what Bobby and I did."

"Brian, you are fifteen-years-old. There's a lot of things you're thinking about. There's a lot swimming around inside your head. A lot has happened to you in this past year. It would leave anyone reeling. But you survived. That's a testament to your strength. You are a strong, strong kid, Bri."

Vicky said, "I can't tell you how much I enjoy watching you and Bobby together. Your friendship is incredible."

Brian shifted on the couch and stared at Vicky and said, "But are you going to look at Bobby and me and think, 'They're gay!' when you see us? When we go to bed, are you going to think, 'I wonder what they'll be doing?'"

"No, Brian, I won't be thinking that. I'll be thinking that two of my sons are the very best of friends. I'll be looking at the two of you and hope that all the other guys can have as close a friendship as you and Bobby have. That's what I'll be thinking. That's what both Jeremy and I will be thinking. That's a promise."

The three of them sat in silence. Brian stared at the fire. He gripped Vicky's hand with his, and he leaned his head on Jeremy's shoulder.

In a small voice, Brian said, "I'm sorry about having sex with Cat. I know you don't want us to until we know we love someone. You said that."

"I know I've said that, Bri. But I also know that sometimes you guys will be in situations and things will happen. The trick is to try to avoid those situations as much as possible until you're ready and sure of yourself and your feelings," Jeremy said, giving his shoulder a squeeze.

Brian nodded and said, "I screwed up."

Jeremy had to stifle a chuckle at the unintended pun.

Brian turned to Vicky and said, "Yesterday I was rude to you."

"How's that?" Vicky said.

"I never said goodbye to you yesterday morning, and I never talked to either of you after the game. I'm sorry."

"Why didn't you?" Vicky asked.

"I was embarrassed. I was afraid you thought I was gay. I didn't want you to think that. I didn't want you to think I was weird or that I would hurt Bobby."

Vicky reached both arms out and said, "Brian, come here."

Brian sat up, and the two of them embraced, neither wanting to let go.

Vicky shifted and placed both hands on Brian's cheeks. She looked at him and said, "Brian, I love you more than you can imagine. I don't think any less of you today than I did yesterday or the day before. I'm proud you're my son. You're not weird, and I know you'd never hurt Bobby. I doubt you could hurt anyone intentionally."

Brian nodded, and Vicky kissed him on the nose.

"I'm going to say a couple more things, and I want you to listen, okay?"

Brian nodded.

"First, if you're going to have sex with Cat, you have to take precautions."

"She's on the pill. She has bad cramps when she has her period, and the pill helps with that." He shrugged and said, "That's what I was told."

Vicky nodded and said, "That's true. Okay, that's some precaution. But it wouldn't hurt to use a condom. It will be important if you and Bobby decide to experiment any further."

"That won't happen."

Ignoring that statement, she asked, "Do you know how to put one on and take one off?"

Brian nodded and said, "Sean showed me." He blushed and immediately regretted throwing Sean under the bus.

"Okay, so your dad is going to get you a box of condoms. You don't have to tell the other guys or Bobby for that matter. Put them somewhere where they won't be seen or where someone will find them. Now, I'm not giving you permission to have sex with Cat, but as a precaution, you need to take one or two with you when you go out with her. Okay?"

Brian nodded.

"Again, that's not permission to have sex. Both your dad and I would prefer you didn't, okay?"

He nodded again.

"And, if you and Bobby go beyond what you've done, both of you will need to protect yourselves. That's just common sense," Vicky said.

Brian blushed, but managed to say, "Okay." He paused and asked, "How did you know Bobby and I did anything?"

Jeremy smiled and said, "You need to keep the door closed."

"Oh. Yeah."

"The last thing is this. It doesn't matter to me, and it doesn't matter to Jeremy if you're gay or not. I don't think you are and neither does Jeremy. I think you and Bobby were experimenting and got caught up in a moment. I think you love each other, and I think that's beautiful. I want each my sons to have someone love them as much as you and Bobby love each other. If at some point you come to the decision that you are gay, I'm going to love you as much as if you weren't. That's a promise."

Brian wanted to believe her. He said, "I don't think I am, but I'm not sure. I liked what Cat and I did last night."

"I get that. But you have to be careful. You can't use her, just like you can't allow yourself to be used, either."

Brian nodded. "I won't."

"Are we good?" Jeremy asked.

Brian sighed and nodded, feeling a lot more relieved than when he first walked into the office. He said, "I just don't want you to think I'm weird. I love Bobby. I won't hurt him. Ever. I promise. And I like Cat a lot. But I'll be careful. I'll try not to," he tried to think of the best way to put it and settled on, "be in situations with her like that."

"Good. You're a good decision maker, Bri. Keep making good decisions. Vicky and I know that there will be times when that might not be possible. Just be smart and be careful."

"Promise."

"Okay, then. Anything else?" Jeremy asked.

Brian glanced at Jeremy and then at Vicky and said, "What do you want me to do for a punishment?"

"For what?"

"For having sex with Cat and for being rude to you and Mom."

Jeremy smiled and shook his head and said, "Brian, what you and Cat did might not have been the smartest thing in the world, but it happens. We're not going to punish you for that."

"What about for being rude to you and Mom?"

Vicky took his hand again and said, "Brian, I'm sorry you felt embarrassed and felt I might be angry with you, but you don't have to worry about that anymore."

"But I was rude to you."

"Okay, perhaps you were. Do you think that will happen again?"

"No, I promise."

"A promise is a big commitment," Jeremy said with a smile.

Brian nodded and said, "I promise to try not to do that again. I love you, and I didn't mean to hurt you."

Vicky kissed his forehead and said, "Apology accepted, and no punishment is necessary because I think you mean it."

"I do. I love you." He turned to Jeremy and back to Vicky and said, "I love both of you."

First Vicky and Brian embraced and exchanged kisses, and then Brian and Jeremy did the same.

Jeremy held his face and said, "I'm proud of you, Brian."

"Why?"

"Because it took guts to walk in here and tell us what's in your heart. Sharing your heart can be a scary thing. You showed us your toughness, but even more importantly, you showed us the beauty in your heart."

Brian nodded, and the two of them embraced again.

Jeremy asked, "Are we good?"

He felt Brian nod against his chest. He kissed the top of Brian's head and said, "I love you so much, Bri. Please believe that."

He nodded again, relieved.

"Do you know where Bobby is?"

"Not sure, but he's around here somewhere," Jeremy said.

"I have to go talk to him," Brian said with a sigh.

"Be as honest with him as you were with us. Honesty goes a long way. With all of us," Vicky said.

Brian nodded and left the room already rehearsing how he might start.

Chapter Thirty-Two

Waukesha, WI

It was not hard to find Bobby. All he had to do was follow the sound of the acoustic guitar and a high melodic tenor, almost alto voice, not that Brian knew the difference between the two. He knew Bobby could play and he could sing, and when most people heard him, they stopped what they were doing to listen.

Much of the time, there would be two guitars and two voices in close harmony. Randy sang melody, and Bobby sang high harmony. They alternated from time to time, one sounding as good as the other. Together, they were unique.

This time, however, it was Bobby by himself, picking and singing with the bedroom door open a crack.

As he did outside the office, Brian leaned against the wall and shut his eyes and took a deep breath. He could not stop shaking. He placed both hands on his head and tilted his face to the ceiling. He brought both hands down and wrung his arms.

Bobby began the last stanza of Miranda Lambert's *Tin Man*. Almost over except for the guitar work. Brian knew from watching him practice this song, Bobby's eyes would be closed, so he hesitated. He did not know if it would be better to wait until the song was over before he walked through the door or if he should be standing in the doorway when Bobby opened his eyes.

He decided to wait until the song ended, and then he entered the bedroom he shared with Bobby and shut the door behind him.

Bobby got up off the bed and set the guitar in the corner by the dresser and sat down cross-legged on the bed, leaning against the headboard. He was barefoot and wearing a gray Nike t-shirt with black Nike nylon sweats.

"Can we talk?"

Bobby cocked his head but said nothing.

Brian sat down on the side of the bed, toward the middle with one leg under him and the other on the floor. He sat facing Bobby but had his head down.

Bobby said, "I sent you seven texts, and I called you three times, and you never answered any of them." He let that sit there between them and then he asked, "Why should we talk now?"

"I'm sorry."

"That hurt, Brian. I didn't do anything to deserve that."

"I know."

"So, what are we talking about? You chewing my ass out after the game for no reason? You not answering my texts? Not answering my phone calls?"

Brian felt like crying. This was not the way he had pictured it going. He expected Bobby's anger but not the calmness with which Bobby spoke to him. Brian would have preferred being yelled at. He could have even accepted a punch or two. Bobby was not like that. He had a temper, but Bobby was gentle. Bobby's pain, if not his anger, was visible to him.

"Why were you so pissed at me last night?"

There it was. Brian knew the question was coming. He had tried to prepare for it. He had rehearsed an answer. In the end, however, all his words failed him. He had nothing.

Brian shook his head and said, "I was jealous."

"Jealous?"

Brian shrugged.

"You don't even know Megan that well. I thought you liked Cat?"

Confused, Brian was, at first speechless. His mouth opened and closed, but in the end, all he did was shake his head.

Then the light went on for Bobby. His eyes got big, and his mouth formed a perfect O. He sat back against the headboard and chose not to say anything and let Brian explain.

"I was at the free throw line, and I looked for you. I made the first one, and I saw you kissing Megan."

Bobby nodded.

"I was jealous."

"How do you think I feel every time you kiss Cat? Do you think that's easy for me?"

The two boys locked eyes. Brian had never suspected Bobby felt like that.

Bobby stretched out onto his back while Brian rolled onto his stomach next to him.

"I couldn't help it. I saw you kissing her, and I got jealous. I could hardly concentrate on the game."

Bobby turned to look at him and said, "You missed two shots, Bri. Both were early in the third quarter, and they were back to back. Other than that, you were perfect from the floor and perfect from the line. Do you know how hard that is? And you couldn't *concentrate*?"

"I wasn't thinking about basketball, and I wasn't thinking about the game. I was thinking about you. And Megan. I ... was jealous."

"So are you saying you can kiss Cat, but I can't kiss Megan? That's not fair."

"I know, it's not fair," Brian agreed. He took a deep breath and said, "There's something else."

"Bri, you know I love you, right?"

"I know, Bobby. And I love you. Honest. I love you more than anyone. I mean that, but there's something else I have to tell you."

Bobby snaked an arm under Brian's head and hugged him. He moved closer and put his head next to Brian's. It made it all the more difficult to tell him what he needed to.

"What?"

"Please let me finish before you say anything, okay?"

Bobby rolled over onto his stomach, put his arm around Brian, and said, "Okay."

Brian wept as he said, "It's hard."

Bobby said nothing but kissed his cheek.

"Last night ... Cat and I ..." Brian could not finish.

Shocked, Bobby said, "*What?*"

"I'm sorry. It just ... happened."

Bobby rolled away and leaned up on an elbow and stared at him.

"You had sex with Cat? But you got jealous when I kissed Megan? How the hell does that work?"

"I'm sorry. It just happened. I wasn't planning it. I don't know what's wrong with me."

Bobby sat up and moved away from Brian, leaned against the headboard, and stared at the wall near the door.

"So, you say you love me. You say you were jealous. But you had sex with Cat."

Brian did not know what to say to that.

"Is that all? Is there anything *else* you want to tell me?"

"I'm sorry. I mean it when I say I love you more than anyone else. I know it might not mean anything to you now, but I do love you."

"Who else knows about this?"

"Mom and Dad. And Sean."

"Sean?"

Brian nodded and said, "Cat told him that she wanted to do it with me."

"So it was her idea?"

"Well, yeah, I suppose. I could have said no, but I didn't. I was hard. My jeans were open. Her shirt was up, and her pants were open. She told me she wanted to. I asked if she was sure, and she said, 'Yeah.' But I don't think I could have stopped if I wanted to."

"You had sex with Cat. You must have been making out, and you felt each other up. She beat you off. And then you had sex." He paused, shook his head, and said, "And you're jealous because Megan and I kissed. And you say you love me." Bobby shook his head again and said, "I don't get it."

"I don't either."

"What did you tell Mom and Dad?"

Brian could not look at Bobby when he said, "Everything."

"Everything."

"I told them that we hardly do anything, and we only did it a couple of times. I told them that I love you and that I would never hurt you." He looked at Bobby and said, "I would never hurt you, Bobby. Honest."

He paused and then continued. "I was afraid they thought I was gay. I don't know if I am or not. I don't think I am, but, Bobby ..."

"They never thought we were gay, Brian. They never thought either of us was gay. All Dad wanted was to make sure that if we do anything more than what we did, we take precautions. And make sure the door is closed. That's all. Guys do stuff. Friends do stuff. We aren't gay. Period!"

Brian sighed. He was not sure even after having sex with Cat and despite what Sean had said. He looked up at Bobby and said, "Are you grossed out that I was jealous?"

Bobby shook his head, folded his arms across his chest, and thought for a bit. He jumped off the bed, went to the sock drawer, pulled out a pair, and said, "Right now, I'm angry. I have to think."

"Bobby, I'm sorry," but Bobby left the room without turning around, and he shut the door behind him.

Brian grabbed a pillow, lay on his stomach, and wept into it. He did not know how long, but in time, he stopped. He still felt miserable. He believed deep down that Bobby did not, maybe could not, understand. How could Bobby when he did not understand either?

He was afraid that he lost a friend. And if that was the case, maybe he lost the friendship of the other guys too.

He rolled over onto his back and stared at the ceiling, hoping no one would come through the door.

Chapter Thirty-Three

Waukesha, WI

Billy made himself a ham and cheese sandwich with spicy brown mustard and poured some chips out of a bag onto his plate. George took a bite out of Billy's sandwich without Billy protesting, and he took a couple of Billy's chips too. It was something they had done to each other ever since George had moved in. George made himself the same sandwich, added chips, and Billy helped himself to them. Jasmine, their dog, was fed surreptitiously by both Billy and George.

Brett peeled an orange, dropped the peels into the garbage disposal and ran it, and then sat down at the table with them. Randy and Bobby wandered in looking for lunch and settled on mac and cheese, splitting the chef duties. For someone who was pretty gregarious and who could speed talk with the best of them, Bobby was unnaturally quiet.

Vicky came into the kitchen and said, "Everyone get enough to eat?"

Mouths were full, so heads nodded except for Brett who declared he was still hungry but did not know what else to eat. Billy suggested Fry Bread, George's specialty from Navajoland, and everyone, including Vicky agreed, so as soon as George finished with his sandwich and chips, he started putting the ingredients together.

Brian limped into the kitchen carrying a soccer ball followed by his dog, Jasper. He stuffed his indoor soccer shoes and two orange oval cones into a small gym tote along with soccer socks and dropped it in the hallway by the back door. He saw all the food, and his stomach growled, but he was not about to join them at the kitchen table.

"Where are you going?" Billy asked.

Brian busied himself by tying up the boots he wore when he and George went to the stable, so he did not look up when he said, "Take care of the horses and work out."

"I took care of the horses early this morning," George said.

Brian did not respond.

"Bri, you're limping quite noticeably," Vicky said. "Where are you hurting?"

Brian blushed. He was not about to tell her that in addition to his knee, his elbow, and his hip that his balls ached. "My hip. I'm a little stiff, that's all."

"I'd like to take a look at it."

"I don't think it's that bad."

"Please?"

Brian looked up at her, sighed, and said, "Okay. Where?"

"Let's go into the bathroom in the hallway," Vicky said, already heading there.

Brian pushed himself up to his feet and limped after her. Brett and Jasper followed them.

When they had left the kitchen, Bobby said, "What happened to his hip?"

"You didn't see it happen?" Billy asked.

"I guess not," Bobby said.

"I don't know how," Billy said. "At the end of the first half, Bri gets wiped out going for a layup. Ruiz got a T for it. But Bri jammed his elbow and knee."

"I thought he was going to break his wrist," Randy said.

"And then in the second half, Brian's shooting a three, and Buddy Welch throws him into the bleachers." Billy demonstrated on Randy. "Welch gets a T and is ejected."

"I thought Bri had hit his head. I thought for sure he wasn't going to play after that," Randy said.

"So how did you miss that?" Billy asked again.

"I don't know." He lowered his eyes and refused to look at anyone.

George stood at the stove silently, watching Bobby throughout the exchange. Bobby did not know it, but George had seen him with Megan. George had tasked himself with watching over each of his brothers ever since he had moved in during the summer of death. More so after the gang mess they found themselves in a couple of months previous.

In the hallway bathroom, Vicky said, "Bri, take down your pants and boxers and lift up your shirt."

Brian turned six different shades of red but did as he was told. He tried to cover himself, but there was too much to cover.

"Brian, this looks awful!"

He tried to turn so he could see it, but the angle was too severe, and he forgot all about covering himself up.

Brett noticed him trying to see it, so he gave him a play by play.

"It's dark blue, maybe black, and it covers an area high up on your hip," he said tracing the area on his leg, "and down to here on your thigh. And it goes from here," he said brushing his pubic hair, "to here on your butt."

"Bri, I'm going to probe it. I need you to tell me where it hurts." She ran her fingers over the area alternating looking where her fingers touched and at Brian's face.

He gritted his teeth but otherwise said nothing until Vicky touched the hip joint. He sucked in his breath and hissed.

"Bingo!" Brett said. "Scale of one to ten, how bad?"

"Eight."

"Brett, can you get Dad? He's in the office."

Brett had to move Brian out of the way so he could get out of the bathroom, smacked Brian's bare butt, and then almost tripped on Jasper as the pup waited just outside the door.

He bent down to pet the pup and said, "He's okay, Jasper. He's okay."

"It's not that bad," Brian protested.

Jeremy and Brett came back, but this time, Brett stayed out in the hallway with Jasper because it was too crowded in the bathroom. As Jeremy entered the bathroom, Brett said, "Brian's hip is hurting."

"A little," Brian added.

"More than a little," Vicky said raising an eyebrow at Brian.

Jeremy took one look at it and said, "Geez, Brian. Why didn't you say something to us?"

"I didn't think it was that bad." To Vicky, he asked, "It's not that bad, right?"

The other guys gathered in the hallway, each sticking his head in trying to catch a peek.

"Vicky, do you think we should take him in?"

"No, please. It's not that bad. I still have range of motion, see?"

Brian placed a hand on the wall, lifted his right knee and turned it out and then in. Then he lifted his knee up and down and then kicked forward and back.

"See?"

Vicky and Jeremy stared at one another as Billy said, "It looks like he can move it."

Jeremy said, "Bri, maybe we should take you in just to have it checked. The doc could look at your elbow and your knee along with it."

"But we have a game on Thursday. If the doctor doesn't clear me by then, I can't play. And I might not be able to play Friday if we win on Thursday, and I might not be able to play on Saturday if we win on Friday."

"But I'm thinking about your long-term health. I'm thinking about your ability to play soccer," Jeremy said.

"But Dad ..."

"Wait! Just wait," Vicky said.

She had been around athletic injuries ever since Brett and Bobby were little. And before that when her pervert brother Anthony- the child molester- played middle school, high school, and collegiate sports.

"Bri, I want an honest answer, okay?"

Eager and sensing something positive, Brian nodded.

"When you get injured, how fast do you heal?"

"Pretty fast. But I've never been injured, though."

"Hardly ever?"

"A sprained ankle. A jacked-up knee. Maybe a shoulder. Nothing much."

"What about this?" Vicky said, pointing at his hip.

"I think it'll be okay. It's just stiff. Honest."

"Before you go to the stable, I want you to take four Motrin for the swelling. When you get back, I want you to put ice on it," and then with a slight nod at his testicles, she said, "And anywhere else that's sore. After that, you jump into the hot tub. I'll stay away so you can go in with or without a suit."

He blushed, covered himself, and said, "Okay."

"And I want you to tell me if it doesn't get any better by Monday morning. And I want honesty. Fair enough?"

Brian smiled and said, "That's fair."

"Jeremy?"

Jeremy smiled and said, "Sounds like a plan."

Forgetting his pants were at his ankles, Brian first hugged Vicky and then Jeremy.

Both laughed, and Jeremy said, "You might want to pull up your pants, Bri."

"Oh, shit, I mean shoot," he said, yanking everything back into place.

Vicky and Jeremy were still laughing as they left the bathroom.

It was Billy who said, "You not flashed Mom and Dad, and you hugged them both with your pants down. Smooth move, Bri." All the boys laughed. Brian, however, was mortified.

The boys walked back to the kitchen. Vicky and Jeremy kissed in the hallway, and Jeremy disappeared to the office while Vicky headed up the stairs.

"Are you still going to the stable?" George asked.

"Yeah. I want to work out."

"You want company?" George asked.

"No, I'm okay. Jasper will come with me."

He finished getting ready and headed out the door without looking at anyone. He chose to walk rather than take one of the four-wheelers.

The boys stared at the closed door.

Billy walked to the window above the sink and watched Brian limp down the path to the stable with Jasper by his side. He turned around, faced Bobby, and said, "Why didn't you do the butterflies, Eskimo, and regular thing you two do?"

Bobby blushed, searched the room for a friendly face but found eyes with a hundred questions, and said, "He's just going to the stable."

Billy said, "You two do that when one of you leaves a room for a second. What's up?"

"Nothing."

"Are you fighting?" Brett asked.

Bobby was rescued by the doorbell before he had to lie. He said, "I'll get it." He got up and hot-footed it to the front door, opened it, and found Pat O'Connor.

"Hey, Pat. What's up?"

"Well. I." He started and stopped. It was a quirk that most found amusing while a few others found frustrating. "I came to see you and Randy. With your dad's and mom's permission."

Bobby stepped aside and let him in. Jeremy came out of the office, walked down the hallway, saw Pat, and greeted him with a handshake.

"Hi, Jeremy. I was hoping to talk with Bobby and Randy. With your permission, that is."

"Jamie called and let me know you'd be coming. It's fine."

"Thank you."

"What's up?" Randy asked.

"Can we sit down?"

"Boys, why don't you take Pat into the family room," Jeremy suggested.

Vicky had come back down the stairs and said. "Can we get you anything? You drink Diet Coke, right? Or water ... iced tea?"

"A Diet Coke would be fine, thank you."

Brett walked back into the kitchen, refrigerated the Fry Bread George was preparing, grabbed a Diet Coke for Pat and a bottle of water for himself, and walked back into the family room.

"What's up?" Randy asked.

"Before we start, we need to go ice fishing again. Right after basketball season and before track," Brett said.

O'Connor nodded and said, "We can do that. You, George, Bri, and Gav?"

"Yeah, but ask Jamie and Earl Coffey if they want to go, too."

Coffey was a Marinette County Sheriff who was on one of the teams rescuing the kids from the ring during the summer of death. He had befriended Brian, Brett, George, and Gav because, like him, they were hunters and fishermen. Real outdoorsy.

Pat looked around the room and asked, "Where's Brian?"

Eyes flicked to Bobby, and Randy said, "He went to work out at the stable."

"Oh, okay. Well, I have something I want you and Bobby to read."

"What is it?" Bobby asked.

"It's a notebook of poems and short stories. They were written by a fifteen-year-old boy, Michael Staley."

"That's the guy who was shot in the alley," Brett said.

O'Connor nodded, pushed his long hair back behind his ears, and said, "Yes, that's the boy."

"He was fifteen-years-old?" Randy said.

"Does this have to do with the serial killer?" Billy asked.

"Guys, let Pat talk," Jeremy said.

Pat smiled at him and said, "Thanks." He turned to the guys and said, "Michael Staley was shot in an alley, but I'm sure you all know that because Brett and George were told not to tell anyone, right?"

Nothing but grins and not one was hidden.

"Okay then. So you know all about it. At least most of it." He continued after he opened the soda and took a quick swallow. "Staley was adopted when he was twelve."

"Just like Randy and me," Billy said.

"Shhh," Randy said.

"Evidently, it didn't go as well for him as it did for you two." Pat looked around the room and said, "Or as well as the rest of you for that matter. I don't want to say too much more than that because that's why I want you to read this." He indicated the notebook.

"What are we looking for?" Bobby asked.

"Not sure. I want you to read it and see what it tells you about the Staley boy. About his family. I want to know as much about him as possible."

"About the serial killer, have you checked into the adoption angle?" Jeremy asked.

O'Connor frowned and said, "No, because as far as we know, he's the only one who was adopted. The other victims were older and some, like the middle school principal, were in their fifties. So that doesn't seem to be a plausible factor."

"Can we read it?" Brett asked. "I mean, Billy, George, Brian, and me?"

"Brian's good with stuff like this," Billy said. "He should read it."

"That's fine. But under one condition and you have to follow my directions. It's too important to have you screw around on this."

"What?" Brett asked.

"That you read it independently of one another. That you don't share your thoughts, your notes, or your ideas. When you're done, I'll come back with Paul, and we'll record it," Pat said looking at each boy. "No one talks about it with anyone else because I don't want you poisoning the well."

"What?" Billy asked.

"He doesn't want any of you influencing each other. He needs to have your own thoughts and your own insights," Jeremy explained. "Guys, this is important, and you have to agree to this. It's important to the investigation. Got that?"

"We can do that," Randy said.

"How much time do we have?" Brett asked.

"Do you think you can finish it by Tuesday or Wednesday? The sooner, the better. We need to find out all we can about Michael so we can catch this guy."

The boys looked from one to the other and nodded, and it was Randy who said, "We'll do that."

"Hope so," O'Connor mumbled. "We need to close this case."

Chapter Thirty-Four

Brookfield, WI

Having decided to go back to his original target, The Man smiled. He made the decision as he was shaving. He never made decisions on a whim. He liked things neat and orderly, planned and perfect. Like his home. Like his life.

No unnecessary emotions. No unnecessary relationships. No complications.

The Man finished shaving and clipped several long nose hairs. Inspected his fingernails and decided they could wait another day. Not overly long, but clean.

He dressed for warmth, but not overly so. He had to fit in with the rest of them.

Them.

Meaningless drones busying themselves in what they think are important tasks. Running. Stretching. Not meaningless of and by themselves. However, when these same imbeciles go out afterward and suck down beer, eat mega amounts of red meat and fatty foods, and perhaps smoke or imbibe in illicit activities, it defeats the purpose of their running and stretching. Perhaps they justify all their self-defeating activities because they run.

Silliness. A waste of time.

Whatever. He had no time for them and did not care about any of them, except her.

This target intrigued him. He knew she was dedicated. He knew she did not do anything that would defeat the purpose of her running.

She was in all things, positive, cheery, and smart.

The Man would kill her. Simply put, she should not have done it.

Chapter Thirty-Five

Cudahy, WI

The Man took off in the opposite direction so that she would run toward him. So if he timed it right ... And he expected just that. He had planned for it.

Jenna Meyers kept her pace steady, but she pushed herself a little more than usual. Her mind was clear and sharp. Her legs were strong, her breathing easy. She felt she could run forever. From experience, Jenna knew she was experiencing runners high, and she felt she could conquer the world.

There were other runners here and there plodding along the trail, some faster, many others slower, but she was alone. Silence, other than her own footfalls was the only thing she heard on this gray, cold morning. Yet, she never felt alone when she ran. Running gave her time to think, to appreciate, and to pray. To give thanks for the life she had. Feeling blessed.

Jenna shortened her stride as she started up a twisting incline. Shrubs and small trees lined her way. In the distance, she thought she heard Lake Michigan waves crashing ashore, but she knew it was her imagination. Waves would not be crashing onto shore in February's chapter of winter. That was a summer chapter, an enjoyable chapter to look forward to. She smiled at the thought.

Approaching the crest, Jenna lengthened her stride once again.

He appeared in her path. Not moving. Standing. His arm outstretched.

Annoyed, Jenna tried to run to her left, but he moved to block her. She changed course to run to the right, but he stepped in her path again. They performed an awkward dance until she gave up and stood in front of him with her hands on her hips. Angered at his rude behavior. So un-runner-like.

The Man smiled, cold, much like the gray morning, and offering no warmth. And in that moment, there was recognition of him and what he held in his hand.

"You," she said. "What ..."

The Man fired twice, and Jenna's run, like her life, had ended.

One more off his list. One fewer in the world.

Chapter Thirty-Six

Cudahy, WI

"According to her license, her name is Jenna Meyers. She's forty-two," Pete said. "Two joggers, Nora McDeere and Chelsey Van Lannen, found her as they came up the hill and rounded the bend."

Summer considered the body. Similar to the Staley boy. She came upon the shooter, and he took her by surprise, just like Staley.

"Same as Michael Staley," Jo Weist said.

"I was just thinking that," Summer said. "Surprise. She wasn't expecting him, just like Michael wasn't expecting him."

"But, in both cases, he was expecting them."

Dahlke worked the crime scene but found nothing of importance. He took pictures of footprints, but they were partials, and most were smeared with prints on top of prints. Still, there were some possibilities.

Cleve Batiste quick-walked up the path from the direction Meyers had come. Previously, he had canvassed the path from the direction of the shooter.

"No witnesses. Can't find one and I talked to everyone I could find."

"How did I know that was what you were going to tell us?" Kelliher said.

He looked around the area. They began to gather outside the police line. The curious or the morbid. Maybe one and the same. At least he did not see any cells out recording or taking pictures. That would have pissed him off.

"Jo, do we have an ETA on the husband?" Kelliher had tasked Weist with calling him once she had been identified by the Cudahy police.

"I'm guessing he should be here anytime now."

To the cops on the scene, Kelliher said, "Keep the crowd back. No cameras or reporters. No TV."

The group of cops turned at a commotion coming from the parking lot end of the run. They watched as a middle-aged man, frantic, voice strident, gesticulating earnestly, if not stridently, tried to charge past the police guarding the path. Cleve left the group and came to his rescue and escorted him just short of the death scene. He motioned for Storm, Kelliher, and Weist to join him.

"You are Russ Meyers?"

His eyes were red and tear-filled. His nose red from a combination of cold air, crying, and nose blowing. He never answered her. A hand covered his mouth, and he seemed to murmur, but it was nothing coherent.

"I'm FBI Agent Storm. This is Agent Kelliher, Agent Batiste, Agent Weist, and Agent Dahlke. I'm sorry for your loss."

"Who ... who did this?"

"We don't know. Yet. But we're working on it."

"Mr. Meyers, can you tell us approximately what time your wife left to run?" Kelliher asked.

He shook his head and appeared not to have heard the question.

"Sir?"

"About ten, maybe ten-thirty this morning. It's a ten- or fifteen-minute drive from our house to Warnimount." He paused, shook his head, and wept. "She loved coming here to run. I tried to get her to run in our neighborhood, but she loved the peace and quiet." He stopped, wept, and shook his head.

"I know this is difficult, and I'm sorry for asking these questions," Summer said. "Do you know of anyone who had a grudge against your wife? Anyone who might have cause to have done this?"

Beyond crushed, Russ Meyers said, "Can I see her? Please?"

Kelliher and Storm turned around to make certain the body was still covered. Thankfully so.

"Mr. Meyers, we can't allow that just yet. We're still finishing up the scene here. It would be better to wait until we get her to the medical examiner's office."

Russ pointed at the sheet-covered body with a shaking hand and said in a not so controlled voice, "That's my wife. My wife! I want to see her."

Jo stepped in and said, "Mr. Meyers, I know you do. And we want you to. It's just that right now, it isn't a good time. Let us have some time, and I promise you, you will be able to see her yet today."

Meyers wiped his eyes and nodded meekly.

"Can I drive you home?"

"I brought my car," he sobbed.

"That's fine. Agent Batiste can drive your wife's car, and we can talk at your house. Is that okay?"

Meyers took one last long look at his wife and headed toward the parking lot with Weist and Batiste following.

"Cleve, can I speak to you a minute?" Summer said.

"Before you take her car, I need you to take one of the cops with you and do a once over on it, inside and out." She turned to Skip Dahlke. "Skip, are you about done here?"

"Yeah, not much to report. Even the autopsy won't yield much that we don't already know. Point of entry is the same as the others. Under the right eye and bridge of the nose. Looks like a .38."

"Go with Cleve and check out her car as a secondary crime scene. But do it quickly. I don't want her husband to get suspicious."

Dahlke and Batiste left together but at a pace slower than Weist and Meyers, arriving in the parking lot as Jo and Meyers were getting into his car. They slowed and began a search, not expecting to find anything.

"Excuse me. Are you cops?"

"Sir, please step back and let us do our job," Cleve said as politely as he could, his impatience poking through.

"This is Jenna's car. I know her."

This got their attention. Cleve and Skip turned around, and it was Cleve who said, "And who are you?"

"I'm Stan. Stan Loth. Is it true? Is Jenna dead?"

Cleve had a decision to make. Stan either was the shooter or, if he was not, had some information the unit might need. Perhaps not.

Batiste judged Loth to be five-ten and about a hundred-sixty. Another runner, not much to him. A little shorter than what they projected the shooter to be. A little lighter and a little thinner than the video at the middle school showed. Cleve made an educated guess.

"Yes, it appears so. Who are you to Mrs. Meyers?"

"An acquaintance. A friend. I run, and I met her running." He paused, looked up at the gray sky, and said with all sincerity, "Who did this? I mean, Jenna wouldn't hurt anyone. She loved everyone."

"Do you know anything that might help us?"

Loth fidgeted, danced from foot to foot. His hand brushed his forehead and then both hands, palms up, reached out to Batiste.
"Look, I don't know if it's something or nothing."

"What?" Dahlke asked, as interested as Batiste.

"A couple of days ago ... it was late in the afternoon. A weekday. That's when Jenna liked to run. You know, leave her job. Run. Blow off some steam."

Impatient, Cleve said, "Yes, go on."

"Well, I saw her or thought I saw her running ahead of me. I tried to catch her, but I'm coming off a knee injury and couldn't catch up. She got to the parking lot ahead of me. She was talking to this guy. He wasn't a runner. I mean, he wasn't dressed like us." He spread his arms out and looked down at nylon sweat suit and expensive running shoes. "He wasn't a runner."

"Do you know who this guy was?" Cleve asked as he took out a small notebook and a pen.

"That's the thing. It was weird. They were talking by her car. Almost right here. She parks in almost the same spot each time she comes here, and she always runs here. Always. So they were talking. I saw Jenna, and I came over to say hello."

"What did the other guy do?" Dahlke asked.

"She and I hugged. It was a while since we'd seen each other. I mean, we weren't close friends. Just running acquaintances, I guess you'd call us." He shrugged.

Impatient, Cleve said, "What did the guy do?"

"I apologized for interrupting them. He turned to leave, and I think I apologized again. Jenna says something like, 'Who are you?' And he says, 'It was a mistake.' And he left."

Cleve squinted at Loth and said, "He left."

"I asked Jenna who it was, and she said she didn't know. But then she said something strange. She said that he knew her name."

"Some guy Jenna didn't know knew her name?"

"Yeah. It was weird. I could tell she was creeped out."

Cleve's heart rate picked up, but he tried not to show his excitement. "Did you happen to see his car, maybe a license plate?"

Loth shook his head and said, "Not the license plate, but it was a black or dark blue BMW. I think it was new."

"How did you know it was a new BMW?" Dahlke asked.

"I'm not a gearhead or anything, but I recognized the BMW emblem. And the car was shiny. New looking."

Cleve nodded. Dahlke turned around, stepped away, and called Summer saying, "You and Pete need to get here right now. I think we have something."

Chapter Thirty-Seven

Cudahy, WI

Pete knew the way Summer's mind worked, having been her partner for years before her rise to the near top of the pyramid within the FBI. She was not there yet, but she was on the upward trajectory.

She was a farm girl born in the back of a station wagon during a raging thunderstorm. Her parents first thought her name should be Hailey but instead chose Summer because they liked the way the way it sounded: Summer Storm.

She was plucked from the University of Louisville Law School by the FBI after she graduated at the top of her class. A first-class mind and a first-class person. That was the consensus by all who knew her.

Like a shark sensing blood in the water, Summer moved decisively, her mind in hyper-drive. In the cold with the wind picking up off Lake Michigan, they stood in the parking lot. None of them, except for the patrol cops, felt the cold.

"We need to check Gustnecky. I want to know his whereabouts this morning, and I want to know what he drives," Summer said. "Do we know where Jamie, Pat, or Paul are?"

"Pat was headed out to Jeremy's house. He was going to get the notebook to the boys," Skip said. "Haven't heard from Jamie or Paul."

"I thought we ruled out Gustnecky after Pat and I interviewed him in Richfield," Batiste said.

"We did. For the most part, that is," Summer answered. "I want to make sure."

"I know Pat has him on soft surveillance, so I can check on it," Cleve said. He turned away to call O'Connor.

"Skip, I want you to check the tire treads from the alley where the Staley boy was murdered against tread on tires on BMWs. That way, we confirm the vehicle of our shooter."

"But, what if it was just some guy who wanted to talk to the Meyers woman?" Skip asked.

"Once we find him, we can rule him in or out. Right now, this guy is our lead. We need to follow it until he proves otherwise," Pete said. "And I think once Jo is finished with Mr. Meyers, she needs to get to the ... where are we?"

"Cudahy. East of Milwaukee," Skip said.

"Okay, once Jo is done with Meyers, we need to get her to the Cudahy police station and interview this Stan Loth. We need him to sit with an artist, get the guy's picture. If we release it, we might get more tips."

"As a person of interest, though, right?" Batiste said. "Not as the shooter."

Summer smiled at him and said, "Let's go to work, people. I don't want to waste any time on this."

Chapter Thirty-Eight

Shorewood, WI

The Man smiled, though he was to have been concentrating on lowering his heartbeat. Vivaldi played through the speakers. A fire glowed in the fireplace. He sunk into his couch comfortably. Iced water sat on the coaster on the side table. And most importantly of all, another was gone.

Now to plan for the next.

He breathed slowly and deeply. He smiled, and though he was relaxed at the thought of another kill, he felt his heart quicken.

The Man considered himself to be an exceptional planner. Detailed. Efficient. Exacting. Thorough. Professional. He doubted he would ever be caught.

The Man did not believe for a nanosecond that the FBI was a match for him. He was certain local law enforcement was far beneath him, beneath his abilities and beneath his intellect.

No, he would not be caught. He would finish his business here and then move elsewhere and begin again.

The Man focused on the problem. Not necessarily a big problem. But a tricky one. His next two targets lived in the same house. A large, *family*, if one could call it that. A further complication was that he did not know enough about them.

Yet.

He would take his time. The authorities would be frustrated at the lag time between kills. They would be afraid that the "trail," as they called it, would get cold. Ironic, he thought, in that as far as the FBI and local law enforcement were concerned, they were working to stop him from killing. Yet at the same time, without The Man killing another, they could not come close to catching him. A Catch 22.

He smiled.

Let them play their games. He would play too. He was the master of games. Let them have their folly. He was their foil. Let them fret. He would cause it. And so much more.

He lay his head back on the couch and thought.

How best to go about collecting information on these two? And how would he do so without raising suspicions?

The best way would be to blend in, to become a part of it. Them. Built-in reconnaissance, if you will. And he was so good at blending in. One of his many talents. A chameleon.

And when he was ready, two more would be dead. Two more of them would be gone.

Chapter Thirty-Nine

Waukesha, WI

Billy grabbed the loaf of bread out of the bread box, the spicy yellow mustard, the Colby-Jack cheese and the turkey out of the refrigerator, along with a tomato and some lettuce. He grabbed a cutting board from the cupboard and sliced the tomato, eating one or two slices as he did. And he built a thick sandwich and placed it in a sandwich bag.

"Are you still hungry?" Vicky asked as she packed the dishwasher.

"No. This is for Brian. He hasn't eaten lunch."

"That's thoughtful."

"I'm going to take it to him. He's hungry."

Brett asked, "Why don't you wait until he comes back? He could eat it then?"

Billy shook his head and said, "I don't want him to be alone."

"Maybe he wants to be alone," Brett mused.

Billy stopped what he was doing, turned around, and said, "No one should be by himself. Not you or me. Not Bobby or Randy. Not George and not Brian. You should know that better than anyone." He referred to the almost two years Brett spent in isolation while he had been kidnapped.

Randy had gone to the living room to begin reading the notebook O'Connor had brought over. George wanted to finish up his paper for English before the Badger game, so he left for the study. Bobby hung out in the kitchen, glancing out the window above the sink every so often.

"You know, Billy, you have your father's heart," Vicky said.

Billy glanced over his shoulder and smiled at her.

It had taken time for her to tell the difference between Randy and Billy. Physically, they were identical. There were habits and interests she had picked up that separated the twins. Small things an outsider would not know. Billy had a crooked smile, and his eyes danced with playfulness. Randy's smile was warm, but his eyes conveyed the pain, the sorrow, and the worry that rose from his life before Jeremy.

"You and your father are fixers," Vicky continued. "You don't like to see people hurting, and you'll do just about anything to fix it," she laughed. "I like that about both of you."

"Brian is hurting?" Brett asked.

Vicky said, "Maybe, maybe not," and left it at that, not wanting to go into it because it was not anyone else's business.

"He might need water," Brett said. "I didn't see him take any with him."

Billy packed a thermal lunch box with a sandwich, chips, and two bottles of water.

"He likes cookies," Bobby added. When he said it, his eyes darted from Billy to Brett to Vicky, and then he left the room. Billy and Brett looked at Vicky for answers, but she betrayed nothing.

As Billy left the kitchen, he said, "I'll be back, but I'll wait for him until he's finished."

He decided to walk the short distance but was surprised at how cold it had gotten. He hunched his shoulders and picked up his pace. Only two hundred yards away, it was not long before he reached the stable. He could hear the irregular pounding of a ball being kicked against something but could not place the sound.

He entered and shut the door. Brian had stripped down to shorts and a long-sleeved t-shirt. Brian's face was beet red, his hair was mussed and he was dripping in sweat. It had to be from his workout, because the stable was rather chilly.

If Brian knew he was there, there was not any indication. Brian shuffled from one cone to the other but kept the ball between his feet without losing it, moving efficiently. His eyes were straight ahead and not down at the ball. Billy noticed that each time Bri shuffled, he winced, but he could not tell if it had hurt more when Brian moved to his right or to his left.

Brian stopped shuffling and without any break, toe-tapped the ball, almost like he was running in place. He would circle to the left, then circle to the right, and Brian would wince with each step, but not slow down.

The last exercise was to kick the ball up from behind his back to the front, dribble using both his left and his right foot, and then turn around doing the same thing. Billy counted twenty of these and was impressed with the ball control and how closely Bri was able to drop the ball at his feet.

He stopped and bent over at his waist with his hands on his knees. He straightened up and placed both hands on top of his head. When he had sufficiently caught his breath, Brian glanced at Billy.

"I can't believe how good you've gotten. No wonder you made varsity as a freshman."

Brian said, "Thanks, but next year, Mario, Cem, Mikey, and Garrett will try out for varsity. Stephen will end up as the goalie. But there will be a lot more competition at striker and midfield than there was this year."

"Nobody's going to take your place."

Brian shrugged and said, "Never know."

"I brought you lunch."

"Thanks."

"And water. Brett couldn't remember if you took any with you."

Brian shook his head, walked over, and sat down on the same bale of hay Billy sat on. He took one of the bottles of water and almost drained it in three gulps, water spilling down his chin and neck.

"Looks like you've been working," Billy said with a laugh.

Brian flashed him a maybe -maybe not look.

"Your hip is killing you, isn't it?"

"Don't tell anyone. I can work through it."

Billy raised his hands in surrender.

Brian's stomach growled as he took the sandwich out of the bag and bit into it.

"I forgot fruit, but if you count the tomato as fruit, which technically it is, then I didn't forget fruit."

Brian flashed him a "what-the-hell" look, shook his head and smiled and kept eating.

"Bobby made me bring a cookie."

Brian's eyes flicked to him, but he kept chewing the sandwich.

"He said to bring you one, but I brought you two. So if you only want one, I can eat the other."

Brian laughed, almost choking, and handed Billy one of the cookies.

"I want the other one. It has more chocolate chips."

"No, that one's mine," Brian laughed elbowing Billy.

Billy waited, took a bite, and with his mouth full said, "What's with you and Bobby?"

"Nothing."

"Something."

"Nothing."

"You left, and you didn't do butterflies, Eskimos, and regulars. That's something."

Brian shrugged.

"Are you fighting? Maybe I can help."

"We're not fighting, and you can't."

"You two are perfect."

Brian looked at him, shook his head, and said, "What's that supposed to mean?"

"We have a cool family. We're all friends, and we like each other. You and Randy and me, we've been friends since what, fifth or sixth grade? And you go hunting and fishing with George and Brett. Gav too, but he's not family. And Randy and I are twins, and we think alike."

"*A lot* alike," Brian agreed.

"And Bobby and Brett, well, they're close."

"They should be. They're brothers."

"But you and Bobby are special. Everyone who sees you knows you two are close. Everybody. There's something special between you two. If something were to happen to one of you, the other would go crazy. All of us would, but you two especially."

Begrudgingly, Brian nodded.

"So, all I have to say is this ... whatever is between the two of you, it needs to be fixed. No matter what, you have to stay as close as you are, as close as you have been. You have to."

Brian looked off in the distance at the horses. What Billy said was not altogether wrong.

"I'm not sure it can be."

"That bad?"

"Maybe."

"I hope not."

"Me too."

Chapter Forty

Waukesha, WI

"What do we have so far?" Summer asked.

They were back at the Waukesha Police Station, and the same group that had met before was there again, almost sitting in the same spots. Missing were Skip Dahlke and Nelson Alamorode.

"Who wants to start?" Pete said.

Eiselmann popped up the picture the artist drew from the description Loth had given. It showed a man in his thirties or forties, dark hair, dark eyes, about six-foot-one, medium build.

"Here's our guy, according to the witness," Paul said.

The group remained silent as they studied the photo. It was Graff who said, "We know this guy. He looks familiar somehow."

"Looks like any guy out on the street," Gonnering said.

O'Connor shook his head and said, "Jamie's right. We've seen him."

"He's not our guy yet," Pete said. "Right now, he's just a person of interest."

"Are we releasing the photo to the media?" Batiste asked.

Summer nodded and said, "In time for the five o'clock news. Maybe they'll run it again at ten and eleven, and hopefully, the newspapers will run it tomorrow morning. But Pete's right. This guy is just a person of interest. We want to find out what he was doing in the park and why he was talking to Meyers."

"What did you find out on the tires?" Pete asked, looking at both Eiselmann and Dahlke. They had decided to work together.

"The tires fit a 2017 BMW 328d Sedan Luxury Package. They match a Bridgestone Potenza REO50 RFT," Eiselmann said.

"Huh," O'Connor said. "That's pretty specific."

"Give credit to Skip. Great pictures and the treads match to a BMW."

"Do you have anything else for us?" Pete said.

"I went into DMV records and pulled any BMWs in the Milwaukee Metro area as far north as Mequon and as far south as Caledonia and as far west as Waukesha. We have two- hundred and thirty-seven BMW owners. I subtracted female owners, and that left us one hundred and ninety-six. Then, I subtracted any married couples, along with anyone younger than twenty-five or older than fifty."

Eiselmann looked up from his computer screen and said, "I can adjust the parameters if you want."

He waited for any objection, and there were not any, so he plunged on. "We have seventy-three possibilities. We can try matching the sketch with driver license pictures and see if there's anything close and that might narrow it down further."

"Seventy-three," Kelliher muttered. "I had hoped it would be less."

"What about our boy from Richfield?" Batiste asked.

"Gustnecky does not own a BMW," Eiselmann answered.

"And he doesn't look anything like the sketch," O'Connor said. "Not even close. But to be certain, I checked with the sheriff up there, and Gustnecky was in Door County since last Tuesday. At the time of the Staley murder, he was in a hot tub at Stone Harbor in Sturgeon Bay, and at the time of the Meyers murder, he was eating lunch at the Inn at Cedar Crossing. He's not our guy."

"It was a longshot anyway, but we had to be certain," Summer said. Still, she sounded deflated. She sighed, put on her best game face, and said, "Anyone else have anything?"

"Carlos and I interviewed Michael Staley's counselor, Jane Breslin." Gonnering lifted his hands up and said, "She had to look him up in a computer. She had no clue who he was. Nada."

"His file had a registration form, emergency card, and a transcript from Monroe Middle School in Monroe, Wisconsin. All B's and A's." Lorenzo said. "Why did his grades change from A's and B's to C's?"

"We met with Rodney Garibaldi, the principal, and he knew even less than Breslin. The assistant principal that covers letters O through Z was Pat Carroll. Michael had no discipline, no referrals, nothing," Gonnering said.

"It's like the kid was a ghost," Lorenzo said.

"Jo and I interviewed Penny Faulkner, Michael's English teacher," Batiste said. "She described Michael as creative and quiet. More of a listener than a talker. He'd contribute to class discussions if he was called upon but wouldn't volunteer anything."

"We asked if he had any friends, anyone who he hung around with, and she couldn't think of anyone," Jo said. "Sad."

"It's like he had no one," Greg said.

"His parents didn't care about him, maybe even didn't like him, at least according to his little brother, Carson," Jo Weist said.

"The boy had no one," Batiste said. "And he was shot and killed, and he died alone."

Jo thought that Cleve summarized the boy's life in one sentence and nailed it. It was more than sad and depressing. It was everything and at the same time, nothing. He left no mark, no trace. The kid was gone before he was dead.

Chapter Forty-One

Brookfield, WI

George had a feeling. It was not specific, but a vague thought. A concern, perhaps. It was not there, and then it was.

The feeling occurred as they drove into the parking lot of Dick's Sporting Goods in Brookfield near I-94 and Highway 41. Jeremy drove Brett, Bobby, and George to get shoes for the upcoming track season. Randy had decided to stay back and finish reading the notebook. Brian and Billy were soaking in the hot tub and did not want to get out anytime soon.

As he stepped out of Jeremy's red Expedition, he stretched and casually looked around the parking lot, hoping to spot someone other than Alex Jorgenson, a Waukesha County sheriff deputy whose turn it was to watch over his family. Of course, it was not supposed to be known that Jeremy's family was being protected. But George had spotted a rotation of sheriff deputies Tom Albrecht, Brooke Beranger, and Alex Jorgenson over the course of the last several days.

George had not noticed anyone that would concern him, but still, he trusted his instincts that were born and bred into him from childhood. His grandfather taught him to notice changes in weather, in the landscape, in people and in all things while living in Arizona raising sheep on the Navajo Reservation. Those instincts had paid off more than once.

His eyes met those of Jorgenson, and while there was a hint of recognition that passed between the two, to any outsider, no one would have caught on. He caught up with his brothers and father, walked between Bobby and Brett, and slung both arms across their shoulders and hugged them.

The original plan was to spend the afternoon watching the Badger basketball team host the Purdue Boilermakers, but the lure running shoes for George and Brett and everyday shoes for Bobby proved to be overwhelming. Jeremy agreed to drive them to the store.

Before entering, George stopped to bang the snow and ice from his cowboy boots on the cement outside the door.

"I'll catch up," George said as the others walked in.

When they had entered, he stepped to the side and snatched his cell from his pocket and texted Jamie Graff. *Why are we being watched?*

It did not take long for his cell to ring.

"Who do you see and when did you notice?" Graff asked without a hello.

"A couple of days ago. I saw Tom and Brooke. Jorgy is with us now."

"How noticeable?"

"Not very. I don't believe anyone would notice. They are good."

Graff smiled because George spoke formally when he was all business. He paused and then asked, "Is everything okay?"

The hesitation before George responded was not lost on Graff, who said, "George?"

"There is something. A feeling."

"Your grandfather?"

"No, my grandfather has not come to me. I have not had any dreams. Just a feeling."

"When did it start?"

"Today in the car as we pulled into the parking lot," George said with a smile trying to cover up the conversation in case anyone was watching.

"What parking lot? Where are you?"

"Dick's Sporting Goods in Brookfield. We are shoe shopping."

Jorgenson, all six-foot-four or five of him, short-cropped red hair uncovered by a hat, walked past him and into the store without any hello or eye contact. George went along with it and pretended not to pay any attention.

Graff said, "Do you see anything? Anyone?"

Play-acting, George smiled, shook his head, and said, "No one."

"Keep me posted. You have Tom's, Brooke's and Jorgy's numbers?"

"Yes."

"Keep them handy."

"I will."

"George, you know I love you and the guys."

"Yes, I know that. Thank you."

The call ended, and it occurred to George that Graff had never answered his question as to why they were being watched. His hand went automatically to his hip feeling for his knife, but he had not worn it. He had decided he would have it with him whenever possible.

George entered the store and walked back to the shoe section where he hooked up with Brett and Bobby. They stood in front of the shoe stacks picking up shoes, looking them over, and then putting them back. Jeremy stood behind them. Jorgenson stood at a rack looking at Dri-Fit socks. George knew Jorgy was an avid outdoorsman like himself, Brett, Brian and Gavin.

George had always been on the conservative side because he had grown up in poverty. Even now, shopping for luxuries was foreign to him. Even for new shoes.

His hogan in Navajoland did not have running water or electricity. His Navajo family used an outhouse. He shared a bed with two of his brothers. His clothes had been patched over and over until the thread and fabric had been so worn the patches would not hold. All of that being said, he had been happy and content, and if given the opportunity, would not have traded that life for any other. The fact that his family had been murdered and little ranch burnt to the ground took away any options he had.

Brett had one shoe in his hand, but he looked at two others, both cross trainers. Bobby stood next to him, eyeing the same type of shoe. Both were close to $150 each. George walked to the sales stack and looked over what was available. The type of shoe he wore lasted four to five months, depending upon the number of miles he put in. Each time he went shoe shopping with Jeremy, he offered to pay for half, but Jeremy would smile and say, "No, I have it." And he was sure that would be the response this time also.

He knew that if he wanted to run at his best and keep improving his time, he had to take care of his feet, and shoes were integral to that. The shoe he wore, Brooks Ghost 10, was not ever found in the sales stack because they were popular. Nonetheless, he checked there first. He shook his head, glanced at Jeremy, and then went to the display model. The cost was $120. He glanced at Jeremy again, who smiled at him and nodded his approval.

"I can pay for half," George offered.

"No, I have it. Get what you need."

"I can pay for Dri-Fit socks."

Jeremy smiled and said, "No, that's okay."

Feeling guilty, George asked the sales clerk for a size nine in a black and gray color combination. Brett chose a Nike Free RN Motion Flyknit 2017, which was thirty bucks more than the Brooks.

Bobby chose an Asics GT-1000 5 for half the price of either Brett's or George's explaining, "I don't do the number of miles you guys do, so I don't need anything fancy."

Each boy picked up a pair of Dri-Fit socks as they headed to the checkout. Jorgy trailed behind, stopping at a rack of Nike t-shirts. He selected two in size Hulk. He added them to the two pair of Dri-Fit socks in what looked to be the size of something one would hang from a mantle at Christmas. George knew they would have to be in order to fit his size-ungodly shoes. He chose the checkout opposite George, his brothers, and father. He finished first and exited, but strolled casually to his car, making sure Jeremy and the boys were not too far behind.

As they got into the car, George took one last long look around the parking lot but did not see anything of note. Still, the feeling he had was evermore present, and it was disconcerting.

He pulled out his cell and texted Jorgy, *Picking up pizza from Michael's on Grand Ave.*

To which Jorgy responded with a thumbs up.

As Jeremy drove out of the parking lot, as calmly as he could, George surveyed cars, shoppers walking to cars, and other vehicles pulling in behind the Expedition. He watched for any lagging behind for no apparent reason. One, in particular, caught his eye.

Chapter Forty-Two

Waukesha, WI

Disgusted, The Man shook his head. Their father indulged them with expensive shoes and clothes that could have been bought at Target or Walmart. Instead, he drove them to a trendy store with shoes and clothes that were extravagant and over-priced. And for what? Why? To win their love and respect? That would never happen. He knew that from experience.

This counselor was supposed to be smart. Certainly not as smart as he was. But for someone whose intelligence was above that of a drone, the counselor should have been smarter than he displayed. Supposed to be, according to the newspaper article highlighting his virtues. He was supposed to have compassion. He was supposed to be a role model.

The Man knew the article was propaganda to encourage others like him. Encourage them to do what he had done. And what he was about to do.

The Man had picked them up down the highway from their house. A big, fancy house. How could he afford that on a counselor's salary? Even if he added what his soon to be wife, a surgical nurse, made, the amount of money would not come close to the money needed to purchase that house. Or the cars they drove.

And they throw away money on over-priced shoes and name-brand clothes in the hope that they would be appreciated, that they would be loved.

In a rage, The Man slammed his fist on the steering wheel and regretted it. He knew better than to lose control. Control was everything. Control was the key. He shut his eyes and, breathed deeply and slowly.

He pulled into the line of cars exiting the parking lot, four cars back, and followed them. Still angry and more than a little determined. Yes, these two would be his next, and two more would be gone.

Chapter Forty-Three

Waukesha, WI

Eiselmann was not one to get excited easily. As control for O'Connor, it was his job to provide security and, at times, backup, and both roles required calm, clear thinking and poise. But when he reexamined the data that spit out of his laptop, his heart chugged away like a runaway freight train. To be safe he checked it again, and then once more, and then he called Graff.

"Jamie, I have something. I got the results on those college students who were killed. You know, the cold cases? The first ones?"

"What do you have, Paul?"

"Tory Wriblowski, Nathan Gruening, and Callie Putzer had one psychology professor in common. Dr. Bryce Miller, Jr. He taught Psych 205 – Personality, and Psych 407 – Personality Theory. Each of those students had these classes with this same professor."

"All three victims had this Miller?"

"Yes and for the same two classes. But there's something else," Paul said, as he stood up and began pacing around his small kitchen.

"What?" Graff asked.

"He's missing."

Graff set his coffee down on the counter before he dropped it on the floor. He took the cell away from his ear, stared out the window above the sink thinking, *One dead end after another.*

"Jamie, are you there?" the distant, tinny voice coming through the cell phone Graff had at his side.

Graff raised it back up to his ear and said, "Yeah, I'm here."

"On Monday, Pat and I will head over to UWM and talk to their Human Resources Department. We'll see if any other professors might know him or his whereabouts. I'm doing a search of DMV records. I'll ask Summer and Pete if the FBI can do a social security check and try to search for him that way." Even he sounded deflated. "It's all I can think of at the moment."

"Try to get a picture of him and see if it matches our guy," Graff suggested.

"You mean our person of interest."

"Him too."

Chapter Forty-Four

Waukesha, WI

The bedroom door was shut, so being polite, George knocked. It was something he had done since he began living with Jeremy and the twins, and would always do. He even knocked when a door was open.

"Yeah?"

"Can I come in?"

Brian sighed. He was not in the mood to see or talk to anyone. But because he recognized George's voice, he said, "Sure."

He had been laying with his head at the foot of the bed on his stomach reading one of Jeff Limbach's novels. He was not sure if *Fright* was an early work, a work in the middle of his writing career, or a work from a more recent time. Brian knew it was not part of a series. He remembered watching the movie, but the book was better.

George entered the room and shut the door behind him. He held four ice packs in one hand and four Motrin in the other.

"Mother sent me," he said by way of explanation. "You have water," he added pointing to half-full bottle at the foot of the bed next to Jasper.

Brian reached out and took the pills, put them in his mouth, and washed them down with water from his bottle. He set it back down on the floor, gave Jasper a scratch behind the ear, and used the book cover flap as a bookmark. He closed it and set the book on the floor next to the bottle.

George sat down on the end of the bed next to Brian and said, "Four icepacks. Elbow. Knee. Hip. And what?"

Brian glanced at George and punched his leg when he saw George smirking.

"Don't start."

"A little too much fun last night?" George said with another smirk, and Brian punched him in the leg again.

Brian flipped over onto his back and placed an icepack on his knee. He started to tuck one under his shorts on his hip when George said, "Let me see your hip."

Brian pulled his shorts and boxers down to his knees and rolled toward George so he could get a better look. George touched it here and there on the outer fringes of the bruise and then touched the darkest spot on the hip itself.

"Hurt?"

"Not as much as it did this morning. I think the footwork I did in the stable and soaking it in the hot tub helped loosen it up. I think it'll be fine by Monday."

He helped Brian pull up his boxers, took two of the icepacks from Brian, and placed one on Brian's hip, telling him to hold it in place. He placed one on top of Brian's boxers and then he placed one on Brian's elbow.

George said, "Twenty minutes," and he checked his watch.

He stretched out next to Brian and said, "Brett and Billy want to know why you're hiding up here." He looked over at Brian and said, "Their words, not mine."

"I'm not hiding. I took a nap, and I was reading. I'm not hiding," he repeated again.

George said nothing. He had another reason to come up here besides delivering ice packs and Motrin. He had been thinking of the best way to ask Brian what he wanted to ask ever since the shoe shopping expedition. But before he could ask, Brian said, "I need to ask you a question."

"Sure."

"You have to answer honestly no matter what, okay?"

On his stomach with his arms under his head, George turned to face him.

"This is hypothetical, but I'm wondering. Say you had a friend. A good friend. Maybe not your best friend, but you're pretty close to him.

You hang out. Hunt and fish and stuff. And you've been friends for a while."

Brian licked his lips before continuing and then said, "And then you find out he might be gay. This friend of yours isn't sure, but he might be. He never did anything, you know, to you. He never thought of doing anything to you. But he has a girlfriend, and he's done stuff with her. But he's wondering if he might be gay."

He stopped, licked his lips again, and said, "What would you do?"

George turned his head, stared at the door, and then turned back to Brian.

"The *Dine'* believe that homosexuality is against nature. That sex should be between a man and a woman."

Brian sighed. He already knew that because he had Googled it. He had hoped that George would not think that way.

"My grandfather was a *Haatalii*, a medicine man. The Navajo elders referred to him as *Hosteen* Tokay, a term of respect. My family was from the *'Azee'tsoh dine'e,* which translates to *The Big Medicine People Clan*. It is one of the oldest clans among the *Dine'.* So, because of that, elders and the *Dine'* listened to him.

"My grandfather argued with the other elders telling them that going against one's heart was also against nature."

He looked at Brian and then back at the door.

"Do you remember when you and Cat first started seeing each other?"

Brian nodded.

"You said you were sorry about Cat liking you instead of me, and I told you that a horse chooses the rider. The rider doesn't choose the horse."

"I remember."

"My grandfather believed that if one heart finds another, and if the two are meant to belong to each other, that is how nature intended it. He believed that as long as two people love each other, it doesn't matter if they are not a man and a woman."

He turned to Brian and said, "I believe that too."

"So, you'd be okay with a friend being gay."

George smiled and said, "Brian, you are my friend and my brother. You will always be my friend and my brother. I love you as much as I do Brett or Billy, Randy or Bobby. None of us believe you or Bobby are gay."

Brian blinked and said, "How ... when ...?"

George smiled and said, "There are no secrets in our family."

"Great. Just great," he muttered.

The two were silent until Brian said, "Have you ever, you know, done anything, you know."

"That is private, but no, I have not."

"I just wondered," Brian said with a shrug.

"Now, I need to ask you a question," George said. "I would like it to be private, just between the two of us. For now."

Brian shrugged and said, "Sure."

"Has your brother, Brad, visited you or spoken to you recently?"

Brian frowned, shook his head, and said, "No. He's never spoken to me ever, and he hasn't visited me in a while. Why?"

"I was wondering, that's all."

Brian propped his head on his hand and elbow and said, "Has your grandfather spoken to you? You had any visions?"

George shook his head and said, "No."

"What's going on, George?" Brian's voice had changed to a whisper.

"I am not sure. Something." He paused, thought about how to word it, and then said, "If your brother comes to you in a dream or if he speaks to you, tell me. It could be important."

Brian licked his lips, nodded, and said, "I will, George. Promise."

"And we will keep this just between the two of us."

Puzzled, if not concerned, Brian said, "Promise."

Chapter Forty-Five

Waukesha, WI

The Man searched the Internet for anything he could find on the family and came across several articles. He read them thoroughly and took notes on each in his painstaking manner. He preferred long-hand on a legal pad rather than the clickity-clack of the computer keyboard. A second, perhaps better feature, was that The Man could destroy his notebooks if he needed to easier than he could wipe a computer's memory.

Not one to give in to an excess of emotion, he was pleased with what he had found.

The counselor was once a social studies teacher who taught psychology. Something The Man had in common with him. The Man smiled. A former basketball coach with quite a bit of success. The Man was indifferent to that because he viewed participation in athletics as a form of self-gratification. Almost masturbation in public. A win, the climax.

He became a counselor the year after he quit coaching. It was not long when after that he entered the foster system as a single parent and adopted his first, a twin.

The first one was abused by his first adoptive family. He ran away and was picked up by two perverts who abused him sexually. The second came along a year or so later after his parents divorced and his father died. It was unclear why the second did not go to live with his mother. He made a citation in his notebook to do some digging in the court system. If the records were not sealed, he would find out.

The counselor was a paid consultant of the FBI, the National Center for Missing and Exploited Children, and several law enforcement agencies. Interesting. The Man made a note to dig for the counselor's coursework to see what, if any, training he had in that area.

The rest of the article contained bullshit about what a wonderful guy he was, how he helped high school kids and his two *sons*. A mentor. A hero. All crap and all propaganda are written so that others might follow in his footsteps.

The next article The Man read after he Googled the counselor's name was from *CNN* that ran two summers previous. It detailed the raid and the rescue of thirty boys from three different brothels. The counselor was mentioned because he had worked with the boys and their families while the boys were in the hospital. Again, he made a note to check on the counselor's qualifications for such a task. In his mind, surely these boys had been damaged mentally, emotionally, and physically. According to one source, there were boys who had been held captive for more than two years. *What background, what course of study did this counselor have that would make the FBI, the National Center for Missing and Exploited Children, and law enforcement agencies to think he was remotely qualified?*

The most recent article dealt with one of the targets and how his parents committed a murder-suicide. Interesting. It talked about how his twin brother had died during the previous summer. After the boys were freed from the brothels, a terrorist machine-gunned down men, women, and children at a soccer game. *Could it be that this target, damaged by the death of his brother and his parents, inflicted this damage on the counselor's family?*

One problem The Man encountered was that there was not any information on the other target. No matter where he searched, he could not find anything. There was a vague reference to Arizona, but that was it. It was as if the target did not exist. As if the target did not have a life before he began living with the counselor. How was that possible? Surely there should be something, somewhere. Odd. Puzzling. The reference dealt with his running prowess in track and cross country. *Another runner.*

The Man placed his pen on the notebook, tented his hands in front of his face, and considered his dilemma.

There were several questions for which he had to find answers before he made any move. The Man had to plan this without getting caught. Not that he was worried about the FBI and the Keystone Cops catching him. He was far too smart for them.

As soon as he had the plan put together, and The Man was sure he would have something unique soon, he would act. He had no doubts that the result would be the same as the others.

Chapter Forty-Six

Waukesha, WI

The evening drew onward. Some hamburgers were grilled by Billy and Brett, each taking turns because it was colder than cold. The wind had picked up and threatened to put out the fire and freeze fingers and faces. Still, hunger had won, and they had volunteered to make dinner, if someone else made the salad and set the table up. That fell to Randy and Bobby. Brian and George cleaned up the mess after.

They waited for them to finish in the kitchen before they popped in the James Bond *Skyfall* DVD. As they waited, they talked about Packer football and Badger basketball and speculated on North's chances in the playoffs. In between, Brett and Billy wrestled over the couch until they settled on sharing it. Partly in jest, Brett made Billy promise not to fart because Billy lay up against him. Brett did not seem too concerned since he had an arm slung over Billy's chest.

George and Brian turned off the lights in the kitchen except for the light over the sink. George checked the alarm system. The panel showed red, indicating the system was armed and working. Brian watched him in silence, his mind working overtime.

Sensing Brian's unspoken question, George said, "Just to be certain."

"The dogs will have to go out before we go to bed."

"You or I can disarm it, let the dogs out and let them back in, lock the door, and arm it again."

They left the kitchen to join the other guys in the family room. Jeremy and Vicky were in the office.

Before entering, George turned to Brian and said, "Tell them to start the movie. I'll be right there."

Brian watched George walk down the hallway to the study and then he continued into the family room.

"George said to start the movie. He went to talk to Mom and Dad."

"We can wait," Billy said.

Brian did not know where to sit. The couch was taken. Randy sat in the recliner. Bobby lay on the floor near the recliner. Most any other night, Brian would lay down next to Bobby and share the blanket with him. That was not an option. He sat on the floor at the foot of the couch holding his knees to his chest.

"Doesn't that hurt your hip?" Randy asked.

"I'm okay," was all he said, staring at the TV.

George came back in, grabbed two pillows off the back of the couch, tossed one to Brian, and lay down on the floor next to Bobby.

"Lay down here," George said, patting the floor between him and the couch.

Brian did so.

"Can you throw me a blanket?" George asked.

"You can share mine if you want," Bobby said.

"There won't be enough for all three of us," George said.

Randy threw a blanket from the back of the recliner, and it landed on top of George's head.

"Good shot," Billy laughed.

George smiled as he spread the blanket over Brian and him, and the six of them settled in for the movie.

Brian did not know why, but he felt out of place and on an island. He was not sure if it was his own making, Bobby's making, or maybe just his imagination. He knew the guys were watching the movie, but he could not help but feel as if silent stares watching him and Bobby.

It was not long before his eyes got heavy and he dozed off with his head against George's shoulder. George let him sleep, staying as still and as quiet as he could so as not to disturb him. Even the gunshots and explosions on the TV did not wake him. Brian was out.

Toward the end of the movie, Jeremy and Vicky popped their heads in to say goodnight.

"Church tomorrow. Regular time," Jeremy said.

"Get some sleep, guys," Vicky said. "We have company coming tomorrow for a late lunch or early dinner."

Calls of goodnight and love you followed. Still, Brian had not moved.

Vicky lingered in the doorway and said, "George, how is Bri feeling?"

George glanced at Brian and said, "I think he's okay."

There were glances cast at Bobby and Brian before they stared at the TV.

"Well, okay. When Bri wakes up, ask him when he took Motrin last. If it was six hours or more, he should take four, but he should have something to eat with it. Otherwise, he might get an upset stomach." She waved goodnight, turned, and left the room following Jeremy up the stairs.

The movie ended, and the boys got up and stretched and yawned. All except for Brian who continued to sleep in virtually the same position he had been in when he first lay down.

George shook his shoulder and said, "Bri, let's go to bed."

Brian blinked, yawned, and tried to go back to sleep, but George shook him again and said, "Come on, Bri. Time for bed."

This time, Brian's green-hazel eyes opened and did not close. First, he sat up and looked around the room, and then he stood up, taking the blanket, folding it, and placing it on the back of the recliner.

While the other boys traipsed up the stairs, George and Brian made the rounds downstairs going room to room making certain the doors and windows were locked.

George deactivated the alarm system and called the dogs to go outside. Momma came down the stairs to join Jasper and Jasmine at the back door off the kitchen. George watched them from the door while Brian watched them from the kitchen window. None of the dogs indicated there was anything or anyone out there. They did their business and trooped single file back to the door. George let them in and wiped their feet off with a towel that was set by the door just for that purpose. Then he activated the alarm, and the LED glowed red just as it did when he set it after cleaning up the kitchen.

"When was the last time you had Motrin?" George asked Brian.

"About four or so."

George calculated the time and said, "Better take four more, but Mother said to take it with something to eat."

Brian did as he was told. He washed four capsules down with a full glass of water, grabbed one peanut butter cookie and one chocolate chip cookie, and ate them as the two boys walked up the stairs.

Bobby was nowhere to be seen. He was not in the bathroom he and Brian used, and he was not in the bedroom they shared. Brian shrugged to no one, stripped down to boxers, threw on a t-shirt, and went into the bathroom. He peed, washed his hands, his face, neck, and ears, and then he brushed his teeth.

By the time he walked back across the hallway, Brett was in his bed waiting for him.

"I didn't want to sleep by myself tonight," Brett said with a yawn. "And I didn't think you wanted to either."

Brian said nothing as he crawled in on the right side, the side Bobby usually slept on. Though to be fair, Bobby slept almost on top of him.

"Sleep closer," Brett said, holding out his left arm.

Brian scooted over, and Brett placed his arm across Brian's chest. He gave Brian's underarm hair a tug, and Brian swatted his hand away and chuckled.

Brett bounced a finger on Brian's chest and asked, "How is the hip? Honest!"

Brian turned his head toward Brett and said, "Honestly, much better. Everything is better," he said flexing his arm at the elbow and his leg at the knee.

"Let me see your hip."

Brian pushed the covers down, then his boxers and rolled onto his left side so Brett could take a closer look.

"Still looks pretty nasty, Bri." He touched the circumference at the outer edges and worked his way to Brian's hip. Watching Brian's face for any wince or grimace, Brett touched the hip and did not draw much, if any, reaction.

"Seems better."

Brian started to pull up his boxers, but Brett stopped him. He pointed to Brian's sack.

"Any pain? Are your balls sore?"

"No."

Brian felt himself getting hard and hoped Brett would not notice. It did not take long for him to get erect.

"Now how do your balls feel?"

"Okay, why?"

"When I was in Chicago with the perverts, my balls would ache and then it would go away. The next time I got hard, they hurt again. That's why I asked."

"I'm okay."

Brian pulled up his boxers and stared at the ceiling.

"What are you thinking about?"

"Nothing."

"You have to be thinking of something."

Brian shrugged and said, "Nothing much."

Brett tweaked one of Brian's nipples.

He said, "Okay, what about now?"

Brian laughed and said, "You're a dork!"

Brett smiled and said, "But at least I'm a fun dork, and you're my friend, so I get to be as dorky as I want to be around you."

Brian laughed and elbowed him the stomach.

"You know, between you and George and Randy and Billy and Bobby, I have the best friends."

Brian turned his head, and said, "I feel the same way."

"I love you, Bri. Nothing will change that. Ever. I mean that."

"Love you too, Brett. Always."

And the two boys fell asleep and did not move the rest of the night.

Chapter Forty-Seven

Waukesha, WI

He was awake, but he did not move, and he hardly breathed. Instead, he listened to everything and anything. Billy, on his side and snuggled up against him. George still had his arm around his chest.

He could hear Jasmine panting on the rug next to the bed, and George knew Jasmine waited for a signal.

George was not sure what it was that woke him up. There was not a defining noise, or was there? Perhaps a feeling? Part of a dream?

His grandfather had not come to him. He was sure of that. Neither had his littlest brother, Robert, nor had Brian's brother, Brad. George concluded that the threat, if there was a threat, was not imminent.

Still ...

He crawled out of bed and tucked the sheet, blanket, and comforter around Billy to keep him warm. Billy had not moved, still sound asleep.

George slid his feet into his moccasins, pulled on a sweatshirt, grabbed his knife and leather scabbard, and walked to the door. Jasmine stood, tail wagging, hoping to tag along. George gave her a signal to stay, and without a sound, she lay back down on the rug. It was only his imagination, but it looked like she was sulking. He smiled, opened the door, and shut it to a crack.

He stood in the hallway and looked left and right. No one or nothing, except for Momma laying on the landing at the top of the stairs, protecting the family from whatever and whomever.

No sounds other than normal night sounds from the big house and from the wind outside.

George tiptoed down the hall, put his ear to Jeremy's and Vicky's closed door, and heard nothing. He stepped kiddie-corner to Randy's room where Randy and Bobby were asleep. The door was shut tight, so George opened it and walked in.

Randy slept in his normal pose. Arms spread to the side, one knee up, and head off the pillow. Bobby was curled in a ball against him.

George smiled. Every night, at just about any time of night, Randy would be found like this.

George gave Randy a gentle nudge, and he rolled over and placed an arm protectively over Bobby. Bobby did not move. George tucked them in and left the room, closing the door behind him.

Brian's door to the bedroom he shared with Bobby was shut. He opened it. He spied Jasper on the rug on the side of the bed just like his sister Jasmine had been in his own room.

Brett lay on his side with what looked to be an arm over Brian, who slept on his back next to him with their heads toward each other, foreheads touching. Neither moved. Both peaceful, at least on the surface. George knew both had, at times, tortured dreams and thoughts whether asleep or awake.

He tucked both in as gently as he could because he knew Brett slept so lightly a breeze might wake him, certain that a sound or a touch would. George knew it stemmed from Brett's life in captivity where he learned that he dare not sleep too soundly, where he learned to listen even though he was asleep.

Sure enough, Brett blinked his eyes open, turned his head, and stared at George. His face softened as he recognized his friend and brother, and he smiled.

George smoothed the bangs off Brett's forehead.

Brett's eyes squinted in silent question, and George bent low and whispered, "Go back to sleep. Just checking the house."

He mouthed, "Why?"

George smiled, and whispered, "Sleep."

Brett stared at him and then turned back on his side snuggling up to Brian, who had slept through it all. George covered them up, lifting up the covers just enough to move them and keep them warm.

He left their room and continued down the hallway toward Momma at the top of the stairs. He sat down, scratched her behind the ear, and bent low to kiss her head. She rewarded him with a kiss of her own, and that caused him to smile. He petted her one more time and then moved down the stairs.

He tiptoed to the front door to check both the door lock and the deadbolt. Satisfied, he moved to the kitchen, checked the back door and then the alarm system. It still glowed red, so it was on and activated.

He left the kitchen walked down the hall and into the family room. The slider was locked. George looked out into the night at the snow-covered landscape of trees and bushes and patio, where earlier that evening hamburgers were grilled. The ground was undisturbed. No sign that anyone had been outside the door.

He left the family room and walked down the hallway to the study, opened the door, and entered. The curtains were not drawn so he could look out. It was woods on this side of the house. Though there was a small stone patio with two metal chairs and a metal table, there was not a defined path through the trees and scrub bushes beyond it, which was just what Jeremy had wanted when the house was built.

George had never mentioned it to anyone, but he loved this room as much as Jeremy did, but for different reasons. Jeremy saw the room as his getaway, his sanctuary, while George loved the room because of the view beyond the sliding glass door.

There were birds of all types, and they flew to the three feeders that George had mounted among the trees. At times, a deer would appear. At night, raccoons might scrounge for something to eat.

George smiled and stepped to the side and the gun cabinet. He checked the lock to make sure it was secure, and it was. It was then he thought he saw a shadow.

At first, he stood still trying hard not to make any sudden moves. He stepped to a space between the gun cabinet and the wall adjacent to the slider. He controlled his breathing and forced himself to focus.

Perhaps it was a bird or other critter? He stared, looking for any shape that did not belong, searching for any movement that was not caused by the wind or an animal.

At his angle, he could not see as clearly as he wanted to, but he dared not move any closer. He dared not expose himself any more than he already was. He had no weapon other than his knife and had the glass slider between him and whoever was out there. If someone was out there.

Without warning, Momma appeared at his side. She had moved soundlessly, and George had not noticed her until she had brushed up against his bare leg. She stared in the same direction as he did.

They waited together hardly breathing.

They saw him at the same time. At first, just a shadow. Then he tripped on a tree root, his pant leg caught on a bramble bush or on a rose bush. They watched him tug his pant free.

And he trudged up to the slider. The moonlight glinted off the handgun in his hand.

It was smaller than the Glock 19s that were in the locked metal case in the locked gun cabinet. George thought it might be a .38 or a .22. Brett would know because he was better with handguns than George was.

The figure, who George judged to be a man, stood about six feet tall. Maybe taller. It was hard to tell because of the jacket he wore, but George thought he might weigh one-seventy or one-eighty. About the same size as Detective Graff, though not in as good of shape. It was not Graff, and it was not Tom Albrecht who normally took night duty if they were being watched and protected. He was not Alex Jorgenson because the man did not have the hulk-like look of the sheriff deputy.

As the man came closer, the clumsier he became, fighting with the bushes and roots, his head dodging a feeder hanging from a tree.

George did not think this man was used to the outdoors as he, Brett, and Brian were. He judged him to be a city man.

He and Momma pushed themselves against the wall to make sure they were not seen as the man pressed his face to the glass to get a better look inside the room. Before he stepped away, he used his gloved hand to wipe the area on the glass where his face was pressed against it. Then he backed away and moved along the side of the house to where the family room patio was.

When George was certain the man was out of view, he tiptoed out of the room and down the hall to the family room. There was not any door, so if the man was at the glass and if George stepped into the room, he would be exposed. Instead, he and Momma crouched down as close to the floor as they could and looked into the room toward the slider.

Sure enough, the man appeared and, as he had done at the study slider, pressed his face against it. He stood there for five or ten seconds and then like he did at the study slider, he wiped the glass with his gloved hand and moved away toward the front of the house where the living room and front door were.

George and Momma crept down the hallway.

He had a decision to make. There were glass panels in the front door and narrow windows on either side of the door. If George and Momma stayed where they were, the man would see them as soon as he checked the door.

George signaled to Momma, and the two of them duck-walked to the kitchen. There was one window above the sink, but there were plenty of places to hide. He chose the small mudroom off the kitchen where the alarm was. He and Momma crouched down and waited.

Sure enough, a shadow appeared that crossed the kitchen table, indicating that the man was, indeed, there. It was there a second or two, and then George heard noise at the back door, inches from him and Momma. The door handle moved, but it was locked, and the deadbolt was set.

They waited. They did not make any noise. It took time, but they were patient. When George felt there had been enough time for the man to leave, George stood and retraced his steps, rechecking doors and windows. And as he did so, he wondered who the man was and who he was after. After, he crawled back into bed, but he did not sleep.

Chapter Forty-Eight

Waukesha, WI

George got up at his normal pre-dawn time for a light run and his knife exercises, followed by his morning prayers to Father Sun. He was not sleeping anyway, so he thought he would put his time to better use. First, he had some tasks to complete before anyone else woke up.

Dressed in his Gore-Tex running gear, George crept down the stairs to the kitchen, opened a utility drawer, and took three sandwich bags. In the cupboard under the sink, he took a pair of latex gloves his mother sometimes used for cleaning. They were the same kind of gloves doctors and nurses used in surgery, which is where his mother got them. He turned off the alarm system because he did not want to set it off.

He entered the study, opened the sliding door, and retraced the intruder's steps to the bush that caught hold of the man's pant leg. It looked like a wild rose bush, something that was not planted by Jeremy or Vicky. George would know because he and Billy had planted many of the non-wild bushes.

George searched the plant and was rewarded with finding a bit of blue fabric, something other than blue jeans, impaled on one of the burs. At first, he thought of taking the single bur, but changed his mind. He thought that perhaps some skin or blood might also be on the bur along with the bit of thread. So instead, George took a three-inch stem that included the bur and the fabric and hopefully some DNA.

He searched outside the house taking the same path as the man in the middle of the night and came across two preserved boot prints. He did not recognize them from any of his brothers or from Jeremy, so using his cell, he snapped off three pictures of each. He removed one of his shoes and managed to keep his balance as he placed it next to one of them, and took a picture of the two together. That way, Detective Graff and Agent Storm would be able to get an accurate measurement.

Satisfied, he stowed his cell and the sandwich bag containing the stem, bur, and fabric into the side pocket of his Gore-Tex top and zipped it up, replaced his shoe and tied the laces and then took off on a quick run. It would have to be quick since the sun would rise soon and he would have to say his prayers. A fast two, maybe three-mile run would do it. That would mean that he would have to run between a six- and seven-minute mile, but that was something he would have done before.

He ran along the side of the road on the shoulder in the opposite direction of oncoming cars, though traffic was nonexistent for the most part. He let his mind flit from topic to topic, random thoughts, to clear his head. The thoughts came one after another in no particular relation to the other. He thought of Rebecca and his love and friendship with her. Of Brian and Bobby and their friendship in a rough patch. Of Brett and his honesty and his friendship with him. He thought of Brian's adoption and his own, similar yet different. He thought of Jeremy's and Vicky's marriage, though an actual date had not been set yet.

George's mind bounced back to Rebecca and their love and the sex the two of them had together. Almost without wanting to, yet needing to, his thoughts drifted to Navajoland, and the last time he had been with her, made love with her. It had been after he had killed three men who had come to kill him and Jeremy high up on Shadow Mesa. The mesa that the locals, his people- the- *Dine'* -named after him because each morning he would say his prayers with his grandfather, and his voice would echo throughout the desert.

It was while camping with Billy and Randy and Danny, who was a friend but more like a little brother, and his friends Charles and Rebecca when late in the night, his last night in *Diné Bikéyah,* he and Rebecca made love. And after, she went back to Billy and shared the blanket with him. He was certain that even after she and he made love that one last time, she and Billy made love. It was Billy who had her love now. Not George. And that was one of his most painful realizations, the beast of a memory he had wrestled with late at night or early morning on more than one occasion.

He wept.

It stunned him. His emotions were neither high nor low. Part of it was the tiredness he felt after a near-sleepless night. A good share of it was the new threat to his family that the midnight visitor presented. His family who had been through so much already.

He grappled with how best to explain to Jeremy and Vicky and his brothers what he had stumbled onto during his midnight rounds. And he knew he would have to share it with Detective Graff and with Agent Summer and Agent Pete.

As he ran, he wiped his eyes while keeping his pace. If anything, his pace picked up. Angry that his emotions had gotten the best of him. It was not like him. Not at all like him.

He hit the one-and-a-half-mile mark according to his step counter on his watch, so he turned around and headed back home. He would begin his prayers and end them with the rising sun. Hopefully, he would be finished weeping by the time he returned home.

Chapter Forty-Nine

Waukesha, WI

Brett woke up a little groggy. He still had his arm across Brian's chest. Sort of on him, but off at the same time. He rolled onto his back and stretched, taking the time to sniff an armpit. The smell of Aqua Reef faint but present. Nothing a shower and fresh coat would not help. He knew his breath was at the least tired, at the worst smelled of dragon poop. He smiled and stretched again.

He thought over George's visit during the night and wondered what that was all about. He would have to have a talk with him at some point.

Brett scratched his belly and then his crotch. He rolled back to his original position with his arm across Brian's chest. He saw that Brian was awake and looking at him without expression.

He smiled at him, and Brian smiled back.

"How do you feel?" Brett asked.

"Fine."

Brett scratched an itch on his chest and then held onto his friend. Brian noticed an odd expression and was curious.

"What's wrong, Brett?"

At first, Brett said nothing. He pursed his lips and considered what he wanted to say. He nestled his face on Brian's shoulder.

Jeremy had spoken to the boys about personal boundaries, asking them to consider their words and actions including the appropriateness of their demonstration of affection. But he also knew that his boys were unusually close and overly and genuinely affectionate, and he and Vicky reasoned they would rather have that than frosty distance and no emotion. In the end, he and Vicky reasoned that the pendulum of their personal boundaries and respect for each other would eventually swing back more toward the middle. He had to admit that he could be accused of being overly affectionate and demonstrative himself.

In answer to Brett positioning his face on his shoulder, Brian said, "My breath might not be too great."

Brett put his nose close to Brian's mouth and declared, "Not bad. Just tired," as he repositioned his head.

"I was thinking how lucky you are."

Brian asked, "How do you mean?"

"Well, on Wednesday, you're going to be Brian Evans. Legally, I mean. Not just in name. You'll be Dad's son."

"You and Bobby are his sons too. You know that."

"Not legally. I don't know if we ever will."

Brian tried to turn his head, but because Brett was so close, he could not. "What do you mean?"

"When Randy was adopted, the state had to terminate the first adoptive family's rights. Billy's mom had to relinquish her rights so Dad could adopt him. George didn't have anyone, so the state gave permission for Dad to adopt him after George and Dad contacted the elders of the Navajo people. It was kind of a big deal. And your uncle and aunt had to sign a paper giving Dad permission to adopt you."

"I didn't know that," Brian said. It troubled him. "Are you saying that if they wouldn't have signed it, I couldn't be adopted?"

"There would be a court fight. Your parents wanted Jeremy to adopt you. They made that clear. I think your aunt was okay with it all along, but your uncle wasn't so sure."

"How do you know this?" Brian whispered. His mouth had gone dry, and he felt a chill.

"I heard Mom and Dad talking. It's all cool though. Now. Wednesday, you'll be adopted, and you'll be Brian Evans."

"Huh. I didn't know that. I mean, about my uncle. I knew he didn't want me to change my name. But there's no way." Then he thought for a minute and said, "But you and Bobby will be adopted when Dad and Mom get married, right?"

Brett shook his head and said, "I doubt it. It's not like we don't want to. I know Dad and Mom want to. But Tom won't relinquish his rights."

194 Spiral Into Darkness

"You can't talk him into it?"

Brett backed away from Brian a little and turned Brian's face toward him. To make it more comfortable, Brian rolled onto his side to face Brett, their noses inches apart, their heads sharing the same pillow. Brett brushed a thumb on Brian's lips and then his cheek and placed his hand on the side of Brian's face.

"I'm going to tell you something I've never told anyone. Not Mom or Dad. Not Bobby or George or Randy or Billy. No one. There's one other person who knows, and that's because he overheard me on the phone talking to Tom."

"Who?"

"Pat O'Connor."

Brian waited. He knew Brett well enough that even though he said he would tell him something important, in a flash his mind might change.

Brett gave Brian an Eskimo and said, "How do you think Mom and Bobby and I came to live here? In Waukesha, I mean."

Brian shrugged and said, "I figured you wanted a new start."

Brett smiled. It was a sad smile that matched his eyes. And Brian noticed a tear trickle down a path next to his nose.

"We did. But at first, Tom wouldn't let us."

Brian waited. Brett would tell the story in his own way and in his own time.

"Tom said that Bobby and I were still his sons. He told Mom that if we moved, he wouldn't get to see us as much as he'd like. Something like that."

"What made him change his mind?"

There were more tears, and when Brett did not wipe them away, Brian did.

"The weekend Brad died and the weekend the bomb went off, before any of that happened, I called Tom. Tim was still in the hospital. You weren't there because we didn't know each other yet. I went outside and called him ... Tom. Pat followed because he was keeping watch over us. Me, I guess. I didn't know he was there, though."

Brett sighed and shut his eyes picturing it all over again. Maybe he was gathering up his courage. Brian did not know which.

"I threatened him."

"What? How?"

"There were a bunch of newspapers and TV stations like *CNN* and *ABC* and stuff that wanted to interview me and some of the guys who were rescued from Chicago. We all agreed that we wouldn't. Talk, I mean. But I told Tom that unless he let Mom and Bobby and me move to Waukesha, I would go to them. The newspapers and the TV stations. I would tell them about the night my shithead pervert asshole uncle came to our house to kill us. I would tell them that Tom wasn't there. That he was with his girlfriend and that his girlfriend was a college student. The university would hear about it, and they'd fire his ass because it's against the rules for professors to fuck their students, and that's what Tom did. Over and over again. He cheated on Mom, and he cheated on me, and he cheated on Bobby. Over and over."

Brian reached out, and the two boys embraced, and he let Brett cry into his neck. Brian kissed the side of Brett's head and rubbed his back and said, "It's okay, Brett. It's okay."

Brett shook his head and said, "It's not okay, Bri. It's not. He should have just let us go, but he didn't. I had to threaten him."

"What happened?" Brian whispered, wanting to know, but not wanting to know at the same time.

"Tom told us we could move. But he said that he never wanted to see or hear from me again. Never."

"Oh God, Brett," Brian said as he hugged him.

"I couldn't tell Mom or Bobby because then they wouldn't want to move, and we'd be stuck there with all of our so-called friends whispering behind our backs and pointing their fingers at us and shit. Bobby was already getting shit from guys who were supposed to be his best friends. My best friend, Austin, never called me or came to see me when I got out of Chicago. Not once. Can you imagine the hell we'd be living in? It would almost be as bad as being in that shithole I was in doing perverts."

Brian did not know what to do other than to hold Brett and let him cry. And as strong as Brett was, as tough as Brett was, Brian knew that of all the guys, Brett was the most like him. Like Brett, he hid things, he doubted things, and he questioned things. Like Brett, he kept things to himself. Things he dare not share with anyone until those things got so bad that they threatened to ooze out of the tightly wrapped package he and Brett kept their feelings hidden in.

Brett gathered himself together enough to say, "I think the bad part is that I don't regret it all that much. Mom and Bobby and I are happy. But Dad will never be able to adopt Bobby and me because Tom won't relinquish his parental rights. Unless Dad and Mom take him to court, and I don't think they will. We'll have to wait until we're eighteen and then," Brian felt Brett shrug, "what good would that do?"

"I'm sorry, Brett. I know how much you and Bobby want that."

Brett shrugged again, chuckled humorlessly, and said, "Like Dad says, you can shit in one hand and wish in the other and see which one fills up the fastest."

At last, the two friends separated a little, though they still had their arms around each other. Brian gave Brett an Eskimo.

"Promise me two things," Brett said.

"Sure."

"You'll never tell anyone what I told you. Ever. And that we'll always be friends."

Brian hugged Brett as hard as he hugged anyone in his life. Their bodies pressed together, legs and feet intertwined, and he said, "Never, and always and forever. I promise."

They held their embrace for what seemed like an eternity.

Chapter Fifty

Waukesha, WI

"Victoria, this meal looks and smells delicious. I had no idea you could cook like this," Summer said as she made her way along the buffet line.

Because there were so many mouths, Jeremy and Vicky thought it would be easiest to use the counters to line the food up and everyone could take what they wanted buffet style. And there was plenty to eat. Two huge lasagna dishes, one with a combination of sausage and hamburger and the other with spinach and cheese. There were soft garlic and butter breadsticks and a large salad that would rival Olive Garden. For dessert, there was homemade cannoli. To drink, there was red and white wine, beer, soda, and water with lemon.

"I come from a long line of Italians," Vicky laughed.

"Italian?" Nelson Alamorode asked. "McGovern sounds Irish or Scottish."

"Yes and yes," Vicky laughed. "My maiden name is Dominico, and my ex-husband's roots are Irish and Scottish, among other things."

Turning back to Summer, Vicky said, "This meal was a family affair though. Brett, Randy, and I started the lasagna yesterday afternoon. Bobby and Billy made the cannoli. Brian, George, and Jeremy took care of the salad and breadsticks."

"My compliments to the chefs, young and old," Pete said.

"Hey! Who are you calling old?" Jeremy laughed.

After everyone filled their plates, groups scattered to various locations. Jamie and his wife, Kelli, joined Pete Kelliher, Nelson Alamorode, Summer, Vicky, and Jeremy in the dining room.

Jamie's and Kelli's son, Garrett, had to be wherever George was. George made sure he sat next to him on the floor with Randy and Skip

Dahlke, who talked about forensic medicine and crime scenes and his training at the academy.

Brian felt out of place. He sat on the fringe of a circle that included Brett, Bobby, and Billy who laughed and joked with Cleve Batiste, Jo Weist, and Pat O'Connor. He did not feel like he was a part of this group.

From what Brian could hear from the dining room, Alamorode asked a lot of questions.

"You're Brian, right?" Batiste asked.

Brian snapped his attention back to the conversation in front of him. "Yes, sir."

"You're a helluva shot. You have great form. I think you missed maybe two or three shots all night."

"Two," Brett said as he reached back and smacked Brian's thigh.

"Thank you, but Bobby's a better shot than I am," he said, blushing deep red.

"Oh, I don't know," Bobby murmured.

To Batiste, Brian said, "He could start next year. He's a better ball handler, and he's quicker than I am."

Brett cocked his head at him.

"You showed pretty good quickness to me," Batiste said. "And tough defense too. Nice anticipation."

"I think Brett, Billy, and Randy are better defensively than I am. Brett knows what the offense is going to do before they do," Brian laughed. "I'm just a soccer player."

"Did you know Cleve was all-conference at Purdue?" Brett said. "He was a point guard."

"Wait, was that a compliment? From you?" Batiste feigned shock. "There was a time not too long ago when you said I was from Purpuke."

Everyone laughed.

Brett smiled and said, "Purdue is a good school. And anytime you make all-conference in the Big Ten, that's an accomplishment."

"I do not believe my ears." Cleve faked surprise. "Who are you?"

The boys laughed, and O'Connor and Weist smiled.

"I was only honorable mention, but thanks. Are you still all fired up about the Butler Bullfrogs?" Batiste smiled.

Brett and Bobby laughed, and Brett said, "No, I want to go to Wisconsin and run track."

"Track? I pegged you for a football guy. But you're also tough enough to play basketball for them."

"No, I don't think I'll be tall enough. I like track. It's my best sport. George and I are going to run track this spring. His freshman year he took third at the state meet in cross country. I've been checking times, and I think both of us have a chance to get to state this spring."

Brian tuned out the talk about track and college. As he did, he overheard bits and pieces of conversation coming from the dining room.

Alamorode asked Jeremy, "What kind of training did you have regarding sexual abuse?"

Jeremy shrugged and said, "Some coursework in my master's program and a workshop here and there."

"Hmmm ... I don't understand how you'd be qualified to give therapy to kids. I mean, kids who had been kidnapped. I've read that several were in captivity for nearly two years."

"Brett was one of those boys," Vicky said with an edge to her voice. "Twenty-two months to be exact. He and the other boys have a close relationship with Jeremy that, frankly, I don't see them having with anyone else, doctor or no doctor."

Jeremy blushed and glanced at Graff and then at Kelliher and said, "I don't give therapy. Like you said, I'm not qualified. I offer parents and kids the opportunity to talk, and I listen."

"You've been effective," Summer said. "Which is why we have you on retainer."

"But anyone can listen. Surely there has to be a better option for kids and parents."

Brett, Billy, Randy, Bobby, and Batiste were in the kitchen refilling their plates at the time and overheard the conversation. Brett raised his voice a little louder than he intended, or perhaps raising his voice was exactly what he intended.

"I'd rather talk to Dad than lay down on a couch and tell some jerk who thinks he knows everything I'm feeling."

"Brett," Vicky cautioned from the dining room.

"I can name a dozen guys who feel the same way," Brett said, ignoring his mother.

"I didn't mean any disrespect, and I'm sorry if I came across that way. It's obvious you're a good man, and the kids and parents respect you. You've raised fine young men, and I know you've done plenty of good in the community. I'm just trying to understand how you got involved in all of this with a limited background, that's all."

An awkward silence ensued. No one knew what to say, and no one seemed willing to break it.

It was Summer who stepped up.

"Vicky, I think I want to get some of that cannoli I saw in the kitchen."

"I saw that too, and I'm going to get some along with a refill of white wine," Kelli Graff said. "I'm breaking all kinds of social rules by not drinking the red."

"I'm going to have a beer," Pete laughed. "I think both of us would get thrown out of an Italian restaurant."

Vicky laughed, gripped Jeremy's hand, and said, "Please eat up. That's an order. There's more lasagna and breadsticks too. Unless the boys ate all of it," she added with a laugh.

The adults headed into the kitchen. Alamorode hesitated, still stinging from the mild rebuke, but he ended up following them. He glanced at Brett, who stared the doctor down to the point where it was Alamorode who looked away first.

Brett turned his back to him and muttered, "Asshole," under his breath as he, Batiste, and the boys walked back into the family room. He did not care if Alamorode heard or not. If the doctor did, he did not show it.

"Whoa, little man," Batiste cautioned as he placed a hand on Brett's shoulder as he walked behind him.

"Nobody talks to Dad that way," he spat.

"Your father can take care of himself, Brett," O'Connor said.

Weist watched the exchange. She watched the expressions on each of the boys, and each expression was of anger that their father had been verbally attacked in their own house. She watched the boys eat in silence despite Batiste's attempts to make conversation. All but one of them. She looked around the little circle and noticed Brian was missing.

Brian had hung back in the kitchen waiting for everyone to leave. He looked at the pile of dishes, antsy to get started. No one had told him or asked him or expected him to clean up. It was something he did both at his other home and now in Jeremy's and Vicky's home. Billy teased him about being OCD.

He crossed the kitchen to one of the cupboards below the counter, opened it, and took out some Tupperware containers with lids and placed them on top of the counter. One by one, he brought over the pans of lasagna and placed the remains into the containers, placed the lids on, and stacked them in the refrigerator. What little salad was left also went into a container. He decided to leave the breadsticks and cannoli out, knowing they would not escape his brothers' mouths.

He stood at the sink, plugged it, squirted some pink Dawn dish soap into it and then ran water, hot enough to wash dishes but cool enough so he could put his hands into it without getting burned.

Brian started with the bigger dishes, washing, rinsing, and then placing them in the other sink.

"What are you doing in here?"

Brian smiled, recognizing his voice, but did not turn around and said, "Building a house. What does it look like?"

O'Connor playfully nipped the back of his head, grabbed a dish towel, and began drying. When he finished with one, he would place it on the counter away from the sink and grab another.

"Excited about Wednesday?"

Brian shrugged and said, "Yeah."

O'Connor gave him a small hip-check and said, "Don't be so enthusiastic. Contain yourself, Bud."

"You're such a smart ass."

"Better than being a dumb ass."

"You're that too," Brian laughed, and O'Connor gave him another hip-check, and Brian answered that with an elbow to O'Connor's ribs.

"You have fun Friday night at Cat's house?"

Brian felt his face getting warm. He looked sideways at O'Connor and said, "Yeah."

"Maybe too much fun?"

Brian did not respond.

"You're a little young to be that involved, don't you think?"

"Who told you?"

O'Connor laughed and said, "I'm a cop, and I'm a guy. No one had to tell me."

In a small voice, Brian said, "It was the first time. It just happened."

"Are you taking precautions, Bri?"

"Both of us, yes. I have it covered."

O'Connor stopped drying a dish, turned to Brian, and laughed.

"That came out wrong."

"Yeah, I guess. So, I suppose that has something to do with what's between you and Bobby?"

"Geez, Pat. Don't be a cop with me."

"Can't help it. Being a cop is not only what I am, but who I am. So, what happened?"

Brian stopped washing dishes and rested both hands on the counter. "We'll be fine."

O'Connor considered that and said, "Way back when I was a freshman, I had a fight with Eiselmann. Like you, I spent a lot of time at Paul's house. I liked his family, and it felt like home. His dad saw what was happening, and one night, he sat us both down at the kitchen table. He told us to have it out, either with him there or by ourselves, but get it out and get over it. He said that whatever was between the two of us was affecting the whole family. It had everyone on edge, and he told us it needed to stop."

"It's just between Bobby and me. It's not affecting the whole family."

"Billy and Randy are trying to fix you and Bobby. That's easy to see. Brett is torn between his little brother and one of his best friends. And you and Bobby aren't yourselves. After the game, I thought you were going to haul off and belt him."

"You saw that?" Brian asked. He was embarrassed.

"Yeah, I saw it. Bobby was hurt. Both of you were hurt and pissed off."

Brian shrugged. "I apologized for that."

"I watch the two of you when things are right, and you guys are inseparable. He sits right next to you, if not on you. It's special. Like Paul and me. Don't ruin it."

"I won't."

O'Connor said, "I'm giving you forty-eight hours to fix it, or I'm taking you and Bobby for ice cream or something, and you'll fix it in front of me. It's the same deal Paul's dad gave us."

"We'll fix it ... by ourselves." He did not want anyone, especially Pat, to know what had happened.

"You have to. It's affecting your family. You and Bobby have a special friendship, and you don't want to ruin it. Most people go through a lifetime and never have the kind of friendship you and Bobby have."

"How long have you and Paul been friends?"

"Since third or fourth grade."

Weist had heard almost the whole conversation. She had started listening in the hallway and then entered the kitchen and stood against the wall. Maybe O'Connor knew she was there, maybe not. He wanted to make a point with Brian and was not going to stop until he had it made. She was not going to interfere, fascinated with Pat's relationship with the boy. With all the boys.

There was a point when he talked about what had happened between Brian and Bobby and how it affected the family that struck a chord in more ways than one. And a little bell sounded at the back of her head, but she did not know why. After more than a little thought, she stepped fully into the kitchen.

"Boys, boys, boys," Weist said from behind them. "You're way too serious. Do I have to separate you two?"

"Nah, I can take him," Brian laughed.

"In your dreams."

"If you show me where these go, I'll put them away."

Brian pointed his left red and white Nike toward the cupboards near the double stove and said, "In there."

Jo grabbed a towel and snapped O'Connor's butt.

"Damn, girl!"

"Can't take it?" she laughed.

"I'll show you what I can or can't take."

The three of them laughed. When Weist laughed, it was light and musical, and both Brian and Pat liked the sound of it.

The dishes were done, and the dishwasher packed except for some dessert plates and glasses. Rather than go back into the family room, Brian, Pat, and Jo sat down at the kitchen table.

"So, you're a profiler. Are you like those guys on *Criminal Minds*?" Brian asked.

Weist laughed again. "A little. Kind of."

Brian blushed and asked, "How does it work?"

"Similar to what Skip does with a crime scene. Both he and I pay attention to what is at the scene, but I also look at what's missing from the scene. I watch people and listen to them. I pay attention to what is not being said as much as what is being said." She smiled at him and said, "Do you know you do it without knowing you're doing it?"

"How's that?" Brian was skeptical.

"When you first met Pat, how did you know you could trust him?"

Brian stared at Pat, shrugged, and said, "We're friends. Brett and George and I go hunting with him and Jamie and Earl."

"Yes, but how did you know you could trust him?"

"I don't know. I just did."

She smiled at him and said, "Whether you know it or not, you profiled Pat to be safe. Your conversation with him while you did the dishes told me that."

"You weren't supposed to hear that." He turned to Pat and said, "Did you know she was listening to us?"

O'Connor kept his eyes on Brian, and smiled.

"Geez!"

"And before you moved here permanently, you stayed here on weekends and sometimes during the week. Why?"

"Because ... I wanted to."

"Why?"

"Because I love it here."

"Why?"

"Geez! What do you want?"

O'Connor chuckled and said, "Jo is looking for you to expand on your answers." And then to Jo, O'Connor said, "George and Brian are the quietest of the guys. He doesn't talk much."

Brian thought about it and said, "Well, the guys are my friends. Jeremy is ... he's ..."

Jo and Pat did not let him off the hook. They waited and let Brian swim in the deep end without his water wings.

He said, "Special. Vicky too. I love them."

"And Bobby?"

Brian blushed. He started to get up from the table, but Pat hand onto his forearm, at first firmly, and then when Brian gave up the fight gently. But he continued to hold onto his forearm.

In a whisper, Brian said, "He's my best friend."

Jo smiled at him and said, "Anyone can see that the two of you love each other. So like O'Connor said, you need to fix whatever happened between the two of you."

Uncomfortable with the topic and being the focal point of any conversation, he decided to change it. Brian said, "So what about Pat? What do you know about him?"

Weist put both hands up in surrender and said, "Oh hell, no way!"

"What else do you know about Brian?" O'Connor asked, bringing the conversation right back.

"That he's honest." She turned to Brian and said, "What you said about Bobby's shooting and the other guys' defense, you meant it."

Brian nodded and said, "Bobby's a great shot. Have you ever seen him or Brett move? They're so fast. And yeah, I get a lot of credit for my shooting, but it's because Brett and Billy set me up. And on defense, I get steals because of Brett and Billy and Randy. They make it easy for me."

"You're a great shot too," Bobby said from the doorway.

There was an awkward silence, and Brian felt O'Connor's kick under the table. Brian shot him a glare and then softened as he looked at Bobby.

"What are you guys doing in here?" Bobby asked.

"We did the dishes, and we're just talking," Brian answered.

Bobby hesitated, shifting from foot to foot and then said, "I came to get cannoli. Cleve and Billy and I want some."

"There's a lot left," Brian said.

Bobby loaded up a plate, hesitated, tried on a smile, and then turned around and walked out.

O'Connor smiled at Brian and said, "That's a start."

Chapter Fifty-One

Waukesha, WI

Most of the guests had left. Pete, Summer, and Skip stayed behind and spoke with George, Jeremy, and Vicky in the study with the door closed. Skip, George, and Pete went outside, and George showed them the footprints and walked them through the evening.

None of the guys knew what their meeting was about, but they knew they would find out. Homework had been finished. Billy, Brett, and Randy were nervous about their comparison essays despite having them edited by Jeff Limbach that afternoon. Brian felt good about his.

The rest of the house had been picked up, and in various stages of dress, the boys stood in front of sinks in bathrooms getting ready for bed. Brian was by himself, however. He suspected that Bobby was in Randy's bathroom, which meant that Bobby would end up sleeping with Randy again and that he would end up sleeping by himself.

He thought about O'Connor's ultimatum. There was not much time with Bobby being in one school and him in another. With both of them in basketball practices after school, that left a couple of hours each night to try to work it out. Great. He did not know what he could say or how to say it any differently than he already did, but he would have to think of something.

Jeremy stuck his head in the bathroom and said, "Vicky and I would like to talk to you. All of you. Can you get the others and meet us in the kitchen?"

Puzzled, Brian said, "Sure. Dad, what's wrong?"

Jeremy smiled, placed a hand on his shoulder, and said, "Let's wait until everyone is in the kitchen, okay?"

Brian nodded and walked down the hallway gathering the rest of the guys.

In minutes, everyone sat around the kitchen table wearing expressions ranging from curiosity to alarm. Pete, Summer, and Skip had left.

"Guys, last night, George woke up, checked the house, and found someone walking around the outside looking into our windows and checking for open doors."

All eyes flicked first to George, who sat without expression, and then back to Jeremy.

"Before you ask, he didn't recognize him, but gave a pretty good description to Pete, Summer, and Skip, and he took pictures of boot prints, and he managed to gather some thread or cloth that had been snagged on one of the rose bushes outside the study."

"We're safe," Vicky said. "Pete is going to have Jamie arrange for someone to watch over us for the time being. We think it was a burglar looking to get whatever he could take."

"That isn't uncommon in rural areas," Jeremy explained. "Other than Jeff and Danny, we're pretty isolated out here."

"We let Jeff and Danny know because they live so close to us," Vicky said.

"With our alarm system and Momma, Jasmine, and Jasper in the house, Pete and Summer think we're safe."

"But we have to make sure all the windows and doors are closed and locked and the security system is activated before we leave or go to bed," Vicky said.

"Do any of you have any questions?" Jeremy asked.

Brett looked at George and said, "Why didn't you wake us up last night?"

"I made sure he had left. We were safe."

"Why did you wait until now to tell anyone?" Randy asked.

"Because I did not want to spoil the party Father and Mom had planned."

Brett turned to Jeremy and asked, "Do we need to have the guns ready? Just in case?"

"No, absolutely not," Vicky said.

Jeremy said, "We keep the guns in the gun cabinet, and we keep the gun cabinet locked. Each of us knows the combination if there is an emergency. George has his knife. And we have Momma, Jasper, and Jasmine who will alert us if necessary."

"So no guns," Vicky said again. "I mean that." Her eyes were on Brett, Brian, and George, the hunters. Their heads nodded, their expressions less compliant though.

Jeremy knew there were unasked questions the boys would bombard George with after he and Vicky went to bed. Questions the boys would not necessarily want to ask in front of them.

"It's late, and a school night, so I think you need to head to bed."

"Everyone have their homework finished?" Vicky asked.

The boys either nodded or said yes, and they pushed back chairs and headed up the stairs.

Jeremy and Vicky checked the doors and windows as Momma trailed them from room to room. At last, Jeremy set the security system, and the three of them climbed the stairs. As Jeremy suspected, they had gathered in George's and Billy's room.

"Goodnight, guys. Don't stay up too late. Get some sleep."

Vicky added, "Brian, it was sweet of you to clean up the kitchen. Thank you."

He smiled and said, "You're welcome."

"How is your hip?"

"Fine. It was a little stiff when I first got up this morning, but it's fine now."

One by one, the boys kissed and hugged Jeremy and Vicki. Jeremy pulled the bedroom door closed to give them some privacy.

Billy scratched his armpit and asked, "What woke you up?"

"I am not sure."

"You didn't recognize him?" Randy asked.

George shook his head and said, "I did not get a clear look at him." His face had a faraway look, and he added, "He looked familiar. I believe I have seen him."

"You didn't tell that to Mom or Dad or Pete or Summer, did you?" Brett asked.

"No, because I was not sure."

"So what do we do now?" Billy asked.

"Nothing," Brett said. "We act normal. If this guy is watching our house, he might notice something if we act any differently."

"You think he might come back?" Bobby asked.

"Possibly," Brett answered. "I bet he was casing the house. I mean, we aren't super rich or anything, but our house is nice, and Dad and Mom drive nice cars. So that might make someone curious about what we have inside."

"Father wants none of us to leave the house by ourselves. If we shovel snow, there needs to be two of us," George said.

"You and I shovel snow and plow the driveway," Brian said.

"If any of us goes to the stable to take care of the horses, there needs to be two of us."

"You and I are the only ones who go to the stable," Brian said.

"That also means you can't go off by yourself to work on soccer or be by yourself," Billy said.

"Other than that, we act normal as if nothing happened. If Momma or the dogs warn us or if George or anyone finds someone, we need to let everyone know. Brian, George, and I will get to the gun cabinet," Brett said.

"We can't go to war, Brett," Randy cautioned.

"No, but we can protect ourselves," Brett answered. "And Mom and Dad."

Chapter Fifty-Two

Waukesha, WI

Before the boys went to their rooms, they stood in the hallway saying goodnight to each other with hugs. Jeremy and Vicky heard the commotion, came out of their bedroom and watched from their end of the hallway. Both were happy the boys loved each other enough to not worry about what others thought. It did not matter if they showed their affection in the hallway, before bedtime, or at half court before a basketball game, or at the sign of peace in church, the boys did not care who knew how much they loved one another. Their innocence was at once scary, and beautiful and magical.

"Pretty cool, huh?" Jeremy whispered.

"It is. The boys are so touchy, feely, I think they're becoming more Italian as time goes by," Vicky said with a chuckle. "And I love you, Jeremy."

They kissed, and that was not lost on the boys. Billy nudged Brett and said, "I wonder what they'll be doing tonight."

"God, you're so gross! How am I supposed to sleep with that thought in my head?"

Laughter was his answer.

Brian went to his room, shut the door, and climbed into bed. He left his light on because he wanted to read one more chapter in Jeff Limbach's *Fright*. He was near the end of it, or what Billy called, "the good part." Jasper kept him company as she lay on the rug next to his side of the bed.

He had settled in when there was a soft knock on the door. It opened, and Bobby stepped through.

"Can I come in?"

Without looking up, Brian said, "It's your room."

Bobby shut the door and said, "It's our room."

Bobby crawled into bed, fluffed his pillow and the blankets like he had done a thousand times or more. The difference was that he did not throw a leg over Brian nor did he throw an arm across his chest. Instead, he kept himself separated. Nothing touched, and for Brian, it was awkward.

At first, Brian tried to read his book, but he never read a single word, his mind going a million places at once. He gave up and reached to turn off his light.

"Wait, before you turn off the light, can I see your hip?"

Brian said, "It's bruised, but it doesn't hurt."

He pushed down the covers and lowered his boxers. Bobby pushed Brian's shirt up and ran his hand over the bruised area.

"Geez, Brian. It looks awful."

"It's just the bruise. It doesn't hurt."

"It goes all the way over here," Bobby said as he ran his hand into Brian's pubic hair. "Does it hurt here?"

"It doesn't hurt anywhere."

Brian started to pull up his boxers when Bobby placed his hand on Brian's balls, his fingers warm and gentle.

"These don't hurt?"

"No," Brian answered in a thick whisper. He knew he was getting hard, and he could not prevent it.

Bobby touched it and said, "It looks like it's working." He stared at Brian wordlessly and said, "You can turn off the light. I just wanted to see your hip."

Brian reached up, turned off the light, and then lay back down. He pulled his boxers up and pulled down his shirt.

Brian could feel Bobby staring at him, but he dared not look in his direction.

Bobby inched a little closer. His cold feet a jolt to Brian's warm feet. His legs and torso touching Brian. Still not like he normally slept, but close. He even reached under Brian's shirt and tickled Brian's chest and stomach. A fire burned in Brian's chest.

"I love you, Bri."

Brian nodded.

"Randy and I talked almost all last night. I talked to Mom and Dad before church this morning. I want us to be like we always were. Before yesterday morning, I mean. I don't want us to change."

Brian turned, and his head bumped Bobby's because he did not realize how close Bobby had gotten.

"I tried to tell you that yesterday, but you ignored me for two days. I said I was sorry."

"I know."

"That hurt, Bobby. I would rather have you yell at me or hit me or something. You didn't talk to me and that hurt."

"I know. I'm sorry. I didn't know what to say."

"Were you pissed at me because I was jealous of you, or were you pissed at me because I had sex with Cat?"

Bobby's hand stopped right over Brian's belly button. Brian could see him struggling with what he needed or wanted to say.

"The thing is, whenever I see you with Cat, I get jealous just like you got when you saw me with Megan. I thought I was weird or something. When you told me you were jealous of me for kissing Megan, I figured, okay, maybe I'm not so weird. But then you told me you had sex with Cat, and I felt like I had lost you, like you don't like me as much as you used to."

Brian heard Bobby's voice crack even though he was whispering.

Brian did not hesitate. He reached out and pulled Bobby to him. Without thinking too much about it, Brian brushed his lips across Bobby's forehead.

"Bobby, I love you so much. No one will ever change that. No matter who I date or go out with or ... *do* anything with, I will always love you more than anyone."

Bobby wiped his tears on Brian's sleeve and said, "Are you just saying that or are you telling the truth?"

"I don't lie, Bobby. I don't. I will always love you more than anyone else. I promise."

"Do you think you'll have sex with Cat again?"

"I don't know. I told Dad and Mom I'd try not to. Dad got me condoms just in case."

"What about us? You and me?" Bobby whispered.

"Bobby, I love you. I know we don't do stuff all the time. But I like it when we do."

"You don't feel weird about it?"

"No. Dad and Mom don't seem to think it's weird either. George doesn't think so."

Bobby nodded. Jeremy and Vicky told him the same thing and so did Randy. Brett was blunt about it. He told Bobby to get his head out of his ass.

Brian added, "Bobby, I don't know if I'm gay or not. I mean, I don't feel this way about anyone else. Brett and I slept together last night, and he was just about on top of me the whole night. But we didn't do anything. This is going to sound weird, but there's no other guy I feel like this about. I love you. I want to hold you all the time. I want to be with you. I like kissing you, and I like the stuff we do. The thing is I also like Cat. I liked what we did. I think about it, and I get crazy. But I think about what you and I do, and I feel the same way."

"Mom and Dad think we're just experimenting and that we got caught up in a moment. They said that we should keep dating Cat and Megan."

"I know. Maybe. But I love you, Bobby. I love you more than anyone."

Bobby kissed Brian, mouth open, his tongue probing. Brian shifted, pulling Bobby on top of him, one hand inside Bobby's boxers on his butt pulling him close, the other on the small of Bobby's back. Bobby's hands pushed Brian's shirt up, and then together the boys slid off his shirt and their boxers. They continued to kiss. The rhythm between the two of them increased in pace ending in a warm release. Still they held each other, unwilling to let go, unwilling to separate from one another.

Brian kissed Bobby's neck and managed to say, "I love you, Bobby. I love you so much."

Joseph Lewis   215

Bobby answered with kisses of his own, but in between, almost breathless, he whispered, "I love you, Brian. I always will. No matter what."

"Always," Brian whispered.

"Forever," Bobby said, as he kissed his way down Brian's chest, down his stomach, and between Brian's legs.

He stayed there until Brian arched his back and came again. And then Brian rolled Bobby onto his back and did the same for him.

After, Bobby stayed on his back while Brian held him.

Brian whispered, "Until you, I never thought about doing this with any guy. Ever."

"Me neither. I mean, my pervert uncle made me do stuff, but I didn't like it. I swore I'd never do that again. But then I met you."

Brian kissed him again, passionately. He managed to say, "I don't ever want to stop."

Time was suspended, and both were surprised when the alarm announced a new day. Their positions had not changed, except for Brian reaching out and turning off the alarm.

He raised himself and smiled down at Bobby. "My breath doesn't smell very good."

Bobby kissed him on the lips and said, "I don't care."

They kissed and clung to one another.

Bobby smiled at Brian and said, "Good morning."

Brian smiled and said, "It was a good night too."

Chapter Fifty-Three

Waukesha, WI

Monday mornings were generally busy in the counseling office. Teenage things like breakups and parent-kid conflicts, gripes about a teacher, an occasional pregnancy or runaway, which may or may not be tied together. Sometimes parents were concerned about their son's or daughter's alcohol or drug use that evidenced itself on a Friday or Saturday night. Depending upon the time of year, there might be a rare suicide attempt. All the results of a weekend where kids did not have the structure a weekday presented.

However, this Monday morning was slow. A couple of kids came in for ACT packets for the test administration in March. An overachieving junior came in for a credit check. That was it. The guidance office was a ghost town.

Jeremy had never been a coffee drinker, not even in college when he pulled all-nighters. Nor was he a drinker, if you ignored a glass of wine once a month or two. So, he sat in his office sipping an ice-cold Diet Coke and browsing the Internet and *MSN.com*. He had three bills to pay, but he hated doing things like that on school time. He even felt guilty being on the Internet. That Catholic conscience thing, he supposed.

His phone beeped. Jeremy clicked off the Internet, pushed the button to receive the call, and Kristi said, "Jeremy, you have a visitor."

He ticked off a list of parents who might stop in. Most of them were pleasant while a few, quite the opposite. He stood up and walked out the door and almost fell over.

Sitting in the outer office was Brett's and Bobby's father and the ex-spouse of his fiancée, Vicky. Dr. Thomas McGovern, an English professor at Butler University. Indianapolis was quite a distance away from Waukesha, and Jeremy wondered when he had arrived.

It had been almost two years since he had seen him and even longer since he had spoken to him. He had longish light brown hair and blue eyes. His fair features were soft, like Bobby's, though both Brett and Bobby had a dark complexion and looked more like their mother and her side of the family. He stood six foot, maybe six-one, and looked trim and fit. Not like a weightlifter, but more like a runner or someone who practiced yoga. Whatever brought him to Waukesha and to North high school was beyond Jeremy's grasp.

"Thomas?" Jeremy asked tentatively.

"Hi, Jeremy," Thomas said as he stood up and walked confidently toward him, hand outstretched, offering a handshake.

Jeremy did not know why, but he took a step back as a precaution, recovered, and shook his hand.

"May I speak to you? Privately?"

"Sure," Jeremy answered as he stepped aside and showed him into his office.

At first, Thomas stood there with his hands in the pockets of his overcoat. Under it was a brown tweed sports coat. Jeremy was pretty sure there would be leather on the elbows. He wore a white button-down shirt and jeans with Hedgehog Fastpack Gore-Tex shoes.

"Please, have a seat," Jeremy said.

Thomas shed his overcoat, folded it over his arm, and sat down.

The silence was awkward, but having worked with teenagers for so many years, Jeremy went with it. He said, "How have you been?"

Thomas hemmed and hawed, and said, "Fine. I guess. I miss my sons."

Jeremy nodded. He was not about to tell him that they did not miss him.

"What brings you to Wisconsin?"

Thomas smiled and said once again, "I miss my sons."

"Do they know you're in town?"

He said, "I thought I'd surprise them. I'd like to speak with Brett, if I could."

Jeremy recognized the edge in his voice that harbored anger living just below the surface threatening to raise its ugly head. He also recognized the smugness, the arrogance, and the cock-sureness of the man that was not hidden at all.

He knew his boys' schedules by heart, but to make a show of it, Jeremy hit a couple of keys on the computer, pulling up the student management system. He typed in Brett's name, and his schedule popped up. Honors Biology. He filled out a call slip summoning Brett to the guidance office and then he stood up.

"I'll send for him," Jeremy said as he opened the door and walked the pass out to one of the student aides, who took off out the door and down the hall.

Jeremy had misgivings. Yes, Thomas had joint custody with Vicky, but until now, Thomas had never spoken to Brett and never indicated that he had been interested in him. Jeremy did not know what Thomas's motives were, and as a consequence, was suspicious.

Jeremy walked back to his office and said, "If you like, I can show you to the conference room where you and Brett can talk privately."

"That would be best, I think."

Thomas stood up, and Jeremy led the way around the corner to the conference room. He opened the door, turned on the lights, and said, "Brett should be here in a minute or two. Can I get you water or something?"

"No, I'm fine."

Jeremy left and went back to wait in front of his office, just as Brett walked into the outer area.

"Hi, Kristi!"

"Hey, Brett. Did you have a nice weekend?"

"Yes, thank you."

Brett saw Jeremy, smiled and said, "Hey, Dad, what's up?" He embraced him and kissed his cheek. Jeremy hugged him and kissed the top of his head.

"You have a visitor."

Brett craned his neck into Jeremy's office and saw that it was empty. He looked up at Jeremy, puzzled.

"He's waiting in the conference room."

Jeremy placed an arm around Brett's shoulders, and automatically, Brett slipped his arm around Jeremy's waist as they walked around the corner. They reached the doorway, and Brett stood frozen, refusing to enter.

He gawked at Thomas and then turned and faced Jeremy, not understanding. The shock gave way to anger.

"What's he doing here?"

"Your father would like to see you."

"You're my father. That's just some guy, and I don't want anything to do with him."

Jeremy sighed and gave Brett's shoulders a squeeze. Jeremy kissed the top of Brett's head and said, "Give him a chance. Go on in. I'll be around the corner."

"Only because you asked me to," Brett answered defiantly.

He walked in, but rather than sit down, he stood against the wall near the door with his hands behind his back. When Jeremy went to close the door, Brett said, "You can leave it open." His eyes never left Thomas.

"I'll shut it part way, okay?"

Brett nodded.

As Jeremy walked away, he heard Brett say, "What do you want?"

Chapter Fifty-Four

Waukesha, WI

"A lot of time has gone by, and I missed you."

Brett snorted.

"I would like the opportunity to reestablish our relationship. I would like to go back to being your father and you being my son. I would like that very much. As I said, I missed you."

Brett's eyes blazed, and his mouth clamped shut.

"I watched you play several football games and a couple of basketball games. Both yours and Bobby's games. Both of you are very good. Athletic like your mom."

Brett could not hide his surprise at Thomas's declaration. What games? When? How did Brett or Bobby or Jeremy or Vicky miss him sitting in the crowd?

He regained control, but still refused to speak.

"So, how have you been? Besides excelling in athletics? Are your grades solid?"

Brett had enough, and he said, "Are you done now? I need to get back to class."

"Brett, I am serious when I said I would like to reestablish our relationship. I forgive you for threatening me."

Brett laughed and said, "You forgive *me? Seriously?*" He laughed again and said, "That's a good one, Tom. *You forgive me.*"

Brett came off the wall, leaned on the back of a chair, and said, "*I* don't forgive *you* for cheating on Mom or Bobby or me. *I* don't forgive *you* for not being there when that pervert uncle of ours came into our house to kill us."

"You're being a little dramatic don't you think?"

"Dramatic? He shot and killed an FBI agent trying to protect us. He shot at Mom. So, no, Tom, I'm not being dramatic."

"Brett, please lower your voice."

"I'm done here, Tom."

"I would prefer that you call me Dad or Father."

Brett laughed and said, "Well, that's not happening, *Tom.*"

Thomas looked down at his hands like he was inspecting his nails or something. When he looked up, he said calmly, "I can understand your anger, and I'm sorry. You're right. I should have been there. And despite what you think, I loved your mother, and l loved you and Bobby. I'm not proud of what I've done, and I can't go back and change that. But I can start over and seek your forgiveness for my actions and my words. I would like to make it up to you and Bobby. Somehow. What can I do to prove to you that I want the three of us to start over?"

Brett shook his head. He was not buying it. He was so angry his hands shook as much as his voice.

"What can you do? I'll tell you what you can do. You can relinquish your parental rights so Jeremy, our *real* dad, can adopt us after our *real* dad and mom get married. Or before. That would be even better. And the next thing you can do is go back to Indianapolis and forget about us because Bobby and Mom and I are happy. We're happier than we've ever been. Ever. We never want to see you again. We never want to hear from you again. Ever. That's what you can do."

Thomas shook his head, sighed and said, "I'm sorry, Brett, I can't do that. You and Bobby are my sons, whether you like it or not. I'll never give anyone the right to take my place. I'm your father whether you accept that or not."

Brett shook with anger. Deep down, he knew that would be Tom's answer no matter how much he hoped and prayed. Not just for himself, but for Bobby.

"I'm going back to class. Don't bother trying to speak to me again. I'm not interested. And about you being my dad? Bobby and I have a real dad now. One who loves us. And we love him more than we ever loved you. And I just thought of one more thing you can do."

Thomas did not ask.

Brett said, "You can go fuck yourself."

Chapter Fifty-Five

Milwaukee, WI

UW-Milwaukee has always been in the distant shadow of its big brothers, the University of Wisconsin in Madison and Marquette University in downtown Milwaukee. While it had a large contingent of on-campus students, it had an even larger group of commuter students. And on weekends, it was a ghost town.

It was newer than its two big brothers. Originally built in a northern area of metro suburban Milwaukee, the city grew up and around the university, and it became more urban.

"The Personnel Office is located in the Golda Meir Library on the first floor in the west wing. Room W120A," Eiselmann said looking at his phone. He had Googled it on the drive over.

"Great," O'Connor deadpanned. "All we need to know then is where the Golda Meir Library is."

"Never fear, Hoss. I can Google it."

"How about if I ask a couple of kids?" O'Connor asked as he looked around for a suitable candidate.

"Right. Sure. How many college students actually use the library?" Eiselmann said with a laugh.

"Cynic."

Eiselmann searched his phone, while O'Connor wanted to speed things up. He asked two students who looked bookish where the library was, and they gave him precise directions. A short seven-minute walk later, they entered the personnel office.

"Can I help you?" said a middle-aged, dark-haired, heavy-set woman in a pantsuit. She looked at O'Connor with his long hair, Levi's with a rip in one knee, and a purple Waukesha North sweatshirt under a leather jacket. He looked more like burnout, or a biker than he did a cop. Undercover cop was the look he was going for.

Eiselmann flashed his badge and said, "My partner and I are with an FBI task force, and we were sent here to obtain some information. A warrant can be furnished, but we're hoping that won't be necessary since it will slow us down."

The middle-aged woman's smile disappeared as she glanced at O'Connor, so Pat pulled out his credentials, and she sniffed at it, focusing all her attention on Eiselmann, who was dressed more appropriately in a dressy top coat, brown sports coat, a tan Henley, and jeans.

"What is it you're looking for?"

"We're looking for information on a professor who either teaches here or used to teach here. Bryce Miller, Jr. He taught Psych 205 – Personality, and Psych 407 – Personality Theory."

"It would be nice if we could obtain a picture of him and perhaps names of other professors who might have known him," added O'Connor.

The middle-aged woman thought for a moment and said pointedly at O'Connor, "I'm not sure we can give you this information without a warrant."

Eiselmann jumped in and said, "As I said, the FBI is standing by, and a warrant can be provided if necessary. But it would slow down the investigation, and there have been several deaths already. We're hoping to avoid any more."

"There were deaths?"

"Yes," Eiselmann read her name badge and said, "Linda. Too many. Including children."

Her eyes grew wide, and she said in a hushed voice, "It's that serial killer, isn't it?"

Eiselmann frowned sympathetically and said, "I can't give you any details. I think I might have given you too many already, so I trust you won't repeat anything. It could be considered interfering in an ongoing investigation."

A hand flew to her throat, and she said, "I won't."

"Thank you."

"Can you give me his name again, please?"

Eiselmann pushed a notecard with Miller's name in small, neat handwriting. She glanced at it, and then her fingers flew over the keyboard. She waited a few seconds, frowned, and then clicked a few more.

"Dr. Miller doesn't teach here any longer."

Eiselmann nodded and said, "I was afraid of that. I had done some preliminary research and found that out. Would you have any information as to his whereabouts? An address perhaps or other contact information?"

"And a picture if you have one," O'Connor smiled.

She did not even look at him but clicked away and then walked to the printer, retrieved two sheets of paper, and handed them to Eiselmann.

"As I said, he no longer works here. The address I have on him is the one printed on this. There is a small picture of him in the upper right corner."

The picture showed a young man with unruly salt and pepper hair and thick black eyebrows over dark eyes. His face is longish and narrow. As doctors or professors went, he fit Eiselmann's idea of what one would look like.

The address matched the one on the DMV record, but his vehicles had not been renewed. At least not in Wisconsin. The FBI was performing a broader search for the man.

"Can you tell me, did he have any friends on staff? Anyone he hung around with?" O'Connor asked.

"I wouldn't know."

"Can you tell us who might have been in the psychology department when Dr. Miller worked here?" Eiselmann asked. "Perhaps one of the professors can give us a more complete picture of him."

She nodded and went back to her computer. "There are three professors still in the department." She frowned and said, "When Dr. Miller worked here, he shared an office with another professor. Dr. Alan

Nelson. He'd be a good one to talk to, but unfortunately, he left the following semester."

"Could you print out the information on him, please?" O'Connor asked.

"I don't see why not."

She retrieved a piece of paper from the printer and handed it to Eiselmann.

He frowned and showed it to O'Connor, staring at O'Connor as he did so. He noticed O'Connor's eyes register surprise and shock, the same emotions he felt. The two cops stared at one another without saying a word, yet there were all sorts of messages sent between the two of them.

"Is there anything further I can help with?" a middle-aged woman asked.

The two cops had tuned her out. They studied the picture of a man in his thirties, dark hair, and a thick beard. O'Connor stared at the picture from over Eiselmann's shoulder, which was not hard since O'Connor was way taller.

He frowned and then looked off in the distance. Something about him; the eyes in particular. It could not be, could it? It would change everything. Potentially. Maybe. Perhaps.

Eiselmann, armed with the names of the other psychology professors, thanked Linda the middle-aged clerk and walked out of the office with O'Connor following. Pat started to say something, but Eiselmann held up a hand.

"Don't jinx it. Don't say anything. I want to do some research before we talk about this."

Slow to speak anyway, O'Connor did not say a word. But there was quite a bit of thought going on in his head. Eiselmann's too.

"One thing," Paul said. "Before we say anything to anyone, I do some quiet digging. I want to confirm it for us. I don't want this going sideways."

"Agreed. And sideways it could."

Chapter Fifty-Six

Milwaukee, WI

"Hi, Dr. Trapp. My name is Paul Eiselmann, and this is my partner, Pat O'Connor," Eiselmann said flashing his badge. O'Connor did the same. "I was wondering if we could speak to you about two of your former colleagues if you have a moment."

Jonathon Trapp stood five-six, shorter than Eiselmann. His head had a crown of skin with thin white hair as a halo. O'Connor stifled a grin, thinking the good doc looked like a garden gnome.

Trapp looked at the clock on the wall and said, "I have about twenty minutes before my class. Have a seat. Can I get you some coffee or tea?"

"We're good, thank you," O'Connor said smiling.

Trapp smiled back and said, "Who did you want to talk about?"

"Dr. Bryce Miller and Dr. Alan Nelson," Eiselmann said.

"Miller and Nelson. Interesting pair," Trapp said raising his eyebrows.

"How so?" O'Connor said.

"In psychology, there is a dominant argument. One of many, I suppose. But one of the biggest questions to answer is, are we who we are based upon our genetic makeup, which would be nature, or are we who we are based upon the environment in which we live, which would be nurture."

"Nature versus nurture," Eiselmann said. "I remember that from college."

Trapp smiled. "I would think in your line of work you might come across examples on both sides of that argument."

O'Connor smiled again. He liked this guy. There was something ... cuddly about him.

"Miller believed that nurture had a larger part to play in one's personality. He believed that a family, one's situation, and circumstance can always influence, if not change, one's personality. Nelson, on the other hand, was a diehard believer in nature. That we are given the DNA that would make up our personality regardless of the environment one was raised."

"Regardless of the environment?" O'Connor said.

Trapp smiled and said, "That's what Nelson believed. No amount of research or reason could sway his belief."

"Huh," Eiselmann said.

Trapp smiled and waited, knowing the question would be asked.

"What side of the argument would you fall on?" O'Connor asked.

Trapp smiled and said, "Let's think of it this way. You, Detective O'Connor, are tall and thin. By your dress, I would say you do undercover work. I would say you're quite good at it because if you weren't, you would either be on a desk or dead. Would that be a correct assumption?"

O'Connor nodded.

"You strike me as thoughtful and deliberate. Yet you must have the ability to adapt and be flexible enough and fast on your feet that allows you the ability to do well in your line of work."

Trapp said, "DNA gave you the brains necessary to recognize patterns. You practiced this whether it was in the academy or on the street. I'm guessing the street. And it was the street, perhaps your home in some ways, that shaped what DNA gave you. So, I would say that DNA or nature gives us certain tools while the environment we are raised in and now live in, or nurture, shapes and builds upon what we're born with."

"Kind of sounds like double-speak," Eiselmann said.

"No, I don't think so," O'Connor said. "Look at the two of us. While I'm tall, I'm also plain looking. I'm thin. I'm made for undercover work. But with your red hair and freckles, you're way too noticeable. Not plain enough."

Eiselmann nodded and said, "I see your point." He turned to Trapp and said, "So I take it that Nelson and Miller argued about it?"

Trapp laughed and said, "All the time. One would bring in a study, and the other would counter it. Neither listened to reason or was willing to budge an inch."

"What happened to Miller?" O'Connor asked. "Where did he go?"

"That's quite the mystery. No one knows. He left on a Friday and didn't show up again." He shrugged and spread out his hands and said, "No one knows where he went. Police showed up and interviewed us, particularly Nelson. But no one could explain it."

"How did Nelson take it?" Eiselmann asked.

"Hard. Alan was, I think, genuinely distraught. Despite the arguing, they were friends or at least seemed to be friends. The arguing was more philosophical and theoretical. It's what we hope to do for our students. Cause them to think, to question, to wonder. The great mysteries."

"What happened to Nelson?" O'Connor asked.

Trapp shook his head sadly and said, "Nelson left the university. I think Miller's ... disappearance, for lack of a better word, impacted him in such a way that, perhaps, Miller couldn't take it."

"Huh," O'Connor said, "In a way, it was nurture that impacted Miller."

Trapp smiled and said, "You have a fine mind, young man. Yes. You may be right."

"One last question, Dr. Trapp. Do you know where Dr. Nelson is or where he went?"

"No, sir. I surely don't."

"May I ask one more question?" O'Connor asked.

Trapp waited with a smile.

"Is it nature or nurture that causes somebody to kill someone else? Murder someone, I mean."

Trapp pursed his lips. "For a person to be born a murderer, we're probably talking some sort of psychosis, a mental disorder. Maybe schizophrenia, something like that. For nurture to take over, there would have to be something traumatic, something," he searched for the right word and said, "something impactful to oneself or to a loved one that might cause one to become a murderer." He shook his head and said, "Unless the individual has a psychotic breakdown, some chemical imbalance, or perhaps a tumor intruding on one of the lobes of the brain, I personally don't believe one is born a murderer."

The two detectives stared at the professor, trying to digest his comment. Eiselmann and O'Connor stood up as did Trapp.

Paul reached out his hand and said, "Dr. Trapp, you've been very helpful. Thank you for your time."

Trapp smiled and said, "Perhaps I shouldn't say this, but I enjoyed your company. Come back any time, please."

He shook Pat's hand and said, "Did you study psychology once upon a time?"

Pat smiled and said, "I took a couple of courses. One of my favorite subjects."

"I meant what I said. You have a fine mind. Would you consent to being a guest lecturer in one of my classes?"

O'Connor smiled and said, "I would consider it."

Trapp took one of his business cards, wrote his cell on it, and said, "Let me know when you have some free time. My students would find you interesting."

Chapter Fifty-Seven

Waukesha, WI

"Anything I can do to help?" Kristi asked.

She had seen Brett leave the conference room, enter Jeremy's office, and through the glass window, watched the boy bury his face in his hands and sob using practically a whole box of tissue. She watched Jeremy try to comfort him, but Brett shrugged him off. Brett left the office pale and bloodshot with a tissue clenched in his hand. She had tried to talk to him, but he walked straight out of the office without looking back.

Jeremy shoved his hands into the front pockets of his gray slacks, walked back into his office, and shut the door. He had not come out for almost an hour. A red light on her telephone console showed that Jeremy was on the phone. Fortunately, no student had come to see him.

"Excuse me."

A well-dressed, smiling man appeared in front of her. Kristi did not know when he had shown up, or how long he might have been standing there.

Kristi had not seen him until he had appeared in front of her desk.

"Hi, how can I help you?"

"I was wondering if I might be able to speak to Mr. Jeremy Evans."

The red light on her console was no longer lit, so Jeremy was off the phone. She buzzed him and said, "Jeremy, there is a gentleman here to see you. Are you available?"

She heard him sigh, but he said, "Sure."

They clicked off, his door opened, and Jeremy stood in the doorway. He cocked his head and said, "Dr. Alamorode?"

"Hi, I was wondering if we could talk for a minute. I promise not to take too much of your time."

Jeremy shrugged and said, "Sure. Come on in."

The two men shook hands and then entered Jeremy's office, and the door was closed behind them.

"I had been thinking about your dinner party yesterday and what an ass I was. You and your lovely wife and your kids didn't deserve any of my comments or questions, so I wanted to come by and apologize. I'm sorry for offending you and your family. Very sorry."

Jeremy smiled and said, "No harm, no foul. Honestly. We're good."

Alamorode looked doubtfully at him but accepted his statement at face value. He had wanted to say more, perhaps ask a few more questions, but bit his tongue.

"I'm heading out of town for the next few days. My flight leaves later this afternoon, so I wanted to make sure I had spoken with you before I left. I don't like to leave things hanging. Again, Jeremy, I'm very sorry. Would you please extend my apology to your wife, Victoria and to your kids? I didn't mean to offend them."

Jeremy stood, as did Alamorode. Jeremy stuck out his hand and said, "Apology accepted, and I'll be happy to let Vicky and the boys know you stopped by. Thank you for doing so. It was thoughtful of you."

"Least I could do. Wish I could do more. But this conference in Vegas will have me tied up. Perhaps after I return, I can take you and your wife out for dinner. My treat."

Jeremy smiled and said, "That won't be necessary, but thank you."

Alamorode sat back down and said, "Do you mind if I ask you one or two more questions. It is okay if you don't have time. I'm fascinated with two of your boys, George and Brian. Can you tell me their story and how they came to live with you?"

Puzzled, Jeremy sat down and told him the sanitized and well-rehearsed version as advised by the FBI two or so summers ago.

"The FBI dropped George off at my house to stay with the twins and me while they investigated a murder in Northern Wisconsin, and the murder of George's family. He had nowhere else to go, so he stayed with us, and I adopted him. As for Brian, his parents died, leaving him alone. He could have gone to relatives, but he chose to stay with us. He had been coming over on weekends and sometimes on weeknights anyway.

He and the twins have been friends since, oh I don't know, a long time. Both boys fit perfectly, and we're family."

"How did they impact your family?"

Not sure he understood the question, Jeremy said, "Impact?"

Alamorode smiled and said, "First you have two sons, twins Randy and Billy. And then George comes along. Then, you have the brothers, Brett and Bobby, along with the twins, so I was wondering how George and Brian impacted your family."

Jeremy shook his head, still not understanding the question. But he managed to say, "No real impact other than the boys like each other, get along well, and they're friends. Brothers in every sense of the word."

Alamorode smiled, nodded his head, and said, "Well, what you've done for those boys is humbling. Sincerely humbling."

Alamorode stood, opened the door, shook Jeremy's hand one more time, and said, "Thank you for seeing me on such short notice. I appreciate it. You have a wonderful family and a beautiful home. I particularly like your office or study, whatever you call it. Serene, peaceful."

"Thank you for stopping by."

Jeremy watched him nod to Kristi and leave the office. And the same thought occurred to Jeremy as it did last night as he and Vicky got ready for bed. *Alamorode is a odd guy.*

Chapter Fifty-Eight

Waukesha, WI

"So, have you made up your mind?" O'Brien asked Graff.

Jamie knew the question would be asked. It was Monday, and O'Brien had summoned him to his office expecting an answer. All along, Graff had wanted to do the picking, not the captain.

He nodded and said, "Carlos Lorenzo and Greg Gonnering. I'm already using them for the serial killer thing. And I'd like to ask Alex Jorgenson. He's a county sheriff. Young, but has good instincts."

O'Brien pursed his lips, nodded his bald head, and said, "I don't know Jorgenson, but I think Lorenzo and Gonnering will work out fine." He paused and asked, "I'm surprised you didn't pick Eiselmann and O'Connor or Albrecht and Beranger. Even Desotel."

"We talked about it. They felt that because they're county, they'll be more help than confined to city jurisdiction. Give us broader coverage."

"Okay. So, we continue to use them as we have. I think you've picked a good crew."

"I'm still not real settled on the whole COD -thing, but there isn't a satisfactory alternative."

O'Brien made a face and said, "I know. There isn't anyone else I'd trust."

"Okay then. How do we go about this?"

"Leave it to me. Tell Gonnering and Lorenzo I want to see them. Contact Jorgenson, have a conversation with him and let me know if he's going to accept it or not. If he accepts, let him know I need to see him. There'll be some paperwork, and we'll need to swear him in."

"Can I ask a favor?"

O'Brien eyed him suspiciously and asked, "What?"

"I'd like to keep my office in the pool. I don't want to be separated from the guys just yet. I want to watch reactions, notice habits. Stuff like that."

"You think there will be pushback?"

"Don't know. Maybe, maybe not. I just want to be in front of it if it happens. Be in a position to anticipate it with the three new guys and all."

"Makes sense. Okay, you'll keep your desk. When or if you want to make the move to the office, let me know."

Graff got up to leave, but O'Brien stopped him as he got to the door.

"What is Eiselmann doing in the conference room?"

Graff shook his head. "I was just about to go find out. He said he had something to research. Wouldn't elaborate."

"The serial thing?"

"Gotta be, but I don't know what it is."

"Where's O'Connor? Those two are usually together."

"Couldn't tell you, but I'll find that out too."

Graff stopped at the vending machine, got himself and Eiselmann a Diet Coke, and walked into the conference room. He found Eiselmann hunched over his laptop. Every now and then, he would scribble something on a yellow pad, making faces as he did.

"What is it you're working on?"

Eiselmann jumped at the sound of his voice.

"Damn, Jamie, don't do that!"

"I thought you knew I was here," Graff said, laughing at him. He walked over and set the Diet Coke in front of him.

"I think I might have something. I'm not going to tell you or anyone what it is until I've nailed it. I'm not there yet, but I'm close."

Graff tried to sneak a peek over Eiselmann's shoulder, but Paul flipped the notepad over and shut his laptop, but not before Graff recognized a name. The surprise showed on Graff's face, and that was not lost on Eiselmann.

Paul pointed at him and said, "Don't ask and don't say anything to anyone. I mean it. I don't want to jinx it."

"Okay. I get that. But you better be sure before you do say something."

"I will. Also, I want to reach out to Morgan Billias."

"Billias? I didn't know you knew him."

Morgan Billias was a techy. That was all anyone knew. Chet Walker used him for off the books, semi- or mostly- illegal techy things. Things that most people, including the feds, might get in trouble for.

Whatever was known about him vanished when Walker died on the soccer field along with Brian's brother and any number of men, women, and children. But Walker did not know much anyway. No one else knew anything about him except a phone number given to Eiselmann by Walker, and that number was traced to a burner phone. No one knew where he lived or what he did for a living.

What the FBI and law enforcement did know about him was that Billias was more than willing to help the FBI and law enforcement with anything sketchy that might help them solve a case. He was instrumental in helping crack the human trafficking ring the boys were caught in. What was suspected was that Morgan Billias worked for one of the alphabet groups in D.C. and his name was an alias.

Graff thought it over. Billias was an asset of the FBI, and as such, permission should be obtained from them ahead of the call. But, he trusted Eiselmann. If Paul said he needed Billias's help on something, and Eiselmann seldom needed anyone's help with anything technical, then Billias was the one person who could help with something dicey. He also trusted Kelliher and Storm, and they trusted him. So, he made the decision to seek forgiveness, if necessary, rather than permission. He just hoped it would pan out.

"I'm leaving. When I do, make the call. And at some point, I'd like to know what you and O'Connor are up to, preferably before Pete and Summer. If that's possible."

Chapter Fifty-Nine

Waukesha, WI

"Brett, what the hell is wrong with you? What's going on?"

Harrison watched Brett lay into Randy for not grabbing a loose ball, into Billy for lack of hustle, and Brian for missing a three with two defenders in his face. He stormed around the court barking and yelling, pointing fingers, clapping to get attention, and yelling some more. He brought him to the sideline, let his assistant run the practice while he and Brett walked to the end of the fieldhouse.

"Nothing!"

Harrison's eyes bore holes in Brett's face.

"Look, I give you a lot of leeway. A lot! But I expect you to lead wisely. You're doing anything but and you need to knock it off or I'm sending you to the locker room."

Brett's jaw jutted out, and his chest heaved in and out. His hands were on his hips, and his head was down. Sweat dripped off his face, and his bare chest, arms, and legs were slick with it.

"What's going on? Talk to me."

Brett stood there in the same position, though his breathing was back to normal. He was not about to give an inch.

"If I put you back on the court, are you going to be okay, or is there going to be a body count?"

"I'm fine."

"You're not fine, but I'm willing to give you another chance. But I want to see you lead in a positive, calm manner and not eat your own teammates. Is that understood?"

Brett nodded.

"I asked a question, Brett. Bobbing your head up and down is not an answer."

Eyes blazing, Brett looked up at the coach and said, "I understand."

"Understand what?"

Brett hesitated, then said, "I'll lead."

"Good. Do that!"

The rest of the half-court work was pretty much okay with one slip up on Brett's part. All Harrison had to say was, "Brett?" and Brett calmed down sufficiently.

Harrison ended that session and sent them into a shooting and rebounding drill. He walked around the court, sidled up next to Brian, and asked, "What's with Brett?"

Without looking at him, Brian answered, "No clue. No one knows. He's been like this all day."

"Would your dad know?"

"Maybe."

Harrison walked to the end of the fieldhouse and pulled out his cell.

Chapter Sixty

Waukesha, WI

O'Connor, Weist, Eiselmann, and Batiste sat on the comfortable furniture in the family room while the boys sat on the floor. Jeremy and Vicky brought in chairs from the dining room but stayed out of the way of the cops who wanted to talk to the boys about the notebook.

Brian and Bobby sat next to each other as they did most often, leaning on big throw pillows with Jasper using Brian's shin as a pillow. Randy, Billy, and George sat together, legs crossed. Brett was off to the side and away from the other guys.

"Okay, all of you read the notebook, right?" O'Connor asked.

The boys nodded.

"And I'm sure you've already discussed it among yourselves even though I asked you not to."

The boys grinned, and Randy said, "We made sure all of us read it before we talked about it."

O'Connor glanced at Weist and Batiste with an "I-told-you-so look."

"Okay, tell me what you think. I want to know what was going on in that kid's head. What are these poems and stories telling you?"

It was Randy who spoke up first.

"He was lonely. He didn't have anyone. Not like us, anyway."

The boys nodded, except for Brian. Weist kept her eye on him.

"Why was he lonely?" O'Connor asked.

Billy spoke up and said, "I didn't get a reason out of the poems. Just that he was lonely."

Brian looked up at Billy, then at George, and at Brett. Still saying nothing.

"Brian, what are you thinking?" Weist asked.

Brian sucked on the inside of his cheek. Bobby looked over at Brian and said, "What?"

"He was more than lonely."

"What do you mean?" Eiselmann asked.

Brian got up on his knees, took the notebook from O'Connor, and said, "This poem. The one about the potted marigold on the gray porch. He describes the porch as gray. The porch is old, and the wood is chipped. There isn't any color used in the poem except for the flower in the pot. He goes on and on about how it smells sweet, about the bright yellow and red colors. But everything else is gray and ugly and chipped."

"Because he's lonely," Billy said.

O'Connor waved him quiet.

Brian shook his head and said, "No, he's more than lonely. He's the marigold. He doesn't fit in."

The cops looked at one another, except for Weist, who was intent on Brian.

"Explain," Jo said.

"The other poem, the one about the highway." He flipped a couple of pages until he found the one he was looking for. "He talks about how fast and smooth the gray concrete is. The only color was the yellow line down the middle. But he talks about the path behind the house that winds up the hill and into the woods. He talks about the trees, the bushes, the blue sky, and white clouds. In each of his poems, there is one thing that contrasts with another. One is plain, and dull and gray, while the other has color and taste and smell. I think he's trying to tell us that he doesn't fit in."

"He doesn't fit in," Batiste repeated.

"There's more to it than that, isn't there, Brian?" Weist said with a smile.

Brian blushed, and he looked down at the floor. He looked up and said, "I think he feels he doesn't belong."

"What do you mean by that?" O'Connor asked.

"He was adopted, right? But his parents and his sister didn't like him all that much. He was alone, and he was lonely. But more than that, no matter what he did, he didn't fit in. He was just ... there. Like he didn't belong."

Bobby turned to him and placed a hand on Brian's arm.

"What?" Brian asked.

"You don't feel like that, do you? Like you don't belong? I mean, we're all adopted. Well, most of us." This last he glanced at Brett.

Brian blushed a deeper red, and in a small voice, he said, "Sometimes." He looked at Jeremy and Vicky and said, "Sometimes I feel like I'm visiting."

"Why do you feel like that, Bri?" Bobby pressed.

"It's not all the time. Just sometimes."

George said, "Father, it is like I felt when I first moved in with you and the twins."

Jeremy said, "I remember. You said you felt like you were upsetting the balance. You were afraid of coming between Randy and Billy, and Randy and me, and Billy and me." He smiled.

"Yes," George said. "That is what I felt."

"But you don't feel that way now, do you?" Billy asked.

"No." George smiled. "We are all brothers, and we are all friends."

To Brian, Randy asked, "Do you feel like that, like how George felt?"

Frustrated, Brian shook his head and said, "Not all the time. Just sometimes. The thing is, if I had moved in with Gavin and his mom, I would have felt the same way as Staley. Gav and his mom are best friends. I would have felt like I was intruding." He shook his head and said, "But it's not like I feel like this all the time."

Brett sat up, pointed his finger, and said, "Well hell, Brian! On Wednesday, you get adopted, so you will belong. You won't be visiting anymore, and you won't be intruding. It's all bullshit, so suck it up, Buttercup!"

Brian blinked. Bobby sat back but snuggled up to Brian like a shield. Billy glanced at Randy and then at Jeremy seeking help. Randy cocked his head and squinted at Brett. George did not convey any emotion or outward expression.

"Brett McGovern!" Vicky snapped.

Brett glared at Brian, checked himself, and then got up and left the room.

No one said anything for quite a while. Eiselmann pecked at his laptop. O'Connor ran a hand through his long hair and then over his face. Batiste stared at the doorway Brett had disappeared through. Weist regarded Brian.

"He didn't mean that," Bobby whispered.

Feeling like all eyes were on him and uncomfortable with the spotlight, Brian stood up and headed out of the room.

"Brian, please wait," Vicky said as she reached for Brian's hand.

Brian pulled his arm out of the way and escaped feeling the eyes of each boy and adult on the back of his head.

No one said anything, because no one knew what to say. The boys looked at each other, except for Bobby, who stared at his hands. George scooted over next to him and placed his arm around his shoulders.

O'Connor said, "I. I think we need to go."

He stood up and motioned for Eiselmann, Weist, and Batiste to follow. Weist retrieved the notebook from the floor where Brian had been sitting. Jeremy and Vicky followed them to the front door, shook hands with Wiest, and hugged Batiste, Eiselmann, and O'Connor.

Pat said, "I'm sorry. I don't know what happened."

Jeremy shook his head but could not find any words.

Vicky said, "Brett's father visited him at school. I'm not sure why he decided to show up, and I don't know what was said. I'm sure it upset Brett." To O'Connor and Eiselmann, she said, "You know him. He's not like this."

"Would it be okay if maybe I give him a call tomorrow?" O'Connor asked.

"That would be fine, Pat," Vicky said.

The four cops left, and Vicky shut the door and leaned against it. Jeremy stood in front of her, his eyes searching for any clue as to what she was thinking.

She reached out and took his right hand in both of hers and said, "Let's go talk to Brett."

Chapter Sixty-One

Waukesha, WI

The ride was six minutes to the outskirts of Waukesha and another twenty minutes to the Holiday Inn Express on Bluemound Road, longer if there was traffic. For the first ten minutes, no one spoke. The only conversation occurred between O'Connor and Batiste, and that was about the weather.

O'Connor drove in silence, even turning off the radio. Batiste stared out of the side passenger window at the cold, dark winter evening. Eiselmann busied himself with his laptop, pausing every now and then to glance out the window and then return to his computer screen.

Weist's mind flew. From the moment she had gotten herself seated and belted into the backseat, she opened her leather pad and began writing, drawing diagrams, and drawing arrows connecting one diagram to another and then writing more. By the time they had reached the Bailey house where Sarah and her son, Stephen, and Stephen's younger sister, Alexandra, lived and where Paul spent a considerable amount of time, she had finished her notes.

"Keep me posted," was all O'Connor said to Paul, and the only acknowledgment he received was a hand wave as Paul moved to the side door off the driveway.

"This is where he lives?" Batiste asked.

O'Connor smiled and said, "He will soon. That is, if after he and Sarah marry and they decide to stay here."

By the time the three of them got to the hotel, she had read and reread her notes and contemplated them in the parking lot. Batiste had left the two of them alone as he walked through the automatic doors. Weist had not even noticed he had left nor had she noticed the car had stopped in the circle drive.

"What's the name of the book you're writing?"

No answer, not even a flinch.

"Yo, Jo," O'Connor said, snapping his fingers as he stared at her using his rearview mirror.

"Huh? What?" And then as she caught her bearings, she added, "We're here already?"

O'Connor turned around and placed a long arm on the back of the seat.

"What were you working on?"

"Jotting some notes from the conversation with the boys."

O'Connor regarded her until she shifted uncomfortably in her seat. She made no move to get out of the car.

"Wanna go get something to eat? Maybe grab a beer?" O'Connor asked.

Weist smiled and said, "If I can sit in the front seat and not be driven around like you're a chauffeur or something."

O'Connor smiled, reached over, and opened the front passenger door. Weist hopped out and jumped in.

"Where to?"

"Depends on what you're interested in."

She blushed, smiled, and said, "Not a beer or something to eat."

O'Connor made a show of looking up at the hotel through the front window.

"Too many eyes and too many questions," was all Weist said.

So, O'Connor put the car in gear and drove to his apartment.

Chapter Sixty-Two

Waukesha, WI

Jeremy and Vicky found Brett in his room, laying on his bed staring at the ceiling. Vicky had knocked, but Brett did not answer, so she and Jeremy entered and sat down on either side of the bed. His homework was nowhere to be found. Brett had a habit of doing it while he was in class, seldom bringing any home with him except for a book to read for English. He was so bright he did math in his head. He could look at a problem once, and without any other direction or explanation, solve it. Same with science.

It drove his teachers crazy because he was the only student, *good* student that is, who never took notes. They worked out a deal with him. If one of the administrators came in for an informal or formal observation, he would take notes to make it look good. It never fooled anyone. Bob Farner, one of the assistant principals, called him on it in the hallway between classes one day.

"You were faking it, weren't you?" he had asked with a laugh.

"I can neither confirm nor deny," Brett said laughing at his own joke.

"And you're a smart ass!" Farner whispered, leaning in so none of the other students overheard.

Brett had grinned and said, "That I can't deny."

Farner had walked off laughing.

"What's going on, Brett?" Vicky started.

Brett did not answer, but a tear dripped out of his eye and ran down his cheek.

"What was the conversation between you ..." Brett glared at her, and she corrected herself, "between you and Tom?"

Brett shook his head once and set his jaw.

"Let me take a guess," Jeremy said. "You told him you didn't want anything to do with him. You told him to leave you and Bobby and your mom alone."

Brett's eyes flicked to Jeremy and then back to the ceiling.

"But there's more, isn't there?" Jeremy asked, taking a gentle hold of Brett's hand.

Jeremy had a habit when holding a hand, he would rub a thumb over knuckles. Vicky would tell him to stop. Brett, on the other hand, would grip Jeremy's hand firmly.

"I told him Bobby and I wanted to be adopted by you." A couple more tears fell.

"And he told you he wouldn't agree to it," Vicky said.

Brett nodded.

Jeremy let go of Brett's hand and smoothed the chestnut-colored bangs off Brett's forehead.

"Brett, a couple of weeks before Christmas, before Brian came to live with us, you and I had a conversation in the study. You had asked me if your mom and I didn't marry and if she began dating somebody else and married him, what would happen to you and Bobby. Do you remember?"

Brett glanced at his mom, but it was clear she knew the story because she gave no hint of surprise.

"Yes."

"What was my answer?"

"That if Mom married someone else, Bobby and I would be loved by three men."

"And you asked if I would still be your dad."

Brett nodded, his eyes shifting from Vicky to Jeremy and then back to the ceiling.

"And what was my answer?" Jeremy whispered.

"That you'd still be Bobby's and my dad," Brett answered, his voice breaking, his chin quivering.

"I said that as far as I was concerned, I would love you and Bobby as I always have and that I was proud to be your dad." Jeremy bent down and kissed Brett's forehead. "And I still am. It doesn't matter to me if your name is McGovern or Evans."

Brett nodded, straining to keep his composure that was crumbling by the second.

"Have I ever done anything or said anything to make you feel like I didn't love you?"

"No," Brett whispered.

"Have I ever done anything to make you feel like I loved you less than the twins or George or Brian?"

Brett's mouth formed the word "no," but there was not any sound.

"Of course not, Brett. I wouldn't do that. I love you and Bobby too much to do that. And I love your mom. If I had done that to you and Bobby, I would be betraying your mom's trust in me, and I love your mom too much to do that."

Brett nodded.

Vicky kissed Brett's cheek and said, "We're family. Bobby, you, the twins, George, and Brian," she smiled at Jeremy and said, "and your dad and me. We're family. It doesn't take changing a name to make us any more than we already are. We're family."

Brett nodded again.

Jeremy wiped the tears off Brett's face, kissed his forehead again, and said, "Let's go have a talk with your brothers."

After a hug and a kiss from both Jeremy and Vicky, the three of them left Brett's room, rounded up the others, and headed to the kitchen.

All of them sat at the table. Eyes darted in every direction, except for Brian's, who stared at his folded hands on the table before him.

Vicky nodded at Jeremy to start, so Jeremy began by repeating what he had said in Brett's room.

"Guys, have I ever said or done anything to make you feel that I didn't love one of you as much as I do the others?"

He looked around the room and saw head shakes. No one dared to say anything.

"Have I ever treated any of you less than I ought to? Have I shown any of you less respect than anyone else?"

Again, head shakes.

"Did I not welcome each of you as my sons regardless of your name or background?"

This time, the boys answered with a yes, except for Brian and Brett, who nodded.

"And I think each of you call me Dad, except for George, who calls me Father." Jeremy chuckled. "Right?"

A quiet chorus of "yeses" was heard except from Brian and Brett, who nodded.

"If I treated anyone here as less than my son, I would like to know, and I'll be happy to apologize."

All heads shook no.

"Your mom and I are going to get married. Until then and long, long after, we're family. It doesn't matter to me what your last name is. Billy is Billy Schroeder because he wanted to respect his dad, Robert. George is George Tokay because he wanted to respect his family and his heritage. It never, ever mattered to me that even though I had adopted them, they didn't take my last name. Because a family is a lot more than a last name. It's how we feel about one another. It's how we love one another. It's how we always have each other's back. It's how we care for each other. That's what a family is. We take care of one another."

All heads nodded.

Vicky said, "There might be disagreements. There might be anger from time to time. One might be annoyed with someone. But in the end, we talk it out, we makeup, we say we're sorry, we forgive, and we move on. That's family." Then she added, "That's what makes our family special."

"One of the rules of this house, this family, is that we're honest with one another because if we can't be honest, then we can't trust one another, and if we can't trust one another, we can't have a relationship." He waited a beat or two and said, "Right?"

A chorus of "yeses" again, this time with Brett and Brian's affirmations.

"So, your dad and I are going into the other room. The six of you are going to stay here, and no one is leaving this table until you work it out. All of it," Vicky said. "Is that understood?"

All the boys answered with a yes.

Jeremy and Vicky got up from the table and walked hand-in-hand out of the kitchen, with Momma following them.

Uncomfortable with the silence, the boys sat around the table waiting for someone to begin. Impatient and wanting to get it over with, Randy got up and walked to the refrigerator.

"Anybody want something to drink?"

"Water," Billy said.

"Me too," Brian added.

"I'll get my own juice," Bobby said as he got up and walked to the cupboard where the glasses were.

He poured himself orange juice. Got an orange for Brett and rolled it across the table to him. He went to the cookie jar and got out two chocolate chip cookies, one for Brian and one for George. Done with that, he sat back down.

George smiled at him, and Brian said, "Thanks."

Eyes turned to Brett, who peeled his orange. He looked up and saw the guys staring at him, and he sighed.

"I'm sorry. I was an ass." He turned to Brian and said, "You didn't deserve that, and I'm sorry. I didn't mean it. Honest."

Brian briefly made eye contact but nodded.

"What happened today?" Billy asked.

Brett sighed again, glanced at Bobby, who studied his older brother.

"Tom came to school today during first period." He went on to tell them in general terms what the conversation was, ending with, "so Bobby and I won't be adopted by Dad. He won't let us."

Brian reached over and held Bobby's hand.

George frowned, cocked his head, and said, "But you and Bobby are our brothers anyway. We were meant to be brothers, and Father and Mom were meant to be our parents. Like Father said, Billy's and my last name might be different from yours or Brian's and Randy's, but we are brothers. We are family."

Brett nodded. He felt deflated. The frustration and anger that had built up were gone. He slumped in his chair, eyes intent on his orange that he ate one slice at a time.

"There's nothing Mom or Dad can do to change his mind?" Bobby asked.

Brett shook his head. Brian laced his fingers with Bobby's.

Bobby shrugged. He had wanted it as much as Brett.

"George and Dad are right," Billy said. "We're family. No one can take that away from us. No one."

Brian cleared his throat, let go of Bobby's hand, and shifted in his seat.

"I don't have to get adopted. I can stay Brian Evans without ... all the other stuff."

Randy shook his head and said, "Not really, Bri. The difference is that Brett and Bobby are legally Mom's kids, so she has power to do things. Simple things, like doctors and dentists. Stuff like that. The same with George and Billy and me. Dad has that power. But without you being adopted, technically, there's stuff Dad and Mom can't do for you. Yeah, he has a piece of paper that your parents say he has power, but even Dad and Mom don't know how that might stand up if someone challenges it in court."

"Besides, being adopted is something you want, right?" Bobby asked.

Brian's eyes flicked to him and then to Brett before he nodded.

"So, yes, you're going to be adopted, and legally you'll be Brian Evans," Bobby said, his voice cracking a little.

"And no matter what, we're brothers and we're family," Billy added.

Heads nodded, though Bobby and Brett were reluctant to agree.

"Is that why you were the way you were at practice?" Randy asked.

Brett shifted uncomfortably, nodded, and said, "I'm sorry. I was an ass."

"You were, but we're good," Billy said. "We understand."

"I already apologized to Coach. I'll talk to the team at practice tomorrow."

Sensing the end, Randy stood up and said, "I'm tired, and I have a history test tomorrow. Brian, are you ready for it?"

"Yeah, pretty much."

"Can you quiz me?"

"Sure."

"I'll let the dogs out," George said, standing and heading to the mudroom for a jacket.

"Want me to come?" Billy asked.

"I'll go with him," Brett said. "If that's okay," he said to both of them.

George nodded, and Billy said, "Okay."

George called to Momma, Jasper, and Jasmine, and they lined up at the back door ahead of George and Brett.

The cold night air sucked the breath from them. Their nose hairs froze making it difficult to breathe. George looked up at the sky as the three dogs did their business on the edge of the woods off the path that led to the stable. The air was cold and damp. Thick, not crisp or brittle.

"Cold."

George nodded and said, "It will snow."

"Tonight?"

George shook his head and said, "Tomorrow. Afternoon I think."

Brett looked at George and said, "How do you do that?" He had asked the same question many times, marveling at George's ability to predict the weather, and always received the same response. Again, he was not disappointed.

"My grandfather taught me."

Momma watched her one-year-old pups play in the snow but kept her eyes on the woods beyond. Her body language was relaxed, so George knew she was not alarmed.

"I think I need to talk to Brian," Brett admitted.

George said nothing.

"I didn't mean to jump on him like that."

George nodded.

"He and Bobby are back to normal."

George smiled and said, "Yes. That is good."

"I think so too."

George placed his arm around Brett's shoulders and said, "I love you, my brother."

Brett turned into him, hugged him, and wept.

Chapter Sixty-Three

Waukesha, WI

Jo padded around the apartment barefoot and wearing one of O'Connor's t-shirts that fit like a mini-skirt. A skimpy mini-skirt that showed too much of her bare bottom. She did not seem to mind, and truth be told, O'Connor liked the view.

The apartment was a small two bedroom with one-and-a-half baths. One of the bedrooms had been turned into a storage/office. The boxes piled against one wall had not looked unpacked from the first move, and if this was the first move, O'Connor had not finished unpacking. The kitchen was small. Two bar stools were placed under the island counter, but there was not room enough for a kitchen table. The refrigerator was surprisingly stocked. There were proteins in various forms, yogurt in various flavors, except vanilla, and a lot of veggies and fruit.

There was not any alcohol that she could see, but a number of bottles of water, and different colors of Propel. There were also four cans of Diet Coke, and an unopened twelve pack of the same on the floor tucked beside the refrigerator. The freezer mirrored the refrigerator, except it was colder. There were packages marked venison or trout, some hamburger, and a lot of chicken. There were bags of frozen fruit. Jo glanced at the counter and saw a blender. She smiled and nodded approval.

She left the kitchen and wandered around the small living room. One couch -a not very comfortable one at that- and a well-used and comfy leather recliner. She had tried out each. A smallish flat screen TV was up on the wall. There were not any pictures or other decorations. In fact, Jo had spotted one picture in the whole apartment. It sat on top of Pat's dresser in a battered wood frame. It showed two boys, middle-school aged, she figured, with their arms across each other's shoulders. A man and a woman stood behind them, and all were smiling.

She walked back into the bedroom and stood in front of the dresser examining the photo.

"Seventh grade. Paul's family took me on vacation with them to Canada. One of the best trips I've ever had. That was taken in Mackinac Island just before we rode the ferry back to the U.S."

Jo noticed the wistfulness in his voice, kind of distant like one would savor a fond memory. She knew he was picturing the trip and the day, even the moments before and after when the photo was taken.

He lay in bed, his head propped up by his elbow and pillow. She came back to the bed, turned him over onto his back, and sat down on top of him. She felt him stirring beneath the sheet, and she liked that feeling.

As aloof as he was on the street and as all business as he was in a briefing, he was gentle and tender, caring more for her than for himself. She smiled down at him.

"What?" he asked.

"You know I hardly ever do this, right?"

O'Connor smiled and said, "Honestly, I don't either. In fact, I can't remember the last time."

She cocked her head at him but knew he had told the truth.

"You ever sleep?" she asked.

Pat laughed and said, "Not much."

"Me neither."

She bent down to kiss him, and he put his hands up under the t-shirt she wore, rubbing her nipples with his thumb and then shifted his hands to her backside.

"We're not going to be able to do a whole lot with the sheet between us," O'Connor said with a smile.

She laughed as she climbed under the sheet and stayed on top of him, their pace quicker than the last time. Each made low guttural sounds, almost feral until they collapsed into each other's arms.

She rested her head on Pat's chest. O'Connor loved the smell of her hair, the feel of her soft skin. He ran his hands and his fingertips up and down her back, her arms, and her breasts.

"I was wondering. . ."

O'Connor's answer was, "Hmmm."

"Those boys mean a lot to you, don't they?"

He knew immediately who she had meant. He nodded and said, "Yes."

"Brett, George, and Brian." She looked up at him and asked, "Why those three?"

He shrugged and said, "They're a lot like me, I suppose."

"Quiet. Intense. Big hearts." Jo kissed his neck and said, "Loners."

He shrugged and said, "In a way, I suppose. But loyal."

"Why did you become a cop?"

He kissed the top of her head and said, "A story for another night."

She kissed him once, then twice, and said, "Will there be another night?"

He kissed her, smiled, and said, "I hope so."

O'Connor waited. Neither he nor Weist fell asleep, content to cuddle. "What's your story, Jo?"

"My story?" She knew what he had meant.

"I don't know anything about you."

She rolled off him and a bit away so she would be able to study his reaction.

"Normal childhood until fourth grade. My parents were killed in a car accident. They had gone out to dinner, and I was with a babysitter. I didn't understand much, except that Mom and Dad weren't going to come back. I went to live with my aunt and uncle. They already had two children, both younger than me. It was hard."

"Why?"

"I wasn't theirs."

O'Connor propped his head up using his hand and elbow. He said, "Like the Staley kid."

"Yes, just like him. Just like what Brian and George described, almost to a T. I wasn't lonely as much as I was an intruder. Like I was on an extended visit."

"Sounds sad."

"It was at times. But it's like Brian said. The feeling came and went. My aunt and uncle tried harder than Michael Staley's parents, but that's the way my life had become. I graduated high school, graduated from college with a psychology degree. I stayed in school and earned a master's in psychology and joined the FBI in the Behavioral Sciences Unit."

"Do you like it? The FBI, I mean?"

"Most days. Pretty much."

O'Connor shifted the conversation and asked, "Do you think Brian or George is lonely?"

Jo shifted her gaze past O'Connor out the window, looking but not seeing.

"No, I don't think so. Those boys are so tight, so close to one another. All of them with each other. God help the fool who messes with any one of them. And Jeremy and Vicky are spectacular. I don't know how they do it."

"I wish you could stay longer and get to know them. Those boys are special. And you're right, Jeremy and Vicky are great parents."

"Are you envious?"

"In some ways, yes. I wouldn't mind a son to raise. But not with my lifestyle the way it is right now. But honestly? I can't complain. When I was a kid, Paul's parents kept an eye on me. I guess like Jeremy and Vicky did with George and Brian, Paul's parents took me in. My dad left when I was a kid. My mom did her best. Worked two, sometimes three jobs. Paul's parents filled the void. And then she died."

She kissed him and said, "You said those boys are special. Well, I think you're pretty special too."

He smiled, kissed her back, and said, "I have to ask. That thing you were working on in the car, was that part of the serial murder thing? The notebook and the conversation with the boys?"

"Yes, but I don't want to say much. I have to do a little more checking, and I queried a colleague at Quantico to do some verifying. I should know more tomorrow, hopefully in the morning. And I want to verify it with someone. Alamorode might have an opinion."

O'Connor thought about that and said, "There might be some bias there. He and Jeremy and the boys. Seemed like there was ... something."

"Yes, I caught that too. Still."

"Maybe."

She lay her head back down on his chest, kissed it, and said, "When I'm ready, I'll share it with you and Paul first."

"Deal."

While Pat thought it might be important to read, it was not as important as Jo naked and snuggled up against him was.

Chapter Sixty-Four

Shorewood, WI

The Man did not happen all at once. He evolved. He came into being with the realization that there was no one as unique as he was. No one.

No one could debate him. No one posed any argument, logical or illogical, that could sway him. Indeed, no one was his equal. Even the weakling who had pretended to be his friend once, in a former lifetime ago, was not.

The Man pretended to be the weakling's friend. He had pretended to be the weakling's intellectual equal. The Man had fooled him, just as he had fooled the others.

No, there was no one who could, or would come close to his intellectual prowess, his drive, his ability to think through a problem, a conundrum, and sort it out to its most basic parts to solve it.

Those who he had saved were not his equals since they had not acted for themselves. No, they had to rely on someone else, The Man himself, to take care of the problem for them. And even less were those who he had done away with.

No, none of them were his equals.

There was no one as gifted or as intelligent or as creative as he was.

The Man had perfected his craft. He admitted to himself in quiet, dark moments of doubt that at first, he had been clumsy, even though his early conquests had been successful. But the clumsiness and indecision of his early work gave way to poetry and beauty with each later success. There was purpose in his action.

The Man unfolded his hands and opened his eyes. He opened the drawer and took out the leather-bound notebook and reread the notes on his next two victims. As he read, he came to a startling conclusion based on his notes and on the conversations he had had.

It was more than Darwin, more than the survival of the strong and the domination of the weak. It was more than the weak dying out and becoming extinct.

The parents and well-meaning adults were as much to blame as the others. Weak. Blinded, as it were. His parents were just like them. Not blind in the physical sense, but blinded to the ways of science and of nature. And that is why they were dead.

At first, he had believed it was the fault of the weak. But now he knew that he had been wrong.

The Man took his wonderful pen, balanced and elegant, and in his firm and concise handwriting, formed his thoughts into words.

The Man set his pen down next to his pad. He folded his hands and reread each page, each insight.

He smiled. Satisfied. Satisfied with his thoughts. Satisfied with his plans.

The man was ready. The two would die. Two more done away with.

And so might their parents, real or imagined. They would die too.

Chapter Sixty-Five

Waukesha, WI

Brian blinked himself awake. Was it a dream? He was not sure. Was it a noise? No, not that he could recall. In fact, Jasper lay on the rug beside the bed head down. Of course, the pup could be faking it, but if there had been anything at all, Jasper would be up and at the ready.

Wearing boxers, Bobby lay curled up against him with an arm across his chest and with his leg over him. His cheek lay on Brian's shoulder, his mouth open.

Brian brushed his lips across Bobby's forehead and ran a hand over Bobby's bare shoulder and arm. He loved Bobby beyond words.

He eased himself out from under Bobby but made sure he was tucked in and kissed his forehead. Jasper looked up expectantly, so Brian squatted down and scratched the pup behind the ears. Jasper sniffed Brian's crotch.

"That's not for you, Jasper. Nice try," Brian whispered with a smile.

He opened the bottom drawer of his nightstand, took out the sealed envelope, and shut the drawer.

Brian tiptoed across the hall to the bathroom, held the envelope in his mouth between his teeth, and then peed, flushed, and washed his hands. He stepped back into the hallway where Jasper was waiting for him, expecting to tag along.

At the top of the stairs lay Momma. He sat down next to her, hugged her, and kissed the top of her head. She rewarded him with a doggie kiss of her own. He got up and tiptoed down the stairs. He checked the front door, and it was locked with a deadbolt. He walked into the kitchen, set the envelope on the table, fetched a glass out of the cupboard, filled it with water from the dispenser on the refrigerator, drank it down, and wiped his mouth off with the back of his hand. He set the glass in the sink because the dishes in the dishwasher were clean. He should know because he had packed it, put soap into the little door, and started it up before going to bed.

He checked the mudroom door, and it was similarly locked. He glanced at the security system and saw it was on. He walked down the hallway to the family room, checked the slider, and it, too, was locked. He walked to the study, and as he had suspected, the slider was also locked.

Brian stood at the slider looking out into the cold night. Goosebumps had broken out on his arms and legs, but he ignored them.

He moved to Jeremy's desk and sat down in the leather swivel chair, rocking back and forth and then side to side. He stared at the dark wood of the desk, his palms flat.

It was not quite 1:30 AM, but Brian was not tired.

Even though he had offered to put off the adoption, he did not want to. He was excited, and he found himself grinning. He was happy. Happy with his life. With Jeremy and Vicky. With the twins. With George and Brett. With Bobby. He had a great girlfriend in Cat and could not wait to be with her again, maybe after the game on Friday. Maybe Saturday too. He pictured what he and Cat had done together, and he smiled. He was uncomfortably hard, and it poked through the opening in his boxers, but he did not mind. He touched himself a couple of times, but stopped.

Brian stood up, made sure his t-shirt hung low enough to cover him up, and walked out of the study and back to the kitchen and sat down in front of the table and stared at the envelope.

His father, David Kazmarick, left it for him on the table in his old house on the day he was murdered by his mother. His mother, Nancy, took her own life moments later. A murder-suicide that did not make much sense. Not to Brian and not to Jeremy.

Jeremy had received an envelope also. While Jeremy read it and shared it with Jamie Graff, and Vicky, Brian had not yet read his. In fact, he had not touched it except to move it from the top of his dresser to the bottom of his bottom drawer in the nightstand.

Brian knew there was money inside. Five hundred dollars. At least, that is what the amount was in Jeremy's envelope. His amount could be more or less than Jeremy's, but he could not have cared less.

There was also a letter.

Jeremy had not shared what was in his, though he did urge Brian to read his own. Brian had not been curious enough to do so. The letter from his father. His other father. His dead father.

Still, he would be adopted on Wednesday morning so maybe.

Brian picked up the letter by the corner, tapped the end, slid his fingers down the side, tapped the envelope again and slid his fingers down, over and over.

"It won't open that way," Randy said through a yawn, scratching first his belly, then his arm, and then his belly again. He and his brothers and Vicky all knew about the letter and Brian's refusal to open it.

Randy walked to the cupboard, took two glasses out, and set them on the counter. He walked to the refrigerator, grabbed the milk and filled the two glasses, placed the milk back into the frig and closed it with a gentle thud. He carried the glasses to the table, setting one down in front of Brian and one on the table next to him. He walked back to the counter to the cookie jar, grabbed four cookies and two napkins, and carried them back to the table and sat down next to Brian. He broke a cookie in half and dunked it, then put the whole half into his mouth dripping a little on the table.

Brian broke his cookie in half and did the same, except that he did not drip milk on the table.

"Milk helps you sleep," Randy explained.

"Sugar gets you hyper."

With his mouth full, Randy said, "But after the sugar high, you crash and become tired."

The two boys ate in silence until Randy tapped the envelope with his finger.

"What?"

Randy shrugged and said, "You might want to read it before Wednesday morning."

"Why? What can my dead father and my dead mother possibly tell me?"

Randy swallowed, took a gulp of milk, and said, "Might give you their reasons."

"And that's supposed to give me peace of mind?"

Randy shook his head and said, "I said it might give you their reasons. I never said it would give you peace of mind."

Brian started on his second cookie.

"Bobby would be pissed at you for eating two cookies and at me for giving them to you."

Brian smiled and nudged Randy in the ribs.

They finished their cookies, and Randy finished his milk. Brian had a couple of swallows left. He had never taken his eyes off the envelope.

He asked Randy, "What was it like before you moved in with Jeremy?"

Randy made a face, kind of like a wince, and said, "Hard. I try not to think about it too much."

"What was it like?" Brian pressed.

"Todd would beat me or ignore me. Nothing in the middle. There didn't have to be a reason. Joyce let him." This last he said with a shrug. "It was hard."

"It was different for me. When Brad died, I was just ignored. I think I could have robbed a bank and got the electric chair, and I don't think my parents would have noticed."

"I think you had it worse," Randy whispered.

"How do you figure? My dad never hit me like yours did. Neither of them hurt me."

"They hurt you where it mattered most." Randy tapped Brian's chest and said, "Your heart."

Brian could not deny it. He hated being ignored, which is why he was angry with Bobby for ignoring him after they had talked Saturday morning.

Randy asked, "Do you think of Brad much?"

"Every day. Sometimes I wonder what would have happened if I was killed that day and he would have lived. I wonder if my parents would have ignored him like they did me." He shook his head and said, "I don't think so."

"I think of him too. He and Billy were alike." Randy turned to Brian and said, "I always thought you and I were alike."

Brian smiled and said, "I did too."

Randy paused for a beat and said, "Are you happy, Bri? I mean, living here with us?"

Brian smiled and said, "Yeah, I am." He paused and added, "I know I said that, at times, I feel like I'm visiting, but that's just every now and then. Not very often. I love it here. Who wouldn't?"

Randy smiled and said, "We have a good family."

"I love our family." Brian pushed the envelope a little away.

"Is there money in there?"

"Dad thinks so. There was five hundred dollars in his."

"If you don't want to read the letter, you could just take the money out."

Brian shook his head and said, "It's like, I don't know. If I accept the money, it's like I'm accepting what they did. I can't do that."

Randy did not know what to say to that. He supposed that if he were in Brian's shoes, he might feel the same way. Taking it would not be right.

Brian chugged the rest of his milk, grabbed his and Randy's glasses, rinsed them out, and put them in the sink. Then he grabbed a dishcloth and wiped down the table and dried it off with a towel hanging on the stove handle.

Randy laughed.

"What?"

"Even at," he glanced at the LED clock on the stove and said, "at two o'clock in the morning, you're cleaning up the kitchen."

"Well, Mom shouldn't have to."

Randy laughed again, slung an arm across his shoulders, and said, "To bed!" He glanced back at the table and said, "Don't forget your letter."

Brian stepped back, grabbed the letter, and resumed his position next to Randy so Randy could put his arm across Brian's shoulders. Brian slipped an arm around Randy's waist.

"I haven't told you or Billy or George this enough, but you know I love you, right?"

Randy's answer was to give his shoulder a squeeze.

At the top of the stairs, Brian and Randy bent down to pet Momma.

"What are you two doing up?"

Brian jumped a little, not expecting Brett to be in his doorway. Randy yawned, scratched his belly, and said, "Goodnight."

He hugged both Brian and Brett and tiptoed down the hallway to his room and shut the door.

Brett stood there, first scratching his belly, then his leg, and then his belly again yawning as he did so.

"Just checking the doors and stuff," Brian whispered. He grinned and said, "We had cookies and milk."

"Come to bed," Brett whispered, turning around and walking back into his bedroom as he did.

He slid into his warm bed and patted the side indicating to Brian he was welcome.

Brian shrugged and got in on the other side, but scooted over next to Brett, who threw an arm across his chest and a leg over Brian's, just the way Bobby had done.

It was not long before Brett whispered, "Are we okay? You and me?"

Brian nodded, turned his head, and smiled. "Yeah."

"I was a jerk."

"Yeah, you were."

"Didn't have to agree with me," Brett said.

Brian smiled and said, "Yeah, I did."

Brett tweaked Brian's nipple, and Brian swatted his hand away.

"I could have grabbed something else."

Brian smiled and said, "And I would have had to retaliate and grab something of yours."

The two boys chuckled and relaxed.

"Are you excited about the adoption?" Brett asked.

Brian turned his head and studied Brett's face, searching his eyes.

He did not answer Brett's question and instead said, "I'm sorry you and Bobby can't get adopted by Dad. I know how much you want it."

Brett shrugged. "Honestly, I didn't think it was going to happen anyway. Yeah, Bobby and I want it, but deep down, I knew it wasn't going to happen."

Brian rolled onto his side facing Brett, their heads inches apart, and said, "Maybe someday?" He meant it to be hopeful, but knew it sounded lame.

He shook his head and said, "I'm not angry at you, Bri."

Brian nodded. He did not know what to say to comfort him and knew it would be even more difficult than it was comforting Bobby. After all, Brett was the big brother, not just to Bobby but for all of them. It was Brett who was the leader, the protector, the planner.

"I know, Brett. I'm just ... sorry. For both you and Bobby."

He shrugged and said, "It's like Dad said. Nothing's changed. He's my dad. Mom is my mom. And you guys are my brothers."

Brian nodded. Brett sounded like it was rehearsed, like he was struggling to believe it himself.

Changing the subject, Brett asked, "You like Bobby?"

"I love Bobby. He's like the perfect little brother."

"But you *love* him love him?"

Brian hesitated and said, "It's complicated. Neither of us understand it. I like Cat." He emphasized, "I think about her, and I get a big ol' boner."

"But you love Bobby."

Brian shrugged. "Can't help it."

Brett caressed Brian's cheek and ran a thumb over his lips. "Just don't hurt him."

"Promise."

Brett kissed Brian's cheek, and said, "Or I'll have to hurt you."

Brett shook his head at something Brian did not understand, and then he shut his eyes. Brian snuck his arm under Brett, pulled Brett to him as he did each night with Bobby, and held him. He even brushed Brett's forehead with his lips and then kissed him.

"Bri?" Brett said with his eyes still closed.

"Yeah?"

Brett hesitated, kissed Brian's cheek, and said, "Nothing. Goodnight."

Brian was left wondering what Brett had wanted to say. As he thought about it, he felt Brett's tears on his arm, so he kissed his forehead again and held him until he was sure Brett was sound asleep.

Chapter Sixty-Six

Waukesha, WI

She had not gotten flowers from a guy since her senior year in high school, and that was a wrist corsage and a homely one at that. The bellman, or whatever you were supposed to call him, knocked on the door and gave her a dozen roses and a little card that said, *Thinking of you! Pat.*

Jo smiled, held and sniffed the roses, forgetting the hotel employee still standing in the doorway. She caught his impatience and said, "Oh, sorry," set the roses down on one of the beds, picked up her wallet and pulled out a five dollar bill. "Thank you," she said.

Jo shut the door after he had left and leaned against it. She picked up her roses, sniffed them again, and smiled. Her heart beat like a bass drum in her chest.

It had been a long, long time she felt this way about any guy. O'Connor made her toes curl. She shook her head and smiled broader until her face began to hurt.

Weist thought, *Okay, one good turn deserves another,* and sat down at her laptop and opened up Gmail.

Still smiling, she had promised that O'Connor and Eiselmann would be the first to receive her theory about the serial killer. She had received an email from the colleague at Quantico who agreed with her assessment. Alamorode, however, was more skeptical. She did not care because her colleague and her own intuition carried more weight.

Pat made them both spinach and tomato omelets with wheat bagels, washing it down with orange juice. They showered together, something she had never done before, with him making the same claim.

O'Connor had towered over her. Thin, but muscled. Quiet and gentle. Tender. The thought caused her to smile again, and she rubbed her face because it hurt.

She attached the Word doc that was sent to Rina Bota, six years her senior and who was another profiler with the FBI. The two females hung together, shared ideas, and formed a team in the male-dominated agency.

Bota had concurred with Weist's conclusion in total without any additions or corrections. Jo had felt confident when she had sent it and even more so when Bota responded the way she did. Jo had felt her reasoning was sound. Alamorode, however, wondered why someone would kill strangers over adoption, since the victims ranged wildly in age. It did not make sense to him. Her confidence was not shaken one bit. She knew she was onto something. She felt it as certainly as she knew she had fallen in love.

She cut and pasted Bota's comments in the body of email after a brief explanation from Weist. She decided to keep Alamorode's skepticism out of it.

Here is my theory. I think Brian and George nailed it. They matched my feelings when I read the notebook. Paul, check all the victims for anything pertaining to adoption. If they were adopted. Thinking about adoption. Were pro-adoption. Then look at anyone who held the belief that adoption disrupted the family unit. Any combination or connection. I'm willing to bet there is one. I realize it sounds like a stretch, and I'm not sure if it will catch the shooter, but it might lead us down the path. At the least, it could give us a reason. I pasted a colleague's comments into this also. I'll be at the station in thirty minutes, maybe less.

Jo

Satisfied, she sent it off hoping they would be on it before she arrived. Maybe even have some results.

Surprise and curiosity replaced satisfaction when there was another knock on her door.

Chapter Sixty-Seven

Waukesha, WI

O'Connor frowned and put his cell back into his pocket. He wondered why he had not heard from Weist after receiving the roses. He checked his watch and figured the flowers should have been delivered by now.

"Before we get started today, I have some good news to share," Graff said with a smile. "Our own Paul Eiselmann is engaged to Sarah Bailey, Stephen's mom."

"Oh, hey! Great news!" Summer said.

There was handshaking, high fives, and pats on the back all around among other congratulations by everyone in the room.

"Where are we celebrating?" Kelliher asked. "And when?"

"Tonight at Jake's Restaurant in Pewaukee. It's up the road from you on I-94 a couple of exits. I'll text you the address," Graff said.

Unable to concentrate on the conversation, O'Connor pulled out his cell and tried Weist again, but after a half-dozen rings, it went to voicemail. A tickle of fear traveled up his spine.

"Who's all going to be there?" Skip asked.

"About half the state, I think," Graff laughed. "Half the sheriff and police departments. Mikey Erickson's parents, Mark and Jennifer. Jeremy and Vicky. Jeff Limbach. Ellie Hemauer, you met her son Gav a summer or so ago. We've rented out a back room. We can order off the menu if you want. It's casual drop-in from six-thirty to nine."

"Sounds good," Summer laughed. "We'll all be there at some point, that's a promise." After everyone calmed down and settled themselves around the table, she said, "Okay, so where are we this morning?"

The picture obtained by Eiselmann and O'Connor from the UWM Human Resources department was popped up on a spilt screen broken in thirds. The middle picture showed the drawing that an artist created from Stan Loth's description after Jenna Meyers was murdered in Warnimount Park. The third picture was a still shot from the security video of the Shirley Bodencamp murder at her middle school. It was dark and grainy and not clear.

The cops stared at the three photos. Curiosity changed first to shock and then to anger on the faces sitting around the table. The similarities between the three photos were undeniable.

Batiste shook his head. Kelliher ran a hand over his face and then his flattop. Summer pursed her lips and would tilt her head first one direction and then the other, only to repeat it seconds later. Skip Dahlke squinted at the screen and flipped through notes of crime scenes. Neither Graff's eyes nor his face gave away anything. Because both of them were late to the investigation, Gonnering and Lorenzo sipped coffee and watched and listened without comment or question, though there were many both had wanted to ask.

"What else do you have?" Pete asked. He did not ask it unkindly, but he did ask it out of frustration, if not anger. He did not like to be duped.

Eiselmann's eyes shifted to O'Connor, but it was picked up by Batiste who also glanced at Pat.

"I contacted Morgan Billias because he could go places I couldn't."

Graff said, "I gave him permission. I hope that's okay with you."

Summer said, "Of course." She sounded stiff like it was not okay at all.

"We know he changed his name legally about four months after he resigned from UWM. He's now using his surname as his first name and his mother's maiden name as his last name. We don't know why he changed his name," Pat said. "I have a call into Dr. Jonathon Trapp, the professor Paul and I met with. I'm wondering if he might know why."

"We know his parents were killed in an explosion. A gas leak at their home. We know a sibling died a year previous in a car accident. There was suspicion that someone tampered with his brakes," Eiselmann said.

"We don't have any proof, but we think the deaths are connected," Pat said.

"So, this Dr. Bryce Miller and this Dr. Alan Nelson or whomever ..." Summer said not knowing where she intended to go with her thought.

She shifted in her chair. She stared at the screen, and then her piercing blue eyes shot daggers, first at Eiselmann and then at O'Connor, to the point that both blinked and looked away, Pat to the pictures on the screen and Paul to his laptop. "No one knows where either of them are. Allegedly."

"Miller disappeared. Morgan couldn't find any trace of him. As for Nelson ..." Eiselmann's voice trailed off.

"Seems like Nelson didn't disappear, did he?" Kelliher asked as he pushed his folder away from him.

"What else did you or Billias find?" Summer asked, a bit more gently.

It seemed to Eiselmann that she did not like being duped either. He said, "This Dr. Nelson or ..." something prevented him from saying his name out loud, "owns two vehicles. One is a dark navy-blue BMW. That was the type Loth identified in the Warnimount Park parking lot."

"The same model with the same tires Skip identified," O'Connor said.

"Huh," Kelliher said. It sounded more like a grunt.

"And he owns a .38," Eiselmann said.

"Same caliber as our shooter," Skip said.

The room went still. Folks shuffled papers, except for Kelliher who pushed his stack farther away. Eiselmann, O'Connor, and Graff exchanged uneasy glances. Graff shook his head. Gonnering and Lorenzo dared not utter a word, not in question or in comment, but they found the whole thing fascinating.

"I," Pat started. He stared at his cell and said, "Paul and I just got an email from Jo."

"Where is she?" Skip asked as he looked up. His pale white countenance had a blush to it.

"On her way. She figures thirty minutes or so," Eiselmann said as he checked his watch, "from ten minutes ago."

"She. She checked her work with someone in Quantico and with Alamorode," O'Connor said.

"Where is *he*?" Kelliher asked.

Graff and Eiselmann could not tell if the question was rhetorical.

"He hasn't checked in," Summer said. "We don't know from day to day when he can consult with us. Usually, we leave a message, and he returns the call or comes in."

"Convenient," Kelliher muttered.

Eiselmann frowned at his laptop.

"What?" Jamie asked.

Paul said, "All that shit Trapp talked about … nature versus nurture stuff."

"What about it?" Summer asked.

Eiselmann hit a couple of keys on the laptop and projected Weist's report up on the screen. He enlarged it to make it easier to read. "Let me know when you want me to scroll down."

It did not take long for Summer or Dahlke to reach the bottom of the screen. Batiste and Kelliher were a bit slower. Gonnering and Lorenzo supposed they should be reading along with them, so they did.

"Adoption?" Graff said.

"In the email she sent with this report, Jo asked me to take a look for anything in each of the victims' background related to adoption, like being adopted, having been adopted, having an interest in adoption, or promoting adoption. She feels the connection exists," Eiselmann said. He began to peck away on his laptop, searching files and jotting notes.

"It fits," O'Connor said.

"What? How?" Batiste asked.

"Dr. Trapp told us that Dr. Nelson and Dr. Miller would have long arguments about which had more of an impact, more influence on personality, nature or nurture," O'Connor said. "And then, what the boys told us about the poems in the notebook."

"Loneliness. Not fitting in," Batiste said.

"George and Brian both said that at times they felt like they were visiting, even intruding. Brian said that Michael Staley wrote about not fitting in. Not being a part of the family," Eiselmann said.

"Jo told me the same thing last night. She was adopted by her aunt and uncle after her parents died in a car accident. She said what George and Brian described was exactly how she felt," O'Connor added.

"Shit, Jo is right," Eiselmann popped up some names up on the screen. "Vincent O'Laughlin, the advertising guy, worked pro bono on an advertising campaign promoting adoption for Milwaukee County. Shirley Bodencamp, the middle school principal, served on the Milwaukee County Adoption Board." He looked up and said, "That's the same board the professor, Miller, sat on. Jenna Meyers, the jogger, was one of the case studies. She was adopted, and in the advertising campaign, she told her story and promoted adoption. And Gwen Fortune, the dental hygienist, promoted foster care. She made it out of the system."

Eiselmann looked up from his computer and said, "Of course, you already know about Michael Staley."

Stunned, the group sat trying to digest the information Eiselmann laid on them.

"If you want, I can find an adoption connection or something with all of the other victims, but I think it's all here," Eiselmann said.

"So he was adopted, and he's taking it out on others who support adoption or others who might have been adopted or people who were somehow involved in the foster system?" Batiste said, scratching his head. "What the hell?"

O'Connor shook his head and ran a hand through his long hair. "I think he might have been in a family who adopted. Whoever was adopted pushed everyone else out of the spotlight."

"He likes the spotlight," Skip said.

"Rendering everyone else second best," Summer said. She nodded and said, "Maybe."

"Like the sib who died in the car crash?" Gonnering asked.

All eyes turned toward him and then on each other.

"At the first briefing, Alamorode and Weist came up with an initial profile and said something about erasing the victim. Something like removing the victim like he was never there," Eiselmann said.

"I remember that," Skip said.

"May I ask a question?" Lorenzo asked.

All eyes shifted to him, and he squirmed like a perp in an interrogation room.

"What does this get us? I mean, does it matter why he's killing others? Don't we have enough to pick him up and question him?"

"First of all, determining the reason or the thinking in a shooter's mind doesn't necessarily help us find the shooter," Summer said. "But understanding the thinking could help us prevent other deaths."

"And right now, all we have are a series of suspicious coincidences," Pete added. "I don't believe in coincidence, so it would behoove us to put a tail on him."

Lorenzo nodded.

Kelliher looked around the room and said, "We need to keep the questions coming. Questions like this help all of us understand and could trigger a thought that would lead to the killer's capture or save a life."

Kelliher had learned through his teaching at the academy that New Agent Trainees or NATs as they were referred to, were reluctant to ask questions for fear of appearing stupid or *less than* in the eyes of their fellow trainees or instructors. It was the few who boldly asked questions who showed the most promise. Those few would grow to be the better agents within the bureau.

"Paul, do you and Pat have anything else?" Summer asked.

First Eiselmann and then O'Connor shook his head. O'Connor pulled out his cell and dialed up Jo Weist. After a couple of rings, it went to voicemail. He checked his watch and frowned.

"It's been longer than thirty minutes," Eiselmann said.

"You said she ran it by someone at Quantico," Skip said. "They're an hour ahead."

"But you also said she was going to pass it by Alamorode," Graff said.

"I'm going to the hotel to check on her," Pat said.

"I'll go with you," Batiste said.

Without asking, Gonnering and Lorenzo pushed back their chairs and left the room with them.

"Fuck!" Graff said at the closed door.

"We need to find Alamorode," Summer said to Eiselmann. "Get in touch with Billias if you have to, but we need to find him."

Chapter Sixty-Eight

Waukesha, WI

"Dr. Alamorode, you could have just returned my call. You didn't have to respond in person," Jo said as she stood in the doorway, a little flummoxed.

"Good morning, Agent Weist. Do you mind if I come in?"

He smiled and bowed.

"I was just about to head into Waukesha to the police department," Jo said still not budging from the doorway. "We could go there and talk as a group."

"You had an interesting theory, and I would like to discuss it with you before you present it to our team."

Their eyes locked, and neither backed down. He smiled charmingly, while she gathered her resolve, not understanding her own reluctance to let him in.

"Those are beautiful flowers, Agent Weist," Alamorode said.

She turned away for a second, and he strode past her and into her room, bumping her on his way through the doorway.

Annoyed, she stood holding the door open not wanting to follow him. Every instinct told her to leave. She watched Alamorode sniff the roses and glance at the open card. He then slipped off his leather gloves, his expensive looking overcoat and scarf, and sat down on the made bed.

Frustrated, but resigned, Weist shut the door, crossed the room, and with her back to him, put the card back into the envelope, gathered her roses, and set them on the console next to the TV. When she turned around, she leaned against the console with her arms folded and regarded him. She did not notice the .38 in his hand at first. When she did, she flushed and felt a finger of cold tickle the back of her neck.

"Why don't you sit in that chair by the desk and we'll talk," Alamorode said with a smile.

"I think I'll stand."

Alamorode waved his .38 a little and said, "I would like you to sit down."

"And if I don't?"

"You try to appear braver than you are, but you don't hide your fear well. It is unbecoming of you, Agent Weist. If you don't sit down, I will shoot you where you stand, and we won't get to talk. But as I said, I would like to hear your theory in person. It sounds interesting."

Jo's cell went off. It was on the desk behind the chair where Alamorode asked her to sit. Her eyes flashed in that direction and then back to Alamorode.

"We will just let that ring."

Weist decided that if she sat down, perhaps she could keep him talking long enough until someone arrived. After all, she had been expected at the station, and she was already late.

"What brought you to your conclusion?" Alamorode asked.

"Michael Staley initially. His notebook. Comments by others who had been adopted."

"Michael Staley kept a notebook." Alamorode nodded thoughtfully. He pursed his lips and said, "Adoption doesn't help kids as much as it hurts families. It splits them apart. It creates turmoil. It distances family members who had been happy and close-knit before the adoption."

"Are you describing adoption or your own sad life?"

"You're not qualified to analyze me, Agent Weist. You don't have the intelligence or the experience."

"Answer my question," Jo said with a smile, knowing she had struck gold. "I'm correct, aren't I?"

Alamorode gritted his teeth, and in a quiet, yet determined voice said, "My parents adopted a child who ruined our family. Michael Staley ruined his family. Those two other boys are ruining a fine family. Adoption ruins families."

Puzzled, Weist was not sure who he had referred to. An alarm of sorts went off, but she did not know what it signaled.

She said, "Did you speak to Michael Staley? His parents? His younger brother? I did. The only person who cared about Michael was his brother, Carson. That family was fucked up before Michael was placed there. He didn't deserve his parents or his sister. And he didn't deserve to be killed in an alley by a sociopath."

Alamorode smiled and said, "A sociopath? That's what you think I am?"

Weist remained still. She needed him to keep him talking. Just long enough.

"A sociopath doesn't care about anyone but him or herself. A sociopath doesn't have emotion or feeling. A sociopath is incapable of empathy. I care about the integrity of the family. All families."

"So you see yourself as serving a noble purpose, is that it?"

Alamorode smiled, cocked his head as if he studied a particularly pleasant painting, and said, "You disrespect me, Agent Weist. All I wanted to do was talk, and you needle me with pop psychology and gibberish."

Weist did not respond.

He waved his .38 as he spoke. "You wouldn't know about being forced to live with a stranger and having to call him my brother. You wouldn't know about having parents coddle and tiptoe and placate a perfect stranger. A stranger who was nothing but an ingrate who bullied and used everyone around him."

His chest heaved as he spoke, his face red, his words clipped. Like a switch was flipped, he smiled, and spoke evenly. In control, he said, "You simply can't comprehend. Not because you don't want to. Because you don't have a frame of reference."

Weist made the decision not to say anything about her own adoption. She knew how that might end. Instead, she said, "Help me understand, Doctor."

He smiled, cocked his head, and said, "I'm sorry, we have no more time. I have to pay another visit this morning. A blast from the past, pun intended. And then this evening, I have to pay another visit. This time, two to take care of. Busy, busy, busy. No, I'm afraid you are out of time."

The gun went off, the bullet striking Jo just below her sternum. The pain instant. At first, it was a punch to her stomach that sucked her breath away. And then burning, piercing pain.

Weist lurched backward, her hands grabbing her stomach, blood soaking her blouse. She tumbled out of the chair and collapsed on the floor, groaning and writhing in pain.

She opened her eyes in time to see Alamorode putting on his scarf and overcoat and then his leather gloves.

He smiled down at her and said, "It won't take long, Agent Weist. Relax and spiral into the darkness." He turned on his heel and left her room, closing the door behind him.

She struggled to keep consciousness. She fought the pain and growing numbness in her legs. Jo rolled to her side, crying out as she did so. In her mind, she was screaming for help, but in reality, she only murmured and groaned.

Realizing no help was forthcoming, she used her finger and her own blood to write as clear a message as she could on the carpet above her head. It was simple and direct, though the letters and numbers were jagged. She had hoped that whoever found her would not mistake it or mess it up before it could be deciphered.

And then darkness came and took her away.

Chapter Sixty-Nine

Waukesha, WI

O'Connor's cell had Bluetooth synced to his car radio. He phoned Weist again and again, and each time it went to voicemail.

He treated the surface streets like his personal Indy 500. The red flasher magnetically mounted to the roof just above his door did not help much. Laying on the car horn he sped through busy intersections, dodging side and oncoming traffic. Batiste rode shotgun with his hands in a death grip on the dash. Gonnering and Lorenzo drove behind him in a cruiser with siren and lights, and it helped, though because of Gonnering being cautious, they struggled to keep up.

The car hardly stopped moving before O'Connor and Batiste jumped out without shutting their doors. Flashing badges and side arms, they rushed the lobby.

"We need a key to room 315! Now!" Batiste yelled.

The few hotel visitors scattered to the far corners of the lobby, huddling in groups of two and three. The clerk behind the desk froze and did not move.

"I said, *Now!*"

The clerk grabbed a red plastic keycard and tossed it to Batiste.

Gonnering and Lorenzo raced in guns drawn.

O'Connor waved and shouted, "Greg, cover the lobby. Carlos, cover the parking lot. There's four ways in or out."

Pat took the stairs while Batiste rode the elevator. Gonnering ordered everyone to get into the back room behind the clerk's desk to minimize the potential for collateral damage and then knelt on one knee and his gun trained at the elevator while still being able to see the stairs O'Connor had raced up. Lorenzo positioned himself behind a small blue compact car in the parking lot, so he could see the back lot and the front lot. If Alamorode was still on site, he would have to drive right past him.

O'Connor was the first to reach the third floor and entered at the end of the hallway low, gun pointing out in front of him. From his position, room 315 would be thirteen doors down on the right. The elevator would be halfway down on the left.

Pat duck-walked down the hallway trying each door as he went. He heard the bell indicating that the elevator had reached its destination. O'Connor flattened himself low and against the wall, not wanting to risk an errant shot from his partner. Batiste stepped out of the elevator in a crouch, flashing his gun in both directions.

For a panicky moment, O'Connor thought Cleve would fire on him. O'Connor raised his open left hand and pointed down the hallway. Batiste nodded and moved to the left side of the hall with O'Connor moving up the right side. Both stayed low and tried each door along the way.

They reached room 315, and O'Connor moved to the right side of the door while Batiste stayed to the left.

O'Connor pounded on the door and said, "Jo, it's Pat. Are you all right?"

No answer. No sound.

"Jo, are you all right?" he repeated as he pounded again.

The neighbor across the hall heard the pounding and shouting and stuck his head out of his door. He was greeted by Pat's .45 and that sent him back inside. O'Connor heard the deadbolt click into place along with the safety chain.

O'Connor nodded at Batiste, who said, "Jo, it's Cleve and Pat. We're coming in."

He stuck the card in and out, the door flashed green, and Batiste shoved the door open. He charged through diving to his left. O'Connor entered low. He cleared the bathroom and the side of the bed.

Jo lay on her side unmoving and not breathing.

He rushed to her side, felt her neck for the carotid artery, hoping for any sign she was still alive, but knowing she would not be. There was too much blood on the floor.

"Fuck! Fuck!" O'Connor sat back against the end of the bed and ran a hand through his long hair. "Jesus *Christ*!"

Batiste had already spotted Jo's crude message, and though he had no trouble reading it, he did not understand it.

O'Connor watched Batiste take out his cell and snap a picture. At first, rage boiled up, and he wanted to tear the FBI agent apart. But then, he focused on why Batiste took the picture and, on all fours, crept closer to get a better look.

"Get this to Eiselmann," O'Connor said.

He pulled out his own cell and called Graff.

"Get Skip here with his kit. Tell Paul an email with a picture is coming his way. He needs to get on it. We need someone at Alamorode's place right away."

Jamie did not have to ask how Weist was. He knew.

Chapter Seventy

Waukesha, WI

Gonnering commandeered the security camera system and ran it backward past O'Connor's and Batiste's arrival on the third floor to the time to see Alamorode exit Weist's hotel room. According to the time stamp on the screen, the time differential was sixteen minutes between O'Connor and Batiste's arrival on the third floor and Alamorode leaving Weist's room.

Next, he ran the outside camera backward from the point where O'Connor's car drove into the parking lot and when they got out of the car to where they saw Alamorode exit the hotel and get into his navy-blue BMW. The time stamp showed eleven minutes.

"Could be the difference using the elevator, but I'll check that too."

So Gonnering used the camera system to follow Alamorode out of Weist's room, to the elevator, in the elevator on the ride down with one stop on the second floor, and through the lobby to the parking lot.

He shook his head and said, "It has to be the elevator time differential."

Lorenzo said, "We missed him by sixteen minutes, depending upon how you look at it."

"It doesn't matter, we missed him, and he got away."

Gonnering borrowed a DVD and burned all three videos to it and then added the best still picture of Alamorode from the video to positively ID him.

"The thing is," Lorenzo said, "we have him. We have him in her room. We don't have any camera showing anyone else entering her room after or before he left. In fact, before Alamorode, the only person who enters Weist's room is Weist. The only ones who enter Weist's room after Alamorode are O'Connor and Batiste."

"You're right," Gonnering said. "We have him."

"Call it in to Graff."

Gonnering took out his cell, dialed him up, and explained what he had on film.

"Don't lose chain of custody, Greg. Hang onto it until you bring it to the station."

"We have an evidence bag in the cruiser. We'll make sure it's official."

"Interview anyone in the lobby. Include the workers behind the counter or anyone else in the lobby who might have seen him. Maybe use the print of the picture from the camera system and show it around."

"Will do, Jamie. Carlos and I will walk her hall and knock on doors after we finish with the lobby."

"How is Pat doing?" Graff asked.

Gonnering considered the question and said, "Hard. There was something between them."

"That's what Paul said. Keep an eye on him, okay?"

"Will do."

In Weist's room, O'Connor and Batiste were careful not to touch anything because they knew what they had and did not want to screw anything up for Skip Dahlke. Both of them wanted it airtight against Alamorode.

To any question Batiste asked or any comment he made, O'Connor either ignored him or grunted a response.

Other sheriff deputies showed up. Two directed traffic in and out of the hotel. Two stationed themselves at either end of the corridor to limit foot traffic.

After Dahlke showed up with the Waukesha coroner in tow, everything was matter-of-fact and by the book. Dahlke barked orders at everyone, including the coroner, Mike Eisenhower, who everyone called Ike. He was in his sixties and bald except for a fringe of snow- white hair that ran around the sides and back of his head like a misplaced halo. Ike was short and a little stooped, but his mind was clear and sharp.

Ike let the barking slide because he knew everyone was on edge when a cop was killed.

284 Spiral Into Darkness

At one point, Dahlke sat down on the edge of the bed and hung his head and wrung his hands.

"Son, it won't get better, but you'll live with it," Ike said with a gentle hand on his shoulder.

Dahlke could recite from memory the nightmares, both awake and asleep, he had about the naked boys he had worked on, tortured, beaten, branded, and finally executed with two shots to the back of the head. He could have told him about the Chicago warehouse where twelve and thirteen-year-old boys were forced into prostitution and how Brett McGovern took a bullet saving Pete Kelliher's life. He could have, but he did not. He did not bother to share any of it because words could not match the horror show that played on a continuous loop each time he shut his eyes, or anytime he relaxed enough to let the ugly memories seep into his conscious.

Instead, Skip said, "I know."

After a little more than two hours, Weist's body was zipped into a black body bag. The room had been dusted for prints, but O'Connor, Batiste, and Dahlke did not think they would find Alamorode's. Trace fiber and hair was found, which may or may not match Alamorode, but they would tag it and bag it and file it for a court date, should one come their way.

"Where to now?" Batiste asked O'Connor.

He shook his head, shrugged, ran a hand through his hair, and walked away. Batiste followed him with Gonnering and Lorenzo bringing up the tail.

Chapter Seventy-One

Milwaukee, WI

Dr. Jonathon Trapp leaned back in his leather chair puffing on his pipe. He wore a beige cardigan sweater with a white button-down shirt, collar open, and olive-green corduroy slacks. Typical for him, he arrived early in the morning to his office, though his posted office hours were not until late morning before his one o'clock class. A widower, his house was too empty, and he liked the company of his colleagues and his students. He reasoned that it was the students who had kept him young.

He pondered O'Connor's question that came earlier that morning in a phone call. A question to which Trapp did not have a satisfactory explanation. The truth was that Dr. Alan Nelson, or Dr. Nelson Alamorode, if that is what he was going by now, were not that close even though they worked in the same department and had offices just down the hallway from one another.

Trapp had admired Nelson's mind, the logic with which he approached debate and discussion. But aside from that, Nelson was, well, not friendly with anyone other than Bryce Miller. To think that Nelson might have had something to do with Miller's disappearance was disconcerting.

Lost in thought, he never heard him enter. It was the closing of the door and the lock clicking into place that made him turn in that direction.

"Hello, Jonathon."

Trapp withdrew his pipe, and his face grew pale. He tried to smile, but gave up.

"Alan. Or Nelson. Whatever your name is."

Nelson cocked his head and smiled, though it was as cold as a Wisconsin winter.

"So, you know. The question is, who else knows?"

Trapp did not bother to obfuscate with any answer that would be false. He did not want to answer the question at all.

"How did you find out?" Alamorode asked, choosing a different path.

Trapp puffed on his pipe.

"Not bothering with small talk, are we?"

Trapp shook his head and said, "What did you do to Bryce Miller?"

"We both know the answer to that."

"Why, Nelson? How could you?"

Alamorode smiled. It was dark and made Trapp's stomach lurch.

"How could I?" he laughed dryly. "It was easy. Easier than I thought it would be. I pointed a gun, aimed, and pulled the trigger."

"But why?" Trapp was incredulous and beyond words.

"Because he didn't get it. He couldn't get it because he wasn't that bright."

Trapp shook his head and said, "Get what?"

"It doesn't matter anymore. It was years ago. We disagreed. He wasn't bright, but he didn't realize it, and no one else did either. He inspired others with his beliefs because they weren't very bright. And the rest, they didn't matter because they caused damage and destruction with every breath they took."

"What are you talking about?" Trapp said. He shook his head because Nelson made no sense.

Alamorode chuckled and said, "I never thought you were that smart either, Jonathon."

"I think you should leave, Nelson. We don't have anything to talk about," Trapp said. Ignoring him, he turned to his desk and shuffled some papers.

"That's rather rude, wouldn't you say?"

Trapp did not answer. In fact, he picked up a pen and began reading one of his student's papers, adding comments in the margins.

Alamorode stepped up behind him, placed one hand on his chin, the other on the back of his head, and twisted violently. He heard something snap.

He set Trapp's head on his left forearm as though he was napping at his desk. He extinguished his pipe and turned off the desk lamp. On his way out of the office, he turned off the overhead light, pushed the lock on the handle of the door, and shut it, locking everyone else out and Trapp in.

Satisfied, he left the building he had worked in so many years ago. He did not encounter anyone on his way out except for groups of students who did not bother looking up from their cell phones.

He left by the side door of the building that led to the faculty lot, got into his car, and drove away satisfied, already planning his next two kills.

Chapter Seventy-Two

Waukesha, WI

After Summer's press conference naming Nelson Alamorode as a person of interest in the killings in the Milwaukee Metro Area, she, Pete, Graff, and Skip left with a warrant to search Alamorode's home. None of them expected to find much of anything, but the search needed to be done. That left O'Connor, Eiselmann, and Batiste back at the Waukesha police station to come up with the answer to Jo Weist's cryptic message.

Frustrated, Eiselmann slapped the table with the palm of his hand and shoved his chair backward. He raised a fist and rested his chin on it. His eyes blazed as he stared at his computer. He had performed several searches using multiple search engines, and they came back with the same answer each time.

"The thing is, if it's about murders, I checked the timeline, and there isn't anything recorded for one in the morning. As for two in the afternoon, there are several that are close, but nothing at two. I have no clue what she was trying to tell us."

Eiselmann had the message up on the screen. Each of the men frowned at it, willing it to tell them something.

1 A.M.
2 P.M.

Batiste read it out loud once again. "One AM over two PM."

"It doesn't matter which search engine I use, each time it comes back to one in the morning and two in the afternoon," Eiselmann groused. "I don't know where else to look."

"Could it be a time range of some kind? Like between the hours of one in the morning to two in the afternoon?" Batiste asked.

"No, because several murders occurred outside that range," Eiselmann said.

"Yes, but that was in the past. What if she meant to warn us of something about to happen?"

Eiselmann shrugged and said, "It's possible, I guess. But we don't know who or where."

Throughout this whole exchange, O'Connor had remained quiet. Brooding, angry, but frustrated and sad. He had liked Weist. So much had been taken from him over time. This was one more loss, and it was perhaps the cruelest.

"What was the name of the agent Jo checked with in Quantico?" Batiste asked.

"Rina Bota," O'Connor mumbled. "She's a profiler. Like Jo."

"Don't know her," Batiste said. "Skip might because he works there."

Brow furrowed and jaw set, O'Connor grabbed the phone and dialed her up, and she answered after three rings. O'Connor switched from a private call to a conference call.

They heard someone clearing her throat and then a soft, "Bota."

"Rina Bota?" O'Connor asked.

"Yes, who is this?"

"This is Sheriff Detective Pat O'Connor. With me is Sheriff Detective Paul Eiselmann and Cleveland Batiste with ViCAP."

"What can I help you with?" she asked, clearing her throat again.

Batiste took over and said, "I assume you know about Agent Jo Weist."

There was some hesitation and then a small, "Yes."

"I'm sorry. I know the two of you were friends."

"What is it you want?" Bota answered regaining her professionalism.

Eiselmann said, "If you give me your email address, I'm going to send you a picture of something Jo ... Agent Weist left us. We'd like you to look at it and see if you have any ideas what she might have meant by it."

"Okay, I can try."

She gave them her email address, and Eiselmann sent her the picture, saying, "You should have it."

They heard her tapping her keyboard. After, there was a short pause. O'Connor had hoped Bota would not recognize it was written in blood but figured she would be too good not to.

"I don't understand how this is difficult for you," Bota responded. "I read it as one o'clock in the morning and two o'clock in the afternoon."

Eiselmann sighed and shook his head. O'Connor dropped into a chair and stared off in space.

"Can you think of anything else she might have meant with that message?" Batiste asked.

"No. Jo is ... was always matter-of-fact. Pretty much straightforward."

"Did Jo share anything else with you when she sent her theory on the killings?"

"No, she didn't. She wanted me to look over the theory she had. I did, and I agreed with it. I found her thinking solid and insightful. But that is ... was typical."

"Anything else you can share? Anything you might be able to give us?" Batiste asked, already knowing her answer.

"No, I wish I could. I wish I could give you something that would help you catch this son-of-a-bitch, but I don't have anything."

"If it's any consolation, we know who it is. We just have to find him before he kills again."

"If you have an opportunity to shoot him, do so. The world would be better off. There's no death penalty in Wisconsin. I looked it up."

They ended the call, and O'Connor stood up and slipped into his jacket.

"Where are you headed?" Eiselmann asked.

"Out."

"Want company?" Batiste asked.

O'Connor let the slamming of the door answer for him.

Chapter Seventy-Three

Waukesha, WI

When George was twelve and in science class back on the reservation, he had his first vision of many that would follow. This was not an unusual occurrence given who his grandfather was or the training he had undertaken.

The first time, he saw wavy lines, what looked like heat waves. The distance shimmered. He was not sure what was happening, and it frightened him a little. His teacher, Forest Crandall, an older man who was a little stooped, did not know what to make of it. Neither did his best friend, Rebecca, who had been sitting at the same lab station and who knew him better than anyone besides his grandfather.

George had never heard them asking him what was wrong or if he was sick. He never felt Crandall shaking his shoulder. It was not until he had returned home from school and had an opportunity to speak to his grandfather did he find out that his grandfather had had a similar vision that same afternoon.

On this day, George sat at his desk in English class writing in his journal from the warm-up prompt on the board when he felt it coming. Knowing what was happening, he stopped writing, put his pen down, and then rested his head on his forearms on the desk. He shut his eyes, controlled his breathing, and let it roll.

He was floating with snowflakes above the trees looking down at his house and the woods that separated their property from the stable and Uncle Jeff Limbach's property. George was not sure what he should be looking at or searching for, but as he drifted closer to the ground, he found himself walking in the woods with his back to the highway. He was with someone, but he did not recognize who it was. One of the dogs was with him ... them. Momma.

They carried rifles as if they were hunting, but it was not hunting season. Were they searching for something, for someone? If so, what or who?

Theresa Ebersol touched his shoulder, bent low, and whispered, "George, do you need to go to the nurse?"

At first, like old Mr. Crandall, George did not feel it and did not hear her. She shook him and said, "George, are you okay?"

George raised his head, smiled weakly, and said, "May I go see my father?"

"Not the nurse?"

Awake, George smiled and said, "My father please, if that is okay with you."

"Can you make it by yourself or would you like someone to go with you?"

"I can go by myself. Thank you."

Worried, Ebersol wrote a note in George's agenda.

George left his books and backpack at his desk but grabbed his cell from his backpack. As he stood up, he weaved, took a step, and stumbled. He regained his balance and walked out of the classroom.

"Troy, would you walk with George to the guidance office, please?"

Troy Rivera, who was one of George's and the boys' friends and center on the basketball team, caught up to George, and together they walked out of the classroom.

They made it to the guidance area and entered.

"Hi, George. Hi, Troy," Kristi said with a smile. "What can I do for you?"

To George, Troy said, "If you don't come back by the end of class, I'll bring your stuff to the cafeteria at lunch."

"Thanks."

Troy left and went back to class but texted Brett, Brian, Randy, and Billy before he walked in the classroom.

Kristi looked up expectantly.

"May I see my father?"

"Yup, he's free or reasonably cheap," Kristi said with a laugh. "Go on in."

"Thank you."

George walked through the guidance area, empty except for three guidance student aides sitting at one of the round tables near Kristi's desk, and knocked on Jeremy's door.

"George? What's up?"

George entered, shut the door, and sat down in one of Jeremy's chairs.

"Father, I just had a vision." He went on to explain what had happened and what he saw. Throughout the telling, George was emotionless and explained it as one would describe an everyday occurrence, like doing the dishes or folding the laundry.

Jeremy listened, and when George finished, he said, "Was your grandfather with you? Did he say anything to you?"

"No. I was with someone, but I do not know who."

"Was it one of the guys?"

George considered that question but did not want to embellish on what the vision showed him. "Possibly, but I do not know for sure."

"And you were in our woods?"

"Yes."

"What was the dog doing?"

George shook his head and said, "Walking with us. She was not on alert. At least not that I could tell."

Jeremy thought for a minute and said, "I don't know what to make of it, George. I wish I was better at this for you."

George smiled and said, "I felt I needed to tell you, Father. If something else happens, I will tell you."

As he got up to go back to class, there was a knock on the door. Both turned and through the door panel saw O'Connor.

Jeremy opened it, frowned, and said, "Hi Pat."

O'Connor saw George and said, "Could I get the two of you to look at something for me?"

"Sure," Jeremy answered for both of them.

There was a little commotion in the outer office as the twins, Brian, and Brett came through the door and walked straightaway to Jeremy's office.

"You okay, George?" Billy asked.

"I am fine."

The boys looked doubtfully at George, and then looked at Jeremy hoping for an explanation. It was not until then that they noticed O'Connor.

"What's going on?" Brett asked.

"Guys, let's go to the conference room," Jeremy said, ushering everyone out of his office to the conference room around the corner.

The boys walked in and sat down and like they watched a tennis match, looked from Jeremy to O'Connor waiting for an explanation. Jeremy deferred to Pat.

"I was wondering if you'd look at something and tell me what it might mean."

Without any other explanation, he pulled out his cell phone, brought up the picture of Jo's note, enlarged it a bit, and set it on the table.

Brett was the first to reach for it while the other boys crowded around to see it.

"That's blood," Brett said.

O'Connor said nothing.

"Pretty easy, I think. One o'clock in the morning and two o'clock in the afternoon," Randy said.

The others remained quiet. Jeremy looked over the top of Brian and shrugged agreement.

George, Brian, Brett, and Billy said nothing, and it was noted by O'Connor.

"What are you guys thinking?"

"If that's blood, I think it means more than that. It's too simple otherwise," Brett said.

"What if ..." Billy said as he picked up the phone to look at it closer. "When my dad had to take pills like his heart medicine and his cholesterol pills, the prescription said something like one in the morning and one at night."

Picking up the thought, Brian said, "After Brad died, my mom had to take a sedative, and the bottle said the same thing."

"So what if the message is one in the morning and two in the afternoon or two in the evening, but not like a clock," Billy said.

"You mean, there's one in the morning, and there will be two in the afternoon or evening," Brett said.

The boys looked up at O'Connor, who ran a hand through his hair and stared off in the distance.

"Pat?" Brian asked.

Pat waved him to be quiet as his mind raced. If the boys were correct, it meant that one person would die at some point this morning and two more either this afternoon or evening. Yes, Jo's message was matter-of-fact and clear. The cops just did not read it correctly.

"I have to go," Pat said as he snatched his phone off the table and cleared the doorway.

"I guess we were right?" Billy asked as he shrugged his shoulders.

George met Jeremy's eyes and gave him a slight but definite shake of his head. Just one. He wanted the two of them to keep the vision to themselves for the time being.

Chapter Seventy-Four

Waukesha, WI

O'Connor's conference call to Summer, Pete, Skip, and Graff on Jamie's cell caused quite the stir. Eiselmann and Batiste were already searching for any missing or murdered individuals for that morning but could not find any that matched the search elements involving adoption or any variation of the word.

"If you and the boys are right," Pete said, "someone will die in the next ten minutes or so."

"Unless someone is already dead and hasn't been discovered," Summer said.

"Pat, where are you now?" Jamie asked.

"I'm heading to UWM to talk to Dr. Trapp face-to-face. He hasn't gotten back to me after my initial phone call this morning. He told me he'd think about it and get back to me. And I know he doesn't have class until early in the afternoon."

"Keep us posted on what you find out," Summer said.

The call ended, and the four of them continued to search Alamorode's home, ending in the office area of the living room.

"One thing about this prick is that he's a clean freak," Pete said.

"He's more than a clean freak," Skip said. "He's obsessive-compulsive. I'd bet a paycheck on it. There's nothing out of place. His closet is textbook. Look at his desk. Everything neat, nothing out of place. The whole apartment is like that."

Each wore latex gloves, and the four of them marveled at how neat and tidy the desk was. At last, Pete stepped around the desk, sat down in the chair, and tried to put himself in the mind of a killer. He did not touch anything right away, but took everything in.

"What's that saying about a neat desk being a sign of a psychotic?" Pete asked.

"Neat desk or not, Alamorode is psychotic as hell, if not a sociopath," Summer said.

"Hmmm," Pete said frowning at the drawers.

"What?" Graff said.

"For a neat freak, you'd expect nothing out of place, right?"

Summer, Graff, and Skip walked around to look at the drawers. The bottom drawer was open while the others were shut tight. Odd for someone who was as fastidious as Alamorode was.

Kelliher slid the drawer open not knowing what was in it. He found two one-inch black three-ring binders. One was a ledger of sorts containing dated entries of office visits and payments.

"Shit, he makes more money in two visits than I make in a week," Graff said.

Summer added, "We need to check his account information, maybe see if he has a bank deposit box."

Pete set aside the first binder and looked through the second. It was similar to the first except for the dates were older.

"In this age of computers and spreadsheets," Summer said, "why is he recording everything on paper and pen? Not even a pencil. Pen."

"Wish Jo was here," Skip said. "She could tell us."

"Would Jeremy have any ideas?" Pete asked.

"Maybe," Summer said. "It's a little out of his area of expertise, though."

Pete placed both binders on the desktop and bent low to search the drawer, but found nothing.

Jamie said, "Something was in that drawer that was important enough for him to take, and when he did, he didn't care enough to shut the drawer completely."

Chapter Seventy-Five

Milwaukee, WI

Sirens sang their discordant melody as Graff and O'Connor arrived at UWM at the same time. They parked in the visitor lot and joined the parade of students bundled up in down jackets, gloves or mittens, and scarfs and weighed down with backpacks as they trudged to and from their classes. The weather felt wet and cold with an icy wind blowing in off Lake Michigan.

"Shit, it's cold," Graff said.

His head down, shoulders hunched, O'Connor grunted something unintelligible. His mind was on Jo Weist and what Trapp might tell him about Nelson changing his name to Alamorode. He had his own thoughts on the answer but wanted to verify his thinking with the professor.

They reached the building where psychology was taught and where the professor had his office and saw a flurry of police and security personnel moving in and out of the building.

"This doesn't look good," Graff muttered.

They walked up to a young Milwaukee Sheriff Deputy, flashed their creds, and Graff said, "Can you tell us what happened?"

Uneasy, the cop looked around to see who was within earshot and said, "An older professor died. Not sure how. I heard broken neck."

"Broken neck?" Graff asked. It did not make sense.

The cop nodded and said, "Found sitting at his desk. One of the professors thought he might be sleeping and left him alone. A student came in for office hours, checked on him, called his name, and shook him, and that's how they discovered he was dead." He looked around and muttered, "That's what I heard anyway."

There was no doubt in O'Connor's mind who the professor was and who had murdered him.

They entered the building and had to flash their badges a couple of times to get to Trapp's floor and into his office. Graff had wanted to call Skip Dahlke to have him run the scene, but there were so many cops and security crammed in the office, it would not pay.

O'Connor exploded. "What the fuck? Do you realize this is a crime scene and all of you fucked it up? Jesus Christ! Assholes!"

"Who the fuck are you?" an older cop asked as he strode over to him.

"Someone who knows how to run a fucking crime scene!"

Graff stepped in between the two of them before they came to blows and said, "We're working with the FBI task force on the serial killings. I'm Detective Jamie Graff, and this is Detective Pat O'Connor. Can you tell us what happened here?" When no one said anything, and it did not look like the older cop was going to back down, he added, "Please?"

Graff held his ground as did both O'Connor and the older cop, but a younger guy stepped up and said, "This is Dr. Jonathon Trapp. He died from a broken neck, and we think he was murdered."

"You think?" O'Connor said.

"Listen, smart ass," the older cop said. "We don't need your help."

Graff ignored both of them and said, "Do you have any security cameras in this building?"

The younger cop said, "Yes, there are."

"If we can see them, we can check to see who murdered him and see if it's our guy."

The younger guy stepped up in front of the older guy and said, "I can show you where the office is. I used to work here in security."

Graff guided O'Connor out of the room, and the younger cop followed up from behind just in case a fist might be thrown.

They walked down two flights of stairs to the security office. It was not manned at the moment, so the young cop, Travis Bickel, sat down at the controls, fiddled with the keyboard, and ran it backward to where the student had found him.

"If you run it back from there, we should be able to see the first guy stop and check on him," Graff said.

Bickel did just that. They watched the man knock on the door, try the knob, use a key to open it, and stand just inside the office. He never fully entered. Then he left. The young cop froze it so Graff and O'Connor could take a good look at him and waited until first one and then the other shook his head.

"Who is that?" O'Connor asked. He was not that interested, but thought he would ask.

Bickel shrugged and said, "Don't know him."

"He had to unlock the door," O'Connor said. "Have someone dust the handle for prints, especially if the lock is a button lock."

Bickel called up to the office, spoke with someone, and relayed O'Connor's message.

"Okay, run it back further to see who shows up before him," Graff said.

Bickel ran it back in almost slow motion until Graff saw Alamorode leave the office and shut the door behind him.

"There! Can you freeze it?" O'Connor said.

When Bickel did, O'Connor said, "That's him."

"And no one came near that door after he came out," Graff added.

"Wait, I know him," Bickel said. "He worked here. What's his name?" Bickel snapped his fingers and said, "Nelson, I think. I can't think of his first name."

"Alan," Graff said. "Alan Nelson."

"Yeah, that's right. He taught psychology. And there was another guy, Miller or something. He disappeared. I remember it. I was one of the security guys who brought the Milwaukee cops to interview Nelson."

"Bryce Miller," O'Connor said.

"Yeah," Bickel said. His face registered the proverbial light turning on. "Wait, is this all related?"

"Maybe," Graff said. "Perhaps. We aren't sure."

"Well, shit! I never liked the guy. Pompous, arrogant ass."

O'Connor and Graff exchanged a look over Bickel's head as he worked the security system.

"Can you tell us about the relationship between Miller and Nelson?" O'Connor asked.

"Everyone thought they were friends," the young cop said.

"But not you," Graff said.

Bickel shook his head and said, "Naw, I sure didn't. They argued. It wasn't just school stuff."

"What kind of stuff?" O'Connor asked.

Bickel hesitated and then said, "Miller was on some county board that promoted foster care and adoption. I remember Nelson arguing that what Miller was doing was hurting families. I never understood why, but that's what they argued about. Miller thought he was doing a service for both parents who couldn't have children or wanted more children and kids who didn't have a home."

"And they argued about that?" Graff said.

"Not many folks know about this, but one night in the parking lot, they got into a shoving match."

"How did it end?" O'Connor asked.

"A couple of students were in the lot heading to their cars. The two saw them, and they stopped."

"Simple as that?" Graff said.

"Yeah, that was it."

"But you remembered it," O'Connor said.

Bickel licked his lips and said, "A couple of weeks later, Miller ends up missing. No one knows where he is. Just ... gone."

"What are your thoughts on that?" Graff asked.

"I'd rather not say," Bickel said.

"Because ..." O'Connor said.

Bickel twisted around in his chair, gestured with his hands, and said, "I thought it was odd. I don't believe in coincidences. Miller invited Nelson to join him on the foster or adoption board, whatever you call it. But I never got the feeling they liked each other."

"Did you know if Nelson joined the board?" Graff asked.

"Not sure, but I think so," Bickel answered with a shrug.

"Do you know the name of this board?" O'Connor asked.

"No, but I think it's a Milwaukee County thing. You might be able to Google it," Bickel said.

They ran the camera back and saw Alamorode look both ways in the hallway before he slipped into Trapp's office. According to the time stamp, he stayed in Trapp's office for a total of twenty-two minutes and forty-eight seconds. They watched him step out of the office, but before he did, he again looked both ways, shut the door, and speed-walked down the hall to the stairwell.

"Nelson was the only one to enter the office for any length of time before the guy stuck his head in the office to check on Trapp and when the student found him," Bickel said.

"You sound pleased," O'Connor said.

"Nelson is a prick. I couldn't stand him."

"Can you get us a copy of that video, please?" Graff said. He handed him a card and said, "My email address is on this card. You can send it to me."

Bickel rummaged through one drawer and then another, found a DVD, held it up to show Graff, and said, "I'll burn you a copy now and send a copy to your email."

Less than ten minutes later, Graff and O'Connor left the building and headed to the parking lot. They had asked Bickel to type up a statement of the conversation they had with him, what he saw on the video system, and any other thoughts he might have and send it to Graff via email.

O'Connor leaned against the front of Graff's car as a few weak flurries fell from dark gray clouds. He stood with his head down and arms folded.

"What?"

"I'm thinking Jo was spot on. One kill in the morning."

Graff nodded and said, "That means Alamorode might have told her who he was going after. The thing is, the type of death in Jo's case and Trapp's case isn't consistent with the deaths of his other victims. In each of those cases, his victims were shot in the face. In Jo's case, she was shot just below the sternum and bled out. In Trapp's case, his neck was broken."

"Perhaps because they weren't tied to his original agenda. I'm guessing Jo never told him she was adopted when she was a kid, because if she did, Alamorode would have shot her in the face." O'Connor shook his head and said, "He didn't know it. And I think Trapp was just a loose end."

"Which leads us to two more deaths either this afternoon or evening. Will they be loose ends, or will he be back on his agenda and somehow be related to adoption or foster care?"

Chapter Seventy-Six

Waukesha, WI

He had watched the press conference as it had been broadcast, so he knew he had to lay low. They were actively looking for him.

He bought himself a pair of plain glasses without any correction, a navy-blue watch cap, and an oversized navy-blue down jacket. He did not need nor want the jacket since he had a sleek form-fitting black North Face with matching black leather gloves. He reasoned that if he kept his head covered, the glasses on, and was swallowed up by the heavy down jacket, he would be safe. At least invisible in plain sight. After all, most people were ignorant and did not pay attention to anything or anyone beyond their own cell phones.

On a whim, he headed for a matinee. Alamorode thought of motion pictures as a waste of time, but he wanted a quiet dark spot to take a nap. The rest would do him good because he would be up late taking care of the next two names on his list before he left for another section of the country to begin a new life.

Chapter Seventy-Seven

Waukesha, WI

The snow came down in big, wet flakes. At first, it did not stick to the ground but instead melted on contact. And then as if the earth said, "Screw it," the amount of snow grew. Inches so far, but George guessed they might end up with a foot or two. For Wisconsinites, one or two feet of snow was no big deal, although schools and businesses might be delayed or closed. Maybe. Every kid's wish, even George's. That way, they could go sledding or have a snowball fight.

For a kid who grew up in the desert, snow was both mysterious and a delight. He could sit for hours and watch snow fall. He would catch snowflakes in his hand or on his arm and study them, marvel at them. He would smile.

On this day however, he did not care about snowflakes. He did not care how much snow would accumulate. Restless and anxious, he spent time in the woods separating the Limbach property from the Evans property after they had returned from school and practice. He had started on the shoulder of the highway facing the woods. He did not enter right away, but studied it looking for a path, any path. He did not see one. At least one that showed itself.

At last, he made his way in. Bending this way and that as he avoided breaking brittle limbs and twigs. He looked for footprints as if they would magically appear before him as they did in his dream. In his dream, he did not see footprints. If there were footprints, they would be swallowed up by the rapidly falling snow.

After an hour and covered with snow and disappointment, he made his way back to the house. He beat the snow off his head, his shoulders, and his pants. He stamped his feet on the stoop and bent down to loosen the laces to make them easier to slip off. He entered the mudroom by the back door. He peeled off his jacket and hung it up on the peg on the wall. He threw his scarf, hat, and gloves in the dryer to dry them off. He walked into the kitchen and joined the rest of his family, though he stayed on the fringe and out of the fray.

"Jeff is bringing Danny over and then your dad, Jeff, and I are going to Paul's and Sarah's engagement party," Vicky said. "We won't be too late, but make sure your homework is done. If anyone needs to shower, you want to do it early enough so you're not up too late. And Danny is welcome to spend the night if he wants."

"What are we going to have for dinner?" Billy asked.

"I'm making pasta with garlic bread and a salad," Brett announced. "You can help with the salad."

"What about dessert?" Brian asked.

"Bobby doesn't know it yet, but he's going to bake a chocolate cake, and Randy's going to frost it," Brett said with a laugh.

"A cake?" Bobby asked.

"Yup, chocolate," Brian said.

"Okay, I can do that."

"What cake?" Jeremy asked as he walked into the kitchen.

"The one in the box in the cupboard," Billy said.

"Oh, that one," Jeremy said, sounding disappointed.

"If you're a good boy, we might save you a piece," Randy said. "Not sure about the ice cream because George might eat all of it."

"How is this going to work tomorrow ... I mean, the adoption thing?" Brian asked.

Vicky had noticed that Brian had grown more unsettled as the afternoon wore on. A little more pensive than normal. Less talkative, if that was even possible. He fidgeted, could not sit still, and wandered from room to room ever since he had gotten home from basketball practice. Bobby broke down and gave him two chocolate chip cookies, thinking that might settle him down. It did not. In fact, he ate one and gave the other to Billy.

"We're going to school in the morning. You boys will come to the guidance center after second period, and we'll meet mom at the courthouse," Jeremy said.

"Then we go into the courtroom and you get convicted of being a dork," Billy said jumping in to help with the story.

"But right after that, you become an official member of the family," Randy said.

"But you'll still be a dork," Billy added.

"Goes without saying," Randy said.

"Any other questions?" Billy asked.

George watched Brett and Bobby during the exchange, but their expressions never betrayed the sadness both of them felt. He knew they were sad. He and Brett talked about it, just like Bobby had talked to Brian about it. However, Vicky being their mom and Jeremy being their dad and a counselor knew them better than anyone.

They heard Jeff pull up in his big Suburban. He kept the SUV running as he and Danny rang the back doorbell. Randy answered it and let them in.

"You two set?" Jeff asked.

Danny shed his jacket, hung it up, and threw his backpack in the hallway.

The boys lined up and gave hugs and kisses to Jeremy and Vicky. Jeff received them also, since the boys considered him to be their uncle, and the three adults left the house to the seven boys.

Chapter Seventy-Eight

Pewaukee, WI

There were three distinct groups at Eiselmann's and Sarah Bailey's party at Jake's Restaurant. One group consisted of those outside the tight circle investigating the serial murders. They partied hard and knocked back what seemed like barrels of beer and dozens of shots. The hors d'oeuvres did not last more than an hour, and when they disappeared, food was ordered by those who were hungry, and most of them were. There was laughter and stories that landed on a scale between false and improbable. Eiselmann was embarrassed and Sarah amused.

The second group, those intimately involved in the serial murder case consisting of Kelliher, Storm, Batiste, Dahlke, Graff, and O'Connor tried to enjoy themselves. It was a battle lost before it had begun. They spoke to each other about the case, but in whispers and short phrases and without names. They wanted to keep the mood light and upbeat despite the apprehension they felt. Each wore false smiles and laughed at most of the right times, but otherwise were morose and on edge because they knew one or more would receive a call informing them that bodies had been found.

The third group was the civilians. Jeremy and Vicky, Jeff Limbach, Ellie Hemauer, and Kelli Graff, Jamie's wife, and Mark and Jennifer Erickson. To some extent, Sarah Bailey, though as long as she was around Eiselmann, she was content, so most of the time, she stayed on the cop-side of the room. The non-cops stayed with each other, but spoke with the serial murder case group because of the friendship that had developed out of mutual tragedy a summer or so previous. Small talk about basketball and the Northstar team, the upcoming tournament game, Brian's adoption, the spring season of baseball, soccer, and track. Of course, school. The most interesting topic was the book Jeff had written and was editing in prep for publication. There had been talks of a movie to be made from it, Jeff being adamant that the book had to be published before the movie.

In all, it was comfortable and relaxing and enjoyable. Other than Jeremy, Jeff, and Jamie, who were friends, who met in a school setting and forged a strong bond based upon trust and support that would endure. The others developed friendship because of tragedy, heartbreak, and death. Their kids were all friends who spent nights at each other's houses, ate meals at each other's tables, and who laughed and sometimes wept together. Like their parents, most of the boys met through the same tragedy, the same nightmare one or more got caught up in, and because of that, their friendship would last and endure far into adulthood. And no outsider would ever be able to explain their behavior, their affection for each other, and would never be able to explain their signs of affection in public.

"How is Brian doing?" Ellie asked. She and her son, Gavin, had offered their home to Brian knowing that he would choose Jeremy instead. And there were no hard feelings about that. Brian knew he was welcome in their home, just as Gav was welcome in Jeremy's and Vicky's.

"He's adjusting," Jeremy said. "The guys rally around each other, and he fits in. He's close to Bobby."

"He's nervous about the adoption," Vicky added. "I guess that's typical. He isn't sure what to expect." She turned to Jeremy and said, "George seemed kind of wired tonight. Do you know why?"

Vicky's question got O'Connor's, Graff's, Kelliher's, and Storm's attention.

Chapter Seventy-Nine

Waukesha, WI

After the matinee, Alamorode drove to Lake Geneva, an upscale, high-class resort city south and west of Waukesha. He drove into the Ford-Lincoln dealership, traded in his navy-blue BMW, and drove out in a brand new dark maroon Lincoln MKS with all the luxurious trimmings. He liked the feel and comfort behind the wheel and, of course, loved the new car smell.

At first, he had been a little nervous whether the sales folks had heard or read the press about him, but there had been no questions or knowing looks. Evidently, they were so concerned with selling cars they had not had time for news.

It was already dark, and the snow had been piling up all afternoon with city and county crews fighting a losing battle keeping the roads clear. His wipers beat a regular time, and between them and the defroster on both the windshield and back window, his visibility was marginally fair.

He tuned his radio to a local news station, and all they spoke about was the storm. There had been some school cancellations in the more rural areas and nothing yet in the bigger cities where they were more equipped to handle snow emergencies.

Alamorode did not care about that. He had a task, a mission to accomplish.

According to his GPS, the distance between Lake Geneva and Waukesha was 42.9 miles, and would take an hour and eight minutes. But that was in normal driving conditions. With the heavy snow and poor visibility, it would add time, at least a half hour, if not more. The extra time would give him time to plan, not that he needed it. He was meticulous in his planning.

There was one detail that he had yet to make a decision on, though he had developed several options. How would he deal with the cop or cops watching over the family?

He knew there would be surveillance. He knew there would be protection provided to them. Yet the clown was a small hurdle for him. He had surveilled the property twice. He knew the habits of the kids, and he knew they had three dogs. But the snow and the dark would be his friend this night.

Alamorode was two or three minutes away. Taking a chance, he cut his lights, relying instead on the pile of snow pushed to the side of the road. If he drove slowly and if he did not venture too far toward it, he would be fine.

He pulled to the side of the road about one hundred yards behind the car he suspected held the cop. He put on his watch cap and checked his .38 to make certain it was loaded. It was, and it did not surprise him. He ditched the oversized parka for the black North Face. Lastly, instead of the matching black leather gloves he liked to wear, he pulled on tight-fitting black ski gloves, flexible yet snug. He slid out of the car and shut the door with a barely audible thud. Snow had covered the landscape and covered all sounds.

Alamorode walked behind his car and over the shoulder and into the edge of the woods and sunk almost up to his knees. Because he kept low and paused every fourth or fifth step, his progress, though difficult, was slow but steady as he approached the car sheltering the cop.

Off to the passenger side, fifteen yards ... ten ... five.

Chapter Eighty

Waukesha, WI

"This is good, Brett," Billy said stuffing his mouth with angel hair pasta that he had twirled around the tines on his fork. "I mean, everything's good."

George smiled, shook his head, and said, "How can you eat that much?"

"I'm growing."

"Is that your second or third helping?" Randy asked.

"Third, but who's counting?" Billy finished chewing, took a sip of iced water, and said, "Your grandmother can cook."

"That's who I learned from," Brett said.

"I think I gained twenty pounds last Christmas when we went there to visit," Billy laughed.

"You're her favorite, besides Bobby."

Billy grinned and said, "Yeah, I know. I think she liked George and Brian. She called them the quiet ones."

"And she called Randy the quiet twin and you the loud one," Bobby laughed.

"Did you ever watch G-Man eat?" Danny asked. "I think he eats as much as Billy but gets more on him than in him."

The boys laughed.

"Kind of gross," Bobby said with another laugh.

The rest of the meal went like that. Banter and laughter about this and that. What good friends talk about, laugh about, poke fun at. Bellies were full, and they had not even touched the cake.

"I ate so much, I think I'm going to throw up," Randy laughed. He pushed his chair away from the table and said, "Who's on clean up?"

"Brian and I will take care of it," George said.

Randy stood up, checked the calendar on the side of the refrigerator, and said, "Supposed to be Brett and Billy."

"Brett made the meal, so George and I will clean up." It was Brian's routine after each meal anyway.

"I can help," Billy said.

The boys got up from the table with Billy reluctantly eyeing the last piece of garlic bread. He decided he would had enough, so he helped clear off plates and silverware from the table, stacking them on the counter to the left of the sink. Done with that, he grabbed a dishrag and towel and wiped off the table.

Brian busied himself putting leftovers into Tupperware and placing them neatly into the refrigerator. George ran warm water into the sink, grabbed a sponge, and rinsed off plates and silverware before stacking them into the dishwasher.

Randy, Bobby, and Danny disappeared into the living room. It was not long before the guys in the kitchen heard guitar music and harmonizing vocals.

"I could listen to them all day," Billy said. He listened for a bit and said, "I don't recognize this one though. It must be one of their own."

"It is," Brian said with his back to him. He was restocking the dishes in the dishwasher, not liking the way George had arranged them. "Bobby wrote it. He's been practicing it in our room."

Billy sat down at the table with Brett, and the two of them started on their math. Easy for both of them, especially Brett.

Shadow, you and your brother need to get ready. He is coming.

George looked up, glanced first at Brian, who was still bent down with his head and arms in the dishwasher. Then he turned around to Brett and Billy. They were hunched over their homework discussing algebra.

Which brother, Grandfather?

The quiet one. Be quick now.

That was when they heard it. Muffled, but the sound carried nonetheless, and it was nearby.

Brett and Billy stared at one another and then both turned around to look at George and Brian to see if they had heard it. George held a plate in mid-air, and Brian froze, still stooped from stacking plates in the dishwasher.

"Firecrackers?" Billy asked.

Brett shook his head and said, "Small arms. Sounded like a .38 or a .22."

Focused and in control, George shut off the water, dried his hands, turned to his three brothers, and said, "Get everyone in the family room. We need to open the gun cabinet."

The last to leave the kitchen, George walked into the mud room and made sure the security system was set.

Chapter Eighty-One

Waukesha, WI

Alamorode stayed low and snuck up on the driver's side of the car. Taking a chance that the car was unlocked, he tried the handle and jerked it open in one sudden pull. The .38 was already in his hand.

Stunned, Greg Gonnering turned to his left and threw up his hands. The first bullet went through his cell phone and lodged in his upper chest. He turned away from Alamorode toward the passenger side, and the second bullet hit his left shoulder. Whether it was shock or pain or the bullet wounds, Gonnering slumped over in the seat and was still.

Alamorode did not stick around to see if the cop continued to breathe. Instead, he believed the two shots would do the trick, so he shut the door and disappeared into the woods. He needed to move fast just in case the sound carried to the house. He did not want to walk up the driveway because he would be too exposed.

There was not a path that he could see, and the snow was deep. He stumbled and had to steady himself by holding onto trees. The going was slow, but Alamorode remained focused on his mission. He was going to kill tonight.

Chapter Eighty-Two

Waukesha, WI

"Tell me again what your grandfather said," Brett said.

The boys had gathered in the family room where the gun cabinet was. Brian had already opened it and took out his rifle and injected shells into it. He slipped an additional ten shells into his pocket.

"He told me to hurry. Brian and I need to go out and find him."

"Me? He called me by my name?" Brian asked. He stopped tying up his boots.

"He called you the quiet one. But in my vision, I saw us hunting with rifles," George said.

Brett and Brian exchanged a look, accepting what George had said.

"So what are we going to do?" Billy asked.

"Brian and I are going to find out where the shots came from," George stated. "We need to find him, whoever he is. You and the others need to protect the house. No one can get inside because if he does, no one is safe."

"Shouldn't all of us just stay in the house?" Bobby asked as he stared first at Brian, then at George and back to Brian. "I mean, we have a security system, right? No one can get in without us knowing it, right?"

"Whoever is out there, we cannot let him get near the house," George said loading his 30-06. Like Brian, he took additional shells and shoved them into his pocket.

"Don't you want one of the handguns?" Brett asked.

Brian shook his head and said, "George and I are better with rifles. You and Billy and Randy are better with handguns."

"We do not want to get close to whoever is out there. I prefer to shoot from a distance," George said.

"With our 30-06s, we're more accurate from a distance than someone is with a .38 or a .22," Brian added.

Randy marveled at how calm the two of them and Brett were in comparison to Billy, Bobby, and Danny. Even he felt nervous. Scared.

"Danny, you have a photographic memory, right?" Brian asked.

"Eidetic, yes."

"You're going to use my dad's rifle. It's like mine, a 30-06. Randy, watch this. You're going to use Brad's rifle."

Brian showed them how to load it, where the safety was, and how to fire it.

"The safety is on. Don't forget to flick it off when you need to. It has a kick, so hold it tight against your shoulder. Don't shoot each other, and don't shoot anyone else. George and I have our cell phones. Don't call us unless it's an emergency. We'll call you when we're coming in."

"We will take Momma with us," George said. He turned to Jasper and Jasmine, and with two quick hand gestures said, "Patrol. Protect."

The two dogs raced out of the room soundlessly, while Momma stood at attention, head low, tail down.

"Bobby, use the Winchester .22. I loaded it, and all you have to do is pull the trigger, pull down the lever, pull it back up, and shoot again. You keep doing this until whoever is in front of you is down." Brian stared at him and said, "Do you understand?"

Bobby licked his lips and nodded.

"We need to go," George said. To Brett, he said, "Call Detective Jamie. Tell him what happened. Then call Father."

"Billy, can you turn off the alarm? George and I will leave through the slider in here," Brian said.

"Wait! Just wait!" Bobby said. "Do you have to go outside? Whoever is out there has a gun. What if he shoots you?"

He was near tears. Brian wanted to take him into his arms and tell him things would be fine, but he did not want to embarrass either of them in front of the others, and he had no idea how things might turn out.

He ended up saying, "Bobby, we'll be okay. We need to go."

There was a lot more Brian had wanted to say. Maybe needed to say. He knew he fumbled it and sounded like a jerk. He did not want to think about Bobby while somebody was out there with a gun. He could not think about Bobby because he would never be able to do what he needed to do.

They turned to leave, but Brett hooked his arm with his hand and turned him around to face him.

Like they did so often, they put their foreheads together and Brett said, "You and George need to be careful. If you pull the trigger, aim to kill. No hero shit."

Brian nodded and whispered, "Take care of Bobby. Please." He turned and followed George and Momma outside.

Chapter Eighty-Three

Pewaukee, WI

The group of friends and those working the serial case ate their meals at two large tables. Jeremy and Jamie sat back to back as did Vicky and Kelli. Most of the food was eaten except for the cake brought out honoring Paul and Sarah. Everyone had a piece, though Ellie Hemauer and Jennifer and Mark Erickson opted for a small piece because of diets.

Vicky turned around to Jamie and said, "I'm surprised Dr. Alamorode isn't here."

Jeremy said, "He told me he was headed to a conference in Vegas."

Pete and Summer turned around swiftly, startling Jeremy and Vicky.

It was Pete who said, "When did he tell you this?"

"Yesterday. He stopped in to apologize for Sunday's dinner."

"Alamorode?" Jeff Limbach said. "Isn't that the guy you're looking for in the serial case you're working on?"

Vicky paled and placed a hand on her throat. "What?"

Ignoring both Jeff and Vicky, Jamie said, "What else did he say?"

Flustered, Jeremy said, "That's all. He said he had to catch a plane because he was going to a conference in Vegas."

Vicky took hold of Jeremy's hand, and the two of them looked at one another thinking that a possible serial killer had been in their home.

O'Connor listened and watched. As he did, he pushed his chair away from the table.

"That's all he said, Jeremy? Think back," Summer said.

He blushed, his mouth going dry, and he blinked at Jamie.

"What?" Jamie asked.

"At the end, I thought he was leaving. We both stood and shook hands and then he sat back down. He wanted to know George's and Brian's story." Jeremy paused, looked from Jamie to Pete to Summer and then to Vicky. "You don't think ..."

O'Connor had his phone out and raced out of the room followed by Batiste and Dahlke.

Chapter Eighty-Four

Waukesha, WI

George, Brian, and Momma stayed on the house side of the driveway almost but not quite in the woods. With George in the lead and Brian trailing, they remained in a crouch and moved slowly. Momma stayed between the boys and the driveway. She focused on the woods across the way, which was where Brian stared. He had his safety off and his finger near the trigger, but not on it. He was too good a hunter to make that mistake.

George held up a hand and got down on one knee. Brian did the same. Momma bared her teeth, but there was no sound. She, too, was good a hunter.

The highway stretched out just beyond the lip of the driveway. No cars were seen or heard, not on this night. The snow had gotten heavier, the flakes bigger, wetter. The night still. Cold, but not freezing. Not yet. The freeze would come after the clouds disgorged their contents upon the earth.

George stood up, and they walked to the intersection of the driveway and highway and stood by the mailbox.

Momma whimpered and threatened to run to the car. Neither George nor Brian recognized it, but both thought it belonged to the cop sent by Jamie to protect them. Snow covered the vehicle in a ten-inch layer so that its color, make, and model was not recognizable.

George trusted his feelings, and he did not have a good one. As he approached the front of the car, Brian, down on one knee, trained his rifle on the woods watching, listening, and covering George's back.

Momma crept forward, head low, tail down, teeth bared, and eyes on the woods.

"Brian, come here!" George hissed.

Without taking his eyes off the woods, Brian broke into a hunched trot, rounded the front of the car, and joined George who had the door open. George leaned his rifle against the back door.

George felt for a pulse and said, "He is still alive, but there is a lot of blood." He had recognized him as being one of the cops from the alley where he and Brett had walked the crime scene where Michael Staley had been shot.

Brian glanced in the car, and then quickly looked away. He felt he needed to focus on the woods because that is where Momma stared.

George took out his cell and dialed.

"9-1-1, what is your emergency?"

"My name is George Tokay ..." He went on to give the address. "A policeman has been shot twice, once in his chest and once in his shoulder. There's a lot of blood. We need an ambulance."

"I'm dispatching an ambulance, but it will take time because of the storm. Do you know first aid?"

George glanced at the cop and then at Brian and said, "Yes, but there is no time. I'm driving him to the hospital. I will have my flashers on. When I see the ambulance, I will flash my lights. Tell them."

"No, George, you need to stay where you are. Apply first aid."

"There is no time."

"Do you know who shot him?"

George glanced at the woods where Momma stared and said, "No, but the shooter is nearby."

"How do you know?"

Frustrated and angry, George said, "Because I know. I am hanging up."

"No, don ..."

"Brian, cover me," George ordered as he brushed snow off the windows and hood of the car with his arm. He brushed off both headlights and then ran to the back of the car and brushed off the taillights. He felt his phone vibrating nonstop, and he expected that. It was the 9-1-1 dispatcher trying to get him to remain where he was.

The two boys moved the unconscious cop to the passenger side as gently and quickly as they could.

When that task was completed, Brian whispered, "George, are you sure about this?"

"He will die if I wait any longer." He placed his hand right hand on Brian's shoulder and said, "Listen to me, Brian. You cannot let whoever shot this man near the house. You cannot."

Brian nodded. He knew what George was telling him without coming out and saying it. It was clear what George had expected of him.

"Call Brett and tell him what we are doing. I will call Detective Jamie."

Brian said nothing but nodded once.

George smiled tentatively and in Navajo tongue said, "*Yá'át'ééh.*"

Brian stepped around the back of the car and knelt next to Momma and called Brett. When the call ended, he gave Momma a hand signal and whispered, "Heel and protect."

George drove away with headlights on and flashers blinking, leaving Brian by himself with his rifle and Momma for protection.

Chapter Eighty-Five

Waukesha, WI

Brett had assigned the guys to rooms that had doors to the outside. Randy and Danny had the study. They positioned themselves in the corner of the room behind the desk. Billy sat on the floor of family room near the gun cabinet. Bobby and Brett were together in the kitchen. Bobby faced the back door, while Brett faced the front door. Each waited, listening for gunshots they hoped would never happen. Jasmine and Jasper roamed the house pausing rarely to check on the boys.

Bobby fidgeted. He would alternately stare at the door and then at the clock. The rifle lay in his lap because Brett made him hold it. He did not want anything to do with it.

Every now and then, Brett would whisper something to try to make him feel better, maybe take his mind off what might happen outside. It did not work. In fact, Bobby had wiped some tears out of his eyes. Brett put his arm around him and held him.

Brett's phone buzzed, causing both boys to jump. They looked at the cell as if it were a snake. At last, he picked it up, saw it was O'Connor.

"Yeah?"

"Are you and the guys safe?" Pat asked.

Brett said, "George is driving the cop to the hospital. George said the cop was shot twice and in pretty bad shape. He's planning to meet up with the ambulance. Brian is in the woods with Momma."

"They're *what?* George is driving in this weather? Brian is *where?*"

O'Connor yelled so loudly, Brett had to take the cell away from his ear.

"He's ..."

"I heard you. Get Brian back in the house! *Now!*"

"I can try, but he won't answer his cell. You know how he is when he's hunting."

"Jesus *Christ!*" O'Connor screamed as he pounded the steering wheel. He thought for a minute and said, "Keep trying to reach him. I want him back in that house!"

Brett was going to tell him he would try, but O'Connor ended the call.

Chapter Eighty-Six

Waukesha, WI

"George, where are you?" Graff asked. "Visibility is the shits. You need to pull over and wait for the ambulance."

George glanced at the cop in the passenger seat. Passed out or worse, and bleeding, pale and sweaty.

"I am on Highway 59, a little more than two miles from our house heading into Waukesha." He glanced at the speedometer, and it registered thirty miles an hour. Much slower than he had wanted to drive, but it was the best he could do.

Pete and Summer were in the car with Jamie, and so far, they listened, both anxious.

"George, maybe you should pull over and wait for the ambulance."

"Detective Jamie, I cannot. He will die."

"Okay, listen. I'm going to have Kelliher call O'Connor."

Pete pulled out his cell and speed dialed O'Connor as Jamie gave George directions.

To Kelliher as much as to George, he said, "I'm going to have O'Connor drop Skip Dahlke off when you meet up with the ambulance. They're in Pat's car. I don't know if they are in front of or behind the ambulance, but Skip knows medicine, and he will be able to help Detective Gonnering."

"That is his name?" George asked.

"Yes. If you see a car, any car, flash your lights and keep flashing them. Slow to a stop. If it's O'Connor, Skip will get out. If not, keep driving. Do you understand?"

"Yes, sir."

Jamie wanted to tell him that they could both die if he got them into an accident, but he bit his tongue. He knew George and trusted his judgment in almost all cases. Perhaps this was the best way. Maybe.

"George, okay. I need you to be careful. I need you both in one piece."

"I will, Detective Jamie. Can you call and ask where the ambulance is? And tell them I will flash my lights when I see them." He knew he had already told the dispatcher, but it would not hurt to remind them.

"George, just be careful, okay? Please?"

"Yes, Detective Jamie." He glanced at the cop next to him and said, "Please tell them to hurry."

Chapter Eighty-Seven

Waukesha, WI

Brian was not scared. He was not excited or happy, not like when he went deer hunting. He did not know what he felt, but he knew he felt ... different. This night he was hunting a man who had a gun, and he knew the man, whoever it was, would not be afraid to use it.

He also knew that without George, it would be up to him to keep this man away from the house and away from the others. He loved them, all of them, especially Bobby, and he was determined to prevent anyone from hurting them ... him.

Brian did not know how much of a lead this man had. Lead or not, Brian knew the woods and knew the family property, and perhaps, Momma knew the woods and property even better. He and Momma moved as a team. He felt it.

And he felt something else. He could not describe it, but he felt he was being watched. Nothing spooky or malevolent, nothing sinister. Not at all. None of those things. Just that he was being watched and he felt at peace. Weird.

He did not struggle, but the snow was already up to his knees. Maybe a dog thing or maybe just a Momma thing, but she negotiated the snow with relative ease. She led, and Brian followed. Every now and then, the big dog would stop and soundlessly stare off in the distance.

"Momma, let's move," Brian urged in a whisper.

They moved onward, and this time, the two of them halted together. He heard him, and so did Momma.

Even with the blanket of snow, off in the distance and not too far away, Brian heard twigs snap and a curse. Brian guessed the man was not used to tramping around in the woods, something he and the guys liked to do and did on a regular basis. And he guessed the man was not a proper hunter, something he, George, and Brett were.

Brian judged the man was thirty to forty yards ahead, which meant that he was near the path that ran between the house and the Limbach property. He needed to move quickly in order to stop him from getting that far.

"Momma, come," Brian whispered as he tried to take the lead. Momma would not let him, but sensing his urgency, she moved faster.

Chapter Eighty-Eight

Waukesha, WI

Even through the heavy falling snow, George saw the flashing red, white, and amber lights. As Graff ordered, he flashed his own headlights as he drove to the side and stopped, sliding a little to the right. Still, George kept flashing the headlights in hopes that he would be seen.

He was.

The ambulance pulled to the opposite side of the two-lane highway across from George and Gonnering. George stepped out of the vehicle and waved to the ambulance. He was rewarded with two paramedics, a man and a woman, running with their emergency gear. They went right to the cop in the car and began assessing him, the man on the driver side and the woman on the passenger side. They called out numbers and started an IV of something.

George watched with interest while at the same time stayed out of the way.

"Can you tell me your name and what happened?"

George turned around. The paramedic was young and bundled up against the cold. The plumes of the guy's breath reminded George of a dragon in the Harry Potter movies, except the guy was not breathing fire.

"My name is George Tokay. I am the son of Jeremy Evans."

"You made the 9-1-1 call." It was a statement, not a question.

"Yes, sir."

"What happened?"

"I saw two wounds. One in the chest and one in the back by the shoulder blade. He had a pulse, but it was weak."

The medic wrote notes on a clipboard. He had to shield it from the falling snow, but even then, the paper was already wet and the ink runny.

"How did you find him?"

"My brothers and I were cleaning up the kitchen after dinner, and we heard the gunshots. My brother, Brian, and I went outside and found him."

Another car pulled to a stop in the middle of the road between the ambulance and George. The paramedic and George turned to see who it was, and George recognized O'Connor as the driver. He barely gave George a head nod, much less a hello. Skip Dahlke hopped out of the back of the car, and O'Connor sped off without a word.

"George, are you okay?"

Skip took him by the shoulders and looked him over from head to toe even though George assured him he was.

"Tell me what happened?" Skip said, ignoring the medic.

"Excuse me," the young guy said. "Who are you?"

Dahlke pulled out his creds, flashed them, and said, "My name is James Dahlke. I'm a Forensic Scientist with the FBI out of Quantico, Virginia." He turned to the car and asked, "How is Detective Gonnering?"

"Don't know yet. Still assessing."

The male paramedic spoke into his lapel mic, and two men jumped out of the ambulance with a stretcher. Dahlke took George by the arm and led him to the back of the Gonnering's car out of the way. The young EMT followed.

"George, your parents will arrive here any minute now, and you're welcome to go back home with them. But, this car is an active crime scene. I have to secure it and make sure it's buttoned up. A tow truck is on the way. We'll work the car tomorrow in a heated garage, hopefully," he said with a laugh. "But I was wondering if you'd wait with me until the truck gets here."

Torn, George wanted to get back to the house to see if Brian was okay. He had worried about leaving him in the woods by himself. He

332   Spiral Into Darkness

also did not want Skip to be here on the side of the road in the cold by himself waiting for a tow truck.

Skip noticed George's indecision and said, "It's okay, George. I understand." He turned away and watched the paramedics take Gonnering out of the car and strap him to the stretcher. One held onto the IV bag, and two carried Gonnering to the back of the ambulance.

Skip pulled out his cell, punched in a number, and waited. He said, "What's the ETA on the tow truck out on Highway 59?" He listened, nodded, and said, "Okay, good. Thank you."

He put his cell away, turned to George, and said, "Should be here any minute."

The young paramedic with the clipboard and soggy form asked George some follow up questions and ended the brief interview by asking George for his cell and home phone numbers.

A set of headlights appeared off in the distance.

Chapter Eighty-Nine

Waukesha, WI

Originally, Alamorode was going to walk down the path and right up to the front door. Confident and brazen, his two favorite qualities besides his intelligence. But the cop parked out on the highway changed his thinking. And there were the dogs.

As a consequence, Alamorode had not been prepared for the trek through the woods. He hated the snow, and he hated the cold, and he hated being wet. His face froze to the point where he could not feel it. He wanted to rub it, but his gloves were damp, which meant his hands might be chafed. As a precaution against the cold, Alamorode flexed his fingers, first on this left hand and then after changing the .38 to his other hand, he flexed his right hand. All he needed was two quick pulls of the trigger.

He had slipped and fallen several times, and he was sure his knee and elbow were bloody from his latest fall. He knew he had made an inordinate amount of noise, and the good thing was that he felt certain no one was in the woods with him. The faster he could get out, get to the house and finish his task, the better.

He stumbled on a tree root or rock or something and fell hard, hitting the same knee as before. Snow got into his glove making his hand colder and wetter and making him even angrier.

"Fuck!" he yelled through clenched teeth.

He leaned against a young oak tree and caught his breath. He took off his glove, tried to find a dry spot to wipe his hand, but found everything wet.

"Fuck!" he yelled again, this time without clenching his teeth.

Seldom, if ever, did he curse. Cursing was for small-minded men and whores. Anyone who was beneath him and that was everyone he had ever met.

He pushed himself off the small tree. Limping and moving slower, he tried to pick up his pace, but could not.

"Slow and steady wins the race," he said to himself and chuckled at his own joke.

Chapter Ninety

Waukesha, WI

Brian heard him, and both he and Momma sped up. It was shortly after that when Brian saw movement. At first a shadow, then a silhouette in black against the snow. He judged the man to be thirty to forty yards ahead of him and off to the right. He did not think he could get off a good shot.

Yet.

Brian struggled with the possibility, the probability of shooting a man, another human being. He knew both George and Brett had, though they did not like to talk about it. Brett viewed it matter-of-factly, whereas George was ashamed. Brett was too. Maybe. Different circumstances, same result.

Brian had always been religious and had taken church and his Catholic faith seriously. Even after his mom shot his dad and then took her own life. Even after Brad had died. Perhaps even more so then.

He had talked long into the night with Randy and George about God and religion. A bit odd for freshmen in high school. Brian talked with Jeremy, wept in front of him as he struggled with the concept of forgiving his parents, knowing it was the right thing to do, but not being able to.

Now he was faced with the probability of shooting a man. Killing was against one of the commandments, and he took that seriously. Yet, he knew he was the only one standing between the man and his brothers. Between the man and Bobby. It was that thought that kept him moving.

Ahead, the man had stopped, maybe to catch his breath, maybe to determine his direction.

Momma gathered herself in a crouch, and Brian got down on one knee.

Snow fell heavy and wet and threatened to make the shot more difficult than it would have been. Brian was dead-eye with deer, with pheasant, and with duck. Of the boys, and even with O'Connor, Graff, and Coffey, Brian could hold his own.

This, however, was a man, another human being.

He pushed that thought out of his head, concentrated on the fact that this man had shot and killed others, had shot the cop, and on this night had come to kill his brothers and him.

Like he did with deer, he counted down *3 ... 2 ... 1*, exhaled, and pulled the trigger.

After his 30-06 bucked against his shoulder, he watched the man do a pirouette in the snow and fall clutching his left buttocks. He followed the grim dance with a scream.

"You *FUCKER!*"

The man writhed on the ground. Brian watched him raise his .38, and he dove into the snow. Momma covered him with her body.

Four shots with only one coming relatively close.

Chapter Ninety-One

Waukesha, WI

It sounded like a war outside. Both Brett and Bobby jumped with the first shot and jumped with the four shots after.

Bobby began to cry.

"Brian," he whispered.

"Shhh, it's okay, Bobby. Brian will be okay," Brett said, though deep down, he wasn't sure.

"What's happening?" Billy yelled.

"Quiet, I don't want this asshole to know where we are," Brett yelled back.

Both Jasmine and Jasper ran into the kitchen, checked on Bobby and Brett, and then ran to check on the others.

Bobby stared at the backdoor hoping, willing, for Brian to come back inside.

"What if Brian's hurt? Maybe we should go check on him?" Bobby sobbed.

Brett hugged him, kissed the side of his head, and said, "He'll be okay, Bobby."

And then they heard another shot.

Chapter Ninety-Two

Waukesha, WI

When Alamorode stopped shooting, Brian raised his head tentatively, and he wiped the snow off his face and out of his eyes. Momma gave him a doggy kiss, perhaps for a job well done.

Brian had purposefully aimed low in an effort not to kill, but to stop him.

The man stood, dragged his left leg, and using his arms, to both hold himself up and help him walk, he moved onward.

"Are you fucking kidding me?" Brian whispered.

Brian knelt one more time, aimed low like his last shot, counted down *3 ... 2 ... 1*, exhaled, and squeezed off another shot.

The man went down, screaming and thrashing in the snow. The man raised his .38, and when he squeezed the trigger, there were only clicks.

"Momma!" Brian said.

The big dog turned around. Brian bent low, gave two hand signals, and said, "Disarm and protect!"

Momma took off like a runaway train hurtling over the snow. It took her no time to cover the thirty or forty yards between Brian and the man.

The man screamed as Momma leapt into the air and landed on top of him. Brian heard growling and snarling and watched as Momma's big head twisted and shook the man's arm like a rag.

"STOP! OH GOD! PLEASE STOP!"

Brian took his time to be certain the man would not get up again. He stood, brushed snow off his knee and sighed.

You were always the best shot.

Brian knew the voice. He stumbled and leaned against a tree thinking he was going mad. He shut his eyes. He strained to hear anyone, anything else. He heard Momma's snarls, growls, and the man's curses.

You should check on him and let the others know it's over and that you're okay.

A tear and then more fell. He brushed them away, took off his glove, and held it under his arm while taking out his cellphone from his inner jacket pocket and sending a group text. *It's over. I'm okay.* It was all he needed to say.

He pocketed his cell and replaced the glove on his wet and frozen hand. He did a slow three-sixty. When he turned around, he came face to face with Brad, his smiling twin.

At first, all Brian did was stare. There were so many questions to ask, things he had wanted to say.

Hi, Bro.

Brad's voice was clear and sounded like it always did. He smiled, and his eyes danced. Typical Brad. And Brian wept.

Brad reached out and put a hand on Brian's shoulder, though it did not feel like a hand. It was. . . a feeling of warmth and comfort.

Brian opened his mouth to speak, and Brad said, *You don't need to talk, Bro. Think it.*

Where have you been? Why haven't you come sooner, Brad? It's been a long time.

Brad smiled and said, *I've always been with you, Bri. Always. I never left.*

How is that possible?

Brad laughed, and Brian smiled because as much as anything, it was Brad's smile and his laugh he missed the most.

Brad reached out, touched Brian's chest, and said, *Because I live here, Bri. I've always lived here. I'm with you all the time, just like you're with me.*

'But it's not the same, Brad.' Brian wept out of profound sadness and want. He wiped his nose with the back of his glove. *I. Want. You.*

Brad smiled, gave Brian's shoulder a squeeze- at least that's what Brian thought he did- and said, *When you need me, Bri. I'm here. Like always.*

And then Brad was gone.

Frantic, Brian reached out into the dark, snow-filled night to hold onto him grasping only falling snow. He turned around in a circle hoping to catch one more glimpse, but Brad was gone.

The sound of Momma's growls and the man's cursing broke him out of his ... trance?

Brian wiped his eyes and his nose, and he walked towards Momma and the man. He caught up to them and was not surprised. The man's arm and hand looked like raw hamburger. The man tried to hit Momma with his other hand, and Momma bit down hard on that one too.

Brian commanded, "Momma, heel and protect!" and Momma did just that, her muzzle inches away from Alamorode's face. Bloody saliva dripped onto his face, but Alamorode dared not wipe it away.

Brian flicked the safety on his rifle and pushed it to his back where it hung from the leather strap.

"I'm bleeding to death, you son-of-a-bitch, you little fucker, you cocksucker!" each curse louder than the first.

Brian ignored him. In the distance and in the direction of the house, he heard a car pull up and car doors slam.

"I'm going to sue your ass!"

Brian ignored him and yelled, "I'm in the woods. Take the path. I'll meet you." To Momma, he said, "Here!" and the big dog stepped to him.

Brian took a handful of snow and wiped the blood away from Momma's muzzle. Satisfied, he said, "Protect and guard," with two quick hand gestures.

"I'm coming out on the path. Don't shoot!"

Chapter Ninety-One

Waukesha, WI

Brett jumped up and ran to the kitchen window over the sink and peered out.

"It's O'Connor!" He turned to Bobby and said, "O'Connor and Batiste are here." He yelled to the others, "It's over! Pat and Cleve are here. Put your guns on safety."

Bobby ignored him, pushed the Winchester .22 away from him with enough force that it slid into one of the kitchen chairs. He stood up and walked to the mudroom.

"What are you doing?" Brett called after him. When Bobby did not answer, he followed him.

"Where are you going?"

Bobby flipped off his shoes and stepped into his boots, threw a scarf around his neck, and slipped on his jacket. He grabbed a pair of gloves, pulled them on, and opened the door.

"If you wait a second, I'll go with you," Brett said as he scrambled to find a jacket, boots, and gloves.

Bobby did not wait but stormed out through the door without shutting it.

"Bobby, wait up!" Brett called.

Bobby slipped down the steps but caught himself on the ornate iron railing and then took off down the path following the tracks left by O'Connor and Batiste. They were already filling up with falling snow, but he could see them. He saw the two cops and Brian up ahead.

One of the cops, Bobby assumed it was O'Connor because of his height, left the path and entered the woods. The shorter of the two stayed with Brian but left and followed O'Connor, leaving Brian alone on the path.

342   Spiral Into Darkness

Bobby and Brian saw each other, and Bobby stormed toward him. He reached Brian, placed two hands on Brian's chest, and shoved him backward. Brian did not fall. He squared himself to face Bobby again. And Bobby did the same thing but shoved him even harder. Brian still did not fall.

Brian did not say anything, but when Bobby came at him again, Brian reached out and hugged him. Bobby struggled, but not much. He sobbed, and Brian held onto him, and the two boys hugged each other.

Brett ran up to them, stopped short, and then joined them in a group hug, their heads pressed together. No words were spoken because they were not needed. The three of them knew all they needed to say because they felt it.

Chapter Ninety-Two

Waukesha, WI

Alamorode had been picked up by an ambulance. He had been Mirandized and spouted off about how he was protecting families and how George and Brian would damage Jeremy's and Vicky's family. Fortunately, none of the boys nor Jeremy or Vicky had heard him. O'Connor and Graff did, and they encouraged him to keep talking since whatever spewed from his mouth further incriminated him. Carlos Lorenzo could not take notes fast enough, but that was okay since he used his cell to record him. He rode in the back of the ambulance as an armed guard and to capture anything else Alamorode might say.

Jeff Limbach had dropped Jeremy and Vicky off at the house and then went back to wait with Skip and George. The tow truck arrived and carted Gonnering's car off to the police station where it would be kept in impound until morning when Skip would go over it. The tow truck made a second visit and took Alamorode's car to the same impound. Graff, O'Connor, and Batiste had opened it and did a cursory inspection, careful to avoid touching anything, and after seeing what was inside, decided to leave it alone until they had a warrant.

The Evans's kitchen was jammed with FBI and cops. Summer, Pete, and Jamie decided Graff would conduct the interviews of George and Brian and, to a lesser extent, Brett. Graff had wanted to do them one at a time, but the boys remained together, refusing to be separated.

While Brian, George and Brett sat at the table across from Pete, Summer, and Graff, the other boys sat on the floor or leaned against the wall behind them. Pete and Vicky sat at the kitchen table on either end. O'Connor, Batiste, Skip, and Jeff Limbach stood behind leaning on the counter watching George's, Brian's, and Brett's expressions and body language.

Brian and George had shed their boots, jackets, and gloves. The two boys were still damp, if not wet, and held mugs of hot chocolate made by Bobby. The two sipped them but were too hot to drink. At least the mugs warmed up their cold hands.

George had already gone through his story, so he was puzzled as to why Jamie asked for it again.

"George, what made you decide to go outside after you heard the gunshot?" Jamie asked.

"Because my grandfather said Brian and I needed to go outside to find the man who had come to hurt us."

Pete said, "He used Brian's name?"

"No, he said, 'the quiet one.'"

Jamie's eyes flicked to Brian, who stared back impassively. Brian had already gone through his story once, just as George had. He did not understand why Graff asked the same questions over and over. All he wanted to do was strip out of his clothes and jump into a hot shower.

"So you went with him."

Brian nodded.

"And after George left, you went into the woods by yourself."

"Momma was with me," Brian answered. Momma pushed herself between Brett and Brian and rested her big head on Brian's thigh. Brian obliged her by scratching her behind the ear and gripping her muzzle playfully.

"How did you know where to look for Alamorode?" Pete asked.

Brian shrugged. He did not know Kelliher very well, but both George and Brett liked him.

"I let Momma lead. I followed her."

"And then what?" Graff said.

"I didn't see him at first, but I heard him. He was about thirty to forty feet ahead of me and off to my right. He stopped, and I aimed, and I shot him."

"But you didn't kill him," Pete said.

Brian shook his head. "I didn't have to. I just needed to keep him from getting to the house."

"Why?" Summer asked. "Why was it important to keep him from getting to the house?"

Brian frowned, surprised at the question because it was obvious to him. He glanced at Brett and George and said, "Because that's where the guys were. I didn't want him hurting them."

Graff, Summer, and Pete exchanged a quick glance, but Vicky picked up on it.

"What?" she asked.

Graff waved her off and said, "I'll come back to that." To Brian, he said, "You shot Alamorode twice."

Brian shrugged and said, "He went down, and I thought he'd stay down. After he shot around in the woods, he got back up and kept going, so I shot him again."

"He shot at you?" Bobby asked.

Brian half-turned to face him and said, "He didn't come close."

Pete said, "Brian, you were forty-three yards away from Alamorode. I had it checked after you walked us through the woods. You didn't use a scope. There was a heavy snow. It was dark and cold, probably near freezing, and you hit Alamorode not once, but twice in a non-lethal spot. How?"

Billy giggled. Brett turned around, and Billy said, "Sorry. I think it's funny Bri shot him in the ass."

Billy turned beet red and lowered his head still wearing a smirk. Randy covered his mouth, hiding his own smile, and Danny looked away stifling a laugh. Bobby registered concern.

"You could have just shot him in the back and ended it," Graff said.

Defiantly, his green eyes staring at both Pete and Graff, he said, "It wasn't that hard of a shot. I didn't need a scope, and I didn't need to kill him. I needed to stop him from getting to the house."

Summer smiled at him.

"Then you approached him," Graff said. "You knew he had a weapon. You didn't think that was dangerous?"

Brian had reached his boiling point. It was like Graff thought he had screwed up.

"He shot the cop twice. A .38 has six rounds."

"How did you know it was a .38?" Pete asked.

Brian licked his lips and glanced uncertainly at George before he said, "A guess, I suppose. Anyway, he shot four more times, and I thought he emptied it. After I shot him the second time, he tried shooting again, but it was empty. I heard the hammer on the empty chamber. I sent Momma to disarm him, and she did."

"Two tricky shots and a gamble, don't you think?" Pete asked with a smile.

Brian had had enough. He pushed his chair away from the table and stood up.

"I've been hunting since I was ten. I've hunted with you," he said to Graff, "and you," he said to O'Connor. "I didn't have to kill him, and I didn't do anything wrong." This last he said glancing at Jeremy and Vicky. He bounced a finger on the table and said, "This is my family. This is our home, and this is our property. That shithead came here to kill somebody, and I wasn't going to let him. If you don't like that, tough shit."

"Bri," Vicky said.

"I'm done. I answered your stupid questions twice. I'm going to shower because I'm cold and wet, and I'm tired." He looked at O'Connor and then at Graff and said, "And you can take your ice fishing trip and shove it up your ass. I'm not going."

He stormed out of the kitchen with both Momma and Jasper at his heels. The boys stood up and followed him out of the kitchen. Bobby was the last to leave, and he did so after glaring at Graff.

Chapter Ninety-Three

Waukesha, WI

Brian had both hands on the ceramic tiles letting the water cascade over his head and down his chest and shoulders. The hot water stung, but he did not care. Steam rose in a cloud over him and throughout the bathroom. He had hoped Bobby would check on him, not so much to talk, but just to be with him. He never showed up, maybe would not at all.

At last, he turned off the shower. He whisked water from his eyes, chest, arms, and legs before he grabbed one of the fluffy white towels and dried himself off. Both Bobby and Brett complained that he sucked when it came to drying off, and on this night, it was no different. Brian did not care.

He hung up the towel and stood naked in front of the mirror and sighed.

He regretted what he had said to Graff and the way he had acted in the kitchen. He placed both of his hands on the counter, shut his eyes, and sighed. He remained motionless until there was a knock on the door.

"Yeah," Brian answered.

"Can I come in?" Jeremy asked.

Not too surprised, Brian said, "Sure."

He pulled on his boxers as Jeremy opened the door and stepped inside. He shut the door behind him.

"Are you okay?"

Brian nodded.

Jeremy grabbed a hand towel and dried off Brian's back and then the mirror.

"When you're done here, come down to the kitchen. Mom and I would like to talk to all of you."

Brian nodded again. Their eyes met, and Brian lowered his, and said, "I'm sorry."

"For ..."

He shrugged and said, "For what I said to Jamie. The way I acted."

Jeremy lifted Brian's chin and said, "A lot happened tonight. No one blames you for anything, Bri. You didn't do anything wrong. Maybe you were a little hard on Jamie. He was doing his job, and on a night like tonight, he's a cop first and a friend second."

Brian nodded.

"I just ..." he started and then shook his head.

"What?"

Brian looked up and said, "I didn't want to disappoint you."

Jeremy looked over his newest son. In the two months he had lived with them, Brian had filled out. His chest and arms had grown bigger and stronger and though never fat or even flabby, his stomach was firm and on its way to a six-pack. His face was thinner, and he was growing into a handsome young man from the cute boy he was. But as much as he had grown on the outside, on the inside, Brian was still young in many respects. He gave off the appearance of confidence, and in some instances and situations, he was. In others, not.

"Bri, you haven't disappointed me. You've done nothing but make me proud."

Sadly, Brian looked at his new father and said, "I had sex with Cat, and Bobby and I ..."

Jeremy blushed, smiled, and took Brian into his arms and said, "Brian Evans, things like that happen even when you don't mean for them to. You and I are good, Bri."

"I'll try not to do that with Cat again, but I think of her and I think of ... that, and I just kind of go crazy. And I love Bobby, Dad. Honest."

Jeremy smiled and said, "I know you do, but we've been through this, all of it. All we ask is that you please be careful."

"I will, Dad. I promise. I like Cat and Bobby a lot."

"I know."

The two of them embraced and like Brett and Brian do so often, Jeremy and Brian had their foreheads together, though Jeremy had to hunch over to do so, and he gave Brian an Eskimo.

"Dad, I shot a guy today. I feel awful."

"I know."

"But I had to."

Jeremy smiled and said, "I know."

"Does this ... does this change anything, you know, about me being adopted?"

Jeremy wrapped him in his arms and said, "Of course not, Bri. Of course not."

Brian began to cry. He did not want to, but he did.

"Brian, look at me." When Brian looked up, Jeremy said, "Bri, you protected your brothers from someone who had come to hurt you and them."

Brian said nothing. He could not shake the feeling he had for shooting another human being. It just felt ... wrong to him. And despite what Jeremy had said, he felt he had let Jeremy down, that he had disappointed him. That is what bothered him the most.

"So I'll ask you again, are you okay?"

Brian nodded, though not confidently.

Jeremy kissed his forehead and said, "I love you, Brian Evans. Don't doubt that. Get yourself dressed and come to the kitchen. We'll talk there."

Jeremy turned and left, leaving Brian alone. Brian grabbed the deodorant, smeared some under his arms and walked across the hall to his and Bobby's room, and finished dressing.

He came down to the kitchen and was surprised to see Jamie, Pete, and Summer still seated at the table. O'Connor, Skip Dahlke, and Cleve Batiste drove back to Waukesha, and Jeff and Danny had left for their house. Randy, Billy, and Bobby had hauled three chairs in from the dining room and fit themselves around the table. They had saved Brian's normal spot for him.

Brian could not make eye contact with Jamie. He did not look at Pete or Summer either but instead folded his hands in his lap and stared down at the table.

"We don't want to keep you up any longer than necessary since this is a school night," Summer said. "But we wanted to tell you a little about what we know because we think we owe you an explanation. Your mom and dad gave us permission to share bits and pieces, maybe not all of it, but enough so you understand what took place and why. Does that make sense?"

The boys nodded.

"But please understand, this is confidential. Very confidential. We," she nodded to Pete on her right and Jamie on her left, "think you deserve to know since you were instrumental in catching him."

The boys waited.

"First, we heard from the hospital. Greg Gonnering is going to be okay. He's in critical condition, but is expected to make it." Summer said to George. "Your quick thinking might have saved his life."

George nodded. He had worried about whether or not he had made a good decision.

"Nelson Alamorode or Alan Nelson, he's gone by both," Summer said, "is in surgery. He'll be well enough to stand trial for multiple murders in and around Milwaukee."

She turned to Brian and George and said, "He fixated on you two."

"What do you mean?" Brett said.

"From what we're able to tell, and this is preliminary, Alamorode thought anyone who was adopted ruined the family. That's why he was after you, Brian, and you, George."

"But all of us were adopted," Billy said.

"Well technically, Bobby and I aren't," Brett said.

"But Alamorode saw you and Bobby as already in the family because you're Vicky's sons," Pete said. "And he saw Randy and Billy as already in the family because they're twins and had been Jeremy's sons."

"Well, that's stupid," Randy said.

"Sometimes, there's no explanation for crazy," Graff said with a laugh.

"This is what we think anyway," Summer said. "We're still investigating, but again, I have to remind you this is confidential, and if it gets out, it could jeopardize the case."

"We're trusting you," Pete added.

"It will all come out at the trial, but you have to keep all of this in this kitchen, and it can't be shared with anyone outside your family," Graff said.

The boys nodded, and Brian raised his hand.

Summer and Pete laughed, and Pete said, "The boy with the wet hair in the white t-shirt."

Brian blushed and said, "I shot Alamorode."

Billy laughed and said, "Yeah, twice in the ass," and the boys laughed. It was clear Billy would not let him live it down.

"What's your question?" Pete asked, trying unsuccessfully not to laugh.

"Will I have a record? I mean, I want to be a teacher and a coach like Dad. And I won't be able to if I have a record." Brian grew pale as he said this.

"Brian, it was self-defense," Jamie said.

"Secondly, you're a juvenile," Summer said. "Like Brett's and George's records, yours will be sealed. Tomorrow morning, Pete, Jamie, and I will approach a judge and make that happen."

"Thank you."

"Anything else? Any other questions?" Pete said.

Brian started to raise his hand, thought better of it, and said, "I want to apologize. I'm sorry for what I said before and the way I acted," his eyes on Jamie, but also on Pete and Summer.

Jamie smiled and said, "It was a tough night, Bri. We're good." When Brian did not look like he believed it, Jamie said with emphasis, "Brian, we're good."

Pete said, "Brian, I train FBI NATs ...what we call recruits at the academy. And I have to tell you that I have only two, maybe three, who could have made the shot you made tonight. Under the conditions you had, that was an impressive shot."

Brian blushed. He was not proud of it, and he said, "George is a good shot. He could have made it. Brett too."

Both boys shook their heads, and Brett said, "No way."

To rescue Brian, Billy said, "If you're done, I think we should have cake. We never got to eat it."

"With ice cream," George added.

"If I can have some coffee," Pete said with a laugh. "My fitness test isn't for another month or two." This last he added while patting his belly.

Epilogue

Brian could not turn his mind off. He rethought what he could have done differently with Alamorode, but he could not see any other choice he had. Even though they said he had acted in self-defense and said that his records would be sealed, he did not feel right about it. He felt ... guilty. He could not shake that feeling. It almost made him sick to his stomach.

Bobby was sound asleep, his breathing slow and deep. He had his cheek on Brian's shoulder, a leg and an arm across his body. Their usual sleeping position. Every now and then, Brian would brush his lips across Bobby's forehead and run a hand up and down the small of his back.

He whispered, "I love you, Bobby."

There was no answer, and Brian did not expect one.

They had not done anything except hold each other and weep. Bobby, because he had been scared that something might happen to Brian in the woods. Brian, because of what did happen in the woods.

Brian had not told anyone about seeing Brad, not even Bobby. He wanted to hold onto that just for himself. At least for a while, maybe a long while because that was the best part of the night. It was also the worst part of the night.

Brian eased himself out from under Bobby and tucked him in so he would not get cold. Jasper raised his head expectantly, so Brian bent down to pet him. After, he stood up and tiptoed to the window.

The snow had eased off, but wind had picked up, and he did not have a doubt it would be freezing. Maybe a snow day, maybe just a delay, or maybe nothing at all. Anything was possible. The one thing he knew for sure was that he and George would have their work cut out shoveling the steps and walkway and plowing out the driveway.

Brian pulled on his boxers and then his sweats along with a sweatshirt. He bent down, opened the drawer of his nightstand. He took out the envelope, and tiptoed out of the room.

Momma had planted herself outside his and Bobby's room instead of at the top of the stairs. He sat down on the carpet, took her big furry head in his arms, and hugged her. She rewarded him with kisses. He stood up and walked down the hallway and the stairs with Momma at his side.

Brian tiptoed to the study, turned on a table lamp at its lowest setting, and then lit a small fire for warmth. Instead of sitting on the couch or the chair, he sat down on the floor cross-legged and leaned against the couch. Momma laid down next to him with her head on his thigh.

At first, all he did was stare at the envelope and slap it lightly against his knee. Then he would stare at the fire but continue slapping the envelope on his knee.

He sighed and slipped his thumb inside the flap and opened it, tearing it a little. Inside was money. A lot of it, but Brian did not count it because he did not care. He took it out, along with two typed pages, but stuffed the money back into the envelope.

He pursed his lips, then opened the letter and read it from the beginning to the end and then he read it again.

There were no tears. There was not any anger. Brian did not know what he felt other than that he did not know that he cared all that much.

"What are you doing up?"

Brian looked up and saw Brett and George in the doorway dressed like he was, except that Brett was not wearing a t-shirt.

"Couldn't sleep."

The two boys sat down on either side of him, George on his right and Brett on the other side of Momma.

"You read it?" Brett asked.

Brian nodded.

"So?"

"So nothing."

Brett was not going to push. Brian would either talk about it or he would not. That was his way about most things. George patted Brian's knee and smiled. Brian took that as George's way of agreeing that the letter might not be something to talk about, at least right away.

"What are you guys doing up?" Bobby asked, walking through the door carrying a blanket and a pillow.

"Couldn't sleep," Brian said.

"Move your legs," Bobby said.

Brian uncrossed his legs, and Bobby laid down between them, put the pillow on Brian's lap, and covered up with the blanket.

"Make yourself at home, why don't you," Brett laughed.

"I am," Bobby said with a smile. He shut his eyes, wrapped his arms around the pillow. As he did, he poked Brian once or twice in the stomach causing Brian to laugh.

"Dork."

"Guess what?" Billy said, leading Randy into the room. Both boys carried pillows and blankets and handed them out to Brian, Brett, and George.

"No school tomorrow," Billy said answering his own question.

"That means we don't get to practice. We have a tournament game on Thursday," Brett said.

"We can ask Dad to let us in the gym in the afternoon, maybe," Randy said. "Coach can't be there, but you can run the practice."

"Maybe," Brett said as he stretched out with a pillow and blanket, sharing it with Randy. Momma got up and lay down on the rug in front of the fire.

Billy lay down next to George, leaving Brian sitting up.

"Bobby, I can't sleep like this," Brian said shaking Bobby awake.

Bobby got up and waited for Brian to lay down, but instead, Brian stood up.

"What are you doing?"

The boys' heads popped up from their pillows as they watched Brian take the letter and place it in the fire. He watched it until it was ash. He stood and watched the fire, and then he walked to the desk with the money in the envelope. He took a pen and wrote on it and left it there. After, he came back and laid down between Brett and Bobby.

"You okay?" Brett asked.

Brian thought for a minute, turned his head, and said, "Yeah. More than okay."

Brett smiled, turned toward him, and threw an arm over his chest, as did Bobby. Of course, Bobby added a leg.

The last thing Brian remembered before he fell asleep was that he was happy. That, and how much he loved his family.

Thank you so much for reading one of our **Crime Fiction** novels.
If you enjoyed the experience, please check out our recommended title for
your next great read!

Caught in a Web by Joseph Lewis

"This important, nail-biting crime thriller about MS-13 sets the bar very high.
One of the year's best thrillers." *–BEST THRILLERS*

View other Black Rose Writing titles at www.blackrosewriting.com/books

and use promo code **PRINT** to receive a **20% discount** when purchasing.

CPSIA information can be obtained
at www.ICGtesting.com
Printed in the USA
FFHW021624010219
50361741-55464FF